Irresistibly Exotic Men

PAULA ROE
ANNE FRASER
LAURA IDING

First Published in Great Britain 2017
By Mills & Boon, an imprint of HarperCollins*Publishers*
1 London Bridge Street, London, SE1 9GF

IRRESISTIBLY EXOTIC MEN © 2017 Harlequin Books S. A.

Bed Of Lies, *Falling For Dr Dimitriou* and *Her Little Spanish Secret* were first published in Great Britain by Harlequin (UK) Limited.

Bed Of Lies © 2012 Paula Roe
Falling For Dr Dimitriou © 2014 Anne Fraser
Her Little Spanish Secret © 2012 Laura Iding

ISBN: 978-0-263-92984-3

05-1017

Our policy is to use papers that are natural, renewable and recyclable products and made from wood grown in sustainable forests. The logging and manufacturing processes conform to the legal environmental regulations of the country of origin.

Printed and bound in Spain
by CPI, Barcelona

BED OF LIES

BY
PAULA ROE

Despite wanting to be a vet, choreographer, card shark, hairdresser and an interior designer (although not simultaneously!), British-born, Aussie-bred **Paula Roe** ended up as a personal assistant, office manager, software trainer and aerobics instructor for thirteen interesting years.

Paula lives in western New South Wales, Australia, with her family, two opinionated cats and a garden full of dependent native birds. She still retains a deep love of filing systems, stationery and traveling, even though the latter doesn't happen nearly as often as she'd like. She loves to hear from her readers—you can visit her at her website, www.paularoe.com.

To all those wonderful writers, contest judges and editors who read my original version of Beth and Luke's story many, many (many!) years ago and gave me the encouragement to keep writing: Meredith Webber, Meredith Whitford, Desley and Michael Ahern, Valerie Susan Hayward and Diane Dietz.

One

Trouble.

For a moment, Beth Jones had to steady herself against the kitchen sink, her heart pounding basket-ball-hard against her ribs as she stared out into her leafy front garden. Right into the impeccably dressed, clean-shaven face of trouble.

A man had eased from a sporty BMW parked in her driveway, his tall, broad figure radiating tension. The giveaway signs were as tangible as the lingering heat of the early-October evening—his stiff shoulders and neck, a frown knotting his forehead, the impatient way he slammed the car door.

She swallowed thickly, pushed away an errant curl and continued to stare.

He paused by her letter box, checking something on

a piece of paper, a frown creasing behind those dark sunglasses. His hesitation gave her time to take in a top-to-toe view of an efficient haircut, broad chest encased in a sharply cut suit and long, long legs. And the nerve ticking away in his jaw.

He looked expensive and self-assured, one of those billion-dollar alpha males who automatically command respect.

So, not a reporter. Some business hotshot? A lawyer? Banker?

She sucked in a breath. *Yes.*

Amazingly, it looked like East Coast National Bank had graduated from phone calls to face-to-face intimidation.

A misplaced half a million dollars would do that.

Trouble always came in threes. And if she counted her flat tire this morning and her missing employee as numbers one and two, then the third looked as if he was about to come knocking on her front door.

Luke De Rossi had a whopper of a headache.

It had started up after he'd left the Brisbane solicitor's office and drove south along the M1 toward the Gold Coast, the blasting air conditioner doing nothing to soothe his anger. He'd clicked through a dozen songs on his iPod before giving up, instead letting the thick silence fill the void.

He'd barely noticed when he took the turnoff to Runaway Bay, traffic thinning, the houses becoming bigger and properties more expansive. A couple of times he'd glanced in the rearview mirror, but the car that'd been tailing him had disappeared.

He should be happy about that. Instead, apprehension gnawed like a dog worrying a bone. He could just imagine the headlines now: Lucky Luke Cops House from Dead Gangster Uncle was a particular favourite. The press would put another knife in his back, his reputation would be screwed and he'd lose everything he'd worked for all his life.

He and Gino had never been close, but his uncle had known how much his career meant to him. So what the hell had he been thinking, bequeathing him a house that could effectively sabotage his career?

At the end of the cul-de-sac, sunset spread long-fingered shadows over the sprawling century-old colonial-style two-story, a long, partially hidden driveway and a white letter box emblazoned with the number thirteen. *How apt*.

The house was painted dark green and ochre, the colors blending into the surrounding trees, completely at odds with the modern grandiose Grecian creations he'd passed farther up. For one second, he expected to see a dog bounding away in the front yard and kids playing on the spacious porch. Instead, a comfy swing sat on the polished wooden boards, inviting him to come and take a load off.

He snorted as he got out of the car. Despite its exclusive island location, the place looked…low-key. Something his uncle was definitely not. So what was Gino doing with a perfect slice of suburbia in his possession when he had the pick of any mansion along Queensland's elite Whitsunday Islands?

He'd left the solicitor's office too fired up to hear any explanations. Yeah, he'd gone in already furious and, two sentences into the reading of Gino's will, he'd turned around and stormed right out. He knew if he'd stayed a moment longer he would have done things, said things that weren't his right to do or say.

Yet those words still burned in his brain: *You need to hear this, Luke. You need to make peace with your family.*

Privately, his board of directors had warned him away from the public-relations nightmare that was Gino Corelli. Publicly, they'd called his suspension a "temporary leave of absence due to family commitments." Yet for some crazy reason, here he was.

You need to make it right.

He sucked in a breath. Gino had died because of him. He'd managed to shove the guilt aside for weeks, burying it under his insane workload and long hours until it had all exploded in Paluzanno and Partners' shiny boardroom.

Make it right.

With a soft curse, he shook his head. A week would be enough time to check out the house and put it on the market. Then he'd return the money to his aunt Rosa and get back to his life and his upcoming promotion.

A week. Maybe ten days, tops. Then he was home free. Simple.

He took another step forward, ignored his ringing phone, then stilled when he spotted a red hatchback parked under the porch.

This house was designed to pass under the radar, yet by Sunset Island real estate values alone, it was worth a few million. His brain quickly ran through the possibilities until it landed on an unpleasant thought.

A love nest.

A sour taste lodged in his mouth, something bitter and dark. *No*. Gino had loved Aunt Rosa. They'd been happily married for over fifty years. There was no way he would…

Yet why hadn't Gino willed the house to Rosa then? Why him, if not to keep Rosa in the dark?

He glanced at the house again, his mouth thinning in suspicion. Something was off… something he couldn't put his finger on.

He slammed the car door, rechecked the address then stalked across the yard.

Only to pause at the front steps.

A thin band of worry tripped down his back, following the sweat plastering the shirt to his skin. He scratched the base of his neck and looked over his shoulder. The winding driveway and a dense hedge hid the house from the quiet street. A couple of well-tended lemon trees bent over the front porch like wizened sentries. The lawn was in need of a cut, but the flower beds were turned, indicating where the occupant's priorities lay. And with the exception of the cicadas chirping their repertoire with monotonous regularity, silence reigned.

The remnants of adrenaline from his press encounter surged up a notch.

There were no caretaking arrangements in place. Either he was right about Gino or… His mind clicked, grasping for one other plausible explanation.

Some enterprising reporter was one step ahead.

Luke had always managed to draw the line between unwanted attention and good publicity when needed. Yes, he was the youngest board member of Jackson and

Blair, Queensland's most affluent merchant bank. Yes, he possessed an insane amount of power in the corporate world. But now all people saw was the nephew of alleged mob boss Gino Corelli.

They saw a criminal.

Luke stared at the key in his palm, regret stabbing in his chest. His cousin's deadly accusation at Gino's funeral still festered—*Maybe if you'd done something, my father would still be alive.*

If he only knew.

His hand closed around the key and squeezed. The sharp edges bit into his skin yet he welcomed the pain. Anything that took away, even briefly, from the nagging wound in his heart was a reprieve.

Luke glared at the front door of his legacy—solid, worn…and locked. And felt a frustration so deep it burned a hole behind his eyes.

Despite holding the key, he pounded on the door. Then waited.

Just as he was about to try again, the door opened and his mind went momentarily and uncharacteristically blank.

A human version of Bambi stood there, all mossy wide eyes and long limbs. She was barely dressed in a faded blue tank top and white denim shorts, the frayed cuffs ending midthigh and leaving a long expanse of leg bare. Legs starting at her armpits and running down to the tips of her pink-painted toenails. Legs curved in all the right places, tanned a light honey, with dimpled knees.

Lucio De Rossi was a leg man and he appreciated a quality vintage when he saw it.

He dropped his hand, tipped down his sunglasses and let his gaze run leisurely up her body until his eyes met hers—frosty green eyes that shot down all inappropriate thoughts in flames.

Beth took a step back. The look stamped on this stranger's arrogant features did not bode well. And those dark, dark eyes edged in thick, almost feminine lashes backed up that thought. As he shoved his glasses up and studied her with the intensity and thoroughness of an interrogator, he ran a long-fingered hand over his jaw.

"I take it you're here about Ben Foster?" Beth asked coolly, reining in her churning thoughts.

"Who?"

He glanced past her shoulder and unease flared. She snapped her mouth shut, suddenly realizing the downside in offering too much information.

His eyes returned to her and narrowed. "What are you doing in this house?"

Beth's gut flipped at his barely hidden animosity, but she refused to be cowed. "What are *you* doing?"

He gave her a dark look, brushed past her and strode down the hallway.

Openmouthed, Beth stared after his retreating back. Panic kicked in, hitching her breath and lending speed to her steps.

When she finally caught up, he'd reached the lounge room, pulled the curtains wide and was scanning the shadowed backyard.

"What do you think you're—"

"You people never give up, do you?" He spun, eyes shining with battle. "The tail, the ambush at my apartment—now this little trick. So what's the plan? Bat your green eyes, flash your legs and ask me nicely for an exclusive?" He ran that dark gaze over her so thoroughly Beth might well have been naked. "Those shorts are a good touch, by the way. Distraction by attraction, right?"

She sucked in a sharp indignant breath. "What gives you the right to—"

"Lady, I've had one crappy day and I don't need this. I've blown your cover, but you obviously need the story. So here's the deal—you leave now and I won't charge you with trespass." Stunned, Beth watched him turn back to the window. "Where's your camera crew? Your mikes? Behind the bushes?"

She sucked in a sharp furious breath. "Just *who* do you think you *are?*"

That got his attention. He spun with catlike agility, angry and bristling. A formidable sight with the height and arrogance to back it up. But as his silent scrutiny lengthened, her heart quickened, pounding in heavy thuds against her ribs. She nervously eyed the distance to the kitchen. Sharp knives…a phone…

"Are you trying to be obtuse?" he demanded.

Before she could answer that, he reached into his back pocket, pulled out an expensive leather wallet and thrust his driver's license under her nose. "Luke De Rossi, Miss…?"

"Jones. Beth Jones."

Thin fingers of suspicion spiked through Luke's gut as he watched her reposition herself at the hall entrance. Her eyes, startled green and fringed in long sandy lashes that darted over to the kitchen, finally got him. She rocked on the balls of her toes, poised and ready for flight. Suspicion tightened the muscles in her face. Hell, he could practically smell her distress.

A reporter she definitely wasn't. And squatters didn't live this well. She sounded like a tough nut, looked like a divine gift and wore her defensiveness like a cloak. She was as confused as he was.

So—a mistress, then.

Normally he relied on his immaculate composure to radiate authority, but, along with his seemingly infallible instinct, all three had flown right out the window.

He took a step back, regrouped. "Look, Miss Jones. Maybe we'd better start again. I'm—"

"I know exactly who you are."

Luke exhaled heavily and felt the determined throb of a headache coming on. "I suppose you have some proof this is your house?" he said shortly.

She narrowed her eyes. "Proof? Why?"

"Lady, I'd appreciate a little help here."

"I've lived here for the past three years and—"

"Owner or tenant?"

"What?"

"Do you own it or do you rent?" he enunciated clearly.

Beth bit back a rude comment as anger still simmered. "Rent, but—"

"Work with me, Miss Jones." She watched his jaw tighten. "Who rented you the place?"

"A real estate agency."

"Which one?"

"I don't see—"

"The name, please."

Silently, defiantly, she crossed her arms.

He ran a hand through his hair again, the short strands peaking in the wake of his long fingers. The incongruous action made him seem…oddly vulnerable. Beth nearly laughed at the absurd observation. *Vulnerable? Right. Like a black panther waiting to catch his lunch is vulnerable.*

Vaguely, she recalled an old *Sun-Herald* feature on Australia's leading financial corporations. "Lucky Luke" De Rossi was just one of Jackson and Blair's gifted talent—off-the-charts IQ, Harvard educated. As a corporate suit with the multibillion-dollar merchant bank, he had a perfect employment record, a perfect trust-me-with-your-millions attitude and perfect integrity. Hell, she'd actually admired his professionalism and commitment even if she hadn't agreed with his workaholic drive.

His unwavering gaze held hers in silent stalemate. Then, with a sudden grimace, he rolled his shoulder and rubbed the base of his neck.

Trapezius, she automatically thought. *Tight deltoids. Possible back pain. Definite headache.*

She blinked, confused. Weariness practically oozed from this man's pores, his features etched in frustration. And try as he might to hide it, she could make out the lines of pain bracketing his mouth.

As quickly as her sympathy rose, she tried banishing it.

And still he continued to massage his neck, almost as if it was a subconscious tic. Maybe, she thought grudgingly, high stress levels could send someone temporarily insane.

"So you're renting this place," he finally said.

She held his gaze. "Yes."

The cynicism in his eyes didn't intimidate her one bit. If anything, it spurred her irritation.

"So who's the agency? You have an address? A phone number?"

"Are you going to tell me what's going on?"

"Look, I'm trying to get to the bottom of this and you're not helping."

He was so obviously used to asking the questions, to having ultimate control, that Beth couldn't contain a humourless laugh. She'd dealt with his kind all too often. "How's about *you* help *me* and get out of my house?"

"What?"

"You heard."

"*Your* house?" He narrowed his eyes. "Last time I checked, this place was my uncle's." His dark expression grew thunderous. "Were you and he involved?"

Her breath choked off for one second, then came rushing back in a hiss, face flaming. "First you barge into my house then accuse me of sleeping with your uncle. Are you crazy?"

Luke gritted his teeth, the headache pounding in earnest now. *Jeez, this lady isn't Bambi, she's Godzilla!* "Look, we're not going to achieve anything by yelling at each other."

"That's right." She marched down the hall, leaving him no choice but to follow. "I live here, Mr. De Rossi. If you're telling the truth, then come back with proof."

Exhaustion tugged at his legs, desperate to drag him down. All he wanted was a shower and a decent night's sleep—he'd be willing to commit a felony to get it just about now.

So maybe he could reason with her soft side. If she had one.

Time to change tactics. He took a step toward her, a conciliatory smile teasing the corners of his mouth, palms turned up in supplication.

"I'm sure we can come to some arrangement." Rewarded by her startled look, he continued. "You know who I am, so you know I'm good for—"

"Good for what?" Her calm response had him flashing a real full-on smile, one he knew could melt a few hearts and strong wills when he chose. "And what kind of arrangement did you have in mind?"

As they stood there with the warm evening breeze drifting through the doorway, Luke happened to glance down. Her tank top gaped at the neck, displaying a gentle swell of cleavage. *Bloody hell.* Quickly he dragged his eyes up, but a sheen of sweat dotting her smooth honey throat diverted his attention.

"Just give me a break, Ms. Jones." He swallowed and finally managed to focus on the doorjamb behind her left ear. "I drove down from Brisbane and dodged reporters to get here."

"Not in the car that's being jacked, I hope."

His reaction couldn't have been more perfect. As Luke whirled, Beth put her hand firmly in the small of his back and shoved with all the pent-up anger and frustration bubbling inside.

Luke stumbled through the doorway. By the time he'd regained his balance, she'd locked the security screen.

"Possession is nine-tenths the law. Have a nice night!"

Then she slammed the door in his stunned face.

Two

Tuesday morning rolled in on brilliant beams of spring sunshine, streaking across the cloudless sky and encouraging more than one worker to call in sick.

Luke sat in his parked car and stared across the yard and into the kitchen. Beth moved with purpose—firm, precise and direct. The very thought of tangling with her cranked his warning system up to maximum volume.

Most men would have taken the hint and let the local cops sort this mess out.

He wasn't most men.

He'd called Gino's lawyer and been put on hold for ten minutes. When he'd rung back, the receptionist apologized profusely then proceeded to put him on hold again. With a curse he'd finally hung up.

He should've gone with his first thought and refused the bequest. Except…

Gino always knew exactly what he was doing when it came to his business interests. There was a reason Luke had been named beneficiary and by God, he was going to find out. Even if it meant dealing with a possible mistress.

So, two options—call in the cops or deal with the situation himself.

He sighed. No-brainer. Option one meant publicity, something he neither wanted nor needed. With option two, he'd at least be in control. Which meant he needed more information about Beth Jones.

His neck twinged and he stretched, the muscles pulling painfully taut. As the blinding sun hit his face, he flipped down the visor.

It didn't take a degree in psychology to work out the woman didn't trust easily, especially following his performance last night. He cringed inwardly. He'd suffered an uncharacteristic loss of control, one that wouldn't happen again.

His mouth twitched. Damn, if she hadn't surprised the hell out of him. She was stronger than she looked.

Luke swung open the car door and got out. Lemons. That's what she smelled like. Fresh, citrus and edible. Like the old-fashioned lemonade his aunt Rosa made on hot Sunday afternoons…sharp on the surface yet oh, so sweet when you got down to the sugar pooled in the bottom of the glass.

He scowled. She might smell great and look even better, but he had a job to do. And her guarded suspicion definitely meant there was something she wasn't telling him. He'd bet his upcoming promotion on it.

"Thank you for calling Crown Real Estate," came the tinny message on the other end of Beth's line. "Our office hours are from—" Beth gripped the phone with a tight sigh then hung up. The phone rang almost immediately. She grabbed it. "Yes?"

"Don't hang up. It's Luke De Rossi."

She frowned. "How'd you get this number?"

"It's on the deed. Look outside."

She spun and stared at the long-legged figure in her front yard. "How long have you been there?"

"A few hours." What did he think she was going to do—burn the place down? Do a runner? "We need to talk."

She stiffened, waiting for the catch. Luke maintained steady eye contact. Finally, she said, "I'll come out."

With a coolness belying her thumping heart, she released the blinds. They clattered down with sharp finality.

A burst of nervous energy sent her pacing across the kitchen.

She didn't want to talk. Hell, she'd spent the last ten years keeping her mouth shut. Her idyllic existence was based on a bunch of lies and talking would only leave her wide-open to the past, to what she'd left behind.

Not to mention possible criminal charges for identity theft.

Icy fear skimmed her skin, forcing goose bumps to the surface. The Australian press had a fascination with morbid grand-scale tragedy, especially on the eve of the ten-year anniversary. She rarely read the news but the past few months she'd managed to avoid everything—papers, TV, radio. She'd become adept at sidestepping when her clients brought up current affairs. But her memories couldn't be so easily avoided.

She went over to the counter and poured a cup of coffee from the pot, swallowing the faint acrid taste of panic. No one in her new life knew who she'd been, what she'd done. Yet Luke's appearance brought back all those old fears like the Ghost of Christmas Past.

She quickly slammed the door on her thoughts and focused on the present. Luke De Rossi.

Like an old motor starting up, her heart quickened. In a normal situation, she'd be itching to help this man who practically smoldered with shredded nerves. In a normal situation... But this could hardly be less normal.

Good-looking men always had hidden agendas. Like that reporter she'd trusted when she was eighteen. Like a couple of rich, smooth business types—both married and single—who used her massage services then tried to chat her up.

Like Ben, her missing bookkeeper.

She'd more than learned her lesson about trust.

After she made a quick call to Laura and asked her to open the store today, she went to the front door, cup in hand. With an efficient smoothing of hair and squaring of shoulders, she took a deep breath. *Getting all panicky will do no good.* The agency couldn't give her answers, so maybe he could. And, she realized, Luke De Rossi, Mr. Rich-and-Powerful, could make her life very difficult if she kicked up a fuss.

On that last thought, she opened the kitchen door and stepped outside.

Luke sat on the railing, looking seriously dangerous in the morning light. Even with creased shirt and rumpled hair, everything about him screamed authority and confidence—from the tanned skin revealed by the one loose collar button and strong biceps beneath rolled-up sleeves, to the way he watched her with those darker-than-midnight eyes.

He needs to get rid of that tension bunching up his neck. A few sessions and she could have those muscles massaged into relaxation.

The thought of getting her hands on all that pent-up energy sent an unfamiliar sensation down her spine. What was wrong with her? Sure, she'd seen great bodies before. Pummeled, manipulated and eased any manner of muscular aches and pains. Yet this stranger had a look about him, one that said even though he was fired up about something, he could handle it. He was in control. *Too* in control?

He surprised her by handing her a bunch of letters. "Your mail." As she took them, he nodded toward her porch swing and added, "Those are for you."

Beth's eyes widened. Carnations covered the seat, a burst of vivid yellow, white and pink. Their distinctive fragrance teased her nose, courtesy of a warm easterly.

She glanced from the swing back to him. His expression was subdued, even a little uncomfortable.

"I was out of line last night," he said brusquely. "I don't normally jump to conclusions. I apologize."

"Okay." Her gaze skittered back to the flowers.

"I got them from the garden at the end of the street. I left a note and twenty bucks."

A reluctant smile kicked the corner of her mouth up. "You stole Crabby Craig's prized flowers?"

"Ah." His confident expression fell. "With a name like that, he *will* mind."

She surprised herself by grinning. "He may come looking for you. Apparently, the man's a big-shot doctor."

"Then I'll have to tell him it was a life-or-death situation." When he answered her grin with one of his own, her thoughts mockingly returned. He *was* gorgeous without all that anger—all Italian muscle, aquiline nose and a set of hypnotic eyes.

An awkward silence descended until she remembered the cup she still held. "Here." She saw him hesitate and added drily, "It's not poisoned. Milk, no sugar."

"Good guess." Luke took the cup gratefully. "Why the sudden kindness? I thought you wanted me gone."

"And I thought you'd have a cop with you this morning."

"There are other ways to deal with this."

"Then I should credit you with more self-control than I initially thought."

"Enough for both of us, it seems." Was he teasing her from behind the coffee mug? After that lame attempt to sweet-talk her last night, she didn't doubt it.

His soft, almost seductive tone made her heart thump. Annoyed, she swallowed a sharp retort. Instead, she gave him an abbreviated version of what little she'd discovered that morning.

He took it all in in silence, with no overt display of

emotion except a faint tightening of the jaw, a flash of his dark eyes. Finally, he dragged a long-fingered hand through his hair and rose.

"And what's the real estate agency called?" He fixed her with such a piercing look, she felt the danger tingle down to the roots of her hair.

"Crown. I have a rental agreement… well, it's more like a caretaking agreement—the owners are permanently overseas and I pay minimum rent to keep their house."

"And you've been here three years."

"Yes."

"And before that?"

A myriad of emotions tightened her gut. "A bunch of cheap rentals. Nothing like this."

She'd put so much time and effort into making this house her home. Fixed and replanted the sad garden. Painted the walls. Retiled the bathroom. Put up shelves. All with her own sweat and time and with many a muttered curse. And in a few months, finances willing, she'd even planned to make an offer on it.

It was her sanctuary from the world and no one was going to take that from her without a fight.

"What do you do for work?" he continued.

"I'm a masseuse. I have a store in Surfers…" She glanced at her watch. "One that opens at ten."

He paused and took a sip of coffee, his expression unreadable. "Do you have the agency's address?"

"Highway end of Surfers Mall." She frowned. "What are you going to do?"

"Who's Ben?"

"What?" Beth blinked.

"Boyfriend? Ex-husband?"

"No!"

"You thought I was here about Ben yesterday."

She hated how the seeds of insecurity had blossomed into a full-blown tree of doubt in the last half hour. She didn't want to give in to that. Because if she did, it meant all her efforts to carve out a normal life these last ten years had failed. She didn't want to be suspicious, didn't want to automatically doubt every person she met. But right now, faced with this bizarre situation, she had a strange feeling she *should* believe him. He just gave off that kind of aura.

"Ben's got nothing to do with this," she eventually said.

"How do you know that? He could've been partners with the agency, operating a real estate scam."

"Do you know how ridiculous that sounds?"

"Oh, and what we have here is normal?"

She plunked herself on the porch railing. They stayed like that for a few moments, Luke in anticipatory silence, she with her lips pressed tight. He gave her that look again, that firm, what-are-you-hiding-from-me look. It unnerved her.

"He was my bookkeeper," she conceded tightly, cheeks warming. "When my bank accidentally deposited someone else's money into my business account, he took it and ran."

"How much?"

"Five hundred thousand dollars."

He gave a low whistle, and embarrassment flamed her face. She'd trusted Ben—someone she thought she'd known—and he'd gone and screwed her over.

"I take it you've filed a police report?"

"Not yet." His look only compounded her shame. "The bank gives you twenty-eight days to return the money. It's only the second."

"You think he's going to bring it back?" At her silence, he added more softly, "So. We have a scam *and* a missing person."

"*We* don't. My problems are none of your business."

"And I can see you're handling them just fine."

She shot to her feet, irritated beyond words. He was right. But cops meant an inquiry, one she couldn't afford to have.

"Were you and Foster in a sexual relationship?" he said suddenly.

Beth flushed. "What is it with you and sex? No! He's nineteen, barely out of his teens. A math geek. His mother was a client and he… I…" She faltered at his expression then conceded, "We met twice after work, but it was always about business."

"Did he know that?"

"Of course!" She swallowed as a small sliver of doubt crept in. "Of course," she repeated with less conviction. "Why would he steal from me? And something that's not even mine?"

"Greed's a basic human desire. It's not a matter of need, it's about want. You focus on a victim, build trust and then…"

"Don't you think I know that?"

Luke took in her tight expression and felt a rush of sympathy. "Do you need to sit down?"

"No." As if he'd insulted her, she straightened her back and crossed her arms.

He flipped out his phone and dialed. "Dylan. It's Luke. I need a favor. Information on a Ben Foster. Lives…?"

He paused for an interminably long moment, until Beth grudgingly reeled off an address.

As he gave details, he pointedly ignored Beth's impatient snort. But when she attempted to interrupt, he held up a hand, silencing her. A complex play of emotions flitted across her face—annoyance, indignation—along with a scowl. Obviously she wasn't used to being silenced. Fascinated, he watched her wrestle with the anger banking in her eyes. For a second he wasn't sure control would win out.

"Gotcha," Dylan said. "When do you want this info?"

"Yesterday."

Dylan laughed. "Right. I'm off to Cairns for a court appearance this afternoon, then I'm booked solid until Friday. I could hand it over to one of my guys—"

"No. I'd much rather you handle it."

"Okay. So it'll have to wait until Sunday."

Four days? Luke frowned. "Sure." Then he hung up.

Beth rounded on him. "I didn't ask for your help!" Her eyes narrowed, her expression tight. "Or is poking about in people's lives just something that comes naturally?"

He slowly crossed his arms. "Dylan's a P.I. and can find your runaway a lot quicker than the bank or the cops. I'm not interested in your secrets, Beth," he lied smoothly.

"Just make sure it stays that way." The fire retreated

as she darted her gaze away to a point past his shoulder. "My private life stays private."

Luke swallowed the unspoken question teetering on the tip of his tongue. Somehow he didn't think voicing his opinion on her trust issues would bode well for their tentative truce.

"White-collar crime is more common than you think."

"Gee, that makes me feel so much better."

He ignored her sarcasm and started dialing Gino's solicitor again. "And we need to prove I'm telling the truth."

Luck was definitely not with him. After a few minutes of the busy signal, he clicked off with a foul curse. "I need to see your lease."

Her eyes narrowed then zeroed in on his hand where he'd begun to rub his neck.

"Wait here." But when he stood, she took a step back. "What?"

"Wouldn't have any more coffee, would you?"

She paused. "In the kitchen." Then, reluctantly, "Fine. Come in."

Beth was acutely aware of his presence as she gathered up the carnations then walked into the kitchen. She got an empty vase from the cupboard, filled it with water then arranged the flowers, all the while trying to ignore the whirl of confusing reactions circling inside.

"Mind if I have some toast?" he asked when she finally finished.

She sighed. *What's one more oddity in a day like today?* "Help yourself," she muttered and walked out of the kitchen.

When Beth returned, she paused in the doorway, watching as Luke stood at the counter eating Vegemite-smothered toast.

I'll bet relax *is not in his vocabulary.* Yet despite that small flaw, he was a perfect specimen. He had shoulders broader than a man had any right to have. His Mediterranean skin was a healthy tan and from what she could see, not one ounce of fat insulted that perfect physique. It was a functional, red-blooded, well-kept body…and looked far too warm and touchable for her liking. Despite herself she *wanted* to touch him, wanted to ease out the tension furrowing his brow, trail her hands down those beautiful forearms, over his chest, feel the heat radiating there, maybe even—

Annoyance chased away the threads of attraction. After her past mistakes, she'd vowed never to let anyone get that close again.

And now Luke was making himself at home in her kitchen. He'd even mastered her temperamental toaster, because just as the offending appliance flung a piece of toast high into the air, Luke caught it as skillfully as a Brisbane Broncos halfback.

She'd never been able to judge the trajectory on that stupid thing.

She laid her papers on the kitchen table. "Here's everything. You should also know I have a legally binding tenancy agreement."

She savored the small bittersweet triumph, even as he grabbed the documents and scanned them with a black scowl.

But as she watched him read, that feeling of victory slowly leeched away. Three months. Only a blink away. If he was telling the truth, could he actually sell her home from under her feet regardless of that bit of paper?

This house meant more to her than a roof. It was a home, a sanctuary. It was *her* home. After so many years of not belonging, it was a symbol of how far she'd come and everything she'd struggled for. And there was no way some high-priced banker with a sinful smile would force her out.

She needed expert legal advice—except she couldn't afford it.

She eyeballed Luke still studying her papers, his shirt tight across his shoulders as he leaned over the table. *Amazing how such a large piece of clothing provided so little cover.*

With awareness prickling her skin, she reached for the coffeepot and poured herself a cup. Gently blowing the steam off, she lifted her eyes, only to find his intent on the rim of her cup.

On her lips.

She swallowed, lowered the cup and waved to her papers. "Does that prove I'm not lying?"

"It looks legitimate." He pointed to a signature. "The agency has a management agreement, acting on behalf of the owners."

"That's right."

"So you have no idea who the real owners are?"

"No." From the look on his face he obviously didn't like her answer. "So our next move is…?"

"I'm going to see Gino's lawyers."

"You mean, *we're* going." She put her cup in the sink, the coffee now a tart taste in her mouth.

He flexed his back and grimaced but said nothing.

She scowled. "I'm going to be frank with you, Mr. De Rossi. I am not impressed with you—not by your power or your wealth. I know people like you."

His eyes narrowed. "Really."

"Yes. Men dedicated to their jobs, their own needs. They think that with one killer smile, anyone can be swayed into changing a decision. They have to be in control twenty-four hours a day."

"All that just by looking at me, hey?"

"I've had a lot of practice. And just so you know, don't even think about trying to charm me. I'm immune."

Luke studied her blankly, her stubborn chin tilted up, lips pressed tightly together, hands on hips.

Classic defensive stance.

His sudden smile threw her. "So, apart from my job, my looks and my mere presence, you like me, right?"

A gentle morning breeze took that moment to sweep through the window, curling through the flowers on the windowsill and ruffling her wheat-blond curls. It wrapped around them until Luke wasn't sure if the perfume came from her or the flowers.

Either way, she smelled damn good.

Yeah, hold on there, mate. You need to focus on getting Gino's stuff out of your life, not be swayed by a pair of wide Bambi eyes. She could make things awkward. You still don't know what her part is and you need Beth Jones onside.

Judging by the hostile vibe of her crossed arms and her closed expression, he had his work cut out.

"Surely there must be one tiny thing you like about me, right? Otherwise I wouldn't be standing here."

She tilted her head with a curious expression. "Why is it so important I like you?"

"Because then you can start to trust me."

"I don't trust anyone."

Luke watched her grab a cloth and wipe the table in swift, jerky movements.

He could read people pretty well, yet Beth Jones was an enigma. In direct contrast to yesterday, she was armored up in a green shirt and jeans, her hair efficiently pulled back low on her neck. Defensive, yes. Self-sufficient, definitely. Yet he couldn't quite get a handle on the rest…and loose cannons made him nervous.

Despite her desperation to get rid of him and the mess she was now in, she hadn't mentioned cops or lawyers again. He'd expected tears or anger, not this cool, calm logic. She'd even dug in her heels and dared him to prove his story, which meant she was confident with hers.

His initial hunch was correct—she *was* hiding something.

He crossed his arms and tested his theory. "We do this my way or we hand it all over to our lawyers. And I'm pretty sure you won't like the alternative."

She narrowed her eyes, her smile tight. "So I guess we're about to find out who's trustworthy, aren't we?"

Three

They got into Luke's car and set off in silence.

Instead of thinking about those long fingers changing gears a hairbreadth away, she tried to focus on the things she *didn't* like—his arrogant attitude, the way he took control. Those all-seeing, all-knowing eyes. The tension in his shoulders…hard, firm shoulders… That kissable mouth…

As he changed into third gear, she jumped again, the warmth of his knuckles sending a tingle up her leg. She stole a glance at him. He was looking straight ahead and didn't appear to be having a problem keeping his hormones in check.

"So," he finally said, absently running a finger around his rolled-up shirtsleeve and working the material, bringing Beth's attention to the tanned forearm underneath. "We'll make a stop at the real estate agent's first then head to Brisbane."

"What makes you think they'll tell you anything?"

"Because I can be very persuasive."

Oh, I'm sure you can.

"So how did you find them?" he asked.

"They're local, a few of my clients use them and they had what I was after." She glanced sideways, taking in his expression. "Look, they're a legitimate business with an office, a receptionist and a bunch of listings. It's not like I threw my money at any old bum in the street."

"I've no doubt their operation is professional," Luke said.

"And I have all the right papers, as you saw."

"I also saw you have three months left on your lease." She clamped her mouth shut. She wouldn't have to suffer his presence much longer. Before day's end this would all be cleared up.

She focused back on the road, staring out the window as they moved along Pacific Highway, passing Australia Fair shopping complex before driving over the Nerang River.

Soon, Aphrodite's appeared on the left, all towering glass and concave walls. A replica of the *Venus de Milo* standing proudly atop seemed subdued in the daylight, almost grave in her state of undress. But at night, when all the lights of the casino came on, reflecting on the lake below like a never-ending fireworks display, she glowed with inner beauty. A magnificent spectacle that was still a regular Gold Coast draw twenty years on.

A familiar line of hotels, shops and restaurants

flanked busy Surfers Paradise Boulevard as they crawled along with the rest of the traffic, the pungent smell of exhaust fumes mingling with the familiar saltiness of the Pacific Ocean a few hundred feet away.

She chanced another glance at Luke—deep in thought—and set her mouth in a grim line.

"Why are you getting involved in this, anyway? Don't you have an army of lawyers to do all the legwork?"

The unspoken mistrust hovered, warm and cloying, until he pulled into a parking space across from Cavill Mall.

He switched off the engine and turned to face her.

"For whatever reason, Gino Corelli gave me that house. So—"

"Wait, what? Gino *Corelli? He's* your uncle?" Shock slammed into Beth, choking her breath. She tried to swallow but failed. "The owner of Aphrodite's? The one who's just been under investigation from the gaming commission?"

"Yeah, so?"

At his confused expression, she slumped back in her seat and stared blankly ahead. "Gino Corelli," she repeated slowly. "So you're…he's… My God! You… you… You were in my home…using my toaster!"

His black frown loomed like storm-filled clouds. "I thought you knew who I was!"

"*You,* yes. Not who your uncle is…*was.* I…" The words caught in her throat as his expression iced over.

"The press are wrong. The commission didn't have enough evidence to bring to the Director of Public Prosecutions," he returned tightly.

Beth scrambled out of the car, desperate to dislodge the sour taste in her mouth. What on earth was she in the middle of?

Luke rounded the hood and came toward her.

"You just keep your distance!" she ordered. The brief newsflashes she'd been unable to avoid burst in her mind, robbing her of coherent thought. "Corelli's a crime boss who laundered money and was bribing the cops and..." She scrambled for further details but it was futile. All that stood out was something about insider trading—and Luke worked for one of the largest merchant banks in Australia.

"*Allegedly* bribing the cops. *Allegedly* laundering money." His eyes went stony, his expression grim. A wall of self-protection to hide the blow she'd unthinkingly dealt him. "One disgruntled employee with an ax to grind, and the mighty press finishes the job. And for the record, Ms. Jones, the case was eventually thrown out and I was never formally named. They didn't splash *that* on the front page though, did they?" He spun on his heel and strode across the road.

His words struck Beth like a slap. A wave of shame immediately followed, burning her cheeks as surely as if he'd landed the blow.

She had hurt him. She'd never willingly hurt anyone, yet she'd blurted out those accusations without a thought as to Luke's innocence.

A small groan of dismay escaped as she recalled the scant details. More important, she remembered the overwhelming rush of sympathy she'd felt for Luke De Rossi right before she'd clicked off the TV in frustration. She had avoided the news since then and frankly, the absence of hearsay, rumor and half-truths was wonderfully liberating.

So why was she so willing to believe in Luke's guilt now?

That thought propelled her into action. She dashed across the street to where Luke was impatiently waiting, his eyes hidden by sunglasses.

"Look, I'm sorry," she said quietly. "I overreacted. I…" She shrugged, at a loss for words. "It's not exactly been a normal day for me, okay?"

He sighed, as if suddenly tired of arguing. "Yeah. Me neither. So let's just focus on clearing up this mess."

Then he turned and Beth followed in silence as he stalked down the mall.

By the time they'd made it through the gradually thickening crowd of tourists and office workers, avoided a persistent busker and his jovial crowd then a group of teenagers with surfboards, Beth was slightly out of breath. Luke's purposeful strides left her in the dust. The determined set to his jaw and shoulders screamed "get out of my way." No wonder people stopped to stare as he breezed by, their whispers and odd looks quickly masked as she stabbed them with a glare.

As they approached Crown Real Estate, they both noticed the closed sign and the locked glass doors.

"Open at ten," Luke muttered, glaring at the sign. Still, he tried the handle, then shielded his eyes and peered in. Suddenly he pulled back with a soft curse, a moment too late.

A key rattled and the door opened an inch. A business-suited man, his tie askew, smiled out at them.

"Sorry. Office opens in half an hour."

"Is Jay around?" Beth asked.

"She's doing a bunch of showings until twelve. Hang on." He disappeared for a second then returned with a business card. "Call her mobile." His gaze flicked over to Luke and lingered. "Hey, I know you. You're—"

"No one important. Thanks." Luke turned and took Beth's arm, steering her away.

Beth extracted herself from Luke's grip moments later.

"Well, that was a bust," he muttered.

"Not entirely." Beth took out her phone and punched in the number on the card as they walked back to the car.

"Message bank." She left a brief message then clicked off. "Great. So what now?"

Luke shoved his hands deep in his pockets and tightened his jaw. "We're going to Brisbane."

Two hours later, after meeting with Gino's lawyer, they rode the elevator down to the basement parking lot in silence.

Beth punched the button again, barely sparing him a glance. She glared at the tiny red numbers, her plunging stomach having little to do with their descent.

"So that's it, then. You win."

He glanced up from his phone, still scrolling. "It's not about me winning."

"Isn't it?" She crossed her arms, refusing to look at him.

"No. Probate will take a few months then the estate has to be wound up. That'll take years."

Years. "What about my tenancy agreement?"

"Your lease expires the same time the agency's management agreement does." Luke frowned then tapped the screen.

"I was in that meeting too." She scowled at him. "Both are legally binding—"

He held up a hand and put the phone to his ear. "It's Luke De Rossi."

Man, that was really beginning to bug her! Beth waited in simmering silence until he hung up.

"I'll buy the house from you," she said suddenly. "How much?"

One eyebrow lifted. "I need to get it properly assessed."

"Ballpark, then."

He studied her in total silence before saying slowly, "It'll be way out of your price range."

Her eyebrows shot up. "How would you know?"

"You *do* know a Sunset Island price tag starts at a million? What would you use as collateral?"

"My business. And when I get this thing with the bank sorted—"

"What if you don't?"

"I will. And anyway, I'm there until my lease is up, which gives me time."

"No."

"You're going to keep it?" she asked, surprised.

"Look, it's not personal."

At her blatant skepticism, his expression twisted in annoyance. "Gino's investments took a big hit in the financial crisis, the casino's been hemorrhaging cash and the gaming commission probe scared a lot of people off. I need to sell quickly and quietly so I can get back to my job. Now, unless you have a spare couple of million hanging around, that rules you out."

Her initial surprise quickly transformed into irritation. "So nothing matters except protecting your reputation?"

"Do not—" he narrowed his eyes "—presume to judge me, Beth. We still don't know why you're involved here."

"Well, it's obviously just a massive coincidence."

His silence and flat expression told her what he thought of that. "I can offer you a good price for your lease."

She blinked. He wanted her gone that badly he was willing to buy her out? "I don't want to leave. I *want* my house."

The elevator doors opened then and he walked out without a word.

Wow. Talk about shutting her down. She watched his long legs eat up the distance, taking him farther away with each stride until he paused and turned.

"Coming?"

His voice echoed in the great concrete cavern. A thousand different retorts, all considered then discarded, formed as she stalked toward him.

Her phone rang then, but he suddenly grabbed her arm.

She hissed, twisting in his warm grip. "What do you—"

"Shh. Something's not right."

"But—"

"Move. Now."

Her eyes went in the direction of his nod, to the fire
stairs nestled in a concrete alcove, then widened.

And all hell broke loose.

Four

Like a deer caught in the headlights, she froze.

A second too late.

A handful of reporters surged forward from the stairwell, surrounding them like a fluid entity. Cameras flashed, microphones thrust forward as they yelled out questions and jostled for a better position.

"How are you taking the suspension, Luke?"

"Have you hired Gino's lawyers to defend you?"

"Any truth to the rumor you've been accused of insider trading?"

The air buzzed, frantic and urgent. Luke fought against the sea of bodies, shielding his face as he grabbed Beth's wrist just before a camera slammed into his shoulder. Sucking in a grunt and with Beth firmly in his grip, he turned and ran.

Beth gulped in huge lungfuls of air and picked up the pace, her flat shoes slapping on the concrete as they raced toward their car.

Luke glanced back before aiming his keys at the car. With a pop and flash of lights, the locks disengaged. "Get in!"

She barely had time to close her door before he gunned the engine and took off.

The car flew over a speed bump. Luke spun the steering wheel and the tires squealed, the smell of burned rubber hitting Beth seconds later as she slammed into his shoulder.

"Slow down!" She righted herself from that wall of muscle quickly. "Are you trying to get us killed?"

"Just trying to lose their tail and avoid any pedestrians with a death wish."

He followed that with an abrupt swerve, barely missing a jaywalking youth. Luke ignored the obscene comment and gesture left in their wake. He did, however, inch his foot off the accelerator.

Beth glanced through the back window. A beat-up cream-colored car that had been following was stuck at the now-red light. "You're losing them."

Luke barely managed two more yellow lights before their pursuers were lost in the steady flow of traffic.

He matched the car's speed to the signed limit and Beth finally loosened her grip on the door handle.

"You okay?" He glanced at her.

Her pulse pounded in her forehead, but she gave him a nod, grateful for the blasting air-conditioning. "How on earth did they know where we were?"

"People noticed us at the mall. It only takes one

phone call." He glanced in the rearview then changed lanes.

"Great." Beth sighed and pushed a lock of hair behind her ear as her heart began to slow. "So what do we do now?"

"We're going to the airport."

"The what?"

"Here, take the wheel."

She grabbed the steering wheel as Luke flipped open his phone. "This is Luke De Rossi. I need the plane ready for takeoff in around thirty minutes." He paused, said, "Thanks," then hung up.

"We're *flying?*" She relinquished the wheel.

"Yep."

Her throat tightened, suddenly dry, and she squeezed her eyes shut, the stony walls of frustration lying heavy on her shoulders for one brief second.

It had been ten years. Ten long, full years of triumphs and achievements. She'd worked hard, been in control. She'd overcome enormous hurdles many would have run from. She was living her life.

It made sense to do this. It was the quickest way to leave the tailing press behind.

But a *plane*...

For a nanosecond the awful flashes screamed by, but she refused to let them linger.

She swallowed again and straightened her spine. *You can do this. You have to.*

It was one thing to convince herself while they were driving, but soon they were on the tarmac, the shiny Beechcraft King Air plane awaiting them.

She stared at the clean white lines of the turboprop plane, the large twin engines, the glossy paintwork as her heart began to race.

Pound, pound, pound. The sudden primeval urge to run snaked low as a shaky breath jammed in her throat.

Therapy worked. It stopped those nightmares. It helped to handle the fear and guilt. It can't rule your life anymore.

When she choked down a short groan, she could feel Luke's eyes on her.

"You don't like flying?"

She nodded mutely, her eyes still locked on the plane.

"Soooo…" He paused. "You've never been on a plane at all?"

"Once. It…didn't go well." Boy, understatement of the century. She blinked, filling her lungs slowly then emptying them again, just as she'd been taught.

"After instrument check, it's a fifteen-minute flight to Surfers—we go up, we come down. The whole thing will take an hour. I've made the trip a thousand times."

But it only takes one. She remained silent, her heart battering her tight chest.

When Luke took her hand she nearly jumped out of her skin, her nerves lurching as his fingers laced intimately through hers.

"Okay?"

"No."

"You can do this."

With his hand enveloping hers, she let him tug her across the tarmac, the steady roar of Brisbane airport's air traffic swirling around them.

"Mr. De Rossi." Their pilot stood by the stairs and nodded. "We have clearance, when you're ready."

"Get us up, John." Luke mounted the stairs, still holding her hand. Her viselike grip must have been uncomfortable, but he said nothing. His warm skin, firm fingers and cool authority were a welcome distraction, even if her breath still raced as they walked up the metal stairs one clanky footstep at a time.

But when she stepped into the plane's cool interior, fear was momentarily suspended.

"Wow." Perfectly circular tinted windows let in enough light to display the oval interior to luxurious perfection. She counted six spacious seats in soft honey leather before running her gaze over the polished mahogany paneling and fittings, the immaculate carpet, then the cockpit just beyond. She barely registered Luke's hand slipping from hers as she took one step inside, then another.

"Pretty cool, huh?" he said behind her.

"It looks like a limousine." She slowly ran her hand down one headrest.

Just as soft as it looked. She breathed in a myriad of scents—leather, new carpet, even a faint whisper of cigar smoke. The scent of power and money.

Then Luke shifted behind her and suddenly a luscious hint of ginger and spices, mingled with something all male, flooded her senses.

Her heart kicked up, but whether it was from the impending flight or Luke's proximity, she couldn't tell.

Then his hand was on the small of her back and she had to swallow back her nerves.

"Take a seat and buckle up." He nudged her forward

then took the seat next to hers, the leather squealing in protest.

She could do nothing but follow his lead.

Luke watched Beth squeeze her eyes shut as the plane began to taxi down the runway, her breath coming short and sharp. Sweat beaded across her forehead and her grip tightened on his, threatening to cut off his blood supply. He swallowed a wince.

"Hey. Look at me."

Reluctantly, her eyes edged open. "What?"

"It's better if you don't shut your eyes."

She scowled. "What would you know about it?"

"My aunt hates flying, too—her first and only trip was when she and Gino immigrated here forty years ago. If she can't get to it by car or boat, she doesn't go."

"Oh." She jumped as the gears clunked into place. Then he began to gently stroke her knuckles and she blinked.

"What are you doing?"

"Calming you down."

"That doesn't help."

"No?" He continued, his eyes fixed on her pale face. "When were you in a limo?"

"What?" The plane sped up and she dragged in a raggedy breath, but Luke wouldn't let her look away.

"You said the plane looked like a limousine."

"Yes."

He reached up and twisted the knob for the air-conditioning in the overhead panel, and when the cool air flooded down, she breathed deeply.

"A limo?" he prompted, settling in his seat.

"A bunch of us hired one to celebrate our final year of study. My first and last taste of the high liiiii—!"

The plane swooped up, his stomach quickly following, and Beth's hand gripped his until his fingers began to throb.

He winced and ignored the pain.

Beth swallowed, knowing she was hurting him but helpless to stop. Yet past all that blood-thumping anxiety, his strong hands wrapped around hers and his deep voice murmured gentle inanities that eventually broke through her panic. Yes, she still wanted to jerk her hand away, but the desire to overcome this awful debilitating fear was greater.

She hated losing control. Yet as she kept her eyes focused on Luke, listening to him recite the plane's capabilities and luxurious interior specifications, she felt something shift. It could've been the intimate warmth of skin on skin, or the sensual timbre of his voice. Or maybe it was the promising flicker behind those eyes she wasn't *quite* sure she'd seen.

When he leaned in, she did, too, her gaze snagged on that sensual mouth only centimetres away. But it was his scent that made her tummy flip in a completely different way.

Lord, he smelled wonderful. She took a deep, shaky breath, just to make sure. Yes. Oh, yes. She closed her eyes. Ginger, peppermint. Hint of bergamot. And…

"Are you sniffing me, Beth?"

Her eyes sprang open, her face hot. "I…uh…"

His mouth curved. "We're in the air, by the way."

"What?" She yanked away and whirled to the window, heart reverberating in her throat.

"You don't need to look." He recaptured her hands, forcing her to turn back. "Just keep focusing on me. Just breathe. And tell me about your work."

"My work?"

"Well, how did you get your own business? Did you go to university?"

"No." She swallowed, allowing his eyes to command hers. "I did a course at my local college. Four years and I had my diploma in massage therapy. I—"

The plane banked right and Beth tightened her grip.

"Go on."

She swallowed then continued faintly, "I did a few business courses, worked a bunch of jobs. And here I am."

"Why massage therapy?"

"Because I'm good at it." *And I like the idea of taking away someone's pain.*

"Your family?"

She bit back a familiar sliver of sorrow. "None."

His gaze softened. "I'm sorry."

She shrugged. "What about yours?"

"My parents died when I was fifteen." She noticed the tightening of his expression, the tiny twitch at the corner of his jaw. "Robbery gone wrong."

"That's…" Sad? Awful? Terrible? Beth paused. Any word she chose was inadequate.

Luke took pity on her. "Yeah. Gino and Rosa took me in until I was eighteen."

Beth flicked a nervous glance out the window, to the clouds floating by, then back again. "You were a gifted child, right? Graduated from a seven-year university degree at nineteen."

He moved uncomfortably in his seat. "Yep. I've been working for Jackson and Blair since then."

Despite the air-conditioning, she felt the slow trickle of sweat meander down her back, coming to rest at the base of her spine. She shifted, the heavy echo of her heartbeat drowning out the engine's gentle drone.

After a moment or two, he said, "It's like a roller coaster."

"What is?"

"Flying. You start off real fast, take off and roll with the dips and turns. It's over before you know it."

She smiled suddenly. "I liked the Tarantula better."

"The what?"

"You know, the ride that swoops up and down and in and out as it spins?"

Luke grinned. "Gotta say, I've never tried it."

"Really? You do *not* know what you're missing."

"Tell me."

Beth took one look at his serious expression, debated for half a second then continued.

"My mother used to take me to the annual Bathurst Show. The guy who operated the Tarantula always slowed it down in the middle of your ride and called out, 'Do you wanna go faster?' And of course, we all screamed, 'Yes!' and he'd yell back, 'Let me see your hands!' and then we'd wave our hands above our heads like crazy while he cranked it up, faster and faster." She sighed. "We flew and it just stole your breath, like being out of control but in a good way…" She paused at his grin then added a little self-conscious one of her own. "*Aaaand* I'm rambling. Sorry."

"Sounds like fun."

"It was."

They remained that way, held only by their smiles, until Beth sensed something more, something…kind of dangerous and yet somehow comforting lying just below the surface.

She stared. A shot of desire hit the pit of her stomach and spread, heating her body. His gaze slowly slid down to the swell of her bottom lip and she was too late to steel herself. Her breath stuttered out. As he continued his slow scrutiny, her skin began to tingle, an irritating yet anticipatory buzz that spread up from her legs to her belly in seconds flat.

Arousal—hot, dark and unwanted—body-slammed her, stealing her breath, eliciting a small gasp of dismay.

She dragged her hands from his and leaned away, swallowing a murmur as the plane began to descend.

"We're nearly there," Luke said as he pulled his phone from his jacket and began scrolling. "You did well."

"Thanks."

An intimate, almost tangible silence fell as the plane swooped in for a landing. Beth refused to break it. She couldn't bear to vocalize what had nearly passed between them.

Because there was no way she was going to succumb to the charms of Luke De Rossi, simple as that.

Five

The landing was a gut-clenching, lip-biting affair, but she managed to make it through without completely losing it. A gray limousine—one of Surfers' most common modes of transportation—was waiting for them as they disembarked.

At least it'd provide much-needed anonymity, space and distance from the roadblock in her life that was Luke De Rossi.

She settled in the soft leather seat, buckled up and prayed for the forty-minute drive to be over as quickly as possible.

"Drink?"

She glanced up and he nodded to the bar fridge laid into the dash. "Mineral water, juice, Coke..."

"Tequila?"

He didn't bat an eye. "Sure."

She smiled humorlessly. "Mineral water's fine."

She waited until he'd finished playing host, until he handed her the drink, poured himself a Scotch on the rocks then settled back.

She pointedly turned to the window and drew the icy glass across her cheek with a sigh.

First those cameras, the frenzied questions, everyone pushing and shoving. Then the scary, gut-wrenching flight that felt as if her stomach had been sucked out with a straw.

Yet she'd made it.

Triumph curved her lips in the tinted reflection. She'd done it. With Luke's help, she'd taken that first step into the unknown and conquered some of her fears.

The victory lingered briefly, until the inevitable memories began to seep in. And slowly, she watched her mouth flatten and her eyes harden.

She'd been eighteen—just a kid. Too young to know better, too weak to hold on.

Frustration snaked its way under her skin, making everything achy, her breath like jagged pieces stabbing her throat on the way in. Those months after the crash had been mind-numbingly tough, her desperation for privacy tested by the public's morbid fascination with every gory detail. On the very first anniversary she'd caved and given an interview, naively assuming the reporter would keep her personal details anonymous. In the ensuing press avalanche, she'd gone off the grid, working a dozen different cash-in-hand jobs, living in near squalor in Sydney's far west before reinventing herself. All had been worth it to finally get through night college and earn her TAFE certificate in remedial massage.

She could've joined the other survivors in their class action suit but that would've involved too many questions, too much publicity. For so long the crash had been her first and last waking thought, consuming every hour, every day, every dream and horror-filled nightmare until she'd somehow managed to leave the past behind and focus on her future.

Stop. You can't go back. Only forward.

Beth rubbed at her eye sockets until her face ached, until she managed to shove those memories away and her shoulders slowly relaxed.

When she softly exhaled, the window misted. She wiped it away. Now was not the time and place to lose it, not when she needed all her wits and strength to deal with the here and now.

Through the window's reflection she glanced at Luke, but the melting ice in his drink had his rapt attention.

He handled millions, no, *billions,* on a daily basis, rubbed shoulders and dealt with clients who made ridiculous amounts of money. The sheer scale of the league she was now in blew her away.

"Do you still think I'm your uncle's secret mistress?" she asked quietly, still staring out the window.

He paused, but when she turned to face him, he shook his head. "No."

"Good."

Another moment of silence passed as they studied each other like wary opponents unwilling to concede.

"I'm serious about my offer to buy you out," he

said suddenly. "I can make it worth your while. You can start over in a new place, something closer to Surfers—"

"Let me tell you something." She shifted, crossed one leg over the other and gave him her full attention. "Imagine someone gives you a car—it's old, it's worn, there are a few bumps and scratches on it and a bit of rust. But still you can see the potential behind all that because up until now, all you've ever had were total lemons that weren't even roadworthy. You spend years on improving that car, banging out the dings, replacing the tires, giving it a new paint job. You sweat and obsess because it gives you a purpose, transports you from your studies, from your crappy waitressing and cleaning jobs, and shows you the possibilities that come with a little hard work and determination. It becomes more than just a project—it becomes a part of who you are. And finally, when you've got it running perfectly and that sweet feeling of pride sings through your veins, a guy shows up and demands you turn it over to him. Yes, legally I know I'm just a tenant," she added quickly just as he opened his mouth. "But, Luke, I put my heart and soul into that place when I had absolutely nothing else. Can you understand that?"

After an interminable silence, a faint ring permeated the air. Without a word he pulled out his phone. Beth sighed and went back to staring out the window.

"Connor. What's up?" Luke said by way of greeting.

"I heard about the commotion on the 10:00 a.m. newsflash."

Luke ground his teeth and muttered a curse. "Yeah, we lost them on the way to Brisbane airport."

"Where are you now?"

"Surfers. Pacific Highway."

"What? And who's 'we'?"

Luke glanced at Beth staring out the window then brought his best friend and boss up to speed.

"I see," was all Connor said when he'd finished explaining. Luke cringed. He could just picture the dark, impassive expression on Connor's face.

Luke clamped down on his jaw, grinding his teeth hard. Gino was *his* uncle. Everything he did reflected on Luke, which in turn reflected on Jackson and Blair. And because of that, good men and women had suffered the fallout. Like Connor Blair. The court case may be over, but the securities commission was still determined to put Jackson and Blair through an internal inquiry.

No wonder Connor was on edge.

"So what's Gino's connection to this woman—Beth Jones?" Connor finally said.

"No idea. I called Dylan."

"The ex-con?"

"P.I. now. The guy owes me a favor."

"You're supposed to lay low. In case you missed it, that wasn't a request."

Luke ran a frustrated hand through his hair. "And I can kiss that promotion goodbye if I don't get my name cleared."

"You will. You made a statement and the majority of the Board is behind you. I'm working on the rest of them. Now it's up to the commission next month."

"But—"

"You've never second-guessed yourself before, Luke.

Why now?" Luke remained silent until Connor broke it. "Your cousin still pissed at you?"

"Yep."

"And this Beth Jones. She's not a criminal?"

"Not as far as I know."

"She an ax murderer? A hit man? A *reporter?*" He could barely keep the contempt from his voice.

"What—?"

"Do you have a natural disaster about to open the ground? A flood? A bushfire that will raze the house? Because these are the only things I'll be looking for if I see your name in the papers."

"Mate…"

"I don't want to hear it. This latest news flash is the last straw. The company's under an internal investigation and my soon-to-be vice president is accused of money laundering only because he shares blood with Gino Corelli. Unless your life's in danger, you *are* going to wait this out."

Luke thought of a dozen comebacks, none of them adequate. "How long?" he finally said.

"Take the rest of the month. I'll give you a call when you need to come in for the hearing."

He could hear a faint sound in the background, which meant Connor had grabbed a pen and was tapping the end on the desk. Luke could just imagine the accompanying facial expression—a mixture of weariness and caution.

"Okay," Luke conceded.

"Oh, and Luke?" Connor said suddenly.

"Yeah?"

"Get a massage. Otherwise you'll get a headache."

Luke cut the call then settled back in the seat. Beth was on her phone, pressing buttons. "I missed a called from the agent and she texted me," she said. "We can call her back in an hour." She returned the phone to her pocket. "A bit pointless now, though." She sighed and changed the subject. "So you're up for a promotion."

"Yeah."

"What's the job?"

"Vice president of international investments." He tapped the phone against his knee, thoughts churning.

"Think you'll get it?"

"Right now, I have no idea."

Silence fell. Then, "This is not good, is it?" she asked softly.

Luke finally glanced over and their gazes met.

There it was again, that odd vulnerability. It jarred deep inside, stirring long-buried feelings that set his whole body on alert even as he tried to quash it. He'd given up on that dumb compulsion years ago. But now, looking into Beth's face with those wide green eyes and that guarded expression, he felt the familiar overwhelming urge to protect her from all the world's wrongdoings.

She doesn't need you to look after her. You need her out so you can sell that house and give Rosa the much-needed money. Then things will go back to normal.

"Well," he said slowly, "it's not all bad."

"And what's your definition of 'bad'?"

"No one got hurt and we have some answers." He settled back in the seat and laced his fingers behind his neck. "On a scale of one to ten it'd rank about seven."

"Including the press ambush?"

He arched one dark brow. "Now you see why I wanted to fly solo? The press would eat you alive."

Beth swallowed. How little he knew. And why was he picking her apart with that look? She needed the Luke of last night—arrogant and argumentative—so she had a legitimate reason for disliking him.

For one heartbeat Beth wondered what it'd be like to have all that long-lashed, dark-eyed charm smiling only for her.

She stared at his mouth. A delicious-looking mouth with a full bottom lip. A totally kissable mouth that a woman with half a brain would fantasize about.

Don't even think about it. Luke was definitely a "love 'em and leave 'em" guy. Unpredictable, career-devoted and an attention magnet. Attention she had spent years avoiding. Getting involved with him—however superb the encounter promised to be—was the last thing she needed.

She looked away even as her skin began to tingle annoyingly. "What's our next move?"

"So you're determined to stay?"

"I still have a lease, in case you've forgotten. Legally—"

"Look, if you were in any position to call a lawyer you would've done it hours ago. Right? So if you're not moving out and won't consider my offer, it leaves with me with only one option. I'm moving in."

Her mouth gaped before she snapped it shut. "That's not funny."

"I'm not joking. I've got reporters camped out at my apartment, so I can't go back without leading them to the house. And—" He stopped abruptly, but she already knew what he'd been about to say.

I still don't trust you.

Well, fine. She didn't trust him, either.

"Take it or leave it, Beth. Do we have a deal?"

As the moment stretched in the cool silence, Luke tried to ignore that wide-eyed stare, the frustration and indignation playing out so clearly on her face. Tried, but somewhere inside, something tugged annoyingly on his conscience.

Finally, she said, "Why are you doing this? There's nothing more to find out and the house will be yours in three months."

"Because I'm involved."

"You want to make sure your name stays out of the papers."

"Yes. And because, a long time ago, there was no one there to help me or my family." He deliberately avoided those accusing eyes, lingering instead on her mouth.

Damn. Bad move.

"You were told the owners were overseas, right? So why would they lie to you? Plus, there's the mater of your missing money."

Luke watched her expression go from shock to resentment, her cheeks twin flaming spots of frustration. He could practically see the steam coming from her ears.

"Get on board or leave, Beth." He added, "I can help with your bank problem—"

She pulled out her phone and dialed while Luke remained in frustrated silence.

"So a woman came in claiming she was a friend of the owners requesting the tenant be 'preferably female, single, nonsmoker, employed or owning own business.'"

She nodded, studying him as he proccessed that information. "It's time to pay my aunt a visit."

Luke must have let something slip in his expression because a small frown marred her forehead as she studied him.

"You don't want to see her," she said slowly.

He shrugged. "What makes you say that?"

"Oh, the scowl, the tight jaw. The way you're narrowing your eyes right now. Plus the lawyer told you in no uncertain terms you should."

He remained stubbornly silent until he finally said, "I haven't seen her since Gino's will reading two weeks ago."

"So why—"

"It's complicated."

"I see."

And still she continued to sit there, watching him in silent scrutiny until frustration seeped warmly from his skin.

"First this inquiry, then Gino's heart attack, the funeral. She's been through a lot."

"So have you." When she tilted her head, a blond curl slid across her cheek. "All that anger isn't good. You should see someone."

"I don't need a shrink."

She brushed the curl away. "I *meant* a physiotherapist or masseuse."

"It's nothing sleep can't fix." He stretched his legs,

crossing them at the ankle before eyeing her speculatively. "You know, we're more alike than you think."

"Really?"

He ignored the sarcasm. "We're both work driven, handling a lot of stress, and now we've got this situation messing up our lives. Which brings me back to my original problem. What's our connection, Beth Jones?"

"I know as much as you do." She glanced out the window as they passed the sign to Sunset Island.

"Sure."

"So you think I'm hiding something."

"I'll bet my fifteen years at Jackson and Blair."

"And in fifteen years you've become a master of avoiding a question," Beth pointed out.

"What question?"

"Relaxation? You've got nothing to lose. Unless you *like* having a sore neck."

He gave her a look. "Sounds like you want this for me more than I do."

She blew out a breath and rolled her eyes. "Fine. Ignore the expert." Yet he couldn't miss that fleeting look of concern as she turned back to the window.

He paused, allowing the events of the last day to press oppressively down. If he watched his back, he could hide out until the press frenzy blew over. Maybe. If luck was on his side.

But there was one big problem. A blonde, beautiful, hostile problem.

"Okay. A massage," he said suddenly. But when she turned back to him, a small smile blooming, he added, "A massage for some background information."

She blinked. "Some things are personal."

"And we're in each other's faces, which is about as personal as it gets."

The silence was absolute, a stark and obscene contrast to the noisy thoughts warring in Beth's head.

Damn Luke and his steady chip-chip-chipping away at her defenses. She needed space, much more space than this luxurious interior would allow. Like another continent's worth.

"Look," she finally said, "I'm tired of arguing."

"Then don't."

For one crazy second, Beth thought about walking away and letting him deal with the mess. Quickly, she rejected it. *He's prepared to fight for this. So am I.*

"I promise I'll get to the bottom of this, Beth."

Her mouth opened, but no sound came out.

"And I can pull my weight around the house. I can clean, fix that loose pantry door. I even make a mean lasagna."

A vision of Luke cooking in her kitchen jolted her. Another quickly followed—only this time he was stripped to the waist and teasing her with those come-to-bed eyes.

As if reading her thoughts, he grinned. "You're tempted. The thought of a home-cooked lasagna got you, hey?"

The fantasy scattered. Confusion and pleasure battled for the lead until irritation won out. "Don't think I don't know what you're doing with that seductive smile and I'm-so-charming routine."

His smile dropped. "Hey, I wasn't trying to—"

"And don't insult us both by denying it." She scowled. "You really think that's going to work on me?"

Instead of being insulted, that sensual smile just got wider. "You know what I think? I think you're just trying to pick faults when there aren't any. That you're irritated because you desperately want to dislike me. That—" he held up his hand when she opened her mouth to interrupt "—that despite this weird situation you're actually attracted to me, *cara*."

She floundered for a second or two, trying to wrap her head around his bluntness, her cheeks flaming at his obvious amusement.

"Rubbish!"

He winked. "You sure?"

If a man could purr, Luke would be doing it right now. Coupled with that look and the memory of heat on her skin where his fingers had caressed her, he personified danger with a capital *D*. And he was about to move into her spare room and share her bathroom.

"Positive." She turned away as her body hummed, a low throb reminding her that impending danger was only a couple of feet away.

She sat back in the luxurious leather, trying to put her thoughts in order. Yet she kept returning to the same conclusion. She might not like his methods. His mere presence may set her pulse racing and her internal alarms on high. But short of a miracle, she needed help finding Ben and sorting out her bank mix-up.

Plus, his staying with her was a perfect chance to convince him to sell.

Her mouth tightened as she turned back to him. "We need to set some ground rules."

One eyebrow rose. "Okay…?"

"One. We share whatever information we find."

Luke nodded.

"Two. No physical stuff. I mean it, Luke," she warned as his eyes crinkled. "No touching. No smiling. Definitely nothing else."

"So I can't smile at you now?"

"You know what I mean. No Mr. Charming. Stop it!"

Luke, to his credit, tried to swallow the offending grin. "I can't promise that, *cara.* But I will keep my distance if that's what you want. However," he added, his mouth kinking up, "if you should change your mind…" Her heart beat a little faster.

"I won't be asking."

"Really."

She narrowed her eyes. "Do you doubt my willpower?"

"No." He grinned. "Just questioning why I get you all flustered in the first place."

The arrogance of the man! Beth looked away as the car finally pulled into the driveway and she leaped out as if her life depended on it.

He followed her up the front steps. "Running away won't do any good, *cara.*" His liquid voice dropped to a husky rumble. "You tell me I need to relax, but look at you. You're a bundle of nerves."

Welcoming the cold indignation that started in the pit of her stomach, she whirled on him.

"You ever think maybe it could be *you* stressing me out?" She jammed her keys in the front door and managed to break a nail in the process. Cursing, she glared at him. "I've spent the better part of ten years getting my life just the way I want it and suddenly it's snatched away. Do you know how damn frustrating that is?" She tightened her hands into fists and placed them on her hips, the keys forgotten, dangling from the lock. "It galls me to ask for help but yes, I need it. But let me get something straight—I don't need fixing or saving or anything else. And I'm not going to be your project, so you can get that out of your head, too."

She paused for breath.

"You finished?" Luke asked quietly.

"Yes."

"Good. You got the wrong guy. Playing the knight in shining armor isn't my thing. All I want is to clear my name and get back to my job. And we both want to keep this out of the papers."

The keys suddenly fell from the lock and they both bent for them. Their hands collided. Then their gazes. Luke was so close he could smell her—lemons and freshness and rain—could nearly touch those soft curls that framed delicate earlobes. Could even feel the slow heat humming through her skin.

The woman was a baffling mix of "back off" and steely determination. She didn't want him around, yet she wasn't going to leave. He'd never felt more confused.

She was the first to straighten. She did it so smoothly and with such aplomb that he almost missed the shadow of regret clouding her eyes.

Finally, Beth managed to open the door. *Touching is supposed to be a major release for stress,* she reminded herself as she walked down the hall. *It boosts your immune system, it eases tension. It releases endorphins to help you relax.*

Whoever thought that one up obviously hadn't been touched by Luke De Rossi.

She glanced back. Luke stood in the doorway, looking very large, very male and totally in charge.

The expression on his face made her nerves backflip. "Trust me, Beth, I'll get to the bottom of everything."

Yeah, that's what she was afraid of.

Six

Beth fought the overwhelming urge to pack up her things and drive away until this horrible situation was a distant memory. Instead, she went into the kitchen and watched Luke through the window as he made a few phone calls.

Oh, how she desperately wanted to demand he get a lawyer and she'd see him in court. But that would be supremely stupid, not to mention inflammatory.

Remember who he is and what he could do.

Luke De Rossi. In her home. In the bedroom next to hers.

Letting him in was a mistake. Luke was a very smart man, not to mention determinedly single-minded—and she had so much to lose, so many secrets to guard.

She watched him pace her front yard, phone still attached to his ear as the sun glared down, bathing him from shiny head to toe.

Her stomach made a weird little lurch.

You sure your secrets are all you're worried about?

With a snort she yanked open her cupboard. He could deny it all he wanted—Luke *was* a white knight. He obviously believed they would sort everything out, the bad guys would be caught and justice would prevail.

She did not.

It would be better to think of him as a self-absorbed, perfectionist career junkie instead of the truth—that beneath the tough exterior was a man who wanted to spare his family further heartache, no matter how tainted Gino Corelli's reputation had become. Who held her hand to distract her during that interminable flight.

Who wanted to make her lasagna.

She banged a cup on the countertop with a satisfying crack.

How long since a man had touched her? Wanted her? And he felt so good, smelled like a gift straight from heaven. Celibacy did that to you, made you forget what it was like to need someone.

Oh, boy.

Yanking open the fridge, she pulled out a carton of juice.

Why now, after all those years of denial, all those years spent carving out a life, did she have to start thinking of sex? And with someone like Luke De Rossi, a man whose mere presence could ruin everything?

Because you've got a good-looking guy up close, and you know that abstinence has been too much.

Beth poured the juice with an unsteady hand. She didn't even like him.

She glanced out the window just in time to see Luke bending down to take an overnight bag the driver had retrieved from the trunk. His pants stretched tight, outlining a set of perfectly formed buttocks, and she groaned, turning away.

She would just have to focus on the problem at hand and *not* on that smooth-talking, dark-eyed, divine-smelling, soft-lipped…distraction about to settle in the guest room so unnervingly close to hers!

As Luke walked in, she downed the rest of her juice, muttered, "I'll make up the spare room," and left.

The room that served as her office was a mess. Aromatic oil bottles and bags of fragrant leaves littered every available space on the windowsill and bookcase. She grabbed up a box and stashed them in the wardrobe. Then she put the scattered accounts folders back on the shelves, drew the curtains, returned a pair of sneakers to her room. Even as she pulled out the sofa bed and started to make it, she still couldn't get that flight out of her head. The soft caress of Luke's fingers, the feel of his breath, the burn of want in his eyes. And his pure male smell, all warmth and promise.

It took her breath away.

As if on cue, Luke appeared in the doorway. "Need a hand?"

"No." She fluffed up the last pillow and tucked in the sheets. When she looked up, she caught the tail end of his scrutiny…and a sudden undeniable flame of heat flickering in those dark depths. But the second he realized she was looking, it was gone.

Beth straightened. "Look. I know I'm… I've been a bit—"

"Overzealous? Unbending?"

"Defensive. I like to be self-sufficient. And, well…" She shrugged. "You're obviously a take-charge guy."

The corners of his mouth kicked up. "In many things. Not all."

If he sought to embarrass her, he was hitting the right notes. Picking up an empty cup from the desk, she turned to leave. He crowded the doorway—nasty habit of his—so she had to make a good impression of ignoring that broad chest as she brushed past. Especially ignoring those nerve endings that let up a cheer at his proximity.

"I'm going for a run," she muttered. "Make yourself at home."

Ten minutes later she descended the stairs dressed in a T-shirt and running shorts, her curls tucked under a worn blue cap.

With arms crossed, Luke watched her charge down the hall and slam out the front door.

Just what are you playing at, mate? First that thing in the plane, then the flirting. Now you've moved in. Next, you'll be kissing, and you know where that'll lead.

He swiped back his hair with a quick jerk. No. She had told him loud and clear she wasn't interested. Except…he found himself wanting to believe that the surprised desire in those expressive eyes wasn't just his imagination.

He thought about her mouth, how soft it had looked. How her skin felt, as smooth and unlined as the downy softness of a newborn. And how those mossy-green eyes had tugged at his common sense, dragging him under like a floundering swimmer at the beach.

Luke shoved those thoughts away and went to the foot of the stairs. Work and career had always been his prime objective, even before this mess. Even before he'd entertained the thought that he might make VP one day.

Before Gabrielle?

The faint twinge twisted low before he forced it away. Yeah, even before then. His brief disastrous marriage just proved his theory: you couldn't have a demanding career and keep a relationship alive. One always had to suffer.

No, he liked his life just the way it was. And if he needed sex, he could always rely on a few willing female colleagues who were just as focused on their careers.

No-strings sex. Yep. Nothing like it.

If Luke had been looking in the mirror at the bottom of the stairs, he would've been surprised to see a dark scowl blooming across his face.

Now he stood in the middle of the living room, casting an eye over the spread and cataloguing the details. There were two entrances: one from the short hallway and one via the kitchen. The faint aroma of coffee lingered, mingling with some fresh lemony, floral fragrance. Sunshine streamed through the huge bay window ahead, illuminating sunflower-yellow walls, two overstuffed couches and a coffee table in the center of the room. A small TV, open fireplace, floor-to-ceiling bookshelves and an exposed-beam ceiling completed the comfy look, with colorful rugs spread on polished wooden floors.

This place held nothing of Gino and everything of Beth, which made his mistress theory an even longer stretch.

Luke went over to the photos he'd noticed on a bookcase yesterday. Beth and another female grinning outside a storefront. A shot with beach scenery. And an old black-and-white studio portrait of an icy blonde with a come-hither smile.

In thoughtful silence he picked up an unusually shaped candle in a blue glass holder and sniffed. *Beth.* Quickly, he replaced it.

He'd left his high-rise Brisbane apartment—a three-bedroom homage to every technological advancement—for this. Despite his perfectly decorated rooms, the massive plasma-TV screen and the appliance-ridden kitchen he only used for entertaining clients, there'd been no soul to the place. No warmth, no garden, and now, thanks to the reporters camped on the block, no privacy.

And for the second time in his life he was in a house Uncle Gino had provided.

But you're not fifteen anymore. Not an angry, sullen teenager torn apart by the fury of his parents' pointless struggle and the guilt of hating them for it.

He tilted his head and read the book titles on the shelves. *Handbook of Aromatherapy, The Healing Body, The Small Business Owner's Guide. The Complete History of Cartoons.* And a bunch of sci-fi novels, their spines bent and cracked from use.

He cast another eye around the room and a vague,

warm feeling settled over his shoulders. This was a home. A lived-in, occupied home. If all *his* stuff went up in smoke tomorrow, it could all be replaced by day's end.

Disturbed, he let that uneasy feeling sit there for a second before shucking it off. It wouldn't do any good to start getting off track. This was just a place to lay low until he met with the investigators next month. The situation would be resolved and he'd be back at work. Simple.

He wandered from living room to kitchen. He never let emotion distort his decisions, yet he'd chosen to share his space with a woman who was full of emotion, who had let an abundance of it shape and change her life. Case in point—her can't-get-away-from-you-quick-enough dash when they'd got out the car.

He walked outside and sat on the porch swing. All around, the air was still and warm, no traffic, no urban noise to pierce the silent bubble of the perfect spring day.

Peace. Quiet. Stillness.

He breathed in deep and closed his eyes. Grass. Salty sea. The lemon tree at the end of the driveway.

Beth.

The moment stretched into a handful, until he finally opened his eyes and glanced at his phone.

Thirty minutes had gone by. Thirty minutes in which he hadn't been making a deal or negotiating with clients or worrying about what Gino would do next to screw up his life.

Had Marco's little psych evaluation at Gino's funeral been right? *"You care too much about what's past and what you can't change, Luke. You hold a grudge for way too long. Take it from someone who's been there— you're on the fast track for a spectacular crash if you don't slow the hell down."*

And as he delved into the waters of self-doubt, he didn't like what he saw.

With a soft sigh, he reached for his phone and started to make the first of a handful of calls.

Beth didn't run because she enjoyed it, although sometimes she actually did. She ran because exercise effectively cleared her head like nothing else. And today, she needed the clarity of movement, the pure and honest motion of running.

Even though the afternoon heat embraced her like an exuberant relative's hug, she picked up the pace. She ran all the way to the end of the street then turned east. Trees flashed by; she noted her progress by counting the cats' eyes hammered onto the white guideposts flanking the road. When she got to the small park with the duck lake, she pounded over the footbridge. The sun sparkled off the water in blinding shafts, the air hummed with the noise of the distant highway. Eventually all she could hear was her heaving lungs.

Nearly an hour later, when she finally turned back, her whole body ached from exertion. Sweat pooled in the small of her back, her scalp itched, her T-shirt clung and her legs sang. But the effort had been worth it. Her thoughts had been Luke free.

She got to the top of her street and stopped long enough to stretch her hamstrings, then continued at a brisk walk before pausing at the end of the driveway.

The lawn edges needed trimming. The orange trees were begging for a good prune, too. The porch also had to be swept and that second step was in sore need of a nail or two.

She breathed in a deep sigh, reveling in the warm, perfect stillness of the day. After drifting from one impersonal crowded city to another, this was heaven on earth. Solitude and independence had brought that to her life.

A breeze interrupted the air, tickling along her damp skin.

She loved this place. Giving up and walking away would be like wrenching off a vital piece of herself. It would be like erasing every good memory she had made these last ten years.

If Luke wanted to do that, he was in for a fight.

Determination added steel to her step as she walked in the front door. She didn't have much time on her side, but Luke was obviously not a patient man. After a week or two, he'd get sick of waiting and take her up on her offer. They'd agree on a price, sign on it, and she'd eventually work off her debt.

She was extremely good at waiting.

"Hey."

Beth jumped as Luke appeared from the kitchen. "Can't you make some noise instead of sneaking around?" At his look, she sighed. "What?"

He crossed his arms, leaning against the wall. "We need to talk."

Beth's flushed face suddenly felt like a thousand burning knives. "I have to shower first. I'll be down in fifteen."

"If you're not, I'm coming up to get you."

Beth turned and practically ran up the stairs. He wouldn't dare barge into her bathroom. Would he?

Seven

Ten minutes later Beth stood in the kitchen in a T-shirt and army-green cargo pants, her hair slicked back into a damp ponytail. Luke watched her refill her glass from the kitchen sink, glance across at him then gulp down the water.

Still, he let the silence do all the talking, a technique that not only allowed him to observe her under pressure but also showed she was extremely uncomfortable with his singular scrutiny.

"Is the room okay?" she finally asked.

"Yes. Thanks." Then he added, "Nice house. Lots of space."

She nodded with a small smile. "That's why I chose it. It's the first place I've actually felt at home."

A small pang of guilt twisted in his gut. Not a good

sign, considering the snooping he'd done minutes before.

He'd rummaged through her filing system, her desk and behind the books in her living room, before quickly going through her bedroom. With reluctance dogging every step, he'd been about to give up until he'd hit the back of her wardrobe.

Just who was Taylor Stanton and why did Beth have her birth certificate buried in an old shoe box?

Before he could change his mind, he'd called his P.I. Dylan and relayed the details. Now, with Beth sitting across the table, his conscience took that moment to flare.

That's stupid. It could mean nothing—in which case, she'd never have to know.

His neck began to ache again, sharp darts of pain stabbing his muscles.

First, he'd been suspended from his job then hounded from his apartment. He'd been rendered ineffective, like an illegal vehicle banned from the road. And now he'd resorted to spying. Unease sliced across his chest, but he clamped a lid on it, wrapping his fingers around the cup of coffee he'd prepared moments ago. The scalding heat was a welcome distraction.

"You know you'll have to make a formal statement to the bank eventually," he said.

She sighed. "I know."

"And I made a few calls," he said. "Unless we get the police involved, the real estate agent isn't legally obliged to pursue this any further. So I'm getting a copy of the deed from the titles office, which should take a few days. In the meantime, I need to talk to my aunt."

Beth made a noncommittal sound to cover up her nervousness. This would not do. As badly as she wanted him gone, he was equally determined to keep digging until everything was wrapped up to his satisfaction. But as she watched him brush back his hair with stiff fingers, a wave of reluctant sympathy swelled at the expression on his face. Something was going on here.

"You're not happy about that."

"Gino's investigation may be over but not the fallout," he said slowly. "Everyone's running crazy—the lawyers, investors, my family. I'm not exactly Australian of the Year right now."

"But you are innocent."

His expression remained impassive. "So you don't think I colluded to launder drug money from the casino through Jackson and Blair."

She snorted. "No."

Skepticism riddled his frown. "Why not?"

"Because of what I've seen today. You may be a pushy, overconfident alpha male—" she smothered a grin at his scowl "—but ironically, your ethics work in your favor. There's no way you'd knowingly sabotage your reputation."

If that brief look of surprise hadn't spoken volumes, his silence did. She couldn't help smiling now.

"I see," was all he said.

Then he shook his head and swept a hand through his hair again, a gesture Beth was beginning to equate with pent-up frustration. The coal-black strands stuck up in spikes and she had the urge to smooth them down. Especially when she saw that flash of emotion in his eyes.

In that instant, Beth realized she'd just caught a glimpse of the real man behind the veneer—how his perceived failures ate at his pride, how much his status meant. How totally ineffective he must be feeling.

No wonder his reputation was perfect. He was a driven man and driven men often set impossibly high standards for themselves. And when they failed to live up to them, they frequently crashed to earth.

Something inside her shifted. She had to help him, even though he had something she so desperately wanted. Her compassion, her training, demanded no less.

"I can stop that ache in your neck, you know."

He barely gave her a glance. "Can you?"

There it was again. More than anyone, Beth could understand his frustration. But right now he didn't need empathy—he needed stress relief. She ticked off the telltale signs one by one and knew she couldn't ignore his discomfort any longer.

She stood, reached over and firmly removed his hand from his nape. "Let me help you."

The sudden heat flaring in his eyes disappeared as quickly as it started, yet despite that, it still had the power to warm her belly.

"It's my job," she clarified. "You're no good to anyone burned-out, and I can help you relax."

"You don't need to—"

"Yes, I do. Let me do this, Luke. Please."

They stared at each other for a few seconds before Luke glanced away with a shrug. "Okay."

And, dammit, her pulse began to pick up the pace.

"Go into the living room," she said in a too-thick voice. "I'll get my things."

She hurried up to the spare room, determined to outrun the doubt dogging her footsteps. Right now was not the time to take a close look at her reasons for offering her help. She was a professional and she could do this, no matter that the body she was about to lay her hands on was six foot four inches of hard, warm male.

Beth returned with her oils and pulled the curtains closed, casting the room in half shadows, then pulled out a massage table from under the stairs and unfolded it.

He watched it all in silence.

"So I take it you've never had a therapeutic massage," Beth said.

"Once, ages ago. Now I don't have the time."

"You should make time."

"Before or after I solve world hunger?"

Her mouth tilted. "Take off your shirt and lie face-down."

He did as he was told, settling his face into the cut-out oval of the padded table. Now that his body was within her grasp, she would get to feel every contour, every crevice. A deep breath was needed.

Maybe another.

Pouring some oil onto her palms, she rubbed them together and began.

Her thumbs started gently at his lower back and Luke nearly leaped off the table. "What the hell…?"

He twisted, but Beth placed a restraining hand on his back. "Lie still." She stifled a smile.

"But it hurts!"

"Stop being a baby." She pushed him down and tried again, this time easing back on the pressure.

"You're doing this on purpose!" he accused.

"I'm trying to get the tension out, so yes, I am."

She went as softly as she could, warming up his muscles. She had to hand it to him, he managed to bite his tongue even though a few grunts made their way through his tight control.

"Do you get migraines?" she asked.

"No."

"Panic attacks?"

"You think I get—"

"Performance problems?"

"No."

She bit her lip, swallowing a chuckle at his indignant reply. "Lucky. They're all symptoms of a high-stress environment."

Luke stifled another groan. She was good. In fact, if they gave Oscars for massage, she'd win hands down. She had handfuls of his muscle and used pressure from thumbs, palms and all fingers.

"So how is it," she began, digging deep into his back, "that some lucky woman hasn't already snapped you up?"

A slice of memory twinged, but he thrust it back. "A demanding career and relationships don't mix."

"That's a bit of a broad statement. Maybe you just haven't met the right woman."

"Trust me, I know." He grunted, swallowing a groan as she shifted her hands. "And I meet plenty of women."

"I see."

She continued in silence, and pride demanded he

keep it that way, but when she caught a particularly tight spot, a hiss escaped his clenched teeth. And through the somewhat painful movements, he could feel himself getting aroused.

It was the thought of her standing over him, touching him with her firm, skilled hands that stirred his blood.

Then she reached his shoulders and silence flew out the window with a ragged gasp.

"You're pretty tight up here," she said, concern threading her voice.

Luke muttered something and tried to shake off the pleasant fantasy of Beth naked and massaging him all over. She shifted to stand at the head of the table, her body bent forward over his shoulders while her palms stretched and rubbed down his left arm. Her toes came into view—long, elegant digits with nails painted a soft coral, strapped into well-worn sandals. He also noticed that her second toes were longer than her big ones and the one on the left bore a silver ring with a green stone in the center.

Sucking on those toes would be…

He squeezed his eyes shut as she dug around for such long, agonizing seconds that he wondered if his circulation would cut out. Finally, she took pity on him, easing off until he relaxed with barely disguised relief.

"You should do this more often. It'll hurt less." She gently squeezed his trapezius and was rewarded with a sharp hiss. "See what I mean?"

He grunted.

Beth patted his shoulder. "Don't try to talk. I know it's a big effort holding all that groaning in."

"I'm trying to maintain a dignified silence."

She chuckled, bending close to his ear. "You don't have to. Let it all out."

Her whispery breath sent a shock of heat to his groin. Now all he could think of were their sweaty bodies, Beth groaning beneath him. And above him. All he could feel was the soft brush of her cotton shirt against his hair. And her hands touching every part of him. He itched to reach out and grab a handful of her luscious, rounded butt.

She was driving him crazy, as if punishing him for something.

He felt punished. It was retribution for letting the past weeks build up, for not seeking professional help sooner, just like Beth said.

She walked around the table, returning to his lower back, fingers trailing across his skin. Lust tensed him up. She must have felt it because she said, "No, no. Don't do that."

"What?"

"Tighten your lower back. Here." Her hands began to knead the troubled spot. Luke groaned. It was a different kind of pain this time. His tight groin pressed unbearably against the unyielding table while his mind ran riot. And he couldn't do a damn thing about it.

"You finished yet?" He finally got out.

"Hang on, I've still got to—"

"Thanks. That's okay." He pulled himself up, grabbed his shirt and yanked it over his head.

After a moment's fumbling with the lower buttons, he took a breath, then another, before he got his body under control. And now with his untucked shirt hiding any lingering evidence, he turned back to face her.

She looked astonished and confused while he ached uncomfortably. Dammit.

"I should go and get a shower." Yet he made no attempt to leave.

"Okay." Beth wiped her hands on a towel and tried not to let her disappointment show. He was uptight again and that pretty much kicked all her good work out the window.

She glanced at him, intending only to linger a moment but instead ended up staring. A faint sheen of sweat hugged the shirt to his chest, a chest sprinkled with dark hair that tapered down until the buttons hindered her view.

The breath she swallowed dried her throat.

He was a very large, very muscular man in a pair of crisply cut pants and a creased shirt that probably cost more than a week's wages.

A dark, dangerous-looking man now focused right in on her as if she was some kind of last meal, the musky smell of his sweat and a faint, woodsy aftershave mingling with her oils.

"Beth?"

"Yes?" Her voice came out as an unfamiliar croak.

"If you're going to stop me, do it now because I'm about to break rule number two."

She swallowed as he took those few steps toward her, reached out and slowly tugged her to him, giving her time to protest. But she didn't. She couldn't. She could pull away if she wanted, but resistance felt as appealing as wading through a pool of honey. It was as if he had her hypnotized and all she could do was let him drag his fingers through her hair. Sweep his thumbs over her jaw.

His eyes held hers, unwavering, hypnotic. His thumb pad deliberately caressed her bottom lip, rubbing against the soft contours.

The heat from his body curled into her like a flame. His mouth—so close, so kissable—feathered a warm breath over her bottom lip. Teasing. Testing. Beth felt the full blast of hot, urgent desire and wanted to groan aloud because it felt so good.

She felt like melting right there on the floor when he flicked his tongue out and touched the tip to her slightly parted lips. Every muscle in her body started to sing with anticipation. Her lungs couldn't get enough air and her mind shorted out as pleasure-induced confusion flooded in. His mouth focused on her jawline, placing gentle nips along the length then sliding down into the hollow of her throat.

Oh, sweet heaven.

He nipped at her jaw, following the trail left by his fingers. She let her eyes close in pleasure.

"Is this so bad?" His rough voice against her neck was doing a serious number on her nerves.

"No." *Not bad...so very good.*

"So you have no objections to this?" He reached the base of her throat and gently nuzzled her flesh. She groaned. "Or this?"

His hand slid up her body, past her waist, over her ribs. When he reached the swell of her breast, she released a hiss.

Every tingling pulse rushed through her veins, making it impossible to fight the feeling. She realized she didn't want to fight it. Maybe it was because she'd been alone for so long and had missed the physical side of passion. Maybe she needed to be touched after an eternity of nothing. Maybe she was secretly wishing he would make love to her.

Maybe it was his hot breath whispering in her ear, the urgent press of his groin against hers.

Beth could taste him in every pore. Like a fire that had started in the pit of her belly, her body was hot and molten—and then she was wrapping her arms around his neck, pulling him flush against her heat. She could see him behind her eyelids, could smell, feel, taste him.

It had been so long since she had been kissed.

Been wanted.

No one had touched her like this, in a way that she forgot all reason.

He was caressing the length of her back now and her skin itched for his fingers to touch her all over. Her breath came in short and irregular gasps, barely an inch away from his teasing lips. Was she whimpering like a love-starved virgin? She must be because Luke skimmed his bottom lip lightly over hers and whispered, "You want me to kiss you?"

"Mmm."

Slowly, inch by aching inch, he covered her mouth with his.

Luke De Rossi not only looked like a kissing master, he was hands down one of the best. Her breath merged with his, stirring a long-forgotten ache deep inside, flaring up to lick her body in need. It attacked the part of her mind that controlled rational thought, eating away at her reservations.

He stroked his hands down her arms, creating shivering goose bumps in his wake.

"You want me to stop?" he muttered against her mouth. "I will if you want me to."

She wanted to give in to him, so much that it made her chest ache. "I…"

She wanted him. For the first time in her life she wanted to leap on in and damn the consequences, grab everything he offered—every no-strings-attached kiss, every blood-boiling caress.

But that would mean giving something in return. Something she'd worked ten years to protect.

With a groan, she snapped open her eyes. Luke continued his assault on her neck as she tried to pull back, gasping as his teeth nibbled at her flesh.

Frantically, she pushed. "Stop."

He stumbled but regained his feet quickly. The arousal in his heavy eyes held a shot of confusion.

"Beth—"

"We shouldn't…" She cleared her throat. "This isn't professional. My life is good. I'm happy. I don't want—" She swallowed thickly. "I don't do casual sex."

"There'd be nothing casual about it." His husky timbre sounded like a promise. It made her insides quiver.

"No." She hated the way her denial came out breathy, almost expectant. Anger at her weakness gave her voice more strength when she said, "No. We're in the middle of a crazy situation and I don't need another distraction. Not now."

"Is that all this would be—a distraction?"

"Yes." She glanced away, wrapping her arms around

her waist. She could still feel his heat, still smell his scent on her clothes. She still wanted his mouth on hers.

When he didn't respond, she chanced a look.

He was shaking his head, a frown creasing his brow.

Her restraint faltered and she let out a breath. "Look," she said, shoving a loose lock of hair back behind her ears with an efficient sweep. "What we've got is a basic physiological reaction to a stressful situation. It heightens senses and emotions." She smiled tightly. "When there's a sense of danger, the body's response is to procreate."

"Really."

Beth shrugged. "Hey, it's physiology."

Luke studied her intently, but she just stood there, a firm smile on those lips he'd been devouring not twenty seconds ago. Hell, he ached for her like he'd been celibate for five years and not just three months. So it had to be *something*.

He ran a hand through his hair, wishing it were hers.

"So, no more kissing," he said.

"Right." Beth nodded.

"Yes."

"Mmm."

Luke watched her gather up the oils and refold the table as if she were performing groundbreaking brain surgery. She wasn't bothering to deny their attraction anymore and that should've pleased him. But it didn't. Far from it.

He might have been fooled into thinking she delivered mind-numbing kisses often, ones that chewed up a guy's insides and sent his heart racing. Until he caught a vague look of disappointment as she turned away.

Sure, she could rationalize it all she wanted, but Luke knew the truth.

He wanted her. And she wanted him right back.

Beth Jones was unlike anyone he'd ever met. She didn't disguise the fact that she wanted him out of her life. Yet she was physically attracted, an attraction they both sensed every time he got within arm's length. When every other woman would have told him loud and clear how they felt, she hid it behind a biology lesson. Her blatant denial intrigued him.

Yeah, but you've gotta think with your head, Luke. Your career is everything, always has been. And that's the way you like it. Face it—you're a disaster when it comes to relationships.

And he didn't want to hurt Beth.

"I'm going to take a shower," Luke finally said.

She remained silent until he raised one questioning eyebrow.

"Towels are in the cupboard above the sink."

He took the stairs two at a time and Beth managed to keep her composure. But when he disappeared into the bathroom, she collapsed into the couch with a mutter of dismay.

His skin, the play of his muscles beneath her fingers, had been better than she imagined. A scar in the shape of a circular constellation marred the perfection, along with another silver slash of puckered skin low on his waist. She'd bitten her lip to stop from leaning down and gently kissing away the massage oil.

Beth heard the shower turn on...and an image swam into her mind of Luke naked, water running over his chest, abdomen...

Stop it. Stop it now.

With a grievous sigh, she stood and headed off to the kitchen, unsure and unsettled.

Much later that night, after she'd eaten a quick chicken sandwich alone in the kitchen, Beth ran herself a bath and sank into the warm bubbles with a relieved groan.

Behind her head, scented candles flickered on a small shelf, their reflection bouncing from the huge, gold-edged mirror opposite and ending in a subtle play of light on the water's surface.

The bathroom was her thinking space and she loved it best of all—from the high whitewashed ceiling, the Grecian tiles framing the doorway, the hanging green plants, to the skylight that showed off a clear starry night.

It should have been a haven tonight. But escape was impossible. The house was still and quiet, but an underlying anticipation hung in the air, as if it was waiting to see what changes the newcomer would bring.

Luke dwarfed her spare room, just as he was dwarfing her life, helping himself to a part of it as if she was an amicable participant. She took a deep breath, her lungs filling with steam and scent, and exhaled in a rush.

Luke had to know how out of place he was here, how much he disrupted her sense of order. She'd told him straight what she wanted. Now she had to *persuade*. She'd show him she belonged here, that her stamp was firmly on this place, in every book, every cup, every comfy cushion. It was her task to convince him, so when he went back to work, he'd soon forget whatever attraction this place held and take her up on her offer.

Peace and sanity would return. Even if it meant working long hours for the next twenty years to pay him off, she'd do it.

Yet why did that give her such an unsatisfied feeling in the pit of her stomach? The cooling water washed over her breasts as she shifted in the tub. She shivered and quickly stood, then slowly stepped out.

She *had* to do this. Getting hysterical or wishing the situation could be different wouldn't change anything. At her mother's funeral she'd made a solemn eighteen-year-old vow: never give in to the dark well of depression and self-doubt her mother had suffered, thanks in part to her father's infidelities and mind games.

Well, *she* wasn't going to crumble, Beth decided as she padded into her bedroom. She stood strong and fought for what she wanted.

It was just a matter of waiting it out.

After she put on her pajamas and lay staring at the ceiling for ages, exhaustion that came with thinking too much finally claimed her.

Eight

"Hey, Beth, can I catch a lift with you this morning?"

Her store assistant, Laura, sounded flustered. Beth balanced the phone at her ear as she smeared peanut butter on her toast. "Car troubles again? Have you called the mechanic?"

"Yeah. They won't be here until after ten."

Beth watched Luke walk silently into the kitchen, clad in a pair of jeans and a black T-shirt. Memories of yesterday's kiss came flooding back and with it, heat to parts of her body she didn't want to think of him touching.

"No problem. See you soon." She hung up and poured a glass of juice. "Morning."

"Morning." His all-seeing eyes swept over her, sending her pulse rocketing. "Sleep well?"

"Yeah," she lied. "You?"

"Like a log for once. And I don't have that nagging ache here." He cupped the back of his neck.

"I told you it'd work. Now all you need is a couple more days' rest and you'll be as good as new."

Luke helped himself to coffee, looking much too at-home as he leaned against her counter.

"Going to work?" He nodded, taking in her business shirt, short skirt and flat sandals.

"Yep."

"Is that wise?"

A hell of a lot wiser than being cooped up here with you, no buffer zone in sight. "I have paying clients. And anyway, you can relax better without me around."

Luke looked dissatisfied with her reasoning. "You got something I can do around here?"

"No."

"What about that?" He nodded in the direction of the pantry, where the door was off its hinges and resting against the stove.

"It needs sanding then the hinges need to be re-aligned. I can do it."

"So can I."

"I'd rather you not—"

"Don't make me pull rank on you, Beth." His words were soft but his eyes firm. "I own the place, remember?"

Beth felt her face flush, but shrugged as if it didn't matter. "Fine. Do what you want." Now she sounded petulant and that annoyed her more than anything. But it irked her that he had every right to paint the place in pink polka dots if he so chose.

"I got a call from Dylan last night," Luke said. "He accessed your runaway's cell-phone records. Plus, he's also checking flight schedules."

Beth's heart skipped a beat. "He could've left the country?"

"What would you do if you'd stolen half a million?"

Beth exhaled slowly. "So the money could be gone forever."

"Not necessarily. Let's see what turns up."

She nodded absently, her head whirling. More waiting. She'd be a world champion by the end of it.

"I'll get started on that door, then chop that firewood in the backyard." He massaged his shoulder. "Need to keep busy."

"Not used to being idle, huh?"

"Hate it," he admitted, and as she gave him a small smile, the lines on his face softened. "Lying on a beach with a book was my idea of hell." He put his elbows on the counter and leaned back. "Until that massage."

She knew he wanted to add something more, make some comment about their kiss, but he let his eyes do all the talking.

"I've got to go," she muttered and beat a hasty retreat.

Luke watched her leave, wondering for the umpteenth time since yesterday how one woman could be so damn frustrating.

Connor would say it was because his obsession with fixing things had encountered a brick wall. Marco would add, "Because sometimes things can't be solved with a charming smile, bro!" with a wink and a grin.

Maybe.

He grappled with the real reason, as if by wrestling with it he could reduce it to ashes. But he was plumb out of luck. The answer was purely selfish.

Attraction.

She wasn't his type—too secretive, too stubborn, too take-charge. He liked everything straightforward, out in the open, no surprises. Yet there was something about her that got his blood pumping anyway.

He missed having a woman in his life. Missed the way they felt, their smell, their laughter. Their softness.

It was strange, having a woman refuse his help even when she was so obviously neck deep in problems. But Beth had made it clear she could function perfectly well without him and would continue to do so long after he was out of the picture.

So why did that rub him the wrong way so much?

Beth refused to spoil her day by thinking about her former bookkeeper. Instead, she focused on what she could control: namely, her attraction to Luke De Rossi. So when she picked up Laura she was on the receiving end of a one-sided conversation all the way to work. As she nodded and responded in the appropriate places, her conscience held up its end.

Be honest—you want him. What do you have to lose if you succumb to temptation for once? If you let him kiss you, touch you?

Her control. Not to mention her professional ethics and privacy.

Ha. You were interested long before that massage. And no one can take something from you you're not willing to give.

Sure. It'd only take one eager reporter, one mistake, and your whole life could be exposed. Again.

She focused on the road with exaggerated concentration just as she tried to convince herself she wouldn't care when Luke was gone. She'd be glad. Glad.

A hand waved in front of her face. "Still with me here?"

"Huh?" Beth blinked.

Laura rolled her eyes. "The light's green. I asked if we need to do a double order on our cranberry oils for Christmas."

"No." Beth tempered her abruptness with an apologetic smile and pressed the accelerator. "Sorry. I have a lot on my mind."

Laura shot her a sideways glance. "Anything to do with that sneaky little rat Ben?"

"Got it in one." She smiled weakly.

"Well, thank me for clearing your morning appointments today. I rescheduled everyone so we could go through yesterday's new shipment. Oh, and Jack Benson says he hopes you feel better."

Ahh, Jack, her plantar fasciitis retiree. "Am I sick?"

"Nope. People just assumed anything else wouldn't keep you away."

As the traffic ground to a halt again, Beth gave the younger girl her full attention. Her employee had the kind of personality and looks that could coax a smile from a statue—she'd be dangerous if she were self-centered. But Laura was the nicest person she'd ever known.

"Do you think I'm a workaholic?" Beth asked.

"*Weeeell...* You are. A bit."

And honest to a fault. "I see."

"The last time you took a day off was… Actually, you've never taken a day off. Since when've you had the chance to just lie on the beach and veg? Or come to think of it, been out on a date?"

Beth snorted. "And why haven't you said anything before?"

Laura shrugged. "You never asked before. And you *like* working. The weird thing is you're our target market, but you don't practice what you preach."

"And you think I need a man."

"No. I think you need a little fun." Laura grinned again. "And a little sex wouldn't hurt."

They pulled into the parking lot and Beth wound down her window for the ticket, effectively cutting off Laura's train of thought.

If someone had told her a week ago she'd be sharing a house with Luke De Rossi, running from reporters and hunting down an ex-employee and a missing half-million dollars, she would've laughed in their face.

A shiver shot down her back. Yes, Luke seemed to be helping with her Ben problem. And she was attracted to him. But the issue wasn't physical, it was mental. She didn't want to let him into her life, into her secrets. Her head screamed danger every time she laid eyes on him.

Even if her body screamed the opposite.

At exactly nine-thirty, Beth and Laura walked down the mall toward a darkened shop front.

"Smell that," Laura said softly as Beth unlocked the doors and whooshed them open.

Beth took a deep breath, punching in a security code

as Laura flicked on the lights. "Frangipani, lavender. Lemongrass."

"I can smell coffee," Laura singsonged, dangling a bag of gourmet beans between two fingers. They both grinned.

"You fill the pot and I'll fix things up here," said Beth. She selected a key and switched on the cash register, straightened the flyers on the counter, then placed an errant pen in a cup.

Casting an eye over the familiar interior, she breathed in again with a smile, loving the crazy mix of scents that hit her senses. The place wasn't huge, but she'd made use of every available space. A giant oak tree mural decorated the walls, each branch a protruding glass shelf that displayed various jellies, lotions and powders. Bath bombs, frothies and bottles of shower gel were divided in four tiers on the trunk and a small white sink sat discreetly in the wall, a half-empty body-wash tester bottle on the side.

As usual, everything was in its place.

This was her reality. It was just another normal day. *Please*.

Crossing her fingers, she turned to the office, drawn in by the delicious coffee bean and mocha aroma.

Laura turned from the kitchenette and held out a packet of cookies. "Biscuit?"

"This early?"

"It's never too early for Tim Tams."

Beth grinned, plucked out a chocolate-covered cookie and munched slowly. "You want to check out the stock while we eat and drink?"

"Thought you'd never ask. I've got my eye on those new bath bombs."

* * *

Beth made good use of the internet on her lunch break, searching for anything and everything on Luke De Rossi and Gino Corelli, then making a call to the titles office and local legal aid. Armed with new knowledge, she felt the rest of the day fly by until finally, at five-thirty, she dropped Laura off at her apartment then made her way home.

The sensationalist articles were no surprise. But what she hadn't expected was the absence of Luke in the society and gossip columns.

She sighed, reluctant admiration warring with self-preservation as she pulled into her driveway. Despite how she personally felt about him, Luke was the quintessential high achiever and proud of it. A perfectionist. A man who was doing everything to protect his career. Who still reminded her of every arrogant, demanding suit she'd met, despite the man's overwhelming charm.

Yet he'd still ended up poking holes in her prejudices. He could've stepped back and called in his high-flying lawyers but he hadn't. He could've left her on the airport tarmac. And he could've escaped that reporter crush alone, but instead he'd shielded her from the cameras, even offered to help her with the missing money. For all his alleged faults gleefully detailed in the press, actions spoke louder than tainted words.

And Beth felt like a certifiable ingrate.

As she slammed the car door and strode up the porch steps, the mouthwatering smell of garlic and onions hit her as soon as she swung the door open.

With a thick swallow and deep breath, she walked into the kitchen then peeked in the oven.

Lasagna.

Her smile stretched as she caught sight of the newly hinged pantry door, then the clean sink, the dust-free countertop....

And a bunch of potted gerberas in the center of the kitchen table.

Luke had certainly made himself at home.

"Luke?" She walked slowly into the living room only to finally notice the ominous silence.

"Hello?" She went to the back door and looked out. The silence was so thick she could have walked on it. Despite her quiet reassurances, panic slowly bubbled to the surface.

She was about to race up the stairs, but opted to explore the backyard further. It sloped down toward the riverbank and could obscure her vision of a fully grown man.

Sure enough, when she strode over the rise there he sat on the grass, his back to her, reclining on his elbows, his face accepting the late sunshine in lazy worship.

Beth had to take another inward breath to calm her pounding heart, gently tugging on her necklace as the beat gradually slowed.

Luke must have sensed her, because he turned, sending her a smile that heated her quicker than a January summer's day—and her heart picked up again. "Hey, there."

She swallowed, shading her eyes with a hand. "Hi."

He turned fully this time, sprang to his feet with all the fluid motion of a man who kept his body in perfect shape. "You cooked," she said faintly.

"I did promise you lasagna."

She returned his smile, clamping down on the sudden surge of need. Nervously, she rubbed one palm against her leg.

Luke shoved his hands into his back pockets and the T-shirt pulled taut across his chest, leaving her breath in a hitch as muscles strained against well-worn cotton.

"How was work?"

"Good."

"No phone calls, no problems?"

"If you don't count the usual 'where's our money?' call from the bank."

He frowned. "I can fix that."

Beth shrugged. "I've handled much worse."

"Yeah, but they're not allowed to harass you. Let me deal with it."

Suddenly tired of fighting, Beth nodded. "Okay."

His eyes arrowed in on hers, surprise flaring.

"Why are you so quick to distrust everyone, *cara?*"

She closed her eyes briefly and considered dancing around that question. Honesty seemed less draining.

"Look, my dad was a serial cheater. He left when I was five then came back a year later. My mum took him back and for a while, it was good…until I turned ten and he left again. Mum finally had enough and we moved away and got on with our lives."

If he sensed more to her story, he didn't let on. "And all this—me, your runaway employee—isn't helping, right?"

"Right."

Her gaze skittered away, telling Luke there was more but she wasn't about to share.

The sudden urge to throttle someone flared. Irrational, absurd, yeah, but he felt it nonetheless.

"My parents moved from Italy to Australia when I was six," he said instead, shifting his weight to the back foot. She blinked but said nothing, and Luke continued. "They struggled all their lives to make a living. I mean, really struggled—we lived in a small rural town, trying to survive on the takings from their small fruit-and-veg store. But with the cyclones, drought and rain, plus the huge supermarket chains pushing us out, we were frequently without power and water. It was—" he dragged a hand through his hair, pushing back all those old memories "—frustrating. And after they died, I started to hate them for that."

"Why?"

"Because they never told me about my mother's brother, Gino. Apparently, he'd offered them money, a house and a job when they first got here, but they refused. They were deeply proud and deeply religious, and gambling was a huge sin. So when they died and Gino and Rosa suddenly appeared, it just gave me two more people to blame."

Beth bit down on her lip, watching him shift uncomfortably then glance away. She wanted to go to him, to hold him, to connect and soothe and comfort. She'd even started to move, rolling her weight forward in anticipation, until he suddenly turned to the house and she stopped dead.

"I should go and check on dinner," he said with a half smile over his shoulder. "Coming?"

She tucked her hair behind her ears, feeling foolish. "Yeah."

And then she followed him inside.

They ate dinner in a strange, uncomfortable silence, almost as if Luke had regretted sharing and was waiting for the right moment to take it all back.

That kiss had started it. Since then, their simmering attraction had cooled to arm's-length standoffishness, and despite the good talking-to she'd given herself, Beth felt oddly disappointed.

But instead of meeting the challenge when she felt his eyes infrequently graze over her, she focused on the tabletop, at the small knots and flaws in the heavy pine, at the scores of marks worn into the wood over the years.

Finally she finished her food, and with an inward sigh of relief, stood. Luke followed.

"Let me clear up," he offered.

"There's no need."

"I want to do it."

She clamped down on her frustration. "Okay. You can stack the dishwasher."

They let the mundane task of clearing away the table fill the void, until she went for a plate at the same time as Luke.

Once again their hands met, then their eyes.

Beth didn't know where to look. If she stepped back, he'd know she was nervous, and if she stayed where she was, he'd think she didn't mind him touching her. But the truth was, she was minding less and less.

"Sorry," she muttered and relinquished the plate.

As he stacked the dishwasher, she busied herself with the coffee.

You're hopeless at trying to pretend he isn't affecting you, that his kiss was no big deal.

And for every good reason she came up with for keeping her distance, she had only one very strong one why she shouldn't.

You want him.

"I called Rosa," Luke said suddenly. "I'm seeing her Sunday night."

"Just you?"

At his nod, she shook her head. "Oh, no. You are not leaving me out of this."

"Beth…"

"No, Luke."

He scowled, and finally his eyes revealed something more—anger. "This is personal. To me. Okay?"

Great, throw her words back in her face. "And what about our promise to share information?" The heat from his scrutiny made her cheeks warm, and for a second she stood there in guilty silence, thinking he'd call her on it. "Look, we're in it together. Right?"

Those seductive eyes were blacker than a starless night and revealed nothing. "I don't want you involved in my family disputes."

"A bit late for that. And anyway, just how are you going to stop me?"

Luke's gaze bored into hers, but she refused to back down. Frustration, anger, irritation all flashed in those dark depths, along with something else she was more than familiar with. Guilt.

"I'm stronger," he growled.

She put her hands on her hips and braced her feet apart. "But I can kick."

His eyes narrowed. "You wouldn't."

She gave him a small, deadly smile. "Oh, I would."

For a second they both froze, eyeing each other up in adversarial silence until his sudden bark of laughter broke it. His amusement transformed every worry line and tense muscle into something so compelling that it made her heart jump.

She returned the smile, but realized too late his closeness, his darkening eyes. His sensuous bottom lip.

Time passed. The blink of an eye. But to Beth it stretched, lengthened, heated, teasing out the moment until the lick of flames in her belly flared up and bathed her in a desperate need she could no longer ignore.

Gently, almost wonderingly, she placed a tentative hand on his cheek. The rough one-day growth rasped over her skin, reminding her that this was no dream. He was real and hard, the look in his eyes half warning, half wanting, and she couldn't help herself.

"Beth…" Her name was like a groan on his lips, his eyes devouring her. She paused, her hand still cupping his face.

She wanted to feel the contours of his mouth, touch him, kiss him.

She was going to.

Every muscle in his body flexed and tensed as she edged closer and pressed her legs against his, her hip bumping his groin. She heard his breath catch, the low rumble in his throat barely audible.

"What are you doing?" he said quietly.

"I'm going to kiss you."

Luke swallowed. "You have any idea what you're doing?"

"No," she muttered, her lips hovering close to his, hesitant, waiting.

With a soft groan Luke leaned in and captured her mouth.

There was heat again, that gut-sucking, toe-curling heat licking him from head to feet. She was kissing him back, her mouth sweetly opening underneath his, her arms wrapping around his neck.

They moved up against the counter and his back hit the warm humming dishwasher door. Her damp hands tangled in his hair, her breasts pushed into his chest. As he slid one knee between her legs, he felt himself go hard.

He placed small kisses on her mouth, teasing her bottom lip. He was so deeply intent, transfixed by her smell and delicious taste; her tiny moan of pleasure sent his pulse skyrocketing.

Beth jumped as Luke started exploring her waist with his fingers, then drew his lips along her cheek, grazing it with kisses.

"You smell like that face cream in the bathroom," he murmured, inhaling deeply. "Lemon. Nice."

She shivered with pleasure as his mouth feathered over hers then began a slow descent down her neck.

At some stage he must have hiked up her skirt, because suddenly she felt his hand on her bare thigh, easing up, up, until he was cupping her intimately through the thin cotton of her panties.

She gasped. It felt so good. So reckless. So unlike her sensible, perfectly ordered life.

She wanted more.

With a soft murmur, she eased her legs apart and moved her hips, urging him to continue. And without hesitation, he did, his fingers working under the elastic until suddenly they hit her damp, aroused flesh and she gasped aloud.

He stilled, his eyes black with passion boring into hers. Between their clothes she felt the urgent pounding of his heart, the sear of heat and the rise and fall of his chest.

His breath grazed her cheek. "You want me to continue?"

She stared right into his eyes and fell over the edge. "Oh, yes."

With a low guttural moan, he pulled down her panties, cupped her bottom and slid her onto the countertop. She hissed as the warm top made contact with her sensitive skin, the dishwasher vibrating gently on her calves. Then heat engulfed her as Luke eased her knees apart and slid his finger inside her wet core.

So tight. So hot. Luke's breath hissed out, simultaneously echoing her own ecstasy. His groin was rock hard and throbbing, but he ignored it, instead taking delight in her intimate flesh wrapped around his finger, her arousal as he scraped his palm against her swollen nub. He withdrew then plunged back in, again and again and she threw her head back, a groan of pleasure rolling deep within her throat.

He grabbed the back of her head and dragged her back for a kiss, a deep, soul-searing kiss full of hot passion and desperate longing. She murmured beneath his mouth, her tongue tangling with his as her arms snaked around his neck. Her musky smell, her hot wetness, her murmur of enjoyment surrounded him, infused his skin, burrowed inside until he could feel the pressure build and build. Still he continued to taste, to feel, to tease until she began to tremble and whimper beneath him.

He dragged his lips down her neck and gritted his teeth, begging for control as he finally felt her go over the edge.

The orgasm ripped through Beth, stealing her breath and her control in one thundering swoop.

Joy. Pure unadulterated joy singing in her veins, heating her blood, skyrocketing her heart. It had never, ever been like that before. She felt as if she could take on the world, run a marathon, fly for hours and hours.

She waited out the trembling, until her breath became slower, until her heart calmed and an inevitable wave of uncertainty slowly flooded in.

What on earth had she done?

"Beth."

Her name stirred the damp strands of hair on her cheek, sent a shiver across her skin. He slowly eased his finger from her and she couldn't stop her small disappointed murmur as cool air rushed in. But when he gently closed her legs, reality came crashing back in one disastrous wave.

"Beth," he said again. "Look at me."

Reluctantly she opened her eyes. His were dark and unreadable.

"I…ah…" She paused. Dammit, how could she focus

when he'd taken her on the dishwasher and he'd seen her fall to pieces beneath his hand? With a heated flush, she slid from the counter and scooped up her abandoned underwear. "Okay, so that was a bad idea. We've both been under a lot of pressure and—"

His hands on her shoulders stopped her midsentence, but she refused to meet his eyes, instead looking down.

She drew in a breath, hard. Bad mistake. The telltale bulge in his pants was all too obvious.

With a finger under her chin, he tilted her face up to meet his, but when he went to place a gentle kiss on her cheek Beth pulled away.

"Look, Luke," she began and stepped back, trying to regain control. "What happened here…" She felt her face flush but forged on. "I think it's just… We had a…"

"A purely physiological response under stress."

She blinked, astonished. "Exactly."

Except he now knew what she tasted like, felt like. And she still desperately wanted her house more than ever.

"So let's just focus on what we need to do," he added, then turned back to the table and began stacking the place mats.

She stared at him, her stomach a confusing mixture of uncertainty, relief…disappointment?

He glanced up with a smile. "Right?"

"Right." Nothing had changed. He still wanted to sell her home. And she still couldn't afford it.

But how exactly could she focus on talking him around after *that*?

Nine

As she drove to work the next day, Beth made a firm decision. Avoid Luke whenever possible. There was way too much at risk, a risk that could have the potential to end in disaster.

With new resolve, she got through the day with barely a stray thought to the night before. Yet when she returned home and found dinner warming in the oven and Luke nowhere to be seen, it took all of a few seconds to realize he'd come to the same conclusion.

She wasn't disappointed. No. That would be ridiculous. And anyway, she still saw him later that night, even if it was just in passing, where she couldn't meet his eyes as she awkwardly thanked him for the meal. He nodded with a brief smile and kept right on going, gently closing his door with a soft click.

Still his presence overwhelmed, from the faint cologne that made her senses growl, to the cooked meals and painfully clean state of her kitchen. And with each passing day, the tension wound inexorably tighter until she was itching for something—anything—to happen.

Then it was Sunday night and they were both on their way to the Corellis' in Beth's car.

"Dylan called." Luke finally broke the silence as they drove south on the Gold Coast Highway. "Looks like Foster withdrew big at a Coolangatta ATM then flew down to Melbourne."

"Is he still there now?"

"As far as I know. He's looking into it."

Her stomach swooped, hope fluttering, but with a firm swallow Beth reined it in. Things were far from over. She shifted gears, trying to ignore the brush of her knuckles along Luke's thigh. Her small car did nothing to maintain that distance she'd so determinedly forged these last few days. More irritating, the closer they got to the Corelli estate, the more her body hummed at the thought of Luke in touchable distance for the night.

They'd taken the Ashmore turnoff and were driving along Cotlew Road when Luke pointed to a parked news van ahead.

"Reporters. Take a left at the next corner."

She did, and they passed a few double-storied houses, then a few gates until the road curved again.

"Here." Luke nodded.

They parked on the side of the road and switched off the lights. The street was quiet, streetlamps casting a dim glow in the evening's warmth as upper-class suburbia sprawled on the opposite side. Next to the car, a long, high, brick wall stretched down the road, flanked by trees that swayed and rustled, a ghostly whisper as the wind picked up. All around, the vegetation muttered and moved in the night. Above, black clouds rolled in like waves on a beach. A storm was brewing.

"This is the back end of the estate. We can get in over there." Luke pointed to a large tree. "But we need to climb. Feel up to it?"

Beth looked down at her tailored pants and soft sparkly shift top and nodded.

As they picked their way through the grass and uneven ground, Luke automatically took her hand, tightening his grip when she stumbled. She barely had time to catch her breath before he let her go and began boosting himself up into the tree.

She looked up skeptically at the outspread branches. "You sure this is safe?"

"Who do you think hammered the wooden rungs into the trunk? Frankly, I'm surprised Marco hasn't chopped the tree down. Or at least taken the steps off."

He held out his hand, wriggling his fingers in encouragement.

It seemed perfectly natural to put her trust in him. They climbed the tree slowly, finally reaching a branch that overhung the wall. He placed one foot on the brick surface then turned to her.

"Come on," he gestured. "Come over."

Beth took a deep breath and went for it.

Her heart pounded as she broke out in a sweat. Then she took that step into thin air, just before he grabbed her and pulled her tightly to him.

She took a couple of gulping breaths.

"You okay?"

Beth nodded into the warmth of his chest, breathing in his smell. His arms were a reassuring harbor and slowly her panic petered out.

"I'll go down first, then you jump and I'll catch you."

Beth glanced around, seeing a large estate with glowing night-lights sprawled on the crest of the hill, the perimeter dotted with security lamps. Then she looked down and choked out a nervous laugh. "I'd like to see you try that one."

"You and me both, sweetheart."

A man stepped out of the shadows, accompanied by two beefy security guards.

Luke, to his credit, looked unflappable. "Be a sport and help us down, Marco."

The man laughed sharply then took a drag of his cigarette. "I don't think so. I want to see you manage this one."

Luke gave Marco a scowl, muttered something under his breath then said to Beth, "Hold on. I'm going down."

He lowered himself until his legs were dangling over the edge, then tested the brick and concrete below with his foot. Finding a hold, he settled his toe into the worn hole and slowly picked his way down until he was nearly to the ground. With one push, he jumped the rest of the way.

Beth released her held breath as he landed solidly with both feet. He gave her a grin and a thumbs-up. "Jump down and I'll catch you."

She shook her head. "No. You can't."

"I will," he said, exasperated. "Just jump."

"Come on," Marco said as he ground his half-finished cigarette underfoot. "We haven't got all night."

Beth sighed. "I warned you." And she squatted on her heels, took a breath and jumped off the wall.

With a *whoosh* and a grunt, she landed on Luke. He stumbled, wavering, and she tightened her arms around his neck.

His legs buckled and they ended up sprawling on the grass.

Marco roared with laughter and gave a slow clap. "Well done, Luke! Super catch!"

Beth had a death hold on Luke's neck, her eyes squeezed shut.

"You can look now," Luke murmured.

Her eyes flew open. "Thanks."

"You got a problem with the front door?" Marco was asking as Luke helped Beth up.

"No. Just a problem with the reporters." And he started toward the house.

Marco nodded a dismissal to the security guys then followed Luke, matching him stride for stride. "So the press are finally getting to you." His voice held the gruff resonance of frustration. "Now you know how it feels."

Luke gave a noncommittal grunt. Marco, meanwhile, slowly turned to peruse Beth with hooded eyes.

The eyes and height were Luke's, but that's where the resemblance ended. Marco Corelli was dressed in a light linen suit and cotton shirt, dark hair pulled back into a ponytail that emphasized a stunningly beautiful angular face, complete with sharp cheekbones and sensual mouth.

Beth blinked, frowning. "You look familiar—have we met before?"

"Pretty sure I'd have remembered, *bella.*" Marco winked.

At Luke's sharp look, Marco laughed. "Relax, mate. I'm just winding you up." He turned back to Beth and grinned, offering his hand. "Marco Corelli. And you are…?"

"Beth. Beth Jones."

"Marco plays football for Manchester United," Luke said.

"*Played.* I've retired."

Luke's eyebrows rose. "Since when?"

"Four weeks ago. Too many injuries." He shrugged and kept right on walking, his expression neutral.

"No, that's not it," Beth insisted, frowning. "Have you been on TV or…?"

Luke snorted, choking back a sudden grin. "Underpants."

"Sorry?"

"Marco's the face of Skins. You know, the expensive guy's underwear?"

Of course! She stared at Marco, who was now scowling at Luke in earnest. Tanned, ripped abs, seductive smile, stacked set of y-fronts. He totally sizzled on that huge Gold Coast Highway billboard.

Marco stuck his hands in his pockets. "So where did you two meet?"

"None of your business," Luke retorted before Beth could open her mouth.

"Huh. Always secretive, especially where women are concerned," Marco said. "Ever since Gabrielle—"

"Don't." Luke stopped dead in his tracks, the air crackling with sudden tension. "Don't go there, Marco."

Marco's expression turned dark as he met Luke's angry glare with one of his own. With an inaudible mutter, he shrugged and resumed walking.

"How's Rosa?" Luke finally said.

"Better." Marco kept right on walking, and Beth could just make out the tightening line of his jaw. "Not that you'd know. You've avoided her calls for days."

They emerged from the line of trees, and whatever response Luke gave was lost on the coastal breeze.

The gleaming three-story mansion, all cream-colored pillars, shiny glass and strategically placed downlights, screamed wealth from every nook and cranny.

The immaculate gardens were resplendent with palm trees and native gums. A gently cascading fountain sat in the middle of the circular driveway and behind that, a stucco path led to a pair of huge glass-and-oak doors.

She stood there, admiring the beautiful simplicity, until Luke's gruff voice broke through her thoughts.

"I didn't start this," he was saying.

"But you could stop it."

"No, I can't. I've been suspended, remember?"

Marco snorted. "Last time I checked, you were flavor of the month at Jackson and Blair. Today you can do nothing?"

"It'd only make things worse."

"How in hell could it get any worse?" Marco growled. "Gino is dead, for chrissakes, Luke! He can't defend himself and you *won't* defend him."

"I. Am. On. Suspension," Luke enunciated clearly.

Marco snorted. "That didn't stop you from barging in to see Gino the night he died." At Luke's look, he said, "Yeah, I know all about that."

There was a long pause before Luke said cautiously, "What do you know?"

"Employees talk. And you *were* there when the medics arrived, so you can't deny it."

"So?"

"So I got to thinking—"

"Marco…"

"I wondered why you would risk your precious reputation that night of all nights."

"I don't know what you're talking about."

"Don't you?" Marco's eyes narrowed, his hands going to his hips. "It was the same day Gino's story hit the papers. You went to give Gino a piece of your mind, didn't you? You were furious, that I know. You've always had a problem hiding your anger, Luke. My bet is you and Gino argued, Gino had a heart attack and Lucky Luke hides behind his precious reputation."

"Marco! Lucio! That is *enough!*"

They all turned in unison to the small round figure framed by the huge glass doors. And when she stepped outside, into the full light of the patio, Beth gasped.

"Oh, my God… *Connie?*"

"Beth?"

Luke frowned. "You two know each other?"

"Yes." Beth shoved her hands on her hips, her eyes narrowed as a whirling dervish of questions and suspicion started to swell. "She's one of my clients and her name is Connie Lisone."

Ten

"What?" Stunned, Luke stared at Beth then whipped back to his aunt.

"What are you doing here, Beth?" Rosa said, her face full of bewilderment. "What—"

"What's going on?" Marco said behind them.

"I have no idea—Connie? Or—it's *Rosa*, right?" Beth retorted.

Rosa took a sharp breath, her eyes rounding. "The house. *Caro dio,* the house!"

"Will someone please tell me what the hell is going on?" Marco yelled behind them.

Luke glared from Rosa to Beth, his jaw tight. "Go on then. Let's hear it."

Rosa pushed the doors wider with a shaky hand. "Come in. Please."

Unbelievable. Un-fricking-believable. The anger in Luke simmered as they followed Rosa down the plush hallway, past the familiar blue-washed walls, the classic works of art, the stylish furnishings, before they stopped in the living room.

"Please, sit."

Beth perched on the edge of an elegant Louis XIV chair and crossed her arms. Luke chose to stand.

"Stop glaring at me, Lucio, and sit." She waved to the sofa. With a soft snort, he finally sat.

Rosa sighed, smoothing back her salt-and-pepper hair. "You all know the kind of attention the Corelli name attracts. So for many years I've been using a fake one—for appointments, for bookings." She shrugged. "It allows me a small freedom I wouldn't normally have."

"And what's your connection to Beth? Besides being a client?"

Rosa clasped her hands and turned to Beth. "Remember when you first started your business, *bella?* You mentioned that awful shared apartment you were renting?"

Beth nodded.

"You didn't say much, but I could see how tough things had been for you." She tapped her cheek with a small smile. "It's the eyes, *bella.* All your emotion is locked away behind those green eyes."

"So you set her up?" Luke interrupted.

"No." Rosa looked offended. "I just steered her toward Crown Real Estate. That house had been empty for years and needed a little love and attention.

A word in the right direction and you had yourself a new home."

"So the story about the owners living overseas was a lie?"

Rosa shrugged. "Just a little one."

"You were the 'family friend'," Luke interjected tightly. "And Costas Holdings is one of Gino's?"

"Yes." Rosa turned back to Beth. "You needed help, but were so proud and determined. You'd never have taken charity—" She raised a hand as Beth opened her mouth. "Yes, in your mind my offer would have been exactly that. And I also knew you'd never take the house if you knew who I was." Her lined face creased in a gentle smile. "You reminded me so much of Lucio's mother, in a scary new world and in desperate need of help. How could I not help you?"

"Hang on," Luke interrupted with a frown. "How do you know what my mother needed?"

She gave Luke a tender, sad look. "Every month I drove two hours to see Melina and gave her a little something to meet the monthly bills. Your father never knew."

In stunned silence Luke tried to digest this new revelation. But no matter how many times he played it out in his head, he came up with the same answer.

More lies. More secrets. Dammit, when would they ever end?

His gazed remained unwavering, fixed on Rosa. "So let me get this straight," he said calmly—almost too calmly. "Instead of one simple phone call, both of us ended up racing all over town thinking it was some kind of conspiracy theory?"

"You are *such* an ass, Luke."

Luke whipped around to face Marco's bristling anger. "You've been ignoring *our* calls," he continued tightly. "And then Gino's PR guy advised us to lay low for a few weeks but *that* obviously didn't cross your mind after you were spotted—"

"Boys, please…" Rosa interrupted, her expression torn with concern. "No fighting."

Luke sprang to his feet and began to pace.

Rosa glanced helplessly at Beth, then back to Luke. "I know you are *pazzo* at me, Lucio—"

Angry? If only it were that clear. But Marco was right. Damn guilt got him every single time.

When he finally turned to face his aunt, the soft love mingled with abject worry on her familiar features hit him like a runaway train.

Rosa had tried to be a mother to him, but he'd rebuffed her time and again. Oh, there'd been times when he'd allowed small intimacies—a hug on his birthday, a kiss at Christmas. She'd also mediated the blazing fights between him and Marco and had encouraged him in his studies.

And remained loyal when the reporters had come clamoring for a quote.

He knew she would never deliberately hurt him, just as he had total faith in the honor code he lived by.

The power of that thought stole away his accusations, turning them to dust on his tongue. With a barely audible groan, he sank to the couch and rubbed his temples.

"You know how hard I've worked to get where I am, Rosa." He glanced up, frustration clouding his voice.

"How I've fought for every promotion, made sure I was beyond reproach, because of Gino's reputation. So why did he drag me into this?"

"Lucio. He did not do this to hurt you," came Rosa's soft declaration. "Things have been so crazy around here and I completely forgot about the rental, Gino's bequest to you.

"He had always planned to give it to you," she continued. "It was the house he originally offered your parents when they first came to Australia. Your father turned us down flat."

Luke's gut twisted at the barely hidden grief. The woman had lost her husband, the man she'd loved for over forty years and here he was getting all worked up about a bunch of misunderstandings.

Death had a way of putting everything into perspective.

Rosa's dark eyes, creased with years of life and love, now holding only concern and worry, humbled him. He flushed. She wasn't to blame for the inquiry, or the way the press had focused so thoroughly on him.

"I am so sorry I didn't tell you sooner." Rosa went to Beth and took her hands. "You must have been so confused, thinking you'd been kicked out onto the street." Just as Beth opened her mouth, Rosa added, "I would never do anything to hurt you, Beth. You know that. Don't you?"

As Beth sat there, staring into the earnest woman's big brown eyes, she remembered the moments they'd shared—the laughter, the little gifts on her birthday, the snippets of life advice Rosa had offered. Beth had liked talking to her, had liked her.

"You warm this old Italian woman's heart, Beth," Rosa continued. "You, *bella.* You're smart. You're good here—" she put a hand on one expansive bosom "—you deserve to have someone look after you."

Beth gently extricated herself. "You lied to me, Rosa."

"And what would you have me do, eh?" Rosa's brows shot up. "Sit back and watch you struggle every day? *Pah!*" She snapped her fingers. "You'd never take money from me, so I did the only thing I could."

"After all this time why didn't you say something?"

Rosa shook her head. "I was going to. But you were so happy to finally have a place of your own, and I know how you feel about lying. What if you'd never speak to me again?"

But my lease is up in three months, she was about to say. *I will be out on the street.* But the look on Rosa's face had her choking back the words. Her issue was with Luke, not Rosa, and she sure as hell wasn't about to add to the woman's already heavy guilt.

Suddenly, Beth's heart wasn't in it. She sighed and glanced up at Luke, who had remained oddly silent.

Rosa straightened and turned back to Luke. "Lucio, I know Gino had his faults and you and he never really got along. But he was so very proud of you. As am I." She blinked as her eyes began to tear.

"Rosa…"

"No." She put up a silencing finger, "Your uncle was a proud man and those terrible accusations hit him hard, but he understood what you had to do. He loved you so much." She grasped his hand and squeezed, a bittersweet smile hovering on her lips before she pulled a key from her pocket. "He left you something in his desk drawer. Please, go take a look."

Luke closed the office door firmly behind him and scanned the room. Everything was still in its place, from the large antique desk to the rows of books lining the walls. The faint aroma of expensive cigars and brandy still lingered on the air. He almost expected Gino to be sitting behind that desk, puffing quietly away. Instead, the empty chair matched the hole in his heart.

Quickly, he shoved the key in the desk drawer and unlocked it. The white envelope was addressed to him and the contents yielded a DVD.

A frown furrowing his brow, Luke slowly closed the drawer, went over to the DVD player that sat in the bookcase, shoved in the disc then picked up the remote and clicked on the TV.

He took a seat behind the imposing desk, his finger hovering over the play button.

A clean blotter sat square in the middle, a fountain pen perfectly one inch from the top. Luke picked up the pen and twirled it idly in his hand, a small smile hovering on his lips. Gino was old school, preferring fountain pen and ink for all his correspondence.

Luke replaced the pen, screwed up his eyes and pinched his nose high on the bridge.

Gino's desk at Aphrodite's was identical—same layout, same pens. Same scent of leather, polished wood and cigar smoke.

Every little thing was determined to remind him of that night, even while he'd been trying to forget it. Like a convicted man accepting his fate, he let the memories flood in.

The board had expressed their displeasure earlier that day and Luke had been in a white-hot fury. Regardless of the warnings issued to keep his distance from Gino, he'd stormed into the casino spoiling for a fight. Security had wisely kept out of his way, and frustrated as all hell, he'd slammed into Gino's office.

Luke grunted, remembrance flooding in like waters over a burst dam, too late to stop it.

Those sharp accusations he'd flung at Gino had been like a red rag to a bull, and his uncle had never been one to turn down a fight.

"Dammit all to hell, Gino! Are you using the casino as a money-laundering front?"

Gino shot to his feet, his face flushed. "No! You of all people should know that!"

"Should I?" Luke's eyes narrowed. "I heard the evidence is before the Director of Public Prosecutions. And if he thinks that's enough for a trial then there's probably enough to convict."

"I know the law, Lucio."

"Apparently not enough!"

Gino matched Luke's dark look with one of his own, his breath coming in heavy puffs. "I will not have you stand there and accuse me of breaking the law! *I will not!*"

"Well, that's too bad." Luke shoved his face in Gino's. "Because right now, I don't give a damn if you're fiddling with the tables, cooking the books or ripping off the bloody queen of England. All I care about is that stink rubbing off on me." He slammed his palms down on the desk, his voice deadly calm. "And no one messes with my job."

Every time he relived those few moments, it never got any better. Luke recalled every heated word, every frustrated gesture.

And the outcome was exactly the same every time. Midargument, Gino went bright red, clutched his chest and collapsed.

With a vicious curse, Luke shot to his feet.

The doctors said nothing could have saved him, even if he'd had a heart attack right in the middle of the emergency ward. Still, the guilt had eaten at him until Luke could hardly think straight. CPR was futile; the medics had had to pull him off Gino when he'd refused to believe his uncle had been dead for ten minutes.

Guilt had kept him from seeing Rosa before the funeral. Even then he'd defied a direct order and attended the service, for all the good it did everyone. It had been pure torture. A couple of reporters had been thrown out, Marco had erupted in a rage and all the while Rosa's red-rimmed eyes drilled into his very soul. Still, she'd said nothing, accepted his lame condolences with good grace and said not one word about the argument or Luke's lengthy absence. Which made him feel doubly worse.

Marco had remained uncharacteristically silent throughout the service, but every time his eyes settled on Luke, they'd been bright and angry. Afterward, he'd let it all come spilling out and Luke had deserved it, had welcomed it, even. It was his cross to bear.

Now he focused on the television screen and the remote control he gripped.

He pressed Play and began to watch.

"You and Lucio—you are friends?" Rosa began after she sent Marco off to get drinks then took a seat on the couch beside Beth.

Beth choked down a laugh. "Hardly. I made an offer on the house, but he refused it then moved in. No." Her gaze drifted to the archway where he'd disappeared. "Definitely not *friends*."

"I see." She clasped her hands in her lap. "But he told you about Melina and Salvatore. His parents," she clarified.

"Yes."

Rosa was shaking her head, the pain of remembrance etched in the lines around her eyes. "My brother and his wife were very proud, very strict and devoutly religious. When Lucio found out about us, he blamed Gino for not making an effort, for not coming to their aid when they'd been struggling for so long in near poverty. Stubborn, just like Marco." She smiled, but it quickly disappeared. "Lucio lived with us for nearly three years, holding on tight to that grudge every day. He was such an angry, scared boy, trying so very hard to be a man, and anything we did just pushed him further away. But he was a gifted child and he threw himself into his studies, then his job. It gave him strength, gave him the control and security he needed. And I've seen him barely a dozen times since then."

Rosa's voice broke, but she valiantly held on to her composure. "And now he's living with you."

"Not *living* with me. He's in the spare room."

"So he trusts you." When Beth shook her head, Rosa said, "He does, *bella*. If he didn't, you'd have been out within a day."

"It's not trust that's keeping him there, Rosa. It's suspicion. He thought I was Gino's mistress."

Rosa choked back a laugh. "Really?"

"Yes." Beth bit her lip to stop a smile from escaping. "We both agreed to work this out together and not get the police involved."

"Ah." She tapped a finger on her chin in thoughtful silence.

"Look, there's nothing—"

Marco returned then with a bottle of wine and four glasses, cutting off Beth's protest.

She took the proffered glass, determinedly avoiding Rosa's scrutiny.

"So you're living with Luke, huh?" Marco began, grinning over the rim of his glass as he perched on the couch arm.

Beth swallowed a sigh. "Not that way we're not."

His eyebrows rose. "But you share a house."

Ah, yes. The house. "For the moment, yes."

"There you go." Marco took a swig, rolled the wine around in his mouth then swallowed. "Significant milestone, I'd say."

"You both look good together," Rosa interrupted. "I can see there's something else there than just friends. *Sì?*"

"No!" Beth cleared her throat and tried again. "No, there isn't."

Rosa made a noise that sounded suspiciously like a

snort. "You need a good strong man in your life. I may be old but I know *amore*. Love, it will make your problems go away. It will make you trust again, eh?"

She took Beth's still hands and squeezed. "I know how much you guard your secrets, *bella*. Lucio, he has a few of his own."

Beth blinked, looking from Rosa to Marco grinning behind his wineglass.

Since when had the evening turned into a "what Beth needs is a man" discussion?

She recalled the times Rosa had mentioned her family. On the massage table, clients opened up and talked about the most intimate details of their lives—family feuds, career woes, relationships. Rosa's favorite subject had been her family. She'd boasted of their virtues nearly every session, how talented her son was, how her handsome nephew needed a good woman to slow him down, make him appreciate life more.

Luke suddenly appeared, interrupting Beth's response.

"You found it, Lucio?" Rosa asked, drawing away from Beth.

"Yes." His eyes were expressionless, unreadable. "We should go."

Rosa looked surprised. "You are not staying for dinner?"

"Sorry. Beth?"

Beth threw Rosa an apologetic glance and stood. "Maybe another time?"

"Sì." Rosa kissed Beth on both cheeks, her eyes full of unanswered questions. *"Ciao, bella.* Drive safely."

Eleven

They went back the way they came, this time with a guard holding a ladder against the wall. Luke opted to drive and Beth let him, knowing if they were spotted, he'd lose their pursuers quickly.

"I'm sorry you got messed up in this," Luke said suddenly.

Beth sighed. "Rosa just wanted to help me, Luke. You're not to blame for that."

He shook his head. "I still can't believe she went to all that trouble to help you out."

"I can." She gave a small smile. "Her heart is very much in the right place."

Luke slanted her a look but she remained silent. Was he waiting for her to point out all of this could've been sorted out days ago, if only he'd picked up Rosa's calls?

She never kicked someone when he was down and despite the facade, Luke had been squarely punched.

"I just hope this doesn't turn around to bite us in the ass," he said quietly.

"Then we'll just have to be extra careful," Beth said.

They lapsed into silence. Beth wanted to ask him what he'd found in Gino's office, but if he'd wanted her to know he would have shared. So instead she went with the main question that had been bugging her for the past hour.

"So who's Gabrielle?"

His eyes remained fixed on the road. "My ex-wife."

Wow. She had not seen that one coming. "How did you two meet?"

"In college."

"And were you—"

"Look, Beth, I'd rather not talk about it, okay?"

She watched him work his jaw, his mouth a thin line. "Okay."

The deep rumble of thunder filled the silence. Beth peered out the darkened window. "Might rain."

"Looks like it."

Great. Now I'm resorting to the inanities of weather. She snapped her mouth closed and took a deep breath of moisture-laden air.

The first fat drops of rain began to fall as they arrived home. Inside the house, the darkness was lit only by the warm glow of a small lamp.

When Luke paused in the hallway to retrieve a stray piece of mail that had fallen from the side table, she plowed straight into his broad back.

It was like touching naked flame. She sprang back. "Sorry."

"How are you holding up?"

His concern and silent scrutiny undid her.

It could have been the way his eyes caressed her face, the gruffness of his voice, the way he sensed all those hidden feelings she tried to bury. Or his incredible vulnerability behind an almost impenetrable wall of control. And here she was standing a bare inch away and practically aching to reach out and smooth those creases hovering across his brow. "I'm fine. Just not very tired."

"Do you want a drink?"

"Okay." Inside, her heart was doing a dance on her ribs. "I'll be down in a moment." She went to the stairs, gave him one brief glance then went up to her bedroom.

Dressed in a pair of loose drawstring linen pants and a blue tank top, Beth paused at the top of the stairs. Below lay an abyss of darkness, punctuated only by the candles on the coffee table, their familiar fragrance drifting through the ground floor. The flames danced and teased, as if they knew their purpose was to calm and soothe but deliberately doing the opposite.

She took a deep breath and descended. Luke's long legs stretched out on the floor, crossed at the ankles. His back was cradled by the leg of the couch and in his hand he absently twirled a half-full wineglass.

Swiftly she crossed the room and tugged the curtains apart. "You should really see the sky—it's great on a night like this. See?"

Through the inky blackness, past the fence line, the

river rippled and tossed with the wind. In the distance a brief glimpse of stars glittered, tiny diamonds in indigo velvet, before the rolling black storm clouds gradually engulfed them.

"Here comes that rain."

"Yep." Luke poured some more wine then gestured to the spot beside him. She sat, took the glass he offered then sipped in silence. And slowly, the lull of the alcohol, the slashing rain and the flickering candles began to work their magic.

With a gentle snort, Beth shook her head.

"What?" Luke said.

"Your aunt." At the questioning curve to his eyebrow, she added, "She really loved Gino, didn't she?"

"Yeah."

Beth sighed. "My parents missed out on so much."

Luke watched her contemplate the fabric of her pants, as if they provided an answer only she could decipher.

"Tell me," he said softly.

She shot him a brief glance from under her lashes then focused on her hands, linking her fingers together. *Here is the church, here is the steeple...*

"Oh, just…" She gestured with a shrug. "It's nothing."

"Not nothing."

When her expression tightened, Luke sensed the remnants of something more, something worrying enough to make her shift uncomfortably and straighten her shoulders.

Then she took a deep breath and began to speak.

"I was seventeen and just out of high school while

my mom worked two jobs. Then one day, in the middle of fourth term, she booked us on a flight to Perth with money I knew we didn't have."

She stopped abruptly, letting the silence swallow her confession. Luke remained still, allowing her time to reveal the pieces of her past.

"I had no money, no life and barely a functioning parent," she eventually continued. "For once I wanted to be normal, to travel, to experience new things." He could almost hear her wistfulness as she recalled long-forgotten dreams. "I should've said no but she was so excited. She never got excited about anything, not since my dad left. I couldn't—" she hesitated, then finished lamely "—bring myself to rain on her parade."

I was just a naive teenager, Beth reminded herself. *Wanting an adventure. An escape from the endless boredom of my life.*

Her mouth tilted at the memory. She'd locked her past tightly away and she could try to convince herself that Luke's appearance had forced the memories to surface. But the truth was, her very existence had already begun to turn the key. Now the door gaped wide-open.

Yet her slowly blossoming trust continued to war with a lifetime of secrets. She could feel the warm burn of his eyes and braced herself for the breathlessness and panic to set in. It was there, buzzing faintly in the background, but way less urgent, less dark than before.

That meant something. It had to.

"I was in an accident and people died, my mother included. So about a year later, I met a guy. He seemed nice and I liked him. I was eighteen and of course, you fall in love with every guy you date, right? So one night, after we…uh, were in bed—" she swallowed, embarrassed "—he told me he was a reporter, that he'd been trying to track me down for weeks and could I give him an exclusive."

From the corner of her eye she could see Luke's still profile. The dim light and deep shadows cast his features into sharp angles, doing nothing to hide the flint in his eyes or the tightening of his jaw.

She didn't want to take that step backward, to delve into that pool of loss, betrayal and the inevitable vulnerability that failure had brought her. The past was dead and gone but still had the power to humiliate. Just as she felt a mild panic attack well up in her chest, she recalled the tiny bits of memory she'd shoved away— the irritation on Jack's face when she'd slammed out the door, the hurtful revelation that cut like tiny shards of glass. And the sickening realization she would never truly be able to leave the past behind. She had to get out before it completely destroyed her.

She straightened her back against the hard couch leg. The panic attack faded as she went on. "So, there you go." She drew a stray curl behind her ears with a firm hand. "That's why I don't trust anyone."

When he reached for her, she pulled back. "Don't."

He ignored her and wrapped his arms around her shoulders. "Don't what?" he murmured. "Don't touch you? Or don't care that you've been hurt?"

She buried her face in his chest, her answer muffled. "Both."

"Too late."

As they sat there on the floor cradling each other, she felt the tight constraints of her past begin to crumble.

"You're into touching a lot, aren't you?" she muttered against his shoulder.

"Yep." She closed her eyes as his fingers went into her hair. God, that felt good. "Get used to it."

After an eternity of her against the world, Beth nearly convinced herself he meant that. He'd slowly attacked her defenses, questioned her reasons for being alone. She knew she couldn't hold out forever under this tender barrage. Openness was a luxury she did without, and yet she could feel herself warming to it, welcoming it.

Regretfully, she drew back and felt a surge of terrible loss. But that was dumb. How could she lose what wasn't hers?

"Why do you blame yourself for Gino's death?" she asked after a while.

His eyes watching her over the rim of his wineglass suddenly sharpened. "You really want to go down that road?"

She tilted her chin up. "Yes," then, more softly, "I want to help you."

"I was suspended, I confronted Gino, we argued and he had a heart attack," he stated flatly.

He paused, almost as if he expected her to run screaming from the room. She stayed right where she was.

"Don't look at me like that!" he muttered.

"Like what?"

"Like you're doing right now. I don't deserve it. I don't need it."

Beth sighed. "You don't think you deserve my understanding and support?"

"No. Weren't you listening? I killed my uncle."

"So you said."

Her composure was beginning to irritate him. "So I don't need—"

"Don't tell me what to feel, Luke." She poked a finger in his chest. "You loved Gino. You miss him. How he died doesn't erase a lifetime of good memories. Do you even know what I would've given for a family like yours?"

Luke's scowl matched hers. "They're not saints."

"So whose are? At least they love you."

He shook his head. "You don't understand."

"Whatever taints them taints you, right?" From the look on his face she knew she'd hit a nerve. "And you think bottling up your misplaced guilt is a good way of handling it? If Gino were alive, you'd still have to go through the inquiry. You'd still be on suspension. Nothing would've changed. Would Gino have wanted you beating yourself up about it?" She went on more gently. "With all this craziness around you, you don't need to take the blame for Gino, too. You can't do your job if you don't respect your own decisions. Believe me, I know."

Luke was staring at her, his dark eyes narrowed to speculative slits.

"How do you do that?" he muttered.

"What?"

"Know exactly what—" He looked away.

"What you're thinking?" She gave him a smile. "You've hardly cornered the market on the guilt trip. Don't punish yourself. Tell Rosa how you feel."

Luke snorted. "And have her hate me?"

"She won't hate you. She loves you."

Luke just stared straight ahead, intent on his thoughts.

His profile was perfect—full mouth, strong nose, broad brow. And underneath lurked a vulnerability that tugged at her heart so badly she wanted to wrap her arms around him and never let go.

"You can trust me, too, you know."

Luke tilted the glass to his lips and swallowed, letting her statement hang until it felt like a leaded weight.

"It's gone. I'm over it." Yet the tightness in his shoulders, the gleam in his eyes told a different story.

She reached out and touched his arm. "Okay."

He looked down at her hand, then up to meet her eyes. And gave her a glimpse of pain so raw it stole her breath. "Sometimes it comes back to me, you know?"

"Gino?"

"Gabrielle," he said thickly. "Is there something I could've said or done differently. Anything to stop her from—" He cleared his throat with a scowl. "We were eighteen, she got pregnant. The baby was six months old when she took his life, then her own. I found them both and—" He slashed his gaze to the floor, his jaw working. "It's like I've got a private movie going on here—" he tapped his temple "—and it's an all-night screening."

Instinct kicked in. Going to him in his moment of need seemed perfectly natural. Perfectly right. Beth selfishly absorbed the way he felt in her arms, dragging in the smell of his skin, his warmth.

"When you make it through a day without thinking about it, you feel like cheering," she said softly, her chin on his shoulder. "A week passes, then a month. Before long a year or two's gone by and you forget the way they smiled, or spoke or hummed a certain tune when they were happy. And you wonder if forgetting is the best way to remember them."

"Yeah." He let out a deep breath and drew back and Beth felt suddenly bereft.

"Do you like what you do, Luke? I mean, apart from this last week."

He dragged his fingers through his hair. "My parents died in near poverty, uninsured and in debt. I was determined to be smarter than that. Better. More…" He sighed. "In control."

His soft statement hit a chord inside. He was way too close, evoking emotions he had no right to be evoking. Beth felt her face warm, followed by other, very intimate places.

Luke knew the exact moment everything changed. The melancholy scattered, replaced by a surge of desire that went straight to his groin.

His next question came out rough. "Don't you miss it at all?"

"Miss what?"

"The intimacy. Sex."

"Frankly, no." She glanced away, her discomfort obvious. "It wasn't that good."

"Maybe you weren't doing it right."

She snorted. "What's the saying? 'If it's bad, it's still pretty good.'"

"I think they're talking about pizza."

He grinned at her quickly smothered smile. "Trust me, there's a big difference."

"I see."

The still, warm silence in the room was suddenly more intimate than a caress.

Luke knew Beth was wary, scarred by her past. Hell, he was, too. But this time there was something more, something more than just physical attraction. She intrigued him, her sexy body combined with that don't-touch-me glow. She tried so hard for control and calm yet when you scratched below the surface, complex emotion bubbled out. He wanted nothing more than to dislodge that exterior.

He linked his fingers through hers and watched in fascination as the intimate slide of flesh on flesh sent a shiver over her skin.

Then he reached out and gently removed the glass from her fingers before slowly bending to her mouth.

Her eyes fluttered closed, two dark sets of eyelashes feathering softly against her cheeks. At the last moment he detoured to that cheek, gently lipped the skin, then inched to the corners of her mouth.

Beth's blood pounded as she leaned into him and took a deep breath. Skin, warmth and Luke. Home.

When he finally covered her mouth with his she sighed with contentment. He made her forget the convictions she held on to so tightly. He was heat and passion and tenderness all rolled into one. His lips and teeth and breath did everything his fingers didn't—teasing, testing, savoring her.

When he finally released her mouth, she squeezed her eyes tight.

"Nervous, *cara?*"

She shook her head vigorously, finally opening her

eyes. The passion in his stole her breath away. Gently, he caressed her cheek and her heart broke into a thousand pieces.

"You don't have to live your life because of other people's actions," he said, his warm palm cupping her cheek. "If you do, it means they've won. It means you've allowed them to control you."

He was right. Oh, how he was right. Something so simple should have occurred to her before now, but it hadn't. She didn't like how Luke forced her to take a long, hard look at her life, at herself. She didn't like what she saw.

"I don't know what to think anymore."

"Then don't," he whispered. "Just let go of thinking tonight."

So when he kissed her forehead with infinite tenderness, then each cheek, then her mouth, she refused to think about anything but his lips, his hands and his heat easing its way into every crevice of her body.

He gently drew her down onto the rug, settling her beneath him.

"I'm not sure…" she muttered against his lips.

She felt the curve of his smile against her skin, his breath teasing her sanity. "I am. Let me show you."

Then lips met, tongues gently teasing, coaxing, playing out a sensual game of tag. He slid his hand along her thigh and up to the indentation of her waist. She was so warm and soft! He could touch her forever, those beautiful legs, that hot satiny skin, that gently curving waist. That expressive face with wide green eyes watching his every move.

He yanked off his shirt then went for hers, needing to feel that skin against his.

She reached up and ran her hands over his chest, an expression of wary curiosity on her face. She touched the ridges, the bumps and crevices, caressed the muscle. Gently skimming over his stomach only to pause when he sucked in a breath.

When her eyes met his, passion shoved caution out the window. It made his breath hitch. He lowered himself to lie flush against her, kissing her mouth again, then her neck. She arched back to allow him better access and he teased the skin with teeth, tongue and hot breath. His heart pounded, but he deliberately forced himself to slow down, to take his time. He wanted to imprint the look on Beth's face in his brain, keep her small gasps, the low breathy moans forever in his memory. He wanted to find every sensitive place on her body and kiss it until she begged him to make love to her.

He pulled away, her murmur of protest tightening his groin. But when he stood and silently extended a hand to her, she hesitated, her wide eyes churning with a multitude of emotions.

He smiled and said softly, "Beth. Come here."

That's all it took.

She put her hand in his and let him lead her up the stairs, first into his room where he rummaged around in a bag and came up with a strip of foil packets. She flushed under his smile, nervous, but that flush quickly became an all-over flame when he took her hand and led her into her bedroom.

And then she was in his arms. Their lips met. Then their bodies.

With deft fingers, Luke untied her pants as she peeled his shirt off. She drew in a deep breath, smelling the remnants of his cologne, warm flesh and the musky aroma of male perspiration.

He wanted her, really wanted her.

Mouth on mouth, their sighs mingled, then their tongues.

His skin felt like hot tempered steel under satin and tasted of sin. His hands brushed against her hip and every single sense erupted with awareness and longing as she settled against the length of his body.

Beth gave one desperate moan and knew she was lost.

Nerves crackled to attention, every inch of her skin alert and craving to be touched. A thin sheen of sweat broke out and trickled down the small of her back.

When he sucked on her bottom lip she jumped a mile out of her skin. A jagged breath came in, then out, as he stroked her belly.

She didn't want to get used to his kisses, his touch. Yet she could hardly think straight with his mouth pressed to her neck and expert hands pulling off her panties.

When Luke's palm curled around the moist juncture between her legs, she jerked and grabbed his hand. Stilled it. "Luke... I..."

"What? What is it, *cara mia?*" he muttered against her neck.

"I..." She pulled away to meet his heavy-lidded eyes,

suddenly embarrassed. But all she could get out was, "I'm… not… very good…"

If his tender smile didn't chase all her doubts away, his husky reply did it. "You're beautiful, Beth. You don't need to hide anything from me."

The last remnants of her iron will came tumbling down. She captured his lips and kissed him deeply.

Hard, hot arousal ached between Luke's legs as they continued teasing each other with lips, hands and breath. She let him put his mouth all over her neck. Let him trail his lips toward one sensitive breast. Let his questing hand cup the warmth of her femininity and massage gently. Lost in passion, the growl in his throat was low and predatory.

Her knees trembled as she clung to him, as if she were drowning and he her only hope of survival. And when she let out a husky whimper, it pushed him toward the edge. "Luke… I…"

He swallowed, drew in a breath. "Please don't tell me to stop, sweetheart."

Her eyes opened to his and the passion in them blew him away. Then she let out a contented sigh, then a gentle chuckle that sent his pulse skyrocketing.

"I need you inside me."

With a groan full of pent-up passion, he pushed her back onto the bed then reached for the foil packet he'd put on the nightstand. Beth was doing him in, caressing his arms, rubbing her foot down his legs. With more impatience than care, he ripped the packet open and plucked out the condom. It was only when he was putting it on that he realized his hands were shaking. He glanced up and the sight made him gulp. Beth naked, her glorious breasts beckoning him, the look in her eyes glazed with arousal. He dived at her like a desperate man and began to caress her from top to toe.

He couldn't get enough of the look on her face as he touched and discovered every part of her, as he kissed those rounded, coral-tipped breasts until he had to come up for air.

Beth gasped as he suddenly flipped her over onto her stomach. Then to her utter delight, he proceeded to cover her whole body in kisses. Warm, wet kisses for her shoulder and neck. Tiny lippy nibbles over her shoulder blades. Harder, deeper wide-mouthed bites in the curve of her waist that simultaneously tickled and aroused. And a gentle grazing of teeth and tongue where the small of her back ended and her bottom started to curve.

He flipped her again, but this time Beth was ready for him, wrapping her legs around his waist, tilting her hips up.

"No more," she pleaded. "I need you."

He grinned, his hair flopping forward to tickle her cheek. "Yes, ma'am."

And he grabbed her thighs, angled her body and with one thrust, buried himself in her welcoming warmth.

Luke shuddered, gritting his teeth as her wetness tightened around him. Slowly, second by agonizing second, he released a long breath and began to move. Gently, almost tentatively at first, experimenting with the pace and depth until she was gasping in pleasure, a quivering wild woman beneath him.

"Do you like that?" he murmured, easing out, sliding back in again.

"Oh, yes."

"Do you want to go faster?"

Luke nearly lost it as her luminous green eyes, dark with passion, stared into his very soul. And when she raised her arms above her head, shuddered out a breathy yes and closed her eyes, he nearly lost it again. Instead, he reined in the tiny threads of self-control and kept going. Every soft sigh, every sob of pleasure was a heavenly revelation. She told him how she liked to be kissed. How she wanted to be touched and how she wanted to touch him. She shivered when he drew himself out in long, slow movements that shortened his breath and his restraint.

Dotted with sweat, her skin shone, almost as if inviting him to feel every slick inch. He did, cupping her breasts, flicking his thumb over the peaked nipples. He bent his head and drew one erect bud between his lips, rasping his teeth along the sensitive flesh. All the while he continued his deep stroking rhythm.

And when she tipped her hips up he went even more deeply than he thought possible. It sent a shot of pure lust charging through every bursting vein in his body.

"Luke…" His name was a sigh on her lips. "I think… I feel…"

"I know."

He strained for control as her breath came out in tiny gasps. He wanted to hold back, wanted her to take pleasure first, to see the glorious release on her face.

And a deep and thorough sense of belonging hit him, so sweet and pure it seared his heart.

Pleasure tightened every inch of Beth's skin, inside and out. Blood pounded in her head, between her legs.

She wanted to cry because everything felt so unbelievably good.

She heard his labored breath, felt the heat of it on her face, in her ear. Every emotion on her face was mirrored in his eyes and she reveled in it. And as they moved, her release began to build up inside, something just out of reach but gaining fast. So fast, so overpowering. Her half-lidded eyes sprang open, met his head-on.

She gulped in short gasps, legs trembling as he continued his deep, sure strokes. Part of her wanted to keep on going, to go right over the edge and into oblivion. Another part was scared of what that would truly mean.

He must have sensed that doubt because he grabbed her chin, returned her gaze to his. "Stay with me, *cara*. I want to watch you." His eyes burned into hers, alight with desire and need and fire.

She lost it right then and there. With a final gasp she came in a crashing release, her moans of ecstasy muffled beneath Luke's mouth.

As Beth's wetness pooled around him, Luke finally gave in and followed her over the edge. Buried deep inside her, he rested his hot, sweaty forehead on hers and placed a tender kiss on the tip of her nose. And when she smiled lazily, closed her eyes and ran her hands over his sweat-dampened back, he knew something amazing had happened.

Twelve

The noisy magpies roosting outside the window broke through Beth's halfhearted sleep, and she suddenly realized she wasn't alone in her bed.

Slowly easing out, she grabbed her robe and tiptoed out the door, then headed for the bathroom.

After a hot, unsatisfying shower, she wrapped herself in a towel and swept a hand across the foggy mirror.

She wanted to regret last night. But she couldn't. She'd loved every moment, every touch, every kiss. Loved it so much she desperately wished she could do it all over again.

But the truth was harsh in the morning light.

She and Luke were two vastly different people with two different opinions on what happiness was. Deep down, she was a traditionalist. Despite her past, she still fully believed marriage was the icing on the happily-ever-after cake.

Right. And that's from practice, is it, with years of dating experience behind you?

Confusion and uncertainty flooded every pore as she stared at her reflection.

Luke could break her heart. Of that she was certain. And she was also certain she might not recover.

His career came first, she knew that. And she wanted more than he could offer, like commitment and peace. None of that could happen with Luke being who he was.

She had to build up those walls again, to protect herself from further heartache—which meant giving up this house, this deep and significant part of herself.

The stab of pain deep in her belly echoed across her reflection. Honestly, did she really believe she'd win, with the odds stacked so high against her? Who was she, thinking she could convince a guy like Luke. He'd negotiated tougher situations than this, with people way more experienced than her.

She needed to face reality if she was to survive.

Luke gave up the pretense of trying to sleep about the time the sun sneaked in through the window and brightened every corner of the bedroom.

Instinctively, he cupped the back of his neck, only to stop halfway there. The nagging pain had disappeared.

He sat up, scratched his head then ran a hand over his rough chin while he heard the shower go on.

Hot, erotic memories of last night flooded in and

with them, confusion and a healthy amount of regret. With a jolt, he was on his feet and over to the window.

He blinked into the sunshine and watched a couple of rainbow lorikeets chatter in the tree outside. He refused to think about what had transpired only hours before. How scorching that had been. And how utterly satisfied his body felt.

And how he'd forgotten to protect them both that last time.

Dammit, this wasn't supposed to happen. It had crept up on him like a thief in the night, this place with its pine furniture, brightly painted walls and lovingly worn rugs. A house full of life.

He hadn't seen his cold, perfect apartment in a week. Hadn't missed it, either. He sighed heavily, drained from his solitary life of sleek furniture and fifteen-hour days.

That was insane. He loved his work. Loved the challenges, the deals, making money for his clients. But he didn't miss the late-night food, 3:00 a.m. mornings, the stress headaches that came with the territory... And the steady stream of office chatter about relationships, renovations and family holidays.

Yet the tiny doubts he'd been studiously ignoring slowly began to gain momentum, until they were way too big to overlook.

Since when had he wanted something more? But somewhere along the line he had. He wanted space, privacy. A bath with a claw-foot tub.

A dog. He'd never had a dog—his parents could barely afford to put food on the table let alone feed another mouth.

Perched on the edge of the windowsill, Luke stared out at the blue, blue sky, breathing in the rain-drenched air.

He hadn't expected to want this so much—not until he'd glimpsed Beth's perspiration-soaked cleavage, noticed the way her eyes lit up every time she talked about her work, and the way her long, elegant, kissable fingers splayed almost obscenely around the base of her coffee cup. And the things they did last night...

He'd taken advantage of their situation. Of her emotions. And satisfied his need.

That thought stuck in his craw, choking him.

You're running away from your feelings, Lucio, Gino had said. *I want to help you, be someone you can look up to. Please, these therapists are good people. They will help you.*

And Luke had lashed out with all the guilt and misery and anger a teenager could. *You're not my father! You can't be him! No one can. And I don't need strangers to tell me how to think and feel.*

He winced at the memories. Gino had been right then, just as he had been on that DVD last night. The stern, ten-minute talking-to was so like Gino that he'd ended up smiling all the way through it. Then came a massive flood of guilt all over again. Then another wave of guilt for *that,* too.

Frustration fisted his hands. Everything was such a mess. His problems aside, Beth was still harboring secrets and it was starting to annoy the hell out of him.

He yanked on his pants, scooped up the rest of his clothes and headed for his room. Once there, he rummaged around for his phone and punched in Dylan's number.

"It's Luke. Do you have anything for me?"

"Not a lot. But what I do have is *veeeery* interesting."

Luke rubbed the back of his neck and sighed. "Okay. Tell me."

Beth calmly dressed for work even though her fingers shook doing up her blouse buttons. When she finally walked out of her room she was stronger and more alone than she ever thought possible.

Luke's voice coming from the spare room brought her up short. As she made her way down the hall, her steps slowed to a halt.

Despite her previous conviction, or maybe because of it, something ripped inside her chest.

After a long pause in which she was sure the whole neighborhood could hear her very heartbeat, she heard Luke's colorful curse.

"I didn't see *that* coming. No, she never mentioned it, just said there was an accident. No, I don't think it'd help. I want you to keep this to yourself. I'll do the same. Sure. Bye." He hung up.

Oh. No. Nonononono.

Everything spun to a complete stop, her heartbeat echoing dully in her head as her fingers dug painfully into the banister.

She didn't feel it. The pain in her heart was much, much worse.

Clenching the wooden rail for support, she felt the desperate urge to run pounding through her legs. Anywhere was preferable to staying here. She even took one hesitant step forward, but at the last moment stopped.

She must have made a sound, because Luke spun on his heel, startled black eyes meeting hers. She couldn't move, couldn't speak, just stared at him blankly. She shoved the hurt deep down, tried to regain control over her shattered thoughts. Her face ached with the effort to remain neutral, calm. The giveaway was her cantering heart that she couldn't hope to quell.

Then he smiled and she melted all over again. "Hi."

Those lips curled up, lips that had touched her in all the right places. Damp places. Places that still ached.

She could still feel his breath on her breasts. Every whisper on her skin. And his hands and fingers… Oh, Lordy.

Latent desire fogged her senses and she shook her head to clear them. "Good morning." Schooling her expression into politeness, she hardly noticed the slight waver in her voice.

She walked across the room to retrieve a folder from her desk, skin tingling as she felt his heated eyes roam her back. With a deep breath to bolster her courage, she turned to face him. "Look. About last night…"

"Hmm?" Now that coal-black gaze swept her face, down her neck. Dipped deeper into her neckline, familiar with personal knowledge. She swallowed and noticed the way his eyes focused on her throat. Hoped he couldn't see the pulse beating wildly there.

"Yes…" She swallowed. "Last night was…"

"Great? Exhausting?" Finally, he looked directly at her. The corners of his eyes crinkled in remembrance. "Incredible?" He teased out the last word, his tongue wrapping around every syllable as if he were licking an intimate part of her body.

"A…lapse in judgment."

Beth didn't think silence could be thick and telling. But there it was.

"A lapse in judgment," he finally repeated.

Beth nodded. Before she could blink, he was in her face. She retreated until her back hit the wall. He lifted his hands and for one second she thought he was going to touch her. Instead, he pressed his palms to the wall, either side of her head.

"A mistake?" He got out, studying her as if the truth was scribbled across her flushed skin.

"If you choose to think so."

"If I…" He leaned forward and she was caught up in the depth of his eyes. A faint scent of joined bodies and sexual heat wound around them. Beth tried to ignore it.

"You're lying."

"No."

"So why—"

"Luke, you know why."

"Humor me."

She shrugged, forcing her voice to remain casual. *You can't afford to cave in now.* "We had a good time. End of story."

Something passed over his features, something she couldn't quite get a handle on. "Is that what it was? Just a hookup?"

She gave a small laugh that sounded brittle to her ears. "It was fun, don't get me wrong. But I think we should focus on our situation." Totally aware of the stiffening tension in his body, she continued, "It's clear to me I can't afford to meet your asking price, so I'll be looking for another place this week. There's no need for me to stay when I can afford to rent a—"

"Hang on. That's it?"

She frowned. "Why are you so angry? You won."

"This wasn't a contest, Beth!"

"No. No, it wasn't. But you got the prize anyway."

He yanked away from her and dragged a hand through his hair before turning to pin her with a glare. "After all that talk, all of your 'it's mine and I belong here,' you're willing to just give it up?"

She lifted her chin. "You said it yourself—I can't afford it."

"Bull." His face darkened. "That's not it and you know it. What aren't you telling me?"

"Nothing." She put her hands on her hips as irritation surged. "After last night, you know everything about me."

"Really. So who's Taylor Stanton?"

It was a shocking blow and Luke knew it, right about the second her eyes widened and she gasped.

"You've been going through my things."

"Who is she?"

"You've been going through my *things!*" The furious blast from those green eyes washed over him as if he was something she'd got stuck on her shoe, but he refused to back down. "What else have you been doing? Gathering information to challenge my tenancy? Planning to take me to court for—"

"That's ridiculous!"

"No!" She stabbed an accusing finger at him. "It makes perfect sense. You never trusted me, did you?"

"Nor did you trust me," he pointed out. "Just tell me who she is, Beth."

"No. No!"

Frustration spilled over and suddenly he was all up in her face. "Tell me, goddammit!"

Angry tears welled in her eyes. "She's me, all right? She's *me!*"

Luke felt his jaw sag open in stunned shock. "*You* were on Flight 212?"

"Yes!"

"It was the ten-year commemoration last week. The survivors sued, right, and put OzFlight out of business—"

"I know."

Her small forlorn reply snapped off his flabbergasted ramble midsentence.

What the hell did you say after something like that? Whatever issues he'd gone through were nothing compared to the magnitude of the biggest domestic crash in Australian history. So many things now made absolute sense: her fiercely guarded privacy. Her distrust.

God, he'd practically forced her on his plane.

"Beth…I can't imagine what it must have been like for you—"

Her expression hardened. "No. You can't."

"But I don't understand why—"

"I faked my identity?" She crossed her arms. "I sat next to Beth Jones, a twenty-year-old who was moving to Perth to start a new job. She died in the crash and I ended up with her purse in the ambulance and I…" She paused to swallow, visible proof of the cracks forming in her protective wall. "I was in a coma for a week and they just assumed I was her."

"So you took her name."

She shook her head. "I never planned to. I planned to throw away her purse a dozen times but in a weird way having the reminder was…comforting. I was the last one to see her alive, you see, and she had no one left, no family to miss her, no—" She took a deep shaky breath and recrossed her arms. "I was trying to get my life together but it all just fell apart after that reporter found me. I knew I'd never be able to feel safe as Taylor Stanton again." She looked away, her eyes wide and haunted. "It's so easy to become someone else, did you know that? A gas bill, then a birth certificate, then a driver's license and bang—a whole new person. I've been Beth Jones for ten years. Ten lean, tough years. But damn, they were peaceful."

Her voice wavered for one second before she swallowed and drew her shoulders back. She snorted then, and shook her head. "You know, everyone wanted me to be one of those 'proud survivor' people." When she glanced up through her lashes, Luke thought he detected a shimmer of tears. "You know, the ones who're an advertisement for human endurance? Everyone gushed about this wonderful testament to the Australian spirit, how amazing and lucky I was, how fragile the human race is. And I was barely holding myself together. Things don't stick well when all you have is tape and glue that keeps coming apart."

He had nothing to say to that. Nothing at all.

Her breath came out on a watery, amused smile.

"Funny…all these years and I never could get used to a different birthday. So I never celebrate it."

They remained still for a moment, Luke waiting for more, Beth fiddling with the ties of her blouse with singular intent.

"When is it?" Luke said quietly.

"What?"

"When is your birthday? Your real birthday?"

"August the fifteenth. And I'm twenty-eight, not thirty," she added, as if it was an important detail he needed to know. "And now," she said, then drew in a sharp breath, "I need to go to work."

He dragged a hand over his rough chin. Dammit. There was so much more he needed to tell her. "Beth, I—"

"No, Luke. We both need to focus on moving forward with our lives. Nothing's changed."

But something had. Last night she had clung to him like one of her scented lotions. Minutes ago she'd confessed the darkest secret of her soul. And now she was as cold as a serial liar's conscience.

The stakes have changed, he wanted to say. Since they'd made incredible love and he realized his life wasn't all it was cracked up to be. And that scared the hell out of him.

Everything was so damn complicated. He should tell her what he knew, then do what she asked and walk away. It would leave her free to find someone who would be there for her, be a dependable partner in every sense of the word.

Yeah, but what if you want ties? Complications?

Torn, he watched her descend the stairs, taking heat and light and longing with her.

"Beth. Don't leave."

She paused on the last step, her back still to him. Then, with a breath, she turned. "What can you say that I don't already know? Your career comes first, and me being here totally jeopardizes that. Not to mention, we risk being discovered every day we're together. And I will not got through that again." She gave a soft, humorless snort. "You, me, our combined stories… We're a reporter's wet dream waiting to happen."

"Wait." Damn, he hated that she was right. Hated she had come out and said the words that had chewed him up inside all morning. And hated the fact that he was helpless in the face of that cool logic.

He took the moment to imprint the memory of her in his brain—the curve of her cheek, the curls pushed behind perfectly shaped ears. The remembrance of her kisses and the sweet, welcoming smell of her skin. The strength, the way she refused to fall apart as she confessed her past. That same strength that was shoving him away now.

As every logical bone in his body told him to let her go, he battled with that logic. Something else, something deeper and more urgent demanded he take his shot, lay it all on the line. Damn, he itched to grab her, kiss her senseless and force her to believe in *that,* in their chemistry and how much he wanted her.

But he knew he had to come clean before he even thought about trying to change her mind.

With an inward breath, he measured her. He could live with what Dylan had told him, but at what price? It would eat at him, chip away at his conscience every day until his self-respect became nothing but false words. Worse, it would undermine the trust Beth had placed in him.

But once the truth was out, there'd be no going back.

Girding himself with resolve, he walked slowly down the stairs, not missing the way she straightened her shoulders and tiredly drew herself up, as if reconnoitering for a final bomb to drop even though her strength was at the lowest ebb.

Jesus, he hated doing this to her. "There's more. Dylan found out more."

She blinked. "About Ben?"

"No… Look, there's no way to sugarcoat this. I'll just come right out and say it."

Beth gave a confused frown. "Okay."

He swallowed and stuck his hands in his back pockets. "When your mother was fifteen, she had a baby—a girl—and gave her up for adoption."

Thirteen

Beth's hand flew to the banister and grabbed it for support, eyes wide. *"What?"*

"When that girl was eighteen she put her name on a couple of adoption-search websites," Luke plowed on, "and applied for information on her birth mother via Community Services—"

"Wait! Stop, stop, stop—"

"So she could contact her birth mother. Beth, listen to me." Luke took her hands as she began to shake her head. "That girl is now thirty-eight and lives in Perth. Your mother was taking you both to meet her."

"Oh, no."

"Yeah." Even though he gripped her hands tight, he could feel Beth slipping away from him every second she remained silent. It shredded his nerves until everything felt raw and open. *Say something, anything,* he silently commanded.

Then she firmly wrested her hands from his, took a step back and the distance between them increased like a yawning chasm.

"I…I have to go to work."

"Beth."

She put out a hand, warding him off. "Luke, I can't think right now, okay? I need some time to process this. Just…" She fingered her temple with a sigh. "Just give me some time."

"Okay." His hands went through his hair and he set his mouth in a grim line. "Okay. Take all the time you want."

"And I think it'd be best if I stay elsewhere for a while," she said stiffly.

For the hundredth time Luke wished he could take back last week. But even if he could, he knew he'd do the same things all over again.

Especially last night.

Even as the memory made his blood heat, her shuttered expression froze it. Hell, didn't she see he'd rather take a bullet than intentionally hurt her?

"I can help you. I'll get someone to find out—"

"No." She shook her head, let out a harsh laugh. "No, you've done enough. This is something I have to deal with by myself."

Then she turned, went down the rest of the stairs and strode down the hallway. Grabbing up her handbag, then her keys from the hall stand she marched to the front door, her steps full of purpose, her shoulders ramrod straight.

Luke glared at her back, as if by sheer will alone he could change her mind. It would do no good. She was stubborn and proud and hurting, hiding behind a familiar barrier that had protected her for so long. Seeing that haunted disbelief, how her body had stiffened in shock, made him want to take everything back.

His jaw ached from clenching it so tightly, but he made himself watch her determined progress to the door.

Come on, Beth. Just turn around. You can do it. Just turn.

But there was nothing but the ringing echo of her heels on the wooden floor.

It might have been his heart she was wrenching open as she grabbed the doorknob and yanked. He forced himself to keep watching, until she closed the door softly without a backward glance. Slowly, the sound of her footsteps disappeared and he was left with nothing but unsaid words.

The quiet snick of the closing door was louder than if Beth had slammed out in a fury. If he'd said anything more, given any indication he wanted her to stay, she would have gladly turned and run back into his arms.

But he hadn't.

She took a ragged breath and sagged against her car door. It really was over. She had made it over.

Completely and irrevocably, she'd have to live with her choice.

Alone.

She held up a hand and was surprised to find it shaking. Angrily, she combed her fingers through her hair and tried to force the panic attack back where it belonged. But the trembling in her fingers spread to her whole body. A deep, shaky breath tightened her chest. Then another.

The shock wave hit so suddenly she groaned aloud, a vision swimming in her head as she desperately tried to wish it away.

The cold, drizzly rain outside a cracked window. The putrid smell of leaking fuel, smoke and scorched metal. A woolen blanket that had made her sneeze…and questions, always questions asking if she was okay, how did she feel, what could she remember, on and on and on.

She slapped her hands over her ears and collapsed into her car. Raw emotion coursed through her body now, shaking, stabbing. Her breath caught, sharp and painful.

Then she realized she was crying.

It was too late to stop. She let the tears trail down her cheeks unchecked, uncaring. And with them went her carefully constructed composure, the wall of protection, the hard shell of control. She cried for a lost childhood and a mother she had loved, cried for the sacrifices Angela had made in the face of her depression. Cried for the wasted years alone and the past that had shaped her future.

Finally, she swept her cheeks with a shaky hand, rubbed at her eyes then fumbled in the glove box for a tissue. When she raised her eyes to the mirror, she saw blotchy patches on her cheeks, red-rimmed eyes staring back at her.

You have a sister.

Oh, God. Shock mingling with a tiny blossoming

hope jarred everything inside, her breath whooshing out as she bit back tears.

Who knew what other surprises lay in store? Who else was on the Stanton family tree?

She'd deliberately chopped down that tree ten years ago without a backward glance. But now Luke's shocking revelation only filled her with burning curiosity, not fear. It had the potential to change her life if she chose to follow it through.

But was she going to risk those ten years to find out?

The question remained in her head, waiting impatiently for her answer, as she started the car and set off to work.

Luke remained glaring at the front door, as if by simply staring it'd make Beth reappear. But as the clock counted off the seconds one loud tick at a time, he realized waiting was useless.

He'd well and truly screwed everything up.

Sinking down onto the bottom step, he dragged his hands over his face, then through his hair. Her faint scent still lingered, a bittersweet echo that punched him squarely below the belt. Great. Bloody great. Just another way you've managed to screw up.

But before he could completely throw himself into the pity party, there was a knock on the door. He charged down the hall and yanked it open with a swoop of anticipation.

Then his face fell into a scowl.

"Expecting someone else?" Marco said with a grin.

"Yeah." Luke glanced out the door then quickly closed it behind him. "Did anyone follow you?"

"Oh, will you stop worrying about those damn reporters?" Marco grimaced. "Typical. I've had to defend my reputation for months and all you can think about is your job."

Despite his turbulent thoughts, Luke managed a small smirk. "Oh, c'mon, mate. Everyone's forgotten about you and that cheerleader."

"You'd think so, right?" Marco cocked a dark eyebrow. "But some people can't resist rehashing that whole 'how could he not know she was cheating on him' business. Everyone thinks I'm an idiot."

"Is that all you're worried about?"

"Wouldn't you be?"

Luke threw back his head and laughed at the chagrin on his cousin's face. Then he did something that surprised both of them. He grabbed Marco and wrapped him in a big bear hug.

After a few stunned seconds, Marco returned it. After a few more, he peeled himself away with a snort of nervous laughter.

"This woman of yours has a lot to answer for. Public displays of affection from Luke De Rossi?"

"Don't knock it, cousin." Luke smiled, but soon that disappeared. "Look, I don't mean to be rude, but I have to go and do stuff."

"That's why I'm here." Marco scratched his head, dipped his brow to focus on the floor. "Those things I said back at the house…? About blaming you for Gino's heart attack? You know that was just anger talking, right? I know he'd been to see a specialist. He needed to slow down, quit smoking." He rolled his eyes in self-deprecation. "Don't we all. I told him every day and yet he was so damn stubborn. It wasn't a good idea unless it was his idea, right?" They both nodded solemnly at the shared memory. "Look, the point is, I was shooting off at the mouth. You weren't to blame, I know that."

A heavy, telling silence fell until Marco frowned. "Aw, man, don't tell me you actually believed me?"

"You weren't there, Marco."

"So? Have you told Rosa?"

Luke said nothing. Marco shook his head. "For a child genius, Luke, you can be pretty stupid. Tell my mother and clear your conscience. Or suffer the consequences."

"What consequences?"

Marco grinned. "Me kicking your ass, cousin. Now get into gear and go talk to her."

Rosa.

His family. For better or worse.

Gino had given him the things he'd desperately wanted that his dead parents could not—money, a stellar education and peer respect.

He'd told Beth the truth. Rosa deserved the same. No matter how painful it was for him.

Fourteen

It was Thursday and Beth sat behind her office desk, staring at yesterday's newspaper spread out before her. She had deliberately given Laura errands to run that morning so she could be alone to read the article again.

Now that she was, she felt a tremble chase up her spine and settle in her neck.

De Rossi Reinstated: Inquiry Still on Table.

Jackson and Blair's board had finally come out and publicly backed Luke. A spokesman, someone called Connor Blair, had declared that the company was "looking forward to rigorously defending Mr. De Rossi from these vicious rumors when he gives his statement to the Queensland Gaming Commission in two weeks' time."

She stared at her second cup of untouched coffee, at

the edges of steam curling over the rim. What a difference three days made. A home gone, a heart broken. A mother who'd held on to a secret for years and a possible sister.

That is, if she ever got the courage to actually pick up the phone and call.

She glanced back down at the paper. Luke was moving forward, moving up. His Board of Directors had finally come to their senses and was focusing on clearing his name. She, on the other hand, had had that moving company's quote on her desk for two days. Just the thought of going back there, to her home, to the place she loved above all else and packing up every memory while Luke watched, was still too heartbreaking to contemplate.

There was a soft knock on her door and she glanced up to see a pale Laura.

"What's wrong?"

When Laura swung the door wider, Beth sucked in her shock.

He was leaner and minus the glasses, but everything else about Ben Foster was the same-familiar cargoes, worn Nirvana T-shirt, steel-capped boots. And with his expression a mix of shame and contrition, he looked all of fifteen.

"Hi, Beth," he muttered with a halfhearted wave.

"Hi, yourself." She rose and nodded for Laura to close the door behind her. "So. You've come back."

"Yeah."

Beth felt the weight of a hundred years press down on her shoulders. "Oh, Ben. What on earth were you thinking?"

He shrugged, still unable to meet her eyes. "It was a ton of money."

"But it wasn't yours."

"I know."

She shoved a hip against the desk and crossed her arms with a sigh. "Did you spend it all?"

"No."

"So you're going to give it back?"

"Yeah." His hands went into his pockets and he finally looked up.

His torn expression, the way he held his body as if waiting for her to yell at him, dissolved the dozen reprimands on the tip of her tongue.

She had nothing left. No outrage, no anger, nothing.

It had just been one of those days.

"What made you change your mind?" she finally asked.

He scratched his head. "Your guy."

She frowned. "What guy?"

"The suit who turned up at the Crown Casino. Your guy."

"I didn't send a guy."

"Well, he was under the impression he was working for you."

Beth blinked. "What was his name?"

"Didn't say. Tall dude, dark hair. Italian-looking. Expensive clothes."

Beth's heart did a flip. "And what did he say?"

Ben shrugged. "A few things. Doesn't matter. But he convinced me to do the right thing and come back. I transferred the money back into your business account an hour ago."

"What about what you spent?"

"It's all there, Beth. Every last dollar."

How? Beth frowned but let that go. "You know the bank's probably notified the police. There's bound to be an inquiry."

"Yeah."

Police. An inquiry. She sucked in a breath. Publicity? And yet Luke had plowed right on in, even with the probability of exposure.

To help her. Despite her walking away.

What did that mean?

An overwhelming urge to find out jerked her straight. "I have to go."

"Okaaay?" Ben nodded, confused.

"Sorry." She grabbed her purse from the desk, slammed the drawer firmly shut. Then she put a hand on Ben's arm and looked him square in the eye. "Thank you for coming back, Ben. I appreciate you doing the right thing."

She had no time to think about his sudden flush, the awkward shuffle as he studied his feet with misplaced intent.

She had something she had to do—if it wasn't too late.

Of course, she had as much chance of making it past security and up to Jackson and Blair's executive floors as she had winning the lottery. After three messages and twenty minutes, Beth had to face the fact that Luke had more important things to do than return her calls.

She left the way she came, completely ignored by the scattering of reporters milling around the entrance.

After a ninety-minute drive, Beth checked the house, even though she didn't expect him to be there. Standing still in the cool, long entrance, breathing in the scents and memories, she forced herself to pretend that everything was fine, that this place was still hers. But of course, it wasn't. And whether she chose to accept it now or in three months—nearly two, now—when her lease expired, the result would be the same.

It was never really hers to begin with.

With that final thought, she finally managed to wrench herself away.

As she locked the door behind her, her phone rang.

"Beth. It's Luke." As if she wouldn't know that deep voice reverberating in her ear. It was burned in her memory. "I'm at your store. Where are you?"

"At the house. What are you doing there?" Her heart began to thump harder.

"Stay put. I'm coming to you."

It felt like twenty hours by the time his shiny silver car pulled up in the driveway, time enough for every possible, painful scenario to play out in her head and twist her stomach into knots.

Then he was out of the car and everything fizzled away at the sight of his tall, dark figure dressed in an expensive suit—just like on the first day she saw him.

Her throat was so dry her tongue stuck to the roof of her mouth. She swallowed thickly. There was no way she was going to cry. She'd remained dry-eyed at her mother's funeral and through Ben's betrayal. Even in her darkest moments, five bucks away from poverty, she'd kept it together.

"You didn't need to come out to see me," she finally said.

"I didn't want to talk over the phone." His expression was unreadable.

Oh. "You flew down to Melbourne to find Ben," she blurted out.

"I did."

"Why?"

"Because I made you a promise."

Her heart squeezed painfully in her chest, making it hard to breathe. Until he said gently, "Is that why you've been calling me, Beth?"

Her chin went up as she summoned all her nerve. "I wanted to apologize."

"For what?" He looked confused.

"When you told me about my mother. I…shut you down. I'm sorry."

"You don't need to apologize for that," he said. "Some people handle grief by pushing away those who care about them."

"You…care about me?" she said faintly.

"You know I do."

She was sailing on unchartered waters here and suddenly that nerve left her. She glanced down and spotted his raw, torn knuckles. With a faint exclamation, she nodded to his hand. "You didn't hit anyone, did you?"

"I was fixing that broken step on the front porch." He flexed his fingers.

"Oh. I thought you might have decked a reporter."

A wry smile twitched his lips. "Only in my dreams."

He looked so gorgeous, so noble, that Beth wanted to touch him. She even took a step forward, her hand raised until she realized her folly and instead, laid her palm on the throbbing pulse at her throat.

"I had a long talk with Rosa," he said. "I took your advice and bared my soul." Beth thought she saw a glint of something before his expression dropped back into cool impassiveness. "She doesn't blame me for Gino."

"Of course not." Beth shook her head.

He paused, waiting. Finally she said, "I read in the papers you have the full backing of your Board of Directors."

His smile was brief. "Don't believe everything you read."

"But it's true, right?" At his nod, she added, "So that's good. Now you can move forward, put all this behind you."

He gave her a long, searching look then said slowly, "And how are you doing?"

"I'm...okay."

"Just okay?"

Beth hesitated, the faint, familiar taste of fear clogging her throat. Why should this be easy? If anyone was to attempt to mend things, it should be her.

But who knew it could be this difficult?

"I wanted to thank you for everything. I know I didn't handle a lot of it well, but I just wanted to... well..."

"You're welcome."

"I mean, you didn't have to help me, to put yourself out like that. But you've done more than enough and—"

"You really don't get it, do you, Beth?"

For a second he watched her with curious intensity,

then said, "I never wanted to force you from your home. You should move back in."

As if she could ever live there again without thinking of him. As if she could sleep in her bed without remembering the feel of his skin or him making love to her.

A sudden burst of longing jolted her so hard she ached.

Anyone else would've taken her silence for refusal. Not Luke. With a scowl he said, "You still want me out."

"No, I—"

"Look." He placed his hands on his hips, classic spoiling-for-a-fight stance. "I know I can't promise you the kind of anonymity you've been used to. The fact is, I'm part of the Corelli family and they've always attracted attention. But I do know we have something good—something damn amazing, actually, and I would like to continue that."

She stared at him for a second before finally finding her tongue. "You're asking me to move in with you?"

"Well—" he gave her a sudden grin "—technically, you haven't yet moved out."

She was speechless. Literally speechless.

"Is it so hard to believe I care about you, Beth?" he asked quietly. "That I'd want to help you without any ulterior motive? Hey." He suddenly looked alarmed. "You're not going to cry, are you?"

"No." She blinked and smiled weakly.

"You are."

"Fine, I am. It's the shock, okay? I've been trying to

wrap my head around everything and then you go and do—" she sniffed "—something like this."

"Beth. *Cara.* Don't cry."

"No, let me finish. I was— Oh, I still *am* kind of angry at you for going through my things—"

His mouth thinned. "And I've apologized for that."

"I know. And I probably would have done exactly the same in your situation." She took a deep breath then gave a watery smile. "Damn, this is difficult."

"So let me make it easy for you. Come back, Beth."

Misgiving tugged at Luke as the seconds ticked by and she remained still, just stared at the ground, shaking her head. Stubbornly, he waited, as if by staring at her he could will her into an admission.

She finally glanced up, wide-eyed and begging understanding. Those long elegant fingers skimmed her throat again. The gesture touched him more than he ever thought possible. "I won't settle for just casual sex, Luke."

"Neither will I."

He went to her and took her hands, gritting his jaw as he felt an uncharacteristic tremble in his. His legs, his hip, bumped into hers, and suddenly all he could hear was the roar of his heartbeat echo in his ears. With a thick swallow and a silent prayer, he looked into her face. The wide-eyed expectancy tempered with caution only made his blood pound harder.

"Beth. I know this is going to sound crazy, but I think I love you."

"You *think?*"

He cleared his throat then tried again. "I miss you.

You're all I can think about. And I want you in my bed *and* my life. Come back, okay?"

"Luke…" Lord, the look on her face was killing him a thousand times over. "It would never work. My past, your career—"

"You know what? Screw that." He grabbed her arms, deadly serious. "They're just excuses, Beth, and you know it. If we want to make it work, we can. I want you. I want nights staring out at the stars. I want to make love to you with the taste of wine still on your lips. I want your bra draped over the shower curtain, your face cream dominating the sink…I want to eat lasagna on your battered kitchen table."

His voice dropped lower, almost shaky. "And if you can't see that then you're not the smart, fearless person I thought you were."

He paused, totally vulnerable, totally exposed. The seconds ticked by as Beth searched his face, her wide green eyes staring right into the deepest part of his soul.

And slowly, he saw those eyes fill.

"You want everything I thought you'd run a mile from?" she asked, her voice shaky and uncertain.

He took her left hand in his, bare hope shredding his confidence. He'd never been this nervous before, never pinned his hopes on just one little answer.

"I love you," he said.

Beth choked back a laugh as her eyes spilled over, her hands going to her mouth. Then she curled her arms around his neck and melted against his heat, giving in to the urgent need to touch him, hold him, because maybe this was just a dream and it would all be gone when she woke up. But this was real, as real as Luke's warm gaze washing over her, and the faint residue of the past deflating like a long-forgotten party balloon.

"Say it again."

"I love you, Beth." He pulled back slightly. "Unless it's Taylor?"

"I haven't been her in a long time," she replied firmly. "Taylor Stanton was my past. Beth Jones is my life now."

His warm breath on her mouth was real. The soft, deep words curling around her heart were real.

And the shot of pure pleasure sending her thoughts haywire was definitely real. She inched her lips up to his but gave a soft murmur when he leaned away from her kiss.

"And?" Luke prompted.

"And what?"

"Say it."

She felt herself flush. "I was getting to it. I love you, too."

He tucked a stray curl behind her ear. "I was wondering when you'd come to your senses."

"Were you now?"

"That's a fact. I was waiting in hope."

"For how long?" Her eyes searched his.

"Tomorrow was your last day—until Ben showed up." He grinned. "Then I was going to storm into your store and talk you around."

"Talk, huh." Beth harrumphed. "More like demand."

"Woman, I hope you're not going to nag when we're living in sin."

Her protest was laughingly silenced with Luke's

mouth. When he finally drew his lips from hers, Beth knew she had been well and truly kissed.

"I love you, Beth. Even when you're yelling at me and picking fights, I love you. I want you to say it again."

After that kiss she was willing to admit to anything. "I love you, too. And I'm sorry—"

"Shh…" He put a fingertip to her lips. "You've said it already."

She drew his hand firmly away. "I was wrong not to trust you. I let my past and the people in it influence my judgment instead of thinking for myself."

"Ah, Beth. I made mistakes, too." He still couldn't get used to saying the words, so he said them again with emphasis, in between kisses. "I love you. I love you. I love you."

She laughed, a wonderful sound that filled every part of him with joy.

"And I'd like to be with you if and when you decide you want to meet your sister. You don't have to be alone."

She looked into his eyes, saw the fierce fire behind those dark depths and her breath caught.

"I'm not alone anymore. And I would love to have you with me."

Luke ran his hand across her cheek, nuzzled her shoulder and began to chuckle softly.

Beth tilted her face to his. "Something funny?"

Luke grinned. "For once, the press got something right."

"Hmm?" Beth was placing soft kisses on each corner of his mouth.

"Yeah. Today I am lucky."

She laughed with him. "And," she added with a devilish light in her eyes, "I'll make sure I remind you. Every single day."

Epilogue

What the small wedding lacked in size, it more than made up for in emotion. The bride glowed in a simple off-white satin slip, and the groom wore a fine dark gray wool suit with a snowy cravat and a deep blue silk shirt.

In the backyard of the Corelli estate, the guests gathered under a canopy designed to keep the airborne reporters at bay. Private security saw to the horde of uninvited press on the grounds.

Beth's friends mingled, talked and drank with the Corellis like any ordinary family gathering in the early December morning. And when the happy couple spoke their vows, not a dry eye was present. The celebrant pronounced them man and wife and they kissed long and hard. Rosa beamed, Connor and the rest of Luke's friends laughed and cheered. Even Marco couldn't keep the grin off his face.

But the person who was smiling the most was Luke. The gaming commission had publicly announced its verdict earlier on in the week—cleared of all charges. Of course, as Jackson and Blair's newest vice president, that *may* have held some sway.

He glanced down at Beth, all aglow and grinning, and his heart caught, all thoughts of work scattering on the summer breeze. No, that definitely wasn't the best thing. Because today, he wasn't just getting a wife: in seven months, he'd be a brand-new father.

And finally, everything was perfect.

* * * * *

FALLING FOR DR DIMITRIOU

BY
ANNE FRASER

Anne Fraser was born in Scotland, but brought up in South Africa. After she left school she returned to the birthplace of her parents, the remote Western Islands of Scotland. She left there to train as a nurse, before going on to university to study English Literature. After the birth of her first child she and her doctor husband travelled the world, working in rural Africa, Australia, and Northern Canada. Anne still works in the health sector. To relax, she enjoys spending time with her family, reading, walking, and travelling.

To Rachel and Stewart—my personal on-call doctors—
and to Megan Haslam, my supportive,
patient and all-round fabulous editor.

PROLOGUE

IT WAS THAT moment before dawn, before the sky had begun to lighten and the moon seemed at its brightest, when Alexander saw her for the first time. On his way to the bay where he kept his boat, his attention was caught by a woman emerging like Aphrodite from the sea.

She paused, the waves lapping around her thighs, to squeeze the water from her tangled hair. As the sun rose, it bathed her in light adding to the mystical scene. He held his breath. He'd heard about her—in a village this size it would have been surprising if the arrival of a stranger wasn't commented on—and they hadn't exaggerated when they'd said she was beautiful.

The bay where she'd been swimming was below him, just beyond the wall that bordered the village square. If she looked up she would see him. But she didn't. She waded towards the shore, droplets clinging to her golden skin, her long hair still streaming with water. If the village hadn't been full of gossip about the woman who'd come to stay in the villa overlooking the bay, he could almost let himself believe that she was a mythical creature rising from the sea.

Almost. If he were a fanciful man. Which he wasn't.

CHAPTER ONE

KATHERINE PLACED HER pen on the table and leaned back in her chair. She picked up her glass of water, took a long sip and grimaced. It was tepid. Although she'd only poured it a short while ago, the ice cubes had already melted in the relentless midday Greek sun.

As it had done throughout the morning, her gaze drifted to the bay almost immediately below her veranda. The man was back. Over the last few evenings he'd come down to the little bay around five and stayed there, working on his boat until the sun began to set. He always worked with intense concentration, scraping away paint and sanding, stopping every so often to step back and evaluate his progress. But today, Saturday, he'd been there since early morning.

He was wearing jeans rolled up above his ankles and a white T-shirt that emphasised his golden skin, broad shoulders and well-developed biceps. She couldn't make out the colour of his eyes, but he had dark hair, curling on his forehead and slightly over his neckline. Despite what he was wearing, she couldn't help thinking of a Greek warrior—although there was nothing but gentleness in the way he treated his boat.

Who was he? she wondered idly. If her friend Sally were

here she would have found out everything about him, down to his star sign. Unfortunately Katherine wasn't as gorgeous as Sally, to whom men responded like flies around a honey pot and who had always had some man on the go—at least until she'd met Tom. Now, insanely happily married to him, her friend had made it her mission in life to find someone for Katherine. So far her efforts had been in vain. Katherine had had her share of romances—well, two apart from Ben—but the only fizz in those had been when they'd fizzled out, and she'd given up on finding Mr Right a long time ago. Besides, men like the one she was watching were always attached to some beautiful woman.

He must have felt her eyes on him because he glanced up and looked directly at her. She scraped her chair back a little so that it was in the shadows, hoping that the dark glasses she was wearing meant he couldn't be sure she had been staring at him.

Not that she was at all interested in him, she told herself. It was just that he was a diversion from the work she was doing on her thesis—albeit a very pleasing-to-the-eye diversion.

Everything about Greece was a feast for the senses. It was exactly as her mother had described it—blindingly white beaches, grey-green mountains and a translucent sea that changed colour depending on the tide and the time of day. She could fully grasp, now, why her mother had spoken of the country of her birth so often and with such longing.

Katherine's heart squeezed. Was it already four weeks since Mum had died? It felt like only yesterday. The month had passed in a haze of grief and Katherine had worked even longer hours in an attempt to keep herself from thinking too much, until Tim, her boss, had pulled her aside and told her gently, but firmly, that she needed to take time off—especially as she hadn't had a holiday in years. Although she'd protested, he'd dug his heels in. Six weeks, he'd told her, and if he saw her in the office during that time, he'd call Security. One look at his face had told her he meant it.

Then when a work colleague had told her that the Greek parents of a friend of hers were going to America for the birth of their first grandchild and needed someone to stay in their home while they were away—someone who would care for their cherished cat and water the garden—Katherine knew it was serendipity; her thesis had been put to one side when Mum had been ill, and despite what Tim said about taking a complete rest, this would be the perfect time to finish it.

It would also be a chance to fulfil the promise she'd made to her mother.

The little whitewashed house was built on the edge of the village, tucked against the side of a mountain. It had a tiny open-plan kitchen and sitting room, with stone steps hewn out of the rock snaking up to the south-facing balcony that overlooked the bay. The main bedroom was downstairs, its door leading onto a small terrace that, in turn, led directly onto the beach. The garden was filled with pomegranate, fig and ancient, gnarled olive trees that provided much-needed shade. Masses of red bougainvillea, jasmine and honeysuckle clung to the wall, scenting the air.

The cat, Hercules, was no problem to look after. Most of the time he lay sunbathing on the patio and all she had to do was make sure he had plenty of water and feed him. She'd developed a fondness for him and he for her. He'd taken to sleeping on her bed and while she knew it was a habit she shouldn't encourage, there was something comforting about the sound of his purring and the warmth of his body curled up next to hers. And with that thought, her gaze strayed once more to the man working on the boat.

He'd resumed his paint scraping. He had to be hot down there where there was no shade. She wondered about offering him a drink. It would be the neighbourly, the polite thing to do. But she wasn't here to get to know the neighbours, she was here to see some of her mother's country and, while keeping her boss happy, to finish her thesis. Habits of a lifetime were too hard to break, though, and four days into her six-week holiday she hadn't actually seen very much of Greece, apart from a brief visit to the village her mother had lived as a child. Still, there was plenty of time and if she kept up this pace, her thesis would be ready to submit within the month and then she'd take time off to relax and sightsee.

However, the heat was making it difficult to concentrate. She should give herself a break and it wouldn't take her a moment to fetch him a drink. As it was likely he came from the village, he probably couldn't speak English very well anyway. That would definitely curtail any attempt to strike up a conversation.

Just as she stood to move towards the kitchen, a little girl, around five or six, appeared from around the corner of the cliff. She was wearing a pair of frayed denim shorts and a bright red T-shirt. Her long, blonde hair, tied up in a ponytail, bobbed as she skipped towards the man. A small spaniel, ears flapping, chased after her, barking excitedly.

'Baba!' she cried, squealing with delight, her arms waving like the blades of a windmill.

An unexpected and unwelcome pang of disappointment washed over Katherine. So he *was* married.

He stopped what he was doing and grinned, his teeth white against his skin.

'Crystal!' he said, holding his arms wide for the little girl to jump into them. Katherine could only make out enough of the rest of the conversation to know it was in Greek.

He placed the little girl down as a woman, slim with short blonde hair, loped towards them. This had to be the wife. She was carrying a wicker basket, which she laid on the sand, and said something to the man that made him grin.

The child, the cocker spaniel close on her heels, ran around in circles, her laughter ringing through the still air.

There was something about the small family, their utter enjoyment of each other, the tableau they made, that looked so perfect it made Katherine's heart contract. This was what family life should be—might have been—but would likely never be. At least, not for her.

Which wasn't to say that she didn't love the life she did have. It was interesting, totally absorbing and worthwhile. Public health wasn't regarded as the sexiest speciality, but in terms of saving lives most other doctors agreed it was public-health doctors and preventive medicine that made the greatest difference. One only had to think about the Broad Street pump, for example. No one had been able to stop the spread of cholera that had raged through London in the 1800s until they'd found its source.

When she next looked up the woman had gone but the detritus of a picnic still remained on the blanket. The man was leaning against a rock, his long legs stretched out in front of him, the child, dwarfed by his size, snuggled into his side, gazing up at him with a rapt expression on her face as he read to her from a story book.

It was no use, she couldn't concentrate out here. Gathering up her papers, she went back inside. She'd work for another hour before stopping for lunch. Perhaps then she'd explore the village properly. Apart from the short trip to Mum's village—and what a disappointment that had turned out to be—she'd been too absorbed in her thesis to do more than go for a swim or a walk along the beach before breakfast and last thing at night. Besides, she needed to stock up on more provisions.

She'd been to the shop on the village square once to buy some tomatoes and milk and had had to endure the undisguised curiosity of the shopkeeper and her customers and she regretted not having learnt Greek properly when she'd had the chance to do so. Her mother had been a native Greek speaker but she had never spoken it at home and consequently Katherine knew little of the language.

However, she hated the way some tourists expected the locals to speak English, regardless of what country they found themselves in, and had made sure she'd learnt enough to ask for what she needed—at the very least, to say please, thank you and to greet people. In the store, she'd managed to ask for what she wanted through a combination of hand signals and her few words of Greek—the latter causing no small amount of amusement.

She glanced at her papers and pushed them away with a sigh. The warm family scene she'd witnessed had unsettled her, bringing back the familiar ache of loneliness and longing. Since her concentration was ruined, she may as well go to the village now. A quick freshen-up and then she'd be good to go. Walking into her bedroom, she hesitated. She crossed over to her bedside drawer and removed the photograph album she always kept with her. She flicked through the pages until she found a couple of photos of

Poppy when she was six—around the same age as the little girl in the bay.

This particular one had been taken on the beach—
Brighton, if she remembered correctly. Poppy was kneeling in the sand, a bucket and spade next to her, a deep
frown knotting her forehead as she sculpted what looked
like a very wobbly sandcastle. She was in a bright one-
piece costume, her hair tied up in bunches on either side
of her head. Another, taken the same day, was of Poppy
in Liz's arms, the remains of an ice cream still evident on
her face, her head thrown back as if she'd been snapped
right in the middle of a fit of giggles. Katherine could see
the gap in the front of her mouth where her baby teeth
had fallen out, yet to be replaced with permanent ones.
She appeared happy, blissfully so. As happy as the child
she'd seen earlier.

She closed the album, unable to bear looking further.
Hadn't she told herself that it was useless to dwell on what
might have been? Work. That was what always stopped
her dwelling on the past. The trip to the village could wait.

Immersed in her writing, Katherine was startled by a small
voice behind her.

'Yiássas.'

Katherine spun around in her chair. She hadn't heard
anyone coming up the rock steps but she instantly recognised the little girl from the bay. 'Oh, hello.' What was
she doing here? And on her own? 'You gave me a bit of a
fright,' she added in English.

The child giggled. 'I did, didn't I? I saw you earlier
when I was with Baba. You were on the balcony.' She
pointed to it. 'I don't think you have any friends so I

thought you might want a visitor. Me!' Her English was almost perfect, although heavily accented.

Katherine laughed but it didn't sound quite as carefree as she hoped. 'Some adults like their own company.' She gestured to the papers in front of her. 'Besides, I have lots of work to do while I'm here.'

The girl studied her doubtfully for a few moments. 'But you wouldn't mind if I come and see you sometimes?'

What could she say to that? 'No, of course not. But I'm afraid you wouldn't find me very good company. I'm not used to entertaining little girls.'

The child looked astounded. 'But you must have been a little girl once! Before you got old.'

This time Katherine's laugh was wholehearted. 'Exactly. I'm old. No fun. Should you be here? Your family might be worried about you.'

The child's eyes widened. 'Why?'

'Well, because you're very small still and most of the time parents like to know where their children are and what they're up to.' She winced inwardly, aware of the irony of what she'd said.

'But they do know where I am, silly. I'm in the village! Hello, Hercules.' The girl knelt and stroked the cat. Suddenly pandemonium broke out. It seemed her spaniel had come to look for her. He ran into the room and spotting the cat made a beeline for it. With a furious yowl Hercules leapt up and onto Katherine's desk, scattering her papers, pens and pencils onto the floor. She grabbed and held on to the struggling cat as the dog jumped up against her legs, barking excitedly.

'Kato! Galen! Kato!' A stern male voice cut through the chaos. It was the child's father—the boat man. God, how many other people and animals were going to appear uninvited in her living room?

The spaniel obediently ran over to the man and lay down at his feet, tail wagging and panting happily. Now the father's censorious gaze rested on his little girl. After speaking a few words in Greek, he turned to Katherine. 'I apologise for my daughter's intrusion. She knows she shouldn't wander off without letting me know first. I didn't notice she'd gone until I saw her footprints headed this way.' His English was impeccable with only a trace of an attractive accent. 'Please, let us help you gather your papers.'

Close up he was overwhelmingly good-looking, with thick-lashed sepia eyes, a straight nose, curving sensual mouth and sharp cheekbones. Katherine felt another stab of envy for the blonde-haired woman. She lowered the still protesting Hercules to the floor. With a final malevolent glance at the spaniel, he disappeared outside.

'Please, there's no need…'

But he was already picking up some of the strewn papers. 'It's the least we can do.'

Katherine darted forward and placed a hand on his arm. To her dismay, her fingertips tingled where they touched his warm skin and she quickly snatched it away. 'I'd rather you didn't—they might get even more muddled up.'

He straightened and studied her for a moment from beneath dark brows. He was so close she could smell his soap and almost feel waves of energy pulsating from him. Every nerve cell in her body seemed to be on alert, each small hair on her body standing to attention. Dear God, that she should be reacting like this to a married man! What the hell was wrong with her? She needed to get a grip. 'Accidents

happen, there is no need for you to do anything, thank you,'
she said. Thankfully her voice sounded normal.

'Yes, Baba! Accidents happen!' the little girl piped up
in English.

His response to his daughter, although spoken softly
in Greek, had her lowering her head again, but when he
turned back to Katherine a smile lighted his eyes and
played around the corners of his mouth. He raked a hand
through his hair. 'Again I must apologise for my daughter. I'm afraid Crystal is too used to going in and out of
all the villagers' homes here and doesn't quite understand
that some people prefer to offer invitations.'

Crystal looked so woebegone that Katherine found herself smiling back at them. 'It's fine—I needed a break.
So now I'm having one—a little earlier than planned, but
that's okay.'

'In which case we'll leave you to enjoy it in peace.' He
glanced at her ringless fingers. 'Miss…?'

'Burns. Katherine Burns.'

'Katherine.' The way he rolled her name around his
mouth made it sound exotic. 'And I am Alexander Dimitriou. I've noticed you watching from your balcony.'

'Excuse me! I wasn't watching you! I was working on
my laptop and you just happened to be directly in my line
of sight whenever I lifted my head.' The arrogance of the
man! To take it for granted that she'd been watching him—
even if she had.

When he grinned she realised she'd let him know that
she had noticed him. The way he was looking at her was
disturbing. It was simply not right for a married man to
look at a woman who wasn't his wife that way.

'Perhaps,' he continued, 'you'll consider joining my family one day for lunch, to make up for disrupting your day?'

She wasn't here to hang around divine-looking Greek men—particularly married ones! 'Thank you,' she responded tersely. 'I did say to Crystal that she could come and visit me again some time,' she added as she walked father and daughter outside, 'but perhaps you should remind her to let you know before she does?'

She stood on the balcony, watching as they ambled hand in hand across the beach towards the village square, Crystal chattering and swinging on her father's arm. Even from this distance she could hear his laughter. With a sigh she turned around and went back inside.

Later that evening, after Crystal was in bed, Alexander's thoughts returned to Katherine, as they had over the last few days—ever since the morning he'd seen her come out of the water. It was just his luck that the villa she was staying in overlooked the bay where he was working on his boat.

He couldn't help glancing her way as she sat on her balcony, her head bent over her laptop as she typed, pausing only to push stray locks from her eyes—and to watch him.

And she *had* been watching him. He'd looked up more than once to catch her looking in his direction. She'd caused quite a stir in the village, arriving here by herself. The villagers, his grandmother and cousin Helen included, continued to be fascinated by this woman who'd landed in their midst and who kept herself to herself, seldom venturing from her temporary home unless it was to have a quick dip in the sea or shop for groceries at the village store. They couldn't understand anyone coming on holiday by themselves and had speculated wildly about her.

To their disappointment she hadn't stopped for a coffee or a glass of wine in the village square or to try some of

Maria's—the owner of only taverna in the village—home-cooked food so there had been no opportunity to find out more about her. Helen especially would have loved to know more about her—his cousin was always on at him to start dating again.

But, despite the fact Katherine was undeniably gorgeous, he wasn't interested in long-term relationships and he had the distinct impression that Miss Burns didn't do short-term ones.

However, there was something about this particular woman that drew him. Perhaps, he thought, because he recognised the same sadness in her that was in him. All the more reason, then, for him to keep his distance.

CHAPTER TWO

THE NEXT MORNING, having decided to work inside and out of sight, Katherine only managed to resist for a couple of hours before finding herself drawn like a magnet to the balcony.

Gazing down at the beach, she saw that Alexander, stripped to the waist, his golden skin glistening with a sheen of perspiration, was back working on his boat again. Dragging her gaze away from him, she closed her eyes for a moment and listened to the sound of the waves licking the shore. The sweet smell of oranges from a nearby orchard wafted on the breeze. Being here in Greece was like a balm for her soul.

A sharp curse brought her attention back to the bay.

Alexander had dropped his paint-scraper. He studied his hand for a moment and shook his head. He looked around as if searching for a bandage, but apparently finding only his T-shirt, bent to pick it up, and wound it around his palm.

She could hardly leave him bleeding—especially when, prepared as always, she'd brought a small first-aid kit with her and it was unlikely there would be a doctor available on a Sunday in such a small village.

The blood had pretty much soaked through his temporary bandage by the time she reached him but, undaunted, he had carried on working, keeping his left hand—the damaged one—elevated in some kind of optimistic hope of stemming the bleeding.

'Kaliméra!' Katherine called out, not wanting to surprise him. When he looked up, she pointed to his hand and lifted the first-aid kit she carried. 'Can I help?'

'It's okay, I'll manage,' he replied. When he smiled, her heart gave a queer little flutter. 'But thank you.'

'At least let me look at it. Judging by the amount of blood, you've cut it pretty badly.'

His smile grew wider. 'If you insist,' he said, holding out his injured hand.

She drew closer to him and began unwrapping his makeshift bandage. As she gently tugged the remaining bit of cloth aside and her fingers encountered the warmth of his work-roughened palm, she felt the same frisson of electricity course through her body as she had the day before. Bloody typical; the first time she could remember meeting someone whom she found instantly attractive he had to be married—and a father to boot.

'It's deep,' she said, examining the wound, 'and needs stitches. Is there a surgery open today?'

'Most of them are open for emergencies only on a Sunday. I'm not sure this constitutes one.'

'I think it does.' Katherine said, aware that her tone sounded schoolmistress prim. 'I'm a doctor, so I do know what I'm talking about.'

His eyebrows shot up. 'Are you really? The villagers had you down as a writer. A GP, I take it?'

Katherine shook her head. 'No. Epidemiology. Research. I'm in public health.'

'But not on holiday? You seemed pretty immersed in paperwork yesterday.'

'My thesis. For my PhD.'

'Brains too.' He grinned. 'So can't you stitch my hand?'

'Unfortunately, no. I could if I had a suturing kit with me but I don't. Anyway, you'll likely need a tetanus shot unless you've had one recently. Have you?'

'No.'

For some reason, the way he was looking at her made her think that he was laughing at her. 'Then one of the emergency surgeries it will have to be,' she said firmly. 'I'll clean and bandage the cut in the meantime. Is there someone who can give you a lift?'

'No need—it's within walking distance. Anyway, this little scratch is not going to kill me.'

'Possibly not but it could make you very sick indeed.' She thought for a moment. 'I strongly advise you to find out whether the doctor is willing to see you. I'll phone him if you like. As one doctor to another, he might be persuaded to see you.'

He was no longer disguising his amusement. 'Actually, that would be a bit embarrassing seeing as I'm the doctor and it's my practice—one of them anyway.'

'You're a doctor?' She couldn't keep the surprise out of her voice. She felt more than slightly foolish, standing before him with her little plastic medical kit. If he was a GP he was probably more qualified than she to assess the damage to his hand. Now she knew the reason for his secret amusement. 'You might have mentioned this before,' she continued through gritted teeth.

Alexander shrugged. 'I was going to, I promise. Eventually.' That smile again. 'I suppose I was enjoying the personal attention—it's nice to be on the receiving end for a change.'

'You really should have said straight away,' she reiterated, struggling to control the annoyance that was rapidly replacing her embarrassment. 'However, you can hardly suture your hand yourself.' Although right this minute she was half-minded to let him try.

'I could give it a go,' he replied, 'but you're right, it would be easier and neater if you did it. The practice I have here is really little more than a consulting room I use when the older villagers need to see a doctor and aren't unwell enough to warrant a trip to my practice. But it's reasonably well equipped. You could stitch it there.'

'In that case, lead the way.'

His consulting room had obviously once been a fisherman's cottage, with the front door leading directly onto the village square. There were only two rooms leading off the small hall and he opened the door to the one on the left. It was furnished with an examination couch, a stainless-steel trolley, a sink and most of what she'd expect to find in a small rural surgery. The one surprise was a deep armchair covered with a throw. He followed her gaze and grimaced. 'I know that doesn't really belong, but my older patients like to feel more at home when they come to see me here.'

Not really the most sanitary of arrangements, but she kept her own counsel. It wasn't up to her to tell him how to run his practice.

He opened a cupboard and placed some local anaesthetic and a syringe on the desk, along with a disposable suture tray. He perched on the couch and rested his hand, palm up, on his leg.

He definitely has the physique of a gladiator, she

thought, her gaze lingering on his chest for a moment too long. She shifted her gaze and found him looking at her, one eyebrow raised and a small smile playing on his lips. As heat rushed to her cheeks she turned away, wishing she'd left him to deal with his hand himself.

She washed her hands and slipped on a pair of disposable gloves, acutely conscious of his teasing appraisal as she filled the syringe with the local anaesthetic. Studiously avoiding looking at his naked chest, she gently lifted up his hand and, after swabbing the skin, injected into the wound. He didn't even flinch as she did so. 'I'll wait a few minutes for it to take effect.'

'So what brings you here?' he asked. 'It isn't one of the usual tourists spots.'

'I was kindly offered the use of the Dukases' villa through a colleague who is a friend of their daughter in exchange for taking care of Hercules and the garden. My mother was from Greece and I've always wanted to see the country where she was born.'

'She was from here?'

'From Ītylo. This was the closest I could get to there.'

'It's your first time in the Peloponnese?'

'My first time in Greece,' Katherine admitted.

'And your mother didn't come with you?'

'No. She passed away recently.' To her dismay, her voice hitched. She swallowed the lump in her throat before continuing. 'She always wanted the two of us to visit Greece together, but her health prevented her from travelling. She had multiple sclerosis.'

'I'm sorry.' Two simple words, but the way he said it, she knew he really meant it.

She lightly prodded his palm with her fingertips. 'How does that feel?'

'Numb. Go ahead.'

Opening up the suture pack, she picked up the needle. Why did he have to be nice as well as gorgeous?

'I hope you're planning to see some of the Peloponnese while you're here. Olympia? Delphi? Athens and the Acropolis for sure. The city of Mycenae, perhaps?'

Katherine laughed. 'They're all on my list. But I want to finish my thesis first.'

He raised his head and frowned slightly. 'So no holiday for a while, then? That's not good. Everyone needs to take time out to relax.'

'I do relax. Often.' Not that often—but as often as she wanted to. 'Anyway I find work relaxing.'

'Mmm,' he said, as if he didn't believe her. Or approve. 'Work can be a way to avoid dealing with the unbearable. Not good for the psyche if it goes on too long. You need to take time to grieve,' he suggested gently.

She stiffened. Who was he to tell her what was good for her and what she needed? How he chose to live his life was up to him, just as it was up to her how she lived.

'I must apologise again for yesterday,' he continued, when she didn't reply, 'You were obviously working so I hope we didn't set you back too much. My daughter's been dying to meet you since you arrived. I'm afraid her curiosity about you got the better of her.'

Katherine inserted a stitch and tied it off. 'Your daughter is charming and very pretty.'

'Yes, she is. She takes after her mother.'

'I take it the beautiful woman on the beach yesterday is your wife?' she said, inserting another l stitch.

When she heard his sharp intake of breath she stopped. 'I'm sorry. Did that hurt? Didn't I use enough local?'

His expression was taut, but he shook his head. 'I can't

feel a thing. The woman you saw is Helen, my cousin. My wife died.'

Katherine was appalled. 'I'm so sorry. How awful for you and your daughter. To lose her mother when so young.' She winced inwardly at her choice of words.

'Yes,' he said abruptly. 'It was.'

So he knew loss too. She bent her head again and didn't raise it until she'd added the final stitch and the wound was closed. When had his wife died? Crystal had to be, what? Four? Five? Therefore it had to be within that time frame. Judging by the bleakness in his eyes, the loss was still raw. In which case he might as well be married. And why the hell were her thoughts continuing along this route?

She gave herself a mental shake and placed a small square dressing on top and finished with a bandage, pleased that her work was still as neat as it had been when she'd sutured on a regular basis.

'What about tetanus?' she asked. 'I'm assuming you have some in stock here?'

'Suppose I'd better let you give me that too. It's been over five years since I last had one.' He went to the small drugs fridge and looked inside. 'Hell,' he said after examining the contents. 'I'm out. Never mind, I'll get it when I go back to my other surgery tomorrow.'

'It could be too late by then—as I'm sure you know. No, since it seems that you are my patient, at least for the moment, I'm going to have to insist you get one today.'

He eyed her. 'That would mean a trip to Pýrgos—almost an hour from here. Unfortunately, Helen has taken my car to take Crystal to play with a friend and won't be back until tonight. Tomorrow it will have to be.'

She hesitated, but only for a moment. 'In that case, I'll drive you.'

'Something tells me you're not going to back down on this.'

She smiled. 'And you'd be right.' She arched an eyebrow. 'You might want to fetch a clean shirt. Why don't you do that while I get my car keys?'

But it seemed as if she'd offered him a lift without the means to carry it through. Not wanting to drive down from Athens —she'd heard about the Peloponnese roads, especially the one that ran between here and the Greek capital—she'd taken a circuitous route; first an early morning flight, followed by a ferry and then two buses to the rental company In hindsight it would have been quicker and probably far less stressful to have flown into Athens.

And now she had a puncture. Thankfully the car did have a spare wheel. She jacked it up and found the wrench to loosen the bolts but they wouldn't budge. No doubt they had rusted.

'Problems?'

She whirled around to find Alexander standing behind her. He had showered and changed into light-coloured cotton trousers and a white short-sleeved shirt.

'Puncture. I'm just changing the wheel. As soon as I get a chance, I'm going to exchange this heap for something better.'

The car the company had given her had more dents and bashes in it than a rally car after a crash. She would have insisted on a newer, more pristine model, but the company had said it was the only one they had available.

His lips twitched. He walked around the car, shaking his head. 'They palmed this off on you?'

'Yes, well, I was tired.' She resented the fact that he

thought she'd let herself be taken advantage of—even if she had.

'Which company did you rent this from?'

She told him.

'In that case, they have a branch in Katákolo, which isn't too far from where we're going.'

'Will it be open on a Sunday?'

'The cruise ships all offer day trips to Olympia from there. Like most places that cater for tourists, everything will be open. Once I've been jagged to your satisfaction I'll make sure they exchange it for something better.'

'I'm perfectly able to manage to sort it out myself.' Did all Greek men think women were helpless?

He drew back a little, holding up his hands. 'Hey. You're helping me. And it's not far from where we're going.'

She was instantly ashamed of herself. He'd done nothing to warrant her snapping at him. It was hardly his fault that he made her feel like a schoolgirl with her first crush.

'I'm sorry. It's just that I'm a bit hot.' She sought a better reason to excuse her behaviour, but apart from telling him that he found his company unsettling she couldn't think of one. 'In the meantime, I still have to change the wheel.' She picked up a rock and hit the wrench. Nothing. No movement. Not even a centimetre.

He crouched down next to her, the muscles of his thighs straining against the material of his trousers. 'Let me do it.'

'I can manage. At least I would if the things weren't stuck.'

He took the wrench from her. 'It just needs a little strength.'

'You shouldn't. Not with your hand recently sutured.'

He ignored her and within moments the nuts were off

the wheel. He took the flat tyre off and silently she passed him the spare.

'I probably loosened them.' He looked up at her and grinned. 'I'm sure you did.' He lifted the new wheel into position and replaced the bolts.

'Thank you,' she said. 'I can take it from here.'

He stood back and watched as she lowered the car to the ground.

'I'll just tighten the bolts again,' he said, 'then we'll be good to go. Would you like me to drive?'

'No, thank you.'

Despite the open windows the car was hot; unsurprisingly, the air-conditioning didn't work either. Katherine gripped the steering-wheel, trying not to flinch whenever a car overtook her, the vehicle often swerving back in just in time to avoid being smashed into by another coming in the opposite direction. Perhaps she should have taken Alexander up on his offer to drive? But if he drove the same way as his countrymen did, being a passenger would be ten times worse. She preferred being in control.

Eventually the countryside gave way to denser traffic and by the time Alexander directed her to a parking spot in front of the surgery she was a nervous wreck, her hands were damp and she knew her hair was plastered to her scalp. She was beginning to appreciate why the car the company had given her was badly dented.

He looked relieved as he undid his seat belt. 'This won't take long but why don't you go for a walk while you're waiting?'

'If you're going to be quick I might as well come in with you.' She was curious to see how the medical services in Greece worked.

While Alexander greeted the receptionist, Katherine took a seat in the small waiting room next to an elderly woman with a bandage on her knee and clutching a walking stick. Alexander turned to her and said something in Greek that made her laugh.

'Mrs Kalfas is waiting for her husband to collect her,' he explained to Katherine, 'so I can go straight in. I won't be long.'

A few moments after Alexander disappeared from sight, a man in his early to mid-twenties, staggered in and, after saying a few words to the receptionist, almost fell into one of the empty chairs. He was good-looking with dark curly hair, a full mouth and olive skin, but his jeans and checked shirt were stained and crumpled as if he'd picked them up off the bedroom floor, too ill to care. His cheeks were flushed and his eyes, when he managed to open them briefly, glittered with fever. Perhaps she should have gone for that walk. All doctors knew that hospitals and GP waiting rooms were bad news for the healthy.

Mrs Kalfas tried to strike up a conversation with him, but he appeared to have little interest in whatever she was saying. Warning bells started to clamour in Katherine's head as she studied him covertly from under her eyelids. Now she wondered if his eyes were closed because the light was annoying him—and the way he kept pressing his hand to the back of his neck as if it were sore alarmed her too. He really didn't look well at all. The receptionist should have let the doctors know that he was here.

Katherine was about to suggest it when he gave a loud moan and slid to the floor. Instantly she was on her feet and, crouching by his side, feeling for his pulse. It was there but weak and rapid. She glanced around but annoyingly there was no sign of the receptionist. Mrs Kalfas was staring, horrified.

'I need some help here,' Katherine called out. 'Alexander!'

The door behind which he'd vanished was flung open and Alexander, followed by a short, balding, overweight man with a stethoscope wrapped around his neck, rushed over and knelt by Katherine's side.

'What happened?' Alexander asked.

'He came in a few minutes ago. I was just about to suggest he be taken through when he collapsed. He's been rubbing his neck as if it's painful or stiff. We should consider meningitis.'

Alexander and his colleague exchanged a few words in rapid Greek and the other doctor hurried away.

The man on the floor groaned softly. The receptionist reappeared and came to stand next to Mrs Kalfas, placing a comforting arm around the older woman. Alexander said something to the younger woman and she hurried back to her desk and picked up the phone.

'It could be a number of things but to be on the safe side Carlos—Dr Stavrou—is going to get a line so we can start him on IV antibiotics,' Alexander told Katherine. 'Diane is phoning for an ambulance.'

Carlos returned and ripped open a pack and handed Alexander a venflon. He quickly inserted it into a vein and, taking the bag of saline from his colleague, attached one end of the tube to the needle. When Katherine held out her hand for the bag of saline, Alexander passed it to her and she held it up so that the fluid could flow unimpeded. In the meantime, Alexander had injected antibiotics straight into one of the stricken patient's veins.

As Katherine placed an oxygen mask over his face, she

was vaguely aware that the receptionist had returned and along with Mrs Kalfas was watching intently. Alexander whirled around and spoke rapidly to the receptionist. He translated her reply for Katherine.

'Diane says the ambulance will be here shortly. She's agreed to take Mrs Kalfas home instead of making her wait for her husband. Seeing she's had a bit of a fright, I think it's better.'

Katherine was impressed with the way he'd considered the old woman, even in the midst of an emergency. Their patient was still unconscious but apart from keeping an eye on his airway there was little more they could do until the ambulance arrived. They couldn't risk taking him in a car in case he arrested.

'You have a defib to hand?' she asked.

'Naturally.'

She wondered what had caused the man to collapse. A number of possibilities ran through her head, meningitis being one, but without further tests it was impossible to know. All they could do now was stabilise him until they got him to hospital.

Diane picked up her handbag and helped the old lady out. Soon after, the ambulance arrived and the paramedics took over. They spoke to Alexander before quickly loading the patient into the ambulance.

'Should one of us go with him?' Katherine asked.

'No need. Carlos wants to go. He's his patient.'

The ambulance doors were slammed shut and it drove away, sirens screaming.

'Are you all right?' Alexander asked.

'Perfectly. Could you make sure they test him for meningitis?'

'Bit of a leap, isn't it? Carlos said Stefan—the patient—

is not only accident prone but there's a few bugs doing the rounds. Besides, I didn't see any signs of a rash.'

'Trust me. Communicable diseases are my area of expertise and that young man has all the signs—sensitivity to light, fever, neck pain. The rash could appear at any time.' Alexander studied her for a moment. 'It couldn't hurt to do a lumbar puncture. I'll phone the hospital and make sure they do all the tests. At least he's been started on IV antibiotics. In the meantime, I'm afraid we're going to have to wait here until Carlos returns. Is that okay?'

'Sure.' She smiled at him. 'You can show me around while we wait.'

The practice was as well equipped as any Katherine had seen. In addition to four consulting rooms, one for each of the doctors, one for the nurses and one for their physio, there was an X-ray room and a sleek, spotlessly clean treatment room. All the equipment was modern and up to date.

'You appear to be almost as well set up as a small hospital,' Katherine said, impressed.

'We never know what we're going to get, so we like to be prepared for the worst. We have, as you can imagine, a fair share of road traffic accidents on these roads and sometimes people bring the casualties here as it's closer than the hospital.' Not quite the small family practice she'd imagined.

'We don't do much more than stabilise them and send them on,' Alexander continued, 'but it can make the difference between survival and death.'

'You have advanced life-support training, then?'

'Yes. We all do. It also helps that I used to be a surgeon.' He picked up the phone. 'Would you excuse me while I phone the hospital?' he said. 'I need to tell them to watch out for meningitis, as you suggested, and Carlos was telling me earlier that one of my patients was admitted there last night. I'd like to find out how he's doing.'

'Be my guest,' Katherine replied. As she waited for him to finish the call she studied him covertly from under her lashes. The more she learned about him the more he intrigued her. So he used to be a surgeon. What, then, had brought him to what, despite the expensive and up-to-date equipment, was still essentially a rural family practice? Had he come back here because of his wife? And how had she died? Had she been a road traffic victim?

While he'd been talking on the phone, Alexander's expression had darkened. He ended the phone call and sat lost in thought for a while. It was almost as if he'd forgotten she was there.

'Something wrong?' she asked.

'The patient Carlos was telling me about has been transferred to a hospital in Athens. The hospital doctor who admitted him yesterday sent him there this morning, but he's left to go fishing and can't be reached. None of the staff on duty today can tell me anything.' He leaned back in his chair. 'I'll speak to him tomorrow and find out why he felt a transfer was necessary.' He shook his head as if to clear it. 'But I have spoken to the doctor on call today about Stéfan. She's promised to do a lumbar puncture on him.'

'Good,' Katherine said.

'So what is your thesis on?' Alexander asked.

'As I said, communicable diseases. Mainly African ones.'

'What stage of your training are you?'

She raised an eyebrow. 'Consultant. Have been for four years. I'm thinking of applying for a professor's post. Hence the doctorate.'

He whistled between his teeth. 'You're a consultant! You don't look old enough.'

'I'm thirty-four.'

They chatted for a while about her work and different infectious diseases Alexander had come across in Greece. Caught up in discussing her passion, she was surprised when she heard footsteps and Carlos came in. She'd no idea so much time had passed.

'How is our patient?' Alexander asked in English, after formally introducing her to his partner.

'His blood pressure had come up by the time I left him in the care of the emergency team at the hospital. They'll let me know how he is as soon as they've done all the tests.'

'Will you let me know when they do?'

'Of course.'

Alexander pushed away from the desk and stood. He smiled at Katherine. 'In that case, let's go and swap that car of yours.'

The car rental company did have another car for her, but it wouldn't be available until later that afternoon.

Katherine turned to Alexander. 'I'm sure you want to get home. Isn't there another rental company in the area?'

'I suspect you'll find the same thing there. The cruise ships come in in the morning and a lot of the passengers—those who don't want to take the bus tour to Olympia—hire a car for the day. They tend to bring them back around four.'

'Damn. That's three hours away.'

'We could have lunch,' he suggested. 'Or, if you're not hungry, we can go to Olympia ourselves. It's years since I've been and it's less than thirty minutes from here. By the time we get back, Costa here should have a car for you.'

He smiled. 'You're in Greece now. You'll find life a lot easier if you accept that here time works in a different zone.'

She hid a sigh. She should be getting back to her thesis. By taking the morning off she risked falling behind the schedule she'd mapped out for herself.

Whoa—what was she thinking? Had she completely lost it? He was right. What was the hurry anyway? It was Sunday and an interesting, *single* hunk was wanting to spend time with her.

'I would love to see Olympia,' she said. And she would. It was near the top of her list of places to visit. It would also be less intense, less like a date, than having lunch.

'Good. That's settled, then.' He opened the passenger door for Katherine. She looked at him and arched an eyebrow.

'I think it will be less stressful—and safer for us all— if I drive,' he said. 'I know the roads better.'

She hesitated, then broke into a smile. 'To be honest, if I never have to drive that heap of scrap again it would be too soon. So be my guest. Knock yourself out.'

It wasn't long before she was regretting her decision—and her words. As far as she was concerned, Alexander drove just like every other Greek driver.

'When I said knock yourself out,' she hissed, 'I didn't mean literally.'

He laughed. 'Don't worry. I promise you driving this way is safer.'

Nevertheless, she was hugely relieved when they arrived still in one piece. Alexander found a space in the crowded car park.

'There are two parts to the site—the ruins of the ancient city and the museum. I suggest we start off in the museum, which is air-conditioned.' He glanced at her appraisingly and his lips twitched. She was wearing navy trousers and a white cotton blouse with a Peter Pan collar, which, she had to admit, while neat and professional were almost unbearably hot. 'It'll be cooler by the time we're finished. If I remember correctly, there is very little shade in the ruins.'

She wandered around the exhibits, trying to concentrate but not really able to. She was too acutely aware of the similarity between the physiques of the naked statues and the man close by.

When they'd finished in the museum they walked across to the ruins. Although it was cooler than it had been earlier, it was still hot and almost immediately she felt a trickle of perspiration gather between her breasts. Alexander, on the other hand, looked as fresh and as cool as he'd done since they'd left the village.

As he pointed out the temples of Zeus and Hera, Katherine began to relax. Perhaps it was because, away from the statues, she could concentrate on what Alexander was saying. He knew a great deal about Greek history and was an easy and informative guide and soon she was caught up in his stories about what life must have been like during the Ottoman era.

When they'd finished admiring the bouleuterion, where the statue of Zeus had once stood, he led her across to the track where the athletes had competed. 'Did you know they competed in the nude?'

Instantly an image of Alexander naked leaped into her head and blood rushed to her cheeks. She hoped he would think it was the heat that was making her flush but when she saw the amusement in his eyes she knew he was perfectly aware what she'd been thinking.

It was nuts. After Ben she'd only ever had one other significant long-term relationship—with Steven, one of her colleagues. When that had ended, after he'd been offered a job in the States, she'd been surprisingly relieved. Since then, although she'd been asked out many times and Sally had tried to fix her up with several of the unattached men she or Tom knew, and she'd gone out with two or three of them, no one had appealed enough to make her want to see them again beyond a couple of dates.

Relationships, she'd decided, were overrated. Many women were single and very happy—as was she. She could eat when she liked, go where she pleased without having to consult anyone, holiday where it suited her and work all weekend and every weekend if she wanted to. Until her mother's death, she had rarely been lonely—she hadn't lied to Crystal when she'd told her she preferred being on her own, but that didn't mean she didn't miss physical contact. That didn't mean she didn't miss sex.

She felt her flush deepen. But sex without strings had never been her cup of tea.

God! She'd thought more about sex over these last two days than she had in months. But it was hard *not* to think about it around all these nude statues. Perhaps it hadn't been such a good idea choosing to come here instead of lunch. Lunch might have been the safer option after all.

A replacement car still wasn't available when they returned to the rental company.

'Really!' Katherine muttered. 'It's almost six.' Unlike Alexander, she needed to cool off, preferably with an ice-cold shower. And to do that she needed to get home—and out of Alexander's company.

'He promises he'll have one by seven. If not, he'll give you his own car.' Alexander grinned. 'I did warn you about Greek timing.'

'But aren't you in a hurry to get back?' she asked, dismayed. 'I mean, you've given up the best part of your day to help me out. You must have other stuff you'd rather be doing. And I should get back to my thesis.'

'Nope. I'm in no rush. As I said, I'm not expecting my cousin and Crystal home until later. And surely you can give yourself a few more hours off?' The laughter in his eyes dimmed momentarily. 'Trust me, sometimes work should take a back seat.'

It was all right for him, he clearly found it easy to relax. But to spend more time in his company, blushing and getting tongue-tied, was too embarrassing. Still, she couldn't very well make him take a taxi all the way back home—even if it was an appealing thought. Maybe *she* should get a taxi home? Now she was being ridiculous! She was behaving like someone with sunstroke. She almost sighed with relief. Perhaps that was it? She clearly wasn't herself. She realised he was watching her curiously. What had he been saying? Oh, yes—something about dinner.

'In that case, dinner would be lovely,' she replied, pulling herself together. 'Do you have somewhere in mind?'

'As a matter of fact I do. It's down by the shore. They sell the best seafood this side of Greece.' He tilted his head. 'You do like seafood, don't you?'

'I love it.'

'Good. We can wave goodbye to the cruise ships and more or less have the place to ourselves. We'll leave the car here. It's not far.'

They walked along the deserted main street. Without the hordes of visitors and now that the shopkeepers had brought in their stands that had been filled with tourist souvenirs, maps and guides, the town had a completely different feel to it. It was as if it were a town of two identities—the one belonging to the tourists, and this typically Greek sleepy one.

The restaurant was situated at the end of a quiet cul-de-sac and it didn't look very prepossessing from the rear, where the entrance was situated. Understated was the word Katherine would use to describe the interior with its striped blue and white table runners and unlit candles rammed into empty wine bottles. But when they were guided to a table on the veranda by the *maître d'*, the view took Katherine's breath away. White sands and a blue, blue sea glittered as if some ancient god had scattered diamonds onto its surface. Alexander pulled out a chair for her beneath the shade of a tree and she sank happily into it.

When Alexander chose the lobster, freshly caught that morning, she decided to have it too. And since he was determined to drive they ordered a glass of chilled white wine for her and a fruit juice for himself.

They chatted easily about Greece and the recent blow to its economy and Alexander suggested various other places she might want to visit. Then he asked which medical school she'd studied at and she'd told him Edinburgh. Surprisingly, it turned out that it had been one of his choices but in the end he'd decided on Bart's.

'What made you decide to study in England?' she asked.

'I was brought up there. My mother was from Kent.' That explained his excellent English.

'So you have a Greek father and an English mother. I'm the opposite. How did your parents meet?'

'My mother met my father when she was working in a taverna while she was backpacking around Greece. It was supposed to be her gap year but in the end she never made it to university. Not long after she and my father started dating, they married. They moved to an apartment in Athens and after a couple of years they had me, then my younger brother. But she always pined for England. My father lectured in archaeology so he applied for a post at the British Museum and when he was accepted, we upped and left. I was five at the time.

'My father always missed Greece, though, so we came back as a family whenever we could, particularly to see my grandmother—my father's mother—and all the other family—aunts and uncles and cousins. Greece has always felt like home to me. Dad died when he was in his early forties. My grandfather died shortly after he did and, as my father's eldest son, I inherited the villa I live in now, as well as the land around it. It's been in our family for generations. Naturally my grandmother still lives in the family home.'

Katherine wanted to ask about his wife, but judging by his terse response in the village consulting room earlier that was a no-go area. 'And where's your mother now?' she asked instead, leaning back as their waiter placed their drinks in front of them.

'Still in England,' Alexander continued, when their waiter had left. 'She hasn't been back since my father died. I don't think she can bear to come anymore. She lives close to my brother in Somerset.'

'Doesn't she miss her grandchild?'

'Of course. However, Mother's life is in England—it's where her friends and my brother and his family are. We visit her often and, of course, there's video chat.' He took a sip of his drink. 'That's enough about me. What about you? Is there someone waiting for you in the UK?'

'No. No one.'

He looked surprised. 'Divorced, then? I'm assuming no children otherwise they'd be with you.'

She hesitated. 'Not divorced. Never married.' She swallowed. 'And no children.'

'Brothers and sisters? Your dad?'

'My dad passed away when I was fifteen. And no brothers or sisters.'

'So an only child. Being on your own must have made your mother's death even harder to handle, then,' he said softly.

The sympathy in his voice brought a lump to her throat. But she didn't want him to feel sorry for her.

'As I told Crystal, I like my own company. I have loads of friends in the UK when—if—I feel the need to socialise.'

'No one who could come with you? We Greeks find it difficult to imagine being on our own. As you've probably noticed, we like to surround ourselves with family.'

'Plenty of people offered to come,' she said quickly. 'But this trip was something I needed to do alone.'

He said nothing, just looked at her with his warm, brown eyes.

'I wish I could have come with Mum before she died, though. She always hoped to return to Greece, with Dad and me, to show me her country, but sadly it never happened,' she found herself explaining, to fill the silence.

'Because of her MS?'

'Yes. Mostly.'

But even before her mother's diagnosis the trip had been talked about but never actually planned. Her parents' restaurant had taken all their energy, money and time. At first it had seemed to be going from strength to strength, but then the unimaginable had happened. Dad had died and without him Mum had become a shadow of herself and had talked less and less about returning to Greece.

It had only been later that she'd realised that her father's death and struggling with a failing business hadn't been the only reasons Mum had been listless. She'd hidden her symptoms from her daughter until the evening she'd collapsed. And that had been the beginning of a new nightmare.

'What do you do when you're not working?' he asked, when she didn't expand.

'I kind of work all the time,' she admitted 'It's honestly my favourite thing to do.'

He frowned as if he didn't believe her. But it was true. She loved her work and found it totally absorbing. Given the choice of a night out or settling down to some research with a glass of wine in one hand, the research won hands down.

Their food arrived and was set before them. Katherine reached for the bowl of lemon quarters at the same as Alexander. As their fingers touched she felt a frisson of electricity course through her body. She drew back too quickly and flushed.

He lifted up the dish, his expression enigmatic. 'You first.'

'Thank you.'

'So why public health?' he asked, seeming genuinely interested.

'I thought I wanted to do general medicine but I spent six months in Infectious Diseases as part of my rotation and loved it—particularly when it came to diagnosing the more obscure infections. It was like solving a cryptic crossword puzzle. You had to work out what it could be by deciphering the clues, and that meant finding out as much as you could about your patient—where they, or their families, had been recently, for example. Sometimes it was obvious if they'd just come from Africa—then you'd start by think of malaria—or typhoid or if they'd been on a walking holiday in a place where there were lots of sheep, making Lyme disease a possibility. It was the patients who made the job so fascinating. When you'd found out as much as you could, you had to decide what tests and investigations to do, ruling diseases out one by one until the only one left was almost certainly the right answer.'

She rested her fork on the side of her plate. 'Of course, it wasn't always a good outcome. Sometimes by the time you found out what the patient had it was too late. And what was the point in diagnosing someone with malaria if you couldn't stop them getting it in the first place? I became really interested in prevention and that's when I moved into public health.' She stopped suddenly. 'Sorry. I didn't mean to go on. But when I get talking about work…'

'Hey, I'm a doctor, I like talking shop.'

'Why did you decide to come back to Greece?' she asked.

Something she couldn't read flickered behind his eyes. 'I wanted to spend more time with my daughter,' he said shortly. 'But we were talking about you. How did your parents meet?' It seemed he was equally determined to turn the conversation back to her.

'Mum met Dad when he was in the armed forces. He was stationed in Cyprus and she was visiting friends there. They fell in love and he left the army and they moved back to Scotland. He tried one job after another, trying to find something he enjoyed or at least was good at. Eventually he gave up trying to find the ideal job and started working for a building company. We weren't well off—not poor but not well off. We lived in a small house bordering an estate where there was a lot of crime. When I was eight my father became unwell. He didn't know what was it was—except that it was affecting his lungs. He was pretty bad before Mum persuaded him to see his GP.' She paused. 'That's when I began to think of becoming a doctor.'

He leaned forward. 'Go on.'

'We used to go, as a family, to his doctor's appointments. We did everything as a family.' Sadness washed over her. 'First there were the visits to the GP, but when he couldn't work out what was going on, he referred Dad to the hospital. I was fascinated. Everything about the hospital intrigued me: the way the doctors used to rush about seeming so important; the way the nurses always seemed to know what they were doing; the smells; the sounds— all the stuff that normally puts people off I found exciting.

'Of course, I was too young to understand that the reason we were there was because there was something seriously wrong with my father. His physician was a kind woman. I remember her well. She had these horn-rimmed glasses and she used to look at me over the top of them. When she saw how interested I was, she let me listen to my father's chest with her stethoscope. I remember hearing the dub-dub of his heartbeat and marvelling that this thing, this muscle, no larger than his fist, was what was keeping him—what was keeping me and everyone else—alive.

'I was always smart at school. It came easy to me to get top marks and when I saw how proud it made my parents, I worked even harder. My school teachers told my parents that they had high hopes for me. When I told Mum and Dad—I was twelve—that I wanted to be a doctor they were thrilled. But they knew that it would be difficult if I went to the high school in our area. It had a reputation for being rough and disruptive. They saved every penny they could so they could send me to private school.

'My father had received a payment from the building company when he left—by this time he'd been diagnosed with emphysema from years of breathing in building dust—but I knew he'd been planning to use the money for a down payment on a mortgage to buy a little restaurant—Dad would be the manager, Mum the head cook—and I didn't want them to use their life savings on me, not if they didn't have to.

'I persuaded them to let me apply to one of the top private schools. My teacher had told them that the school awarded scholarships to children with potential but not the funds to go to the school. She also warned them that it was very competitive. But I knew I could do it—and I did.'

'I am beginning to suspect that you're not in the habit of letting obstacles get in your way.'

Suddenly she was horrified. She wasn't usually so garrulous and certainly not when it came to talking about herself. Over the years she'd become adept at steering the conversation away from herself and onto the other person. Now she was acutely conscious of having monopolised the conversation, and when she thought about it she realised she'd made herself out to be a paragon of virtue when nothing could be further from the truth. Perhaps it was the wine. Or the way he listened to her as if she were the most fascinating person he'd ever met. Her heart thumped. Perhaps this was the way he was with everyone. She suspected it was. In which case he'd be an excellent family doctor.

'So how long have you been back in Greece?' she asked when their waiter left them, after replenishing their water glasses. She really wanted to know more about *him*.

'Just over two years.' His gaze dropped to his glass. He twirled his water, the ice cubes tinkling against the side. 'Not long after I lost my wife. I worked at St George's in

London—As I mentioned earlier, I trained as surgeon before going into general practice—but my wife, Sophia, wasn't really a city girl, so we bought a house in a nearby suburb and I commuted from there. And when I was on call, I slept at the hospital.' A shadow crossed his face. 'In retrospect, that was a mistake,' he murmured, so softly she couldn't be sure she'd heard him correctly. 'Why did you change to general practice?'

His expression darkened. 'I gave surgery up when I decided to return to Greece.'

It wasn't really an answer and she had the distinct feeling he was keeping as much back from her as he was telling her. Had he really been content to give up the challenges and adrenaline rush of surgery to return to Greece to be a GP? But bereavement often caused people to change their lives.

'Was your wife Greek?'

'Yes.'

'Did she work while you were in the UK?' she asked. How had she felt about leaving her country and going to a much colder, much greyer London? But, then, she had been with the man she'd loved and who had loved her. No doubt she hadn't cared.

'She was a musician,' he replied. 'She always wanted to play in an orchestra. She gave that up when we moved to England and taught piano instead.'

'Crystal must miss her terribly.'

'We both do. I see her mother in Crystal every day.' He swallowed and averted his gaze from hers for a few moments. 'What about you?' he asked, eventually. 'Don't you want children?'

He was looking at her again with that same intense expression in his eyes.

'Don't most women? But…' She dropped her head and fiddled with her butter knife, searching for the right words. 'It wasn't meant to be,' she finished lamely. Her heart thumped uncomfortably against her ribs. *Keep the conversation on neutral territory,* she told herself. 'I enjoyed the trip to Olympia. You know a lot about Greek archaeology and history,' she said.

He slid her a thoughtful look as if he knew she was deliberately changing the subject.

'My father was an archaeologist and my wife shared his passion,' he said. 'What chance do you think I wouldn't be? I doubt there is an archaeological site in Greece I haven't been to. Every holiday, when we returned here, that's what we did. I think my wife thought it was her mission in life to educate me.' His face clouded and Katherine knew he was thinking of his wife again. He had loved her very much, that much was clear.

What would it be like—the thought almost came out of nowhere—to be loved like that? To know that there was one person in the world who treasured you above all else? That there was someone you could turn to in your darkest moments, share your deepest secrets and fears with?

It was unlikely she'd ever know.

Katherine sank back into the leather seat of her replacement car, grateful she didn't have to drive back to the villa on dark, twisting roads. Alexander switched on the radio, and the soothing notes of a Brahms concerto softly filled the silence that had sprung up between them since they'd left the restaurant. The lights of the dashboard and the occasional passing vehicle revealed a man absorbed with his own thoughts, his forehead knotted, his eyes bleak. He turned the volume up a little more.

'You like this?' she asked. 'It's one of my favourites.'

He glanced at her. 'It is? My wife used to play it all the time. I haven't listened to it for a while...' He looked away, his mouth set in a grim line.

His wife was like a ghostly presence in the car.

Katherine closed her eyes. Deliberately shifting her focus from Alexander, she wondered how Stéfan was faring. If it was meningitis, he could very well be struggling for his life at this moment. She hoped she was wrong and he just had an infection that would be quickly cleared up with antibiotics.

Becoming aware they had entered the village, she sat straighter in her seat.

Tension seeped between them as he brought the car to a standstill outside her villa. They unclipped their seat belts and climbed out of the car.

As he handed her the keys, their fingers touched. She looked up at him from beneath her lashes, wondering if he had felt the electricity too. Would he ask to come in? Or if he could see her again?

Instead, his voice was as neutral as his words. 'I enjoyed today. Thank you, Katherine.'

Disappointment washed over her. But what had she expected? It was clear he was still grieving for his wife.

'I did too. Good night...'

'Good night, Katherine.'

She winced inwardly as she heard the finality in his tone. Hercules, purring loudly, curved his body around her legs as she opened the front door.

He was some comfort at least.

As the door closed behind her, Alexander thrust his hands deeper into his pockets and, before turning for the short walk home across the square, cursed himself for the fool he was.

Throughout the day he had been aware of the rising of desire he felt for this strait-laced, reserved, intelligent and beautiful woman. But hearing the melody Sophia had played so often had reminded him that Katherine would be leaving too. Even if she hadn't he had only ashes to give her.

No, his first instincts had been correct. It wouldn't be right to become entangled with this hurting woman.

CHAPTER THREE

'Yia-Yia says you must come to our house.'

Katherine started. She hadn't been aware of Crystal coming in. Now here she was again, as bold as brass in her sitting room, as if she had every right to be there. But, then, Katherine conceded silently, she had extended what had amounted to an open invitation.

'Excuse me?'

'Yia-Yia says you helped Baba with his hand so she wants you to come to dinner. She says it's not good for someone to be alone all the time.'

'Yia-Yia? Your grandmother?' When Crystal nodded, she added, 'Does your father know you're here?'

The little girl hitched her shoulders and flopped her arms to her side, her hands bumping against her legs. 'I did tell him.' Her sigh was dramatic. 'He's working on his boat again. He also wants you to come.'

Katherine wasn't sure she believed Crystal. She didn't want to impose herself on Alexander's family—particularly if he'd be there. He'd come to the villa the evening after they'd been to Olympia to tell her that her diagnosis had been correct. Stéfan did indeed have meningitis and was in Intensive Care. But Alexander hoped that, because of her alerting them to look out for meningitis, Stéfan would recover.

She hadn't seen Alexander since then but, to her dismay, she'd found herself thinking about him—a lot—during the week and knew she was in real danger of developing a crush on him. An unreciprocated crush, clearly, and someone like him was bound to pick up sooner or later the effect he was having on her. The ending of their evening together had indicated, more than words could, that he wasn't interested in pursuing a relationship with her. No, if the invitation had been extended by him, it had been out of politeness—from one colleague to another.

In which case it would be better not to encourage Crystal to visit too much.

Katherine managed a smile. 'I'm very busy, Crystal, so…' she picked up her pen pointedly '…would you thank your grandmother very much for her kind invitation but tell her I won't be able to make it?'

But instead of taking the hint, Crystal came to stand next to her. 'What are you doing?' she asked.

'It's a paper I'd like to finish before I go back to work.'

'Like homework?'

'Exactly.' Trying to ignore the child next to her, Katherine made a few more notes on the page. But it was clear Crystal had no intention of leaving any time soon.

She suppressed a sigh and put her pen down. 'Would you like some orange juice?'

'Yes, please.'

When she got up to fetch it, both Hercules and Crystal followed her into the small kitchen.

'I told Baba that Yia-Yia and me thought you must be lonely all by yourself and he agreed. So it's good I can keep you company sometimes.'

As Katherine crouched down to give Hercules some food she felt her cheeks grow hot. It was bad enough, mortifying enough, that Alexander had said that, but for him, his six-year-old and his grandmother to be discussing her was too much. Was that what this dinner invitation was about? A let's-keep-the-solitary-woman-company-for-at-least-one-night-so-that-we-don't-have-to-worry-about-her-being-on-her-own? She swore silently.

It made it more important than ever that she stay away from him; she absolutely refused to be the object of sympathy.

'You can tell your father, as I've already told him, I'm perfectly happy being on my own. I'm not in the least bit lonely.' Why was she justifying herself to a child? If she *did* feel a little bereft at times, it was only to be expected after losing Mum so recently. She handed Crystal the glass of juice.

'I could paint your toenails if you like,' Crystal said. She held up a plastic bag. 'Look. I got three different colours for my birthday from Cousin Helen. Baba says I'm too young to be wearing nail polish.' Her mouth drooped. 'Helen shouldn't have given it to me if I couldn't wear it. What was she thinking?'

The last phrase sounded so much like something her friend Sally would have said, it made Katherine smile.

'If you let me do your nails, it'll make you even more beautiful,' Crystal continued plaintively, and apparently without the tiniest hint of guile.

Katherine knew when she was beaten. 'Okay,' she said.

A smile of delight spread across Crystal's face. 'Can I? Really?'

'Yes, but *only* my toes. I don't wear varnish on my fingernails. A doctor has to keep their fingernails short.' She held up her hands and wiggled them.

'Okay. You sit on the couch and put your feet on this

chair,' Crystal instructed, lugging one of the kitchen chairs over.

Wondering whether she'd made a mistake by agreeing to the child's demands, Katherine slid her feet out of her sandals and placed them on the vinyl-covered seat. 'Like this?'

Crystal nodded. She opened the popper of her little plastic bag and very carefully placed three pots of nail varnish on the table. 'What colour would you like?'

Katherine studied the pots of varnish for a moment. One was deep purple and completely out of the question, even if she intended to remove the polish at the first opportunity, the second was deep red and the third a pale, coral pink.

She pointed to the pink one. 'That one.'

'But I like the red.' Crystal pouted.

Katherine bit down on a smile. 'Okay. Red it is.'

She leaned against the back of the couch and closed her eyes. Crystal's little hands were like feathers on her feet and, to her surprise, Katherine found it very soothing.

'There. Done. Look!' Crystal said eventually. She stood back to admire her work. 'I told you it would be pretty.'

Katherine peered down at her toes. It was as if someone had taken a machete to them, lopping them off somewhere below the metatarsals. There had to more nail polish on her skin and the seat of the chair than on her nails. But Crystal looked so pleased with herself that Katherine quickly hid her dismay. 'Mmm. Quite a difference.'

Crystal tugged her hand. 'Come on, let's show Baba.'

'I don't think your father—'

But Crystal was pulling her to her feet. 'Helen wouldn't let me do hers, but when she sees yours, she will.'

'Crystal! I said ten minutes!' Alexander's voice came from below the balcony.

'Coming, Baba. In a minute.'

'Now, Crystal!'

Keeping her toes spread as far apart as possible, Katherine hobbled over to the balcony and looked down. Alexander was wiping grease-stained hands on a rag. His T-shirt clung damply to his chest and his hair was tousled. Yet he still managed to look like a Greek god.

'Hi, Katherine.' His teeth flashed. 'Sorry I'm calling up, but my feet are sandy, my hands grubby and I need a dip in the sea before I'm fit for company. You are coming to dinner, aren't you?'

Crystal bumped against her as she climbed excitedly onto the rung of the balcony. 'She says not to dinner, Baba, but can she come for a visit? She is much more beautiful now! You have to see her.'

Katherine was about to protest when his eyes locked on hers. 'The part I can see of her already looks pretty good.' For a long moment the world seemed to disappear until there were just the two of them. 'Why not dinner?' he asked, breaking the spell.

'Because I've work to do and, anyway, I don't like to intrude on your family.'

'I assume you take time off to eat?'

'Yes, you have to eat!' his daughter echoed.

'My grandmother will be disappointed if you don't. She's already started preparing her best dishes.'

Alexander's family appeared determined to adopt her. She winced at her choice of words and sought desperately for an acceptable excuse. Apart from the effect Alexander had on her, every time she looked at Crystal she was painfully reminded of what she'd lost.

'Yes, *lahanodolmádes* and *patátes yemistés*,' Crystal added. 'Oh, and *baklavás* for afters! What else, Baba?'

'Crystal, could you please stop interrupting everyone?'

He looked at Katherine again. 'Stay for dinner at least and then you can leave.'

It seemed that she had no choice but to allow herself to be dragged out of the house—it would be churlish to continue refusing not only Alexander's pleas but those of his daughter too. And to be honest, her mouth had started to water when Crystal had been listing the menu. It was a long time since she'd tasted home-cooked Greek food like her mother used to make.

'Yes, then. I'd love to.'

Crystal, victorious, clenched her fist and stabbed her folded elbow backwards. 'Yes-s-s! I'll see you at home, Baba. I'll bring her.'

'Not *her*, Crystal. Dr Burns.'

'Katherine is fine,' Katherine said.

He grinned at her. 'You did bring this on yourself, you know, by being so mysterious and elusive.'

Mysterious? Was that how he saw it? That she was the elusive one? She couldn't help smiling back.

'And you did tell Crystal she could visit. My daughter appears to find you irresistible.'

Her heart plummeted. She preferred *him* to find her irresistible.

The pint-sized tyrant wouldn't even let her stop to put on her sandals, saying severely that she would spoil it all if she tried to put them on too soon.

Alexander's home was set back from the village square and up a steep, narrow path. It was several times larger than hers, with shuttered windows, a cobbled driveway and paths and lush, established grounds. He must have a wonderful view from the wide balconies of his clifftop home.

It took a while for Katherine's eyes to adjust to the dim interior after the bright light and blinding white beach outside. The house was cool, probably because it was shuttered against the heat of the day, although now the shutters were spread wide, allowing a breeze to penetrate the rooms. Despite Crystal hurrying her along, Katherine managed to catch glimpses of her surroundings: engraved, dark wood furniture; colourful striped rugs on polished terracotta tiles; and montages of family photographs, old and new, on white, rough-plastered walls. Crystal swept her into the kitchen where Katherine's senses were assailed with the aromas of garlic, herbs and browning meat.

A plump white-haired woman, bent over the pots steaming on an enormous traditional stove, lifted her head. She smiled warmly at Katherine and addressed her rapidly in Greek.

'Yia-Yia welcomes you and says she's happy you are here, visiting our home,' Crystal translated. 'Please sit at the table.' Without allowing Katherine time to reply, she turned to her grandmother and spoke in Greek, pointing excitedly to Katherine's toes. The older woman leant over and exclaimed. Katherine didn't need to understand any Greek to gather she was praising her great-granddaughter's efforts. Crystal's face said it all.

She had barely sat down before a plate of spanakopita was set down in front of her. Crystal's great-grandmother turned back to her stove, muttering happily.

'Aren't you glad you came?' Crystal said triumphantly. 'Look how pleased she is!'

If the child hadn't been so young, Katherine would have suspected her of engineering the whole situation.

'What's your great-grandmother's name?' Katherine asked.

'Yia-Yia, silly.'

Katherine took a bite of the miniature spinach and

feta pie. She flapped a hand in front of her mouth. 'Hot. *Thermo.* Hot. But wonderful,' she added hastily. Two pairs of dark brown eyes studied her 'No, I mean what should *I* call her?'

'The same as everyone. Yia-Yia. She knows your name. Baba told her. I'm just going to get him!' Crystal said, flying out of the door.

Yia-Yia beckoned Katherine over to where she was working and pointed at the leaves of pastry she had laid out on a baking tray. She brought her fingers to her lips and made a smacking sound. It was clear she was showing Katherine what she was making for supper and that it would be delicious. Katherine could only smile and nod in response.

She was almost relieved when Crystal returned, dragging Alexander in her wake. His hair glistened almost black from his shower and he had changed into a bitter-chocolate T-shirt and cotton jeans. 'Show Baba your toes,' Crystal ordered.

Grimacing to herself, Katherine did as she was asked. She saw the leap of laughter in Alexander's eyes as he dutifully studied her feet. 'Very beautiful,' he said to Katherine, before murmuring so his daughter couldn't hear. 'Do you actually have toes at the ends of those feet? Or should I get the suture kit out again?'

Katherine spluttered with laughter, just managing to turn it into a cough at the last moment. But suddenly Alexander was whooping with laughter and she was too. She couldn't remember the last time she'd laughed like that. Yia-Yia and Crystal looked puzzled for a moment then they were whooping too, Yia-Yia's deep brown eyes almost disappearing in her chubby face.

'What's so funny?' Crystal asked, when everyone stopped laughing.

Alexander tweaked her nose. 'If you don't know, why did you join in?'

'I couldn't help it.' She was hopping from foot to foot. 'I just liked hearing you laugh, Baba.'

The atmosphere in the room changed subtly and the light in Alexander's eyes disappeared, replaced by something Katherine couldn't read.

'If you'll excuse me,' he apologised, 'a neighbour is complaining of a tight chest. It's nothing that staying off cigarettes wouldn't help, but his wife is always happier if I look in on him. I'll be back in a little while.' He turned to his grandmother and spoke to her. She nodded, unsmiling.

'Can I come, Baba?' his daughter asked.

'Of course. You know I always like to have my little helper with me. As long as you stay out of the way and as quiet as a mouse.' He caught Katherine's eye and raised an eyebrow. 'My daughter as quiet as a mouse? Who am I kidding?' he murmured, his lips curving into a smile.

Crystal was out of the door almost before he'd finished speaking.

Once again, Katherine was left alone with Yia-Yia. There was an awkward silence for a moment before the older woman beckoned Katherine to come forward. With a series of hand gestures and nods of the head, she indicated to Katherine that she wanted her help to finish preparing the meal.

'I'm sorry, I can't cook,' Katherine protested. There had never been a need to learn. When her mother had been alive and Katherine had been living at home they'd always eaten at the restaurant. And when she'd moved out and into her first flat she'd taken her main meal at the hospital or had eaten simple salads or pasta for supper. Then, when Mum had become too unwell to be on her own and Katherine had moved back home to look after her, she had fetched Greek delicacies from a nearby restaurant—their own having been sold a couple of years earlier—in an attempt to tempt Mum's failing appetite.

But almost before she'd finished speaking she was being passed a bowl of minced lamb and handed bunches of pungent-smelling herbs. Either Yia-Yia didn't understand what she was saying, or it had never crossed her mind that not all women liked cooking.

In the end it was one of the most peaceful and relaxing hours Katherine could remember spending for a long time. With Crystal's grandmother coaxing her along, while keeping a watchful eye on what she was doing, Katherine stuffed vine leaves and baked rich syrupy cakes. Every now and again the old woman would cluck her tongue and shake her head. At other times she'd nod, murmur something in Greek, and smile approvingly.

When dinner had been prepared to her satisfaction, and Alexander and Crystal still hadn't returned, Yia-Yia took her hand and led her outside to a bench in the garden. For the next ten minutes they sat in peaceful silence as the sun sank in the sky.

After a little while Yia-Yia gestured that they should go back inside. By the time Alexander and Crystal returned, a spread that could have fed eight had been laid out on the dining-room table.

Alexander's dark eyes swept over Katherine and he grinned, making her heart skip a beat. 'Somehow I never quite saw you as being domesticated,' he said.

Catching sight of her reflection in the large mirror on the wall, Katherine realised she was still wearing the flowery apron Grandmother had insisted she put on. Added to her bare feet and splotchy nail polish, she must look ridiculous. Her hair was a mess and clinging to her flushed cheeks. And was that a smudge of flour? Liking to appear neat and tidy at all times, tailored dresses with tights and decent shoes or smart trousers and blouses were what she usually wore. Two weeks in Greece and her colleagues would hardly recognise her. *She* barely recognised herself.

But, oddly, she rather liked the look of the woman in the mirror.

She seemed different from the last time he'd seen her, Alexander thought, studying Katherine from the corner of his eye. But if possible she was even more beautiful. Her blonde hair, bleached white-gold from the sun, had come loose from her plait and damp tendrils curled around her cheeks. A tiny wisp of hair clung to the corner of her mouth and he curled his hands inside the pockets of his jeans to stop himself from reaching out to tug it away. His grandmother's apron and the smudge of flour on her nose only added, somehow, to her allure. But those feet! As he'd said, it looked as if someone had bludgeoned her toes with a hammer.

It had been Yia-Yia and Crystal's idea to invite her for dinner. He'd tried to dissuade them, but his grandmother had insisted that not to, after Katherine had helped him, was not the Greek way. He'd had no choice but to agree. And, whatever he'd told himself, he was glad that she was here.

There was something about Katherine that drew him and despite everything he'd told himself he hadn't been able to stop thinking about her. He wasn't sure what to make of her. Her blue eyes were the colour of the sea at its deepest—more so when sadness overtook her. Was it only the loss of her mother that was causing that look in her eyes? She intrigued him. One minute she'd be the cool professional, like when they'd helped the young man who'd collapsed, the next she'd be blushing at something he'd said or refusing to hold his gaze, ill at ease in his company. And then over dinner she'd seemed to relax. At least until he'd asked her about her private life.

When Helen had found out they'd met and she'd sutured Alexander's hand and they'd spent the day together, her curiosity had known no bounds. That Katherine was also doctor tickled her.

'Perhaps she's like you,' she'd said. 'Maybe she has lost her lover and is here to mend her broken heart.' Helen liked to spin stories, usually romantic ones, about people. 'Yes, it has to be a broken love affair, I'm sure of it.' She'd slid him a mischievous look. 'Perhaps together you can mend your broken hearts.'

Despite himself, he'd laughed. 'You know I'm not interested in getting married again.'

'It's been two years, Alexander. A man like you isn't meant to be on his own. Grandmother won't be around for ever. I have my own life in Athens and as much as I love you both, I can't keep making trips down here every weekend, especially when it means leaving Nico on his own. And once we get married…' She shrugged. 'I won't be able to come so often. Crystal needs a mother. Someone who can be there for her all the time.'

'Crystal has me,' he'd replied tersely. 'No one can ever take Sophia's place.'

Helen was instantly contrite. 'Of course not.' Then she'd smiled again. It was hard for his cousin to stay serious for long. 'Anyway, who's saying anything about marriage?'

Typical Greek women. Always trying to matchmake.

'She is good at cooking,' his grandmother said to him in Greek, drawing him back to the present. 'For an Englishwoman. But she is too skinny. She should eat more.'

He grinned at the older woman. If she had her way they'd all eventually have to join a slimming club. 'I think she looks fine.'

'At least she dresses like a good Greek woman. No shorts up to her bottom like your cousin.'

Under the apron, Katherine was wearing a pair of light cotton trousers and a white blouse, neatly buttoned almost to the neck. No wonder his grandmother approved.

Katherine was looking at him enquiringly and he realised they had been speaking in Greek and excluding her.

'My grandmother says you are a good cook.'

'It's been fun—and informative,' Katherine admitted with a wry smile.

'But why does she seem so sad?' his grandmother continued. 'What does she have to be sad about? She is here in Greece, working in my kitchen, making food, and about to eat a fine meal.'

'Her mother died not so long ago,' he replied.

His grandmother's face softened in distress. She pulled Katherine into her arms and patted her on the back. 'Poor girl,' she said. A bewildered Katherine stared at him over her shoulder and he had to fight not to laugh.

He sobered. 'I told my grandmother that your mother died recently. She is saying she is sorry.'

Katherine gently extricated herself from his grandmother's arms. 'Tell her thank you, but I'm all right.'

'And what about a husband?' Yia-Yia continued. 'Where is he? Has she left him in England?' She clicked her tongue. 'A woman shouldn't leave her husband. Where is her ring?'

'She's not married, Grandmother.'

'And why not? She is old not to be married! Is she one of those modern women who think they don't need husbands? Or is she divorced?' Her mouth turned down at the corners. Grandmother didn't approve of divorce.

'I don't think she's ever been married, Yia-Yia.'

She looked relieved. 'Good. Perhaps she will fall in love with you. Would you like that? I think you like her, no?'

Katherine was watching him, waiting for him to translate, but he was damned if he was going to tell her how interested his grandmother was in her marital status—and her suitability as a partner for him.

'Grandmother is saying she is happy to have you here in her kitchen. She hopes you will come often.'

'Tell her it's lovely to be here.'

To his relief, the business of serving them all dinner prevented further comments from his grandmother. Crystal insisted on sitting next to Katherine, her body pressed so tightly against her Katherine had to find it difficult to eat. Yet she said nothing. She laid down her knife so that she could eat with one hand. Crystal was a friendly child but he'd never known her to form an attachment quite as quickly. It wasn't as if she wasn't surrounded by love.

'So you don't work on weekends?' Katherine asked him. They had taken their coffee onto the balcony. She'd offered to help clear away but his grandmother wouldn't hear of it, insisting it was Crystal's job. Or at least that was what Alexander had told Katherine. Grandmother would have been only too delighted to keep their guest in her kitchen while she cooked some more.

'Carlos—my partner, who you met briefly—and I take turns and we have a colleague who fills in the rest of the time. He retired early so he could spend more time on his thirty-footer, but he likes to keep his hand in.'

'What news about Stéfan?'

'He's still in Intensive Care.'

'But he is going to be okay?'

'I don't know.' He rubbed the back of his neck. 'He's on a ventilator. They think it's a rare type of bacterial meningitis that he has. They're still doing tests.' He stood. 'I'm sorry, but you're going to have to excuse me. It's time for Crystal's bedtime and she likes me to read her a story.'

'Of course. I should get back anyway and do some more work before I turn in.' Her cheeks had flushed. 'Please say good night to Crystal and thank your grandmother for me. I had very pleasant evening.'

'You'll come again?' he asked. She was easy company and he found being with her restful. Actually, who was he kidding? He just liked being with her.

'I don't want to keep intruding,' she said, the colour in her cheeks deepening.

'You're not. Trust me.'

She gave him the ghost of a smile and left.

He watched her pick her way down the steps and into the square. He'd found it difficult to concentrate on his paperwork the last few days. His thoughts kept straying back to her, distracting him. Yes, he thought. She was a distraction—a very enjoyable one—but that was all she would ever be.

CHAPTER FOUR

THE FOLLOWING MORNING, just after dawn had lightened the sky and Katherine had taken her coffee out to the balcony, she noticed that Alexander was back working on his boat. In which case she would work inside, at least until she was sure he'd gone. She'd already had more to do with him than was wise. Relationships, particularly brief flings with attractive Greek doctors still grieving for their wives, had no place on her agenda.

But even as she reminded herself of that, she wondered if she could make an exception. It would be so good to feel someone's arms around her again. Good to have company, good to have someone to share walks and trips with, and who better than a man she would never see again once she'd left here?

She shook her head to chase the thoughts away. She suspected he found her attractive, but that wasn't the same thing as wanting even a casual relationship with her. And just how casual did she want it to be? Unbidden, she imagined him naked, tanned body against white sheets, his hands exploring every inch of her.

She retreated back inside and determinedly fired up her computer. Work. That was what kept her sane. Her paper was what she should be concentrating on.

She edited all day, acutely aware that her attention kept wandering back to Alexander. Just before supper she heard the excited voice of Crystal and, unable to resist a peek, peered out at the bay. He was there again, but this time in the water with his daughter.

She watched as he raised Crystal above his head before tossing her in the air and catching her just before she hit the water. The little girl shrieked with pleasure and wrapped her arms around her father's neck. A few minutes later Alexander, Crystal balanced on his shoulders, waded out of the water, his swimming shorts clinging to narrow hips and lean but muscular thighs.

It wasn't just that she found him sexy as hell. She liked the way he was with his child—clearly she was the centre of his universe and that was the way it should be: a child's happiness should always be paramount. Her chest tightened. What would he think if he knew her secret? Not that she was ever to going to share it with him.

She went into the kitchen and made herself a Greek salad with some of local goat cheese and olives, along with plump, ripe tomatoes she'd bought from the village store. Telling herself it was far too beautiful an evening to eat inside, she took her plate out to the lower veranda. Alexander and Crystal had disappeared, no doubt having gone home to have their evening meal. As the sun sank below the horizon, she sighed. Despite everything she'd told herself, their absence made her feel lonelier than ever.

Alexander excused himself from the game of cards he had been playing and, taking his beer, walked over to the small wall surrounding the village square. Crystal was riding her bike around the fountain in the centre in hot pursuit of the neighbour's boy, her little legs pedalling as fast as they could so she could catch up with him.

Alexander smiled as he watched her. He'd made the right decision, coming back. Crystal was thriving, his grandmother was delighted to have her close by and he was…well, content. As long as his daughter was happy he was too—or as much as he had any right to expect. Sometimes he wondered whether Crystal even remembered Sophia. She spoke of her mother periodically, asking if she were still in heaven and telling him that she knew Mama was watching her from the sky. Occasionally he would show Crystal video footage he'd taken of them on the too-rare occasions he'd taken leave and they'd come here. His daughter would lean forward and watch with shining eyes.

What would Sophia think if she knew he was back in Greece? How would she feel about him giving up his job in London? Would she be pleased that he'd finally, even when it was too late, realised what was important? Would she approve of the way he was bringing up their child? God, he still missed her and, God, he still felt so damned guilty.

He sipped his cold beer and gazed out over the sea. It was then he noticed Katherine. She'd just emerged from the water, her long legs emphasised by the black one-piece costume she was wearing. She dried off then wrapped the towel around her and sat with her back to him, knees pulled up to her chest, staring out at the same sea he was.

Under her prim exterior and natural reserve, there was a loneliness, an aura of something so vulnerable about her he found himself, for the first time since Sophia's death, wanting to know another woman better. But what did he have to offer? He wouldn't, couldn't, get married again. No one could ever match up to Sophia.

He took another gulp of his drink and turned away. Why

had the possibility of getting married again even crossed his mind? The moonlight was making him fanciful. His life was complicated—and full—enough.

Crystal whizzed by him on her bike and waved. Right there was everything that mattered. He glanced at his watch. It was time to get his daughter to bed.

CHAPTER FIVE

As had become a habit, Katherine was sitting outside his house on the bench with Grandmother, after spending a couple of hours cooking with her in the kitchen. She'd closed her eyes to savour the sensation of the breeze on her face, but when Grandmother poked her in her ribs with her elbow she opened them to see that Alexander was coming across the square towards them.

Katherine's heart leaped. Frightened of what he would read in her eyes, she lowered her lids until she was sure she could look at him calmly. She could deal with her developing crush on him as long as he never suspected.

'Hello, you two.' He bent and kissed his grandmother on her cheek and said something to her in Greek that made her laugh. Although Katherine's Greek was improving, when the Greeks spoke to each other it was usually too fast for her to follow.

Alexander grinned at Katherine. 'I've just asked her what she's thinking of, sitting down when dinner's due. She says now she has you to help her, sometimes she can take time off to enjoy the Greek sunshine.'

Nevertheless, the old woman got to her feet and retreated back inside, leaving her space on the bench for Alexander. He took a seat next to Katherine and, like she'd been doing earlier, turned his face up to the sun and closed his eyes. 'My grandmother is right. We all need to sit in the sun more often,' he murmured.

His usual vitality seemed to have deserted him and he looked tired.

'Is everything all right?' she asked.

'No, not really. Stéfan—the man with meningitis—died last night.'

'I'm so sorry. I really hoped he would be okay.'

He opened his eyes and turned to face Katherine. 'So did I, but once he developed multi-organ failure...' He paused. 'We've asked for a post-mortem but, according to the pathologist, it might be another week before they can do it. They have a bit of a backlog as his colleague is off on leave.' He rubbed the back of his neck and frowned. 'I was speaking to one of my colleagues in the area today and he tells me he's had a case too—a couple of days ago, a teenager. He's been admitted to a hospital in Athens.'

Katherine's antenna went on red alert. 'Two cases in a week? Doesn't that strike you as odd?'

'He isn't sure his patient has meningitis. He's going to call me as soon as he has the results of the lumbar puncture. But I'd be surprised if they both have it. As far as I'm aware, meningitis normally affects similar age groups.'

'Usually, but not always. It depends on the strain.'

'We'll find out soon enough. They're giving his patient's family antibiotics prophylactically to be on the safe side.'

'Sensible,' Katherine murmured. However, if Alexander's colleague's patient did turn out to have meningitis, it could be the start of something. Something terrifying.

'Any others you're aware of?' she asked.

'I rang around a few of the practices in the area, but no one else has come across any. I've told them to let me know if they do. I'm hoping these two will turn out to be random, unrelated events—supposing David, the teenage boy, does have it and, as I said, that isn't at all certain.'

He could be right, but there was a way she could find out.

She heard Grandmother calling Alexander from inside and got to her feet. 'Sounds like you're wanted.'

'I thought you'd want to know about Stéfan,' he said, rising too 'After I check in with Yia-Yia, I'm going to see the family of one of my other patients who I admitted to hospital after I diagnosed her with a nasty chest infection.' He smiled wryly. 'It's one of the privileges, but also one of the responsibilities, of being in general practice in Greece. Any member of a family becomes unwell and the rest expect you to see them through it as well. And that usually involves late-night tea and cakes and much discussion.'

Although she was disappointed he was going, the care he took of his patients was one of the things she liked about him. Besides, she wanted to do some checking up of her own.

She hurried back to her house. It was after six in the UK but Tim was divorced and rarely left work until much later.

She dialled the number of the office and was pleased when he picked up straight away. After exchanging small talk for a few moments—yes, she was enjoying her break and, yes, she would be coming back to work as planned at the end of September—she repeated what Alexander had told her.

'I've got a feeling about this,' she said. 'Is there any chance you could speak to your opposite number in Athens and ask him if there have been any more cases reported? I realise I'm probably being over-cautious but it wouldn't hurt to find out.'

'I doubt there will be anyone still there at this time. Will the morning do?'

'It will have to. As I said, it's probably nothing but it's best to be on the safe side. Thanks, Tim.'

He called her back on her mobile just before nine the next morning and came straight to the point.

'You were right,' he said. 'I've spoken to my opposite number in Athens and he tells me there have been reports of ten cases in and around the southern Peloponnese, including the two you mentioned. One or two would mean nothing but ten! It certainly suggests there is something to be concerned about.'

Excitement surged through Katherine. Her instinct had been right! 'What ages?'

'It varies. From teenagers to young adults. As you'd expect, it is the youngest who are most seriously affected. One child—a lad of seventeen—is in Intensive Care in Athens and it's not looking good.'

'The boy in Intensive Care—what's his name?'

'David Panagaris.'

Was he the same lad Alexander had told her about? It seemed likely. Her heart was racing. This is what she was trained to do. 'I could look into it. Could you let the department in Athens know I'm here and would like to help?'

'Absolutely not,' Tim protested. 'You're on holiday. They must have someone local they can call on. It's not as if Greece doesn't have public health doctors of their own.'

'Of course they do, but I happen to be here and I'm an expert in the spread of infectious diseases. I'm probably the most up-to-date person in Europe at the moment and you and I both know it's all much more co-operative now than it used to be. Come on, Tim, you know it makes sense.'

There was a long pause at the end of the phone. 'I guess

it does makes sense,' Tim said reluctantly. 'But is your Greek good enough to ensure you ask the right questions and, more importantly, get the right answers?'

It wasn't. But Alexander's was. 'What about the Greek doctor I mentioned? The one who alerted me to the possibility of an outbreak? If he's prepared to take time out to help me, that would solve the problem of my not being fluent in Greek.' She wasn't really sure she wanted to work with Alexander. It was bad enough catching tantalising glimpses of him most days, without being thrust into his company all the time. But she wanted to do this and she couldn't without Alexander's help. 'I'll need to ask him, of course, but I've no doubt he'll say yes.'

'Okay,' Tim conceded. 'I'll suggest it to my colleague.' Katherine released a breath. 'What more info do you have?'

'In addition to the boy admitted to Intensive Care in Athens, there have been two deaths over the last ten days— your man and a woman tourist from France in her teens. Her family have already repatriated her body. No obvious links between the deceased as yet.'

Her excitement drained away. Three families had lost a loved one or were in danger of doing so. And if there was an epidemic, and there seemed little doubt that was what they could be dealing with, if they didn't locate all those who had come into contact with the sufferers and treat them, more people could die. In addition, they needed to find out where it was coming from so they could reach people before they became unwell.

'Could you give me the names and addresses of the patients? Plus the names of their family doctors, or the doctors who treated them?'

'I'll email them to you straight away.'

As soon as she disconnected, she phoned Alexander's surgery only to discover he wasn't expected in until later. She flung on some clothes and, without stopping for breakfast, set off across the square to Alexander's home, praying he'd be there and not out on a visit.

The sun was already blazing down and she was perspiring by the time she reached his door. She found Grandmother in the kitchen, making bread.

'Morning,' Katherine said in Greek. 'I need to speak to Alexander. Is he here?' She didn't have time for the usual pleasantries today.

Alexander's grandmother frowned, wiped her hands on a tea towel and shook her head. '*Nè*. At work.'

'Hello.' It was Crystal, looking sleepy in pyjamas and holding a teddy bear. She said something to her grandmother in Greek and went to stand next to Katherine, slipping her hand into hers. 'Yia-Yia says you're looking for Baba. She says he's gone to his consulting room in the village.' Grandmother had lifted a pot of tea and was holding it up. 'She wants to know if you'd like some tea. And some breakfast? She's just made some.'

'Please thank her for me and say I'd love to stay but I really need to see your father. It's urgent.'

The child relayed it back to to her grandmother, who looked disappointed she'd have no one to feed.

'Is something the matter?' Crystal asked.

'No.' Katherine crouched down and ruffled Crystal's hair. 'At least, nothing for you to worry about. I promise.'

Leaving the house, she headed back down the flight of steps and along the street to the rooms Alexander used as a surgery for the locals.

She tapped on the door of Alex's room and, without waiting for a reply, let herself in. He was sitting at the desk, his chair turned to face the window so that he had his back to her. He swivelled around to face her.

'I'm sorry,' he said. 'This isn't a good time.'

'I heard,' she said softly.

He frowned. 'Heard what?'

'About David Panagaris, that is the name of your colleague's patient, isn't it?' When Alexander nodded, she continued. 'I thought it must be him. I gather he's in Intensive Care. I'm sorry.' Without waiting to be asked, she took the seat opposite him.

'Poor bloody parents. Perhaps if they'd brought him in sooner—' He broke off. 'How did you know he'd deteriorated? He was only admitted to Intensive Care last night.'

'My boss phoned me—I phoned him first. Let me explain.'

Alexander said nothing but leaned forward, placing his folded hands on the desk. He looked even more bushed than he had yesterday. There were dark circles under his eyes and underneath the tan he was drawn and pale. She wondered if he'd been up all night.

'As you know, my thesis for my doctorate is on meningitis and other bacterial infections—its spread and containment. That sort of thing. Our unit is one of the biggest in Europe but we have strong ties with others units across the world. We share information on all matters of public health, especially on infectious diseases. Over the last few years increasing numbers of countries across the world have bought into this collaborative approach. It makes sense to pool our resources rather than compete with one another. Africa, for example, has much better information on the spread of malaria, and so on…'

He nodded impatiently.

'When you told me about your cases it rang alarm bells

so I phoned my boss and asked him to contact the public health department in Athens. Apparently, apart from Stéfan and David, there have been eight other cases all in, or around, this area, including another death—a young French girl' She held out her phone. 'My boss has emailed me a list with all their names.'

'Eight other cases?' Alexander looked instantly alert, all traces of his earlier tiredness having disappeared. 'So there is an epidemic?'

'It appears so. The thing is, I've offered to take the lead in looking into the situation. But I'm going to need help. My Greek isn't good enough for me to do it on my own.'

He narrowed his eyes. 'You want me to help?'

'Yes,' she said simply.

'Of course,' he said with no hesitation. 'I'll need to arrange for Dr Kanavakis—my retired colleague—to cover for me, but I don't think that will be a problem. When do we start?'

'Now.'

He raised his eyebrows. 'Let me make that phone call, then.'

When he'd finished he turned back to Katherine. 'Cover's sorted. Now, what else do you know about the cases?'

'Very little. I have the names and addresses of all the patients. Most live in the southern part of Greece. Two come from Nafplio or very nearby. The French girl was on holiday there.'

He leaned back in his chair. 'Hell, that isn't good. A lot of cruise ships come into Nafplio. That will make tracing contacts more difficult.'

She checked the names on her phone. While Alexander had been on the phone she'd downloaded them into a document. 'What else can you tell me about David?'

'His parents live in a village close to Messini. He'd been snuffly and lethargic for most of the morning. They thought it was a cold, but when he deteriorated they brought him in to see my colleague. Unfortunately, he was already showing signs of septicaemia. He was given intravenous antibiotics and they arranged for an immediate transfer to hospital, but he was already in a bad way.' He raked a hand through his hair. 'He's only young.'

He jumped up and started pacing. 'If we do have an epidemic on our hands, none of the children will be safe.' He stopped in front of her. 'Come on. Let's go to the hospital. I'll let his doctor know what's happening. We need to find where the victims have been and who they've been in contact with.' He paused. 'Unless we should split up? You go to see the relatives of the other cases while I go to the hospital?'

'No,' she said, putting her hand on his arm. 'As I said, I might be the expert and know the questions to ask, but you can speak Greek and you're a local doctor. They'll find it more comfortable to talk to you and they might tell you things they wouldn't tell me. You'll also be able to pick up better than I if they are leaving out information that might be important. But what we should do is make sure the health services in Athens have put all the local family practices on alert, as well as warning the general public. Doctors and parents are more likely to be vigilant if they know what to look out for.'

'I'll speak to them, of course. What is the name of your contact there?'

Even before he put the phone down she could see the conversation hadn't gone the way he wanted. His voice had risen towards the end and he appeared to be arguing with whoever was on the other end. A muscle twitched in his cheek.

'They say they've warned the hospitals and practices to watch out for cases of meningitis but they won't put out a full alert on the radio or in the press. They say that if they do, people will panic and rush to the hospitals. They say the medical services will collapse under the strain and it's too early to take the risk.'

'I could phone my boss and get him to put pressure on them,' Katherine suggested. 'Although I suspect they'd do the same in the UK.'

'Be my guest.' He gestured to the phone. 'I doubt it would do any good. They're unlikely to do anything more until there are more cases. They insist the ones we know about might just be random at the moment—a blip, not connected at all.'

'It is possible,' Katherine said thoughtfully. 'We've noted and recorded many cases of infectious diseases in the past that seemed to be part of an epidemic but that turned out not to be. I think we should talk to the Stéfan's parents before we do anything else. As soon as I get the French girl's parents' contact details I'll call them.'

'Fine with me,' he said, picking up his medical bag. 'And I hope to God you're right about these cases not being connected. Stéfan's family is from a village near Sparta. We could go to the hospital in Athens from there.' He took his mobile from his pocket. 'I'll phone Carlos and let him know what's happening.'

The road leading to Sparta was the worst Katherine had ever been on. Travelling through and over the mountains, it was narrow, with barely enough room for two cars to pass safely. In addition, every few miles the road almost spun back on itself through a number of hairpin bends. She could barely bring herself to look. On her side of the car, the road fell away sharply and there were no road barriers to prevent the car, should it have to swerve to avoid oncoming vehicles, toppling over the side. Incredibly, the road conditions didn't stop drivers from overtaking, whether they could see or not.

'What's Crystal up to today?' she asked, trying to unclench her fists.

'She's having a sleepover with a friend a little way up the coast. Her friend's mother is coming to fetch her.'

'Could you slow down?' Katherine yelped, after they took a particularly sharp bend that she'd thought they'd never make.

Alexander turned to face her and grinned.

'If I slow down, it will only encourage other drivers to try and overtake us. They don't care whether the road is empty or not.'

'Please keep your eyes on the road at least.'

Despite her terror and worry about what they would be facing soon, she couldn't help admire the scenery as they whizzed along. Little villages clung to the side of the mountain, the houses often appearing to spill almost onto the road. Small cafés with old men outside, puffing on pipes or playing board games flew by in a blur. To her consternation, Alexander would often take his hand off the steering-wheel to give them a friendly wave as they passed.

At other times, almost out of nowhere, they'd come upon small farm stalls selling flowers or tomatoes or other freshly grown produce from the roadside. At any other time she might have enjoyed the trip and promised herself that once this emergency was over she'd come back—with her own car, of course—and savour the journey.

As she relaxed a little, her thoughts returned to the task in hand. She unfolded the map she'd brought with her and circled each victim's location with her pen. All of them lived in the Peloponnese, apart from the French girl, who had been on holiday there. Nevertheless, it was still a huge area.

'Is there any facility or event you know of that links the victims?' she asked Alexander.

He waited until he'd slowed down to let an overtaking car coming in the opposite direction pass before he spoke. 'None that I can think of. I'd have to study the map. I don't really keep on top of social events these days.'

A short time later, to Katherine's relief, they turned off the mountain road and towards Sparta and the road became wider and straighter.

'The village is about thirty kilometres northwest of Sparta,' Alexander said. 'We should be there in about twenty minutes.'

Katherine's stomach churned. In a short while she'd be facing two very recently bereaved parents and she wasn't looking forward to it.

'What's Sparta like?' she asked, more to distract herself than out of any burning interest.

'Little of the original city remains. Most of the what you'll see as we pass through has been built on top of ancient Sparta.' He glanced at her. 'You know the stories of the Spartans?'

'Only that they were tough and didn't believe in creature comforts.'

'It's grimmer than that. Under a system known as the *agoge* Spartan boys were trained to be as physically tough as possible. They were taken from their families at the age of seven and made to live in barracks. They were deliberately underfed so they'd become adept at living off the land. The boy babies who weren't expected to make the grade were taken to the top of the mountain and left there to die.'

Katherine shuddered. 'Their poor mothers.'

'It was cruel. I can't imagine how they felt, having their sons ripped from their arms. I suspect some ran away with them, even though they risked death to save them.' He blinked. 'It's what Sophia would have done. She'd never let anything part her from her child.'

Katherine's heart lurched. What would he think if he knew what she'd done? She was glad he would never know.

'You should try to visit Mycenae, though,' he continued, apparently unaware of her reaction. 'It's almost intact. It's very close to Sparta—only a few kilometres at the most. It has a less bloody past.'

'Have you been there?' Her throat was so tight she could barely speak.

He glanced at her and smiled. 'Naturally.'

They turned off onto a minor road and continued. It was much flatter here, the land planted with olive trees and vines. But then they turned a corner, drove up a street so narrow it would be impossible for another car to pass, and into a small village square.

Now they were here, her anxiety about facing the bereaved parents returned.

'Are you all right about doing this?' Alexander asked.

'Yes.' She would be. She had to think of the children whose lives they would save rather than the one who was lost.

They parked the car and asked directions from an older man sweeping the square. He laid aside his brush and gestured for them to follow him. It was just as well because although the village was small, it was unlikely they would have found their way to the house, tucked away as it was behind a crumbling wall and almost hidden down one of the maze-like streets.

The house itself, like many of the others in the village, seemed to be built into the rock face.

A woman in a navy-blue long-sleeved dress answered their knock and after Alexander explained who they were, stepped aside to let them in.

Stéfan's parents were sitting in a darkened room surrounded by family and friends. They clung to each other and Katherine winced at the grief she saw etched on their faces.

This, she thought, was why she was an academic. Facing other people's pain, when she found it impossible to deal with her own, was something she'd spent most of her adult life trying to avoid. But she couldn't afford to be squeamish—or the luxury of dwelling on her own discomfort. However much she hated to intrude on their grief, she knew it was necessary.

Alexander introduced them again and very gently explained why they were there. 'I know this is a very difficult time for you, but we need to ask you some questions.'

Mr Popalopadous nodded. His wife seemed incapable of speaking. 'Please,' he said, 'ask your questions. If we can stop this happening to someone else's child...'

Katherine sat down and took Mrs Popalopadous's hands in hers. 'We need to know Stéfan's last movements—where he'd been before he became unwell and who he'd been in contact with.'

She looked bewildered. 'He was a teacher in the local school, but during the holidays he takes—took his boat out or went to the taverna with his friends. None of them are sick.'

Katherine exchanged a look with Alexander. None of them were sick *yet*.

'Should we quarantine the village?' Alexander murmured to her.

She shook her head slightly. 'Not yet.' She knew there was no point in getting ahead of themselves. What they had to do was retrace Stéfan's movements going back at least a week to establish who had come into contact with him. After that they needed to get in touch with those people where possible and make sure they—and anyone who had spent more than a few hours in their company—were given antibiotics.

When Mrs Popalopadous started sobbing again, Katherine leaned forward. 'I know it's difficult, but can you think of anyone apart from his friends or his pupils he might have been in contact with?' She ignored the warning look Alexander gave her. She wasn't unsympathetic to Mrs Popalopadous's grief but what mattered most now was that no one else would die.

Mr Popalopadous answered for his wife. 'No. No one different.' He wrapped his arm around his wife's shoulders. 'Now, I'm afraid you must leave us. We have arrangements to make.'

His dignity in the face of his grief was humbling. But Katherine wanted to press him further. However, Alexander got to his feet and taking her by the elbow forced her to rise to hers too. He scribbled something on a piece of paper and handed it to the bereaved father. saying something in Greek Katherine couldn't follow.

His hand still on her elbow, Alexander ushered Katherine out of the house and to his car.

'I still had questions for them,' she protested.

'For God's sake, Katherine, they've just lost their child. They've told us all they can.

'You can't be sure of that. It's the things they don't think that are important that might matter most.'

'I gave him my mobile number and asked him to call me, day or night, if anything else does come to mind. I also told them to go to their family doctor and make sure they, and anyone else who might have been in contact with Stéfan, gets antibiotics. I'll call the family doctor to make sure they do—although I'm sure he'll have it in hand,'

'It won't hurt to make sure.' Katherine replied.

After he'd made the call, Alexander turned to her. 'As I thought, he plans to see them later this afternoon. As you can imagine, he's pretty keen that we get on top of this.' He frowned. 'The most likely source of the infection is the high school.'

'But not the only possibility!'

'No, but isn't it better to go with the most likely and work our way out from there?'

He did have a point. 'Perhaps once we've interviewed the other families something will jump out. In the meantime, I'd better get onto my boss and tell him to make double sure that all the medical facilities in the area are on red alert.'

'Shouldn't we do that?' Alexander asked.

'It's more important that we try and locate the source of the outbreak. My boss will liaise with your public heath team in Athens, although we should probably introduce ourselves at some point.'

They got into the car and Alexander turned the key in the ignition. 'Okay. Next stop Athens.'

'How long will it take us to get there?'

'About two and half hours. Less if you stop interfering in the way I drive.'

Katherine gritted her teeth. 'Just get there as soon as you can.'

Happily, it was a far better road to Athens than the one they'd come on. While they were driving, Katherine phoned the French girl's parents. Luckily her French was considerably better than her Greek. But that didn't make the conversation any less painful. Claire's father held himself together long enough to tell Katherine that Claire had been on a short break with her boyfriend in Greece when she'd become unwell. It had all been very sudden—too sudden for the family to make it to her bedside in time. There had been a long pause in the conversation when Claire's father had lost control, but eventually he had, for long enough at any rate to tell her that their family doctor had treated the family and the boyfriend with antibiotics. Katherine repeated what she'd learned to Alexander and they'd sat in silence, each absorbed with their own thoughts. She wondered if Alexander was thinking, like she was, how devastating it was to lose someone you loved—especially when that person was young—like Claire—or Sophia. When, a while later, Katherine's stomach growled she realised she hadn't eaten since breakfast and Alexander would be in the same position.

'I don't know about you but I'm starving,' she admitted.

'Would you like to stop at one of the tavernas?' he asked.

'I'd prefer not to take too long over lunch. I'm keen to talk to David's family.'

'I know a place near here that does pastries and decent coffee. We could pick something up and get back on our way.'

She was pleased he was in just as much of a hurry to get to the hospital as she was. She didn't think she could have beared to have stopped at a café and had a proper lunch, especially when she'd learned that in Greece there was no such thing as fast food served in a restaurant. While most times she appreciated the care they put into their cooking, today wasn't one of them.

When they stopped, she bought some bread rolls and cheese while Alexander downed a couple of cups of espresso in quick succession. She didn't care for the heavy, thick Greek coffee so she bought some fresh orange juice to go with their picnic lunch instead.

She took a few moments to split open the rolls and fill them. Alexander pulled a penknife from his pocket and offered it to her, and she quickly sliced the tomatoes and added them to the cheese. Once she'd done that she handed one of the rolls to Alexander. When she next looked up it was gone. He had to have wolfed it down in a couple of bites.

'Should I get some more?' she asked, astonished.

'No, that will do me for the time being. Shall we get on?'

She wrapped her half-eaten sandwich in a napkin. 'Suits me. I can finish this in the car.'

After they'd been driving for a while she asked, 'How long before we get there?'

He glanced at his watch. 'Another hour.'

She did some calculations in her head. An hour to get there, a couple more at the hospital and then what? A three or a three-and-a-half-hour journey back. They'd be lucky to reach home before midnight and they still had the other families to see.

However, it seemed he was there before her. 'I phoned a colleague while you were in the ladies. He's agreed to contact the doctors on our list and ask the families some preliminary questions. He said he'd call me back as soon as he had some information for us.'

Although Katherine would have preferred to have made the calls herself, she knew that Alexander had made the right decision. Every minute could make a difference— a life-changing difference—for one patient and his, or her, family.

Finally they arrived in Athens. After the peace of the countryside Katherine found the noise of tooting horns and the fumes of the cars that crept along the roads nose to tail almost overwhelming. She craned her neck to see the Acropolis, which dominated the city. It was on her list of places to visit but, like the rest of her plans, it would have to wait.

She was glad Alexander was with her to negotiate his way around the hospital. Although her spoken Greek wasn't too bad now, reading it was a completely different matter and despite many of the signposts being in English, it was still a busy and confusing hospital.

They made their way to the intensive care unit and she listened as Alexander explained to the doctor why they were there. Then he asked for an update on the patient.

'David is holding his own,' he said. 'But the septicaemia means we might have to amputate his hand. We have a theatre on standby.'

Oh, no! The boy was so young to be facing such drastic surgery. His parents must be beside themselves. And indeed, it seemed that they were too distraught to speak to them. The doctor apologised and suggested they come back in the morning when David's condition might have stabilised and the parents be more willing to see them.

'It can't wait,' Katherine protested. 'We have to find out where he's been and who he came into contact with. His family are the only people who can tell us.'

Once more, Alexander took her by the arm and led her away and out of earshot of the doctor.

'For God's sake, Katherine. Their child may be about to go into Theatre. Could you talk to anyone if you were in their position? I'm not sure I could.'

She knew why he was saying that, but she also knew that in circumstances such as these they couldn't afford the luxury of waiting.

'I know it's a bad time, but we need information as quickly as possible.'

'It can wait.'

'No, it can't.' She held his gaze. 'No it can't,' she repeated more softly. 'If you won't talk to them, I'll have to.'

He rubbed a hand across the back of his neck in what, she was beginning to realise, was a habit of his when he was thinking.

'Look, why don't I try to find another, less distressed family member to talk to? There's bound to be at least one here at the hospital—if I'm not mistaken most of the extended family will have gathered by now.'

'Fair enough,' Katherine conceded. 'But if they can't help I'm going to have to insist on speaking to David's parents.'

He nodded and Katherine was left kicking her heels while Alexander went in search of the extended family. While she waited she opened up her laptop and started creating a database. Then she reviewed what they'd learned so far—which wasn't much. They still didn't know what the cases had in common or how they might have come into contact with the virus. It was almost two hours before Alexander reappeared. He looked tired and in need of a shave.

'They decided they had to take David to Theatre and they've just taken him through to Recovery. They had to amputate the fingers on his left hand. Thank God he's right-handed.'

'I'm sorry,' she said. 'But it could have been so much worse.' She waited a few moments. 'Did you find out anything that might help?'

'Not really. I found his aunt, who lives next door to her sister. According to her, apart from school, a party and a trip to the beach he's not been anywhere out of the usual.' He held out a piece of paper. 'She's given me the names of the other kids at the party. None of them are the other victims, though.'

'They might be yet,' she said. 'We need to make sure everyone on that list and their doctors are contacted.'

'I telephoned Diane while I was waiting to hear how David got on in Theatre. She promised to get onto it straight away.'

She was impressed. She'd been right. Alexander was the perfect person to help with the crises.

'What about the other GP? The one you called—has he got back to you?'

'He phoned a few minutes ago. He's spoken to all the doctors, who have agreed to do as we requested.'

Alexander stepped forward and brushed a lock of her hair away from her forehead. The unexpected and tender gesture made her heart tighten. 'We've done all we can for the moment,' he said gently. 'Let's go home. We can discuss what we're going to do next on the way.'

* * *

On the way back. Alexander pulled off the main road. Katherine looked at him, surprised. 'Where are we going?'

'Neither of us have eaten since the rolls we had for lunch. I don't know about you but my brain doesn't work unless it's kept fuelled.'

Katherine had to agree. Now that he'd mentioned food she realised she was ravenous.

A short while later he stopped at a small taverna with tables set out on a veranda upstairs. Despite the hour, and its location, it was thronged with people enjoying meals and drinks in the cool evening breeze of the mountains. Alexander led her over to a table away from the other diners. The view was spectacular. In the crevasses of the mountain hundreds of lights glittered a snaking path downwards towards the sea. When the waitress came Alexander raised his eyebrow in Katherine's direction.

'You order,' she said, reading his meaning. 'I don't care what I eat as long as it's filling.'

Alexander rattled off something in Greek so rapidly she couldn't follow. While he did so she studied him from under her lashes. His earlier tiredness seemed to have disappeared and his usual energy was back. Although she was exhausted, she felt it too. Perhaps it was the urgency of the situation, the need to find answers that was making them both restless.

'So, what next?' Alexander asked, after the waiter had placed their meals in front of them. He'd ordered moussaka and a Greek salad to share. She speared a chunk of tomato on her fork and popped it into her mouth. Delicious.

'We should check in with Public Health in Athens and see if any more cases have been reported.' She laid her fork down, rummaged in her bag, pulled out her mini-laptop and fired it up. 'While you were in with David's parents I made some notes.' She moved it so he could see the screen.

'I've made a table. In the first column I've put the patient's name, the second has the date when they first came to the attention of the medical services and the third has a list of immediate family and friends and anyone else we know of who might have come into contact with them. It's not complete yet—there's bound to be names missing. Next to each name on the list is a column indicating whether they have been given prophylactic antibiotics. The last column is for places they have been in the last couple of weeks and will include swimming clubs, parties, et cetera. By creating a database I can sort the information any way I want. Sooner or later I'm hoping a common link will leap out. In the meantime, I've emailed a copy to my opposite number in Athens.'

Alexander looked impressed. 'You did all that? In, what? A couple of hours. Less.'

Warmth spread through her. Her reaction to him confused her. She couldn't remember a time when she'd felt more at ease in someone's company, yet at the same time her heart raced all the time she was with him.

'It's what I've been trained to do. If I were back at the hospital I'd have access to much more sophisticated programs to do it. On the other hand, entering the data myself helps me to understand it.'

He frowned. 'Is that what they've become? Data?'

'Of course they're not simply data,' Katherine retorted, stung. 'I'm a doctor but also a scientist. Trust me, this is the best way to approach this. Getting too close to individual patients can hinder a person when it comes to seeing patterns.' Hurt, she lowered her glass and pushed her half-eaten meal away. Her appetite had deserted her. 'Give me a moment, will you?' And without waiting for a reply, she stalked away.

Hearing footsteps behind her, Katherine turned. Somehow she wasn't surprised to find Alexander standing behind her.

'Aren't you cold?' he said softly.

'No. It's a perfect evening,' she murmured.

'May I join you?' he asked. When she nodded, he sat down next to her. She could smell his aftershave, almost feel the heat radiating from his body.

'I'm sorry,' he said. 'That was a stupid thing to say. I know you don't see the patients as data.' He grinned sheepishly. 'I'm perfectly aware that underneath the scientist façade beats a soft heart.' He placed a hand over hers. 'Will you forgive me?'

Her heart started pounding so hard she could barely breathe. What was it about him that made her feel that a whole world of possibility lay out there somewhere? She'd accepted that she would remain alone for the rest of her life, which, apart from the sorrow of her parents' deaths and a deep regret about the life she might have had had she made different choices, was a happy one. Then why did she feel she'd been fooling herself all this time?

'What are those lights out at sea?' she asked, to break the tension.

'It's the fishermen. A lot of them like to fish at night.'

'What about you? Is that what you use your boat for? I don't think I've ever seen you go out in it.'

He smiled. 'I've been waiting until I finished repainting it. But normally I go out in it whenever I can. Not just for fishing. I use it to island-hop sometimes. I like taking care of it. It belonged to my father once.' After a pause he continued, his voice soft and reflective. 'When I was a kid and we came to Greece on holiday I used to go out fishing at night with my uncle. Once he wouldn't take me—I forget the reason why. Perhaps he had other plans—but I wanted to go. There was a full moon and only a slight wind—perfect fishing weather. So I waited until everyone was asleep, then I crept out and launched my boat.'

She smiled, imagining the scene. 'Did you catch anything?'

'Tons. There were so many fish I forgot to think about where the boat was, and didn't notice it was drifting. When I looked up I couldn't see the lights on the shore any more.'

'What did you do?'

'I don't know what I was more scared of,' he said, 'being dragged out to the middle of the sea or my father's wrath when he found out I'd been out on my own. I knew the stars pretty well.' He pointed to the sky. 'I knew if I followed the right star it would guide me back to shore. Maybe not here exactly but to somewhere where I could walk or hitch a lift home.'

'And did you?'

'There was only one problem. When I realised I had lost sight of the shore, I jumped to my feet and lost an oar overboard.'

'That must have been a bit of a pain.'

He laughed. 'It was. I tried using the one oar, paddling from one side then the other, but I soon realised that, given the zig-zagging course I was making, it would take days, not hours, to reach the shore. I nearly gave up then. I could have stayed where I was. They would have sent out boats to find me once they discovered I was missing.'

'It's a big sea.'

'And even bigger when you're out there on your own.'

'Were you scared?'

'The thing was, except for the first scary moment, I wasn't. I knew my father would move heaven and earth to find me. I knew whether it took him the rest of his life, whether he had to spend every drachma he had to employ helicopters and search boats to find me, he would.'

'He must have loved you very much.'

'More than life itself.' He turned his head to look at her. 'A parent's love is the strongest love of all. It's only when you have a child yourself that you realise that.'

His words were like a knife straight to her heart. She clasped her hands together and squeezed. He couldn't know how much they hurt her.

'Is that what happened? Did he call the emergency services out?' She was relieved to find her voice sounded normal—cool even.

'No. Thank God he didn't have to. Despite my years in England, I was a Greek boy brought up on legends and myths about Greek heroes. There was no chance I was going to wait for him to come searching for me. I would have died rather than sit there waiting meekly for rescue.' Although he sounded indignant, she could hear the laughter in his voice.

'So, what *did* you do?'

'I decided to try and swim back.'

She laughed. 'You're kidding!'

'It was madness. I know that now, but back then it was all I could think of doing. However I couldn't leave the boat to float out to sea. It was my father's pride and joy. So I threw the fish back. It almost killed me. A whole night's work and the best catch I'd ever had! I jumped out of the boat and, keeping hold of the rope, I swam back to shore.'

'You could have drowned.'

'I knew as long as I kept hold of the boat, I'd be all right. And it worked. It took me a bloody long time but I made it into a small bay just as the sun was coming up. But I still had to get the damned boat back to its proper mooring. So I nicked one of the oars from a boat that was in the bay and rowed home. I've never rowed as fast in all my life. I was determined to get home before my father noticed I was gone.'

'And did you?'

He smiled ruefully. 'Now, that was the thing. I did. At least I thought I did. I crept into bed and a few moments later I heard my father get up. I was pretty pleased with myself, I can tell you. But later, when I went down to the boat again just to check there wasn't any evidence of my night-time excursion, the oar I had pinched was missing and there, in its place, was a brand-new one.' He sighed.

'He must have known what I was up to all along. I bet he was sitting on the wall all night, waiting for me to come home. When he knew I was safe he must have hurried back to bed, and then, when he was sure I was asleep, gone down to check on the boat. Of course, he would have seen instantly that one of the oars had come from another boat and so he made a new one. And you know…' he paused and looked out to sea '…he never once mentioned it. Not ever.'

They sat in silence for a while. 'It sounds as if you have always been surrounded by your family's love. No wonder Crystal is such a happy little girl.'

He looked into the distance. 'I've been lucky, I guess, in so many ways. But the gods like to even the score.' He could only be talking about his wife.

'What about you?' he continued. 'Did you have a happy childhood too?'

Perhaps it was his Greek upbringing that made him talk

like this? Most British men she knew would rather die a hundred deaths then talk about their feelings. Or perhaps it was the night—perhaps everyone found it easier to talk under the cover of darkness.

'Of course my parents loved me. It's just that I think I disappointed them.' The words were out before she knew it.

'Disappointed them? The dedicated, bursary-winning scholar? Did you go off the rails or something when you were a teenager?' He shook his head. 'No, I can't see it. I bet you were head girl.'

Going off the rails was one way of putting it. Off track for a while was perhaps closer to the truth.

She shook her head. 'I was never that popular. Far too studious and serious. I was a prefect, though.'

'There. I was right. And then you went to medical school and here you are about to submit your thesis for your doctorate and one of Europe's top specialists in the spread of infectious diseases. What is there not to be proud of?'

Judging by the teasing note in his voice, he couldn't have known how close to the bone he had come with his questions. She scrambled to her feet. 'I am getting a little cold. I think it's time we went on our way.'

Later that night, she lay in bed listening to the gentle rush of the waves on the shore and thinking about what Alexander had said. She'd tried so hard to make her parents proud, and to an extent she had. Her mother had told anyone who'd listen, sometimes complete strangers, that her daughter was a doctor. In fact, to hear her mother speak you'd think that her daughter was single-handedly responsible for the health of the nation. But what she had wanted most of all, a grandchild she could fuss over, Katherine hadn't given her.

Throwing the covers aside, she went out to the balcony. Alexander was making her think about stuff she didn't want to think about, like loss, and families—and love.

Love. What would it like to be loved by Alexander? It hit her then—she wasn't just attracted to him, she was falling in love with him.

Of all men, why did it have to be him? He was still in love with his wife, that much was obvious. And even if he wasn't, his life was here in Greece and she'd be returning to the UK to pick up hers. But worst of all, if he knew her secret he would despise her. He would never understand why she'd done what she had.

She returned to the sitting room and flicked through the playlist on her iPod. She inserted it into the speakers she had brought with her and as the sound of Brahms filled the room she sat on the sofa and closed her eyes.

What was it with him and this woman? Alexander thought as he stared at the stars from his bedroom window. Why couldn't he stop thinking about her? It wasn't as if he had any intention of having a relationship with her. No one would ever take Sophia's place. Katherine would be returning to the UK soon and he couldn't follow her, she was as much married to her work as he was—there were a hundred different reasons.

Yet he couldn't fool himself any longer that he wasn't strongly attracted to her. Perhaps because he saw his own sadness reflected in her eyes? Or was it because, despite her protestations, he suspected she was lonely and he knew only too well how that felt? It was only when she talked about her work that her reserve disappeared. Her eyes shone and she became more animated. He liked it that she felt passionately about what she did—in many ways she reminded him of the way he used to be. And look how that had turned out.

His mind shied away from the past and back to Katherine.

He liked everything about her—the way she looked, her sensitivity and reserve, the sudden smile that lit up her face, banishing the shadows in her eyes, the way she was with Crystal, slightly awkward but not talking down to her the way many adults did, how she was with Yia-Yia and the villagers: respectful, but not patronising.

When the realisation hit him it was like jumping into a pool of water from a height. Shock then exhilaration. He didn't just like her—he was falling in love with her.

As the plaintive notes of Brahms's Lullaby filtered through the still night air from the other side of the square he went outside and listened. It had been one of Sophia's favourites—something she'd played often. He closed his eyes as an image of Sophia rushed back, her head bent over the keys of the piano, her hair falling forward as her fingers flew over the keys, a smile of pure happiness on her lips. His chest tightened. Sophia. His love. How could he think, even for a moment, that there could ever be anyone else?

CHAPTER SIX

COMFORTED BY THE soothing strains of the music and knowing sleep would elude her, Katherine studied her database, entering the list of names Alexander had given her.

She stopped when she came to Stéfan's name. He had been the first patient to fall ill. Concentrating on him was key.

There was something about him that was tugging at her memory. What was it? Yes! She had it. The day he'd collapsed at the surgery, he'd been sporting a bandage on his right hand. And it hadn't been clean either. It had looked professional, though. Someone had bandaged his hand but not recently. Hercules leaped onto her lap and started purring. She stroked him absent-mindedly as she dialled Alexander's phone. Despite the late hour, he picked up immediately.

'The boy who died. Stéfan Popalopadous? Do you know how he hurt his hand? Did he have it dressed at your practice?' she asked, coming straight to the point.

Alexander mumbled a curse under his breath. 'Hello to you too. No, I don't know how Stéfan hurt his hand. Not without looking at his notes, which, of course, are at the practice. But something tells me that's where I'm going.'

'Would you like me to come with you?' she asked.

'No. That's okay. Keep your phone near you and I'll call you as soon as I have an answer.'

It was over an hour before he called back. She snatched up the phone. 'Yes? What have you found out?'

'He damaged his hand in a winch on his boat. Apparently he often takes people out for trips in the evenings after work. He was treated in Nafplio. He runs trips between there and all the major ports along the coast.'

'Then Nafplio is where we're going. Pick me up on the way.'

Nafplio was pretty, with elegant town houses with balconies that reminded her of Venice. Alexander told her a little of the town's history on the way. During the Ottoman era it had once been the capital of Greece and the Palamayde fortress, which dominated the town, had been a prison during the Greek War of Independence. Now the town was a stopover for some of the smaller cruise ships on their way around the Mediterranean as well as for yachts either in flotillas or in singles. That wasn't good: If one of the transient visitors had come into contact with their patient, who knew where they would be now? Was that how Claire had contracted the disease?

They phoned the doctor of the surgery where Stéfan's hand had been dressed, rousing him from his bed, and discovered that they'd been right. Stéfan had been treated there a couple of days before he'd turned up at Alexander's practice. He'd had a temperature, but it hadn't been raised enough to cause concern.

Now they had their first contact, they could be reasonably confident of tracing the others before they became sick.

Katherine and Alexander exchanged high-fives as soon

as they left the practice. 'You're some public health doctor,' he said.

She grinned back at him. 'I am, aren't I?'

Over the next week, Katherine and Alexander visited all the villages and towns where cases of meningitis had been reported, as well as those of all the contacts they'd traced. Now they knew about Stéfan, it was easier to trace the people he'd come into contact with and their contacts. David, the boy in Intensive Care, had been taken around the coast with a number of his friends as a birthday treat, and the other eight victims, most of whom were recovering, had also taken trips in Stéfan's boat in the days before Stéfan had become unwell. Finally Claire's parents confirmed that their daughter had posted a photo on her Facebook page of Stéfan and his boat shortly before she'd become ill.

Katherine and Alexander set up temporary clinics and spoke to the local nurses and medical staff, advising them what to look out for and what information to give their patients. There had been one new case, but as everyone was more vigilant, she had been admitted to hospital as soon as she'd started showing symptoms and was doing well.

The longer she worked with Alexander the more she admired him. He was good with the patients, kind and understanding with panicked villagers, and authoritative with those who needed to be persuaded to take the antibiotics. It was tiring work and they spent hours in the car, driving from village to village, but she treasured those times most of all. They spoke of their day, what they had to do next, but they also talked about the music they liked and places they wanted to visit.

However, she was aware he was holding back from her, as she was from him. Often it was on the tip of her tongue to tell him about Poppy but the time never seemed right, or, if she was honest, she was too frightened of his reaction. What would he think if, or when, she did tell him? Would he be shocked? Or would he understand? And why tell him anyway? As long as there were no new cases of meningitis she would be leaving at the end of September and so far he'd said nothing, done nothing to make her think he saw her as more than a friend and colleague—albeit one he was attracted to.

She'd caught him looking at her when she'd been sneaking looks in his direction. Unsure of what it meant, she'd dropped her eyes, her pulse racing, finding an excuse to turn away, to speak to someone else.

But apart from the looks, he'd never as much as taken her hand or kissed her good-night. She suspected he was still in love with his dead wife and that no woman would ever live up to her.

The thought of returning to the UK made her heart ache. To leave all this when she'd only just found it. To go back to a life that more than ever seemed colourless and grey. To leave Alexander, his grandmother and Crystal—most of all Alexander—was breaking her heart.

Perhaps it was being here in Greece? Perhaps it was just the magic spell the country had woven around her? Maybe when she returned to the UK she'd be able to see it for what it was: infatuation, brought on by too much sun and the joy of working with someone who cared about what he did as much as she.

But she knew she was fooling herself. She wasn't just falling in love with him—she loved him—totally, deeply and would love him for as long as she breathed. But, he didn't love her. Nothing and no one could replace his wife.

His life was here with his daughter and his family while hers was back in London.

And what if he suspected how she felt about him? That would be too humiliating. Maybe he'd already guessed?.

She threw down her book and started pacing. Perhaps he thought she visited his house as a means to get close to him. And going to the square every evening to share a meal or a beer with him. Wasn't that practically admitting she couldn't stay away from him? God, she'd done everything but drool whenever he was near. She'd virtually thrown herself at him. How could she have been so stupid?

Well, there was only one way to rectify that. She would keep her distance. She wouldn't visit Yia-Yia, she wouldn't go to the square. If anyone asked she would say she was behind with her thesis. That, as it happened, was perfectly true. Besides, what did she care if anyone—least of all him—thought she was making excuses? As long as they didn't think she was some desperate woman trying to snag the local widowed doctor while she was here.

But not to see him? Except in passing? To even think it tore her in two.

She should have known this kind of happiness couldn't last.

Alexander stood on the balcony, a glass of cold water in his hand, his thoughts straying, as they always did these days, to Katherine. He hadn't seen much of her since they'd stopped visiting the affected villages and he missed her. She used to come most evenings to the square but she hadn't been for a while. Was she avoiding him?

Working with her these last weeks he'd come to admire her more and more. She was good at what she did. Very good. If she hadn't been around he doubted that they would have got on top of the outbreak as quickly as they had. Her patience with the affected families, her manner towards the villagers, her determination to speak her faltering Greek to them and the kindness and respect with which she treated young and old alike was very much the Greek ethos. He loved how her forehead furrowed when she was thinking, how her face lit up when she laughed, and most of all the way she was with Crystal. His daughter adored her.

Katherine was almost as perfect in her way as Sophia had been in hers. But she'd be going soon. And the thought of not seeing her again filled him with dismay.

It hit him then. He didn't just like and admire Katherine, he was crazy about her.

So what was he doing here, on his own, kicking his heels when he could be with her?

CHAPTER SEVEN

KATHERINE WAS SITTING on her balcony, watching the sun cast shadows on the sea, when she heard a soft tap on the door. Having come to recognise the sound of Alexander's footsteps, she didn't need to turn around to know it was him. Neither was she really surprised. Deep down she'd known it was only a matter of time before he sought her out.

'Crystal's been looking for you at the taverna these last couple of evenings,' he said softly. 'So was I. And Yia-Yia says she hasn't seen you for a day or two. Are you all right? Not ill or anything?'

The way he was searching her face made her pulse skip a beat.

'I thought I should give company a miss for a while.' Her heart was thumping so hard she was finding it difficult to breathe. 'With everything that has happened, I've fallen behind with my thesis. I'm planning to submit it in the next couple of days.'

He came to sit in the chair next to hers. 'When do you leave?'

'At the end of the month. There's nothing to keep me here longer now the epidemic seems to be under control. I had a phone call from Athens earlier—there's been no more cases reported in the last forty-eight hours. They're pretty confident the outbreak is over.'

'Thank God. If you hadn't got onto it as soon as you did, there could have been more deaths.'

'I was only doing my job. A job I love.'

His expression was unreadable in the light of the moon.

'I never did take you out on the boat, did I?' he said softly.

'No, you didn't,' she agreed. 'But you've been busy. It can't be easy for you, working and being a single father.' God, couldn't she think of anything less inane to say?

'I have Yia-Yia. And Helen when I need her.' He hooked his hands behind his head. 'Although as Helen's getting married in a few weeks it's unlikely that Crystal and I will see as much of her.' He leaned forward. 'I could still take you out on the boat. In fact, we could go later tonight. It's a perfect night for it.'

She didn't think it was possible for her heart to beat any faster but apparently it could.

'You don't have to take me, you know,' she said stiffly.

He looked taken aback. 'Of course I don't have to take you. Why would you think that?' His eyes locked on hers. 'It's not just Crystal who's missed you, I've missed spending time with you too,' he said softly. 'I like being with you. Haven't you realised that by now?' He stood and reached out a hand for hers.

Her heart beating a tattoo against her ribs, she allowed him to pull her to her feet. For a moment she swayed towards him, driven by a need to feel his arms around her. At the last moment she stopped herself and took a step back. Hadn't she told herself she wouldn't make a fool of herself?

He looked bemused, as well he might. How could he

know what was inside her head when she barely did? However, he didn't let go of her hand.

'We should wait until Crystal's asleep, though,' he continued, 'otherwise she'll insist on coming too. If I say no, I wouldn't put it past her to launch a boat of her own and come after us.'

Katherine had to laugh, even if it sounded shaky. 'No one can say she's not your daughter.'

'No.' His expression grew more serious. 'I could do with having you on my own for a bit. My daughter has taken such a liking to you, it's difficult to prise her from your side.'

Her heart catapulted inside her chest.

Why was she worrying about the future? It felt right that he was here, and why not sleep with him if he asked? And she was certain he would ask. She would be leaving soon and although there was no chance of a future for them, why resist snatching a few days of happiness? He need never know her secret. What mattered was here and now and if she could be with him, even for a short while, why not? She'd have plenty time to lick her wounds—to regret what could have been—when she left here. She surprised herself. Greece had changed so much about her.

'We should make the most of what time you have left,' he said, as if reading her mind. 'I could take some leave. We could spend it together.'

'And Crystal? Isn't she expecting to spend time with you?'

'Of course. And she will. I thought the three of us could do some stuff.' He searched her face. 'I know having my daughter around, adorable though she is, puts a spanner in the works, but happily she does go to sleep in the evenings. You do like her, don't you? She's definitely taken a shine to you.'

She wanted to ask him whether he liked to be with her because of Crystal because, much as she was coming to love the little girl, she needed him to want to be with her. But she wouldn't ask him. And what if he said yes? What if he asked her to stay permanently? What would she do then? At the very least she would have to admit that there was a very large part of her life she was keeping secret from him. Perhaps the time to tell him was now, before they got in any deeper. But if she did, what would he say? How would he react?

And what was she thinking anyway? Even if he did ask her to stay, she wouldn't. She couldn't. How could she take on the care of a child after what she'd done? However, didn't he deserve the truth from her, whether she stayed or not?

She was being given a glimpse of a life she might have. A chance to break free from the strait-jacket of the one she'd imposed on herself with its rules, self-denial, hard work and determination. Could she forgive herself—allow herself the joy of loving and being loved? Even for a short while.

He misinterpreted her silence and stood. 'I'll see you about then?'

'What time do you want me to meet you?'

His expression lightened. 'About ten?'

'I'll be there.'

When she arrived at the bay he was leaning against the boat, wearing a black T-shirt and dark jeans with fisherman's boots. He looks a bit like a pirate, she thought, especially with the five o'clock shadow darkening his jaw. He whistled appreciatively when he saw her. She'd been like a cat on a hot tin roof all evening. After discarding several outfits, she'd finally settled on a pair of faded denim shorts and a cheesecloth embroidered blouse she'd purchased in the village. Underneath she wore a lacy bra with matching panties. She'd shaved her legs and moisturised all over.

She couldn't remember the last time she'd felt so nervous and was ready long before she was due to meet him. Unable to change the habits of a lifetime, she'd packed a small bag with a cardigan in the unlikely event it was chilly on the water, and at the last minute had added some fresh fruit and olives, a bottle of wine, a corkscrew and two glasses. It was always better to be prepared.

'Hello,' she whispered. Feeling inexplicably like a naughty child, she suppressed the desire to giggle.

'You don't have to whisper, you know,' he said with a grin. 'It's not as if we're ten years old and stealing a boat.'

'Sorry,' she said in a normal voice. 'Whispering just seemed to go with the moment.'

The boat was in the water, where it drifted gently in the waves, and he was holding on to the rope to stop it being pushed out to sea. 'Why don't you climb in?' he suggested.

She slipped off her sandals and stepped into the sea, shivering as the waves lapped around her ankles, then her calves and above her knees. As her skin adjusted to the temperature, the cool water felt delicious against her overheated skin.

But once she'd reached the boat she stood dumbfounded. How was she supposed to get in? As if reading her mind, Alexander, still holding the rope but gathering it in towards him, waded over until he was standing next to her. Suddenly she felt a pair of strong hands circle her waist and then she was off her feet and he was holding her in his arms. Even in the warmth of the evening air she was conscious of the heat radiating from his body and the clean, fresh scent of him.

He laughed down at her. 'Good thing you weigh nothing.' A slight exaggeration, she thought—she wasn't the smallest of women—but then she was being dropped gently into the boat. A few seconds later Alexander sprang in alongside her. Tentatively she took a seat at the back. He picked up an oar and pushed them away from the shore, before coiling the rope into a neat round and placing it on the bottom of the boat. 'Sit in the front if you like,' he said. 'No, not now!' he added as she stood, making the boat wobble. 'Wait until we're a bit further out. Unless you want us to both end up in the water?'

Feeling a little foolish, she sat back down as Alexander started rowing. The moon was so bright she could see the muscles of his arms bunching with every pull of the oar.

'Are we going to fish?' she asked.

'If you like. But later. I want to show you something first.'

A comfortable silence fell, punctuated only by the creak of the boat against the oars and the lapping of the sea. Katherine trailed her hand in the water.

'Watch out for sharks,' he cautioned.

She pulled her hand out of the water as if she'd had an electric shock. But when she looked at him she saw, from his grin, that he'd been teasing her.

Her skin tingled and she grinned back at him. How she loved this man!

'So, what is it you want to show me?'

'I'm afraid you're going to have to wait and see.' He refused to say any more so she let herself relax, gasping with delight as a shooting star sped across the sky before falling towards the black depths of the ocean. It was if she had been transported into a different world. Happiness surged through her. Everything about being here—being with Alexander—made her feel more alive than she'd ever felt before. As if the person she was when she was with him was a different, more together version of herself on one hand and a wilder, more interesting, version on the other.

It must have been so hard for her mother to leave here when she married. Britain was a colder, greyer place than the one she'd left. Although the way the villagers lived, almost on top of each other and constantly visiting each other's homes, had taken Katherine time to get used to, and she could see how someone used to living in such close proximity with their neighbours, always having someone to call on for support, would struggle to adapt in a strange country with an entirely different culture. Her mother had loved her father very much and, as she'd told Katherine often, she would rather have been with Dad in hell than without him.

A wave of sadness threatened to swamp her mood. At least she was here. In the country her mother had once called home, she felt nearer to her than she'd felt since she'd died.

'You okay?'

Alexander's voice jerked her back to the present. 'Yes. Why?'

'It's just that you looked sad there for a moment.'

She forced a smile. 'Just thinking about my mother and wishing she'd been able come back even once before she died.'

In the distance the tiny lights from other boats bobbed on the sea. Beyond them dark shapes of small islands broke up the horizon.

'Perhaps *you'll* come back—or stay?' he said softly.

Her pulse upped another notch. Was he asking her to?

'I have my work. But, yes, I think will. What about you? Do you think you might ever return to the UK?' She held her breath as she waited for his answer.

'To visit my mother certainly. But I couldn't leave Greece permanently. I couldn't take Crystal away from her grandmother. At least, not until she's older.'

Her earlier happiness dimmed. She could understand him not wanting to separate Crystal from her great-grandmother, not until she was older anyway, but if he felt about Katherine the way she felt about him, wouldn't he want to be with her? Wouldn't he ask her outright to stay?

'Why,' he continued, 'do we always regret what might have been instead of being grateful for the life we have?'

Her heart thudded a tattoo against her chest. She wanted to ask him what he meant. Was he referring to her? What might have been? Or was he talking about his wife?

'Do you regret coming back here?' she asked instead.

'Not at all. It was the right decision for Crystal. Anyway, the UK was too—' He stopped suddenly. 'Too cold,' he finished. She was sure that wasn't what he had been about to say. In unguarded moments his sadness mirrored her own. Even after two years he was still grieving for his wife. But he should find some comfort in the knowledge he had found love—a great love, she suspected—and she envied him for it. More, she envied the woman who had been the recipient.

They lapsed into silence again. Just when she was beginning to wonder where exactly he was taking her, an island with a small bay came into view.

'Is this the place you wanted to show me?' she asked.

'Greece has many beautiful islands, but this is one I like to come to whenever I take out the boat. Not least because no one ever comes here. The only other place I like more is Cape Sounion.'

'Where's that?'

'You mean you don't know? You must have heard of the temple of Poseidon. It's where Byron used to go to write his poetry. I'll take you one day.'

His assumption that they would be spending more time together sent a ripple of happiness through her. She'd waited how many years to find someone like him and she'd had to come to a remote part of Greece to do so. If only she had an inkling of how he felt about her. If only he could love her the way he had loved, and probably still loved, his wife; if only she could make him understand why she'd done what she had, they might have a chance of a future together.

But he would never understand. She was certain of that.

He jumped out of the boat, holding its rope, and held out his arms. She let him swing her into them. As his arms tightened around her she closed her eyes, wanting to savour every last moment. He carried her ashore before standing her gently on her feet.

'So, what's so special about this island?' she asked, when he returned from pulling the boat out of the water. 'You've just told me Greece has hundreds of beautiful islands.'

'Legend has it that a Spartan soldier brought a Trojan princess here when he captured her. I have no evidence that this is the exact place,' he said, holding his hands up as if to ward off her protests, 'but he described it as an island not far from my village whose beauty was only dimmed by the beauty of his wife.' His voice dropped to a murmur. 'He believed if he kept her here, safe, nothing bad would ever happen to her and they could live out the rest of their lives together and in peace.'

'And did they? In your story?' It might only be a legend but she really wanted to know.

His gaze returned to hers, the tone of his voice almost dismissive. 'No. In time he got bored. He missed the excitement and prestige that came with being in the Greek army.'

'What happened?'

'When he was away, fighting in some war or another, his enemies found her here. They captured her and intended to make her a consort. She guessed what they planned so when they weren't watching her, she escaped and ran to the cliff. She threw herself into the sea.'

'Oh, no! And what happened to her lover?'

'As soon as he came back and discovered what had happened, he went mad with grief and guilt. He drowned himself so he could be with her in death.'

Katherine shivered. 'That's so sad.'

He reached for her hand. 'What do you think he should have done? Was he not wrong to bring her here where she was alone and unprotected?' His eyes bored into hers as if her answer really mattered. 'Don't you think he deserved what happened?'

'Well, first of all,' she began cautiously, her reaction was her choice. I don't think she would have agreed to come and live here with him if she hadn't wanted to. She must have known he was trying to protect her the best way he knew how. In the end he was wrong, but that doesn't mean he didn't do what he did for the right reasons. Didn't you say earlier that there is no point regretting what might have been?'

She knew she was talking as much about her own situation as this mythical couple's. 'It's easy to look back on our lives and see what we did wrong, what we should have done—but at the time we can only make the best decision we can in the circumstances.'

'Is that what you really believe? I can't imagine you have much to regret.'

This conversation was getting too close to the bone for comfort. Perhaps it was time to tell him about Poppy. But fear held her back. She couldn't bear it if he judged her or, worse, rejected her. She forced a smile. 'Why do you like the island so much if it has such a sad story attached to it?'

He poured her some wine and passed the glass to her. The touch of his fingertips brushing against hers sent hot sparks up her arm. 'In a way, I guess it is sad. But legend has it that the gods took pity on them and turned them into dolphins. I like to think of them out in the ocean to-gether—always.'

Her heart twisted. So she'd been right. He was still in love with his wife.

He stepped forward and took her face between his hands. 'I don't know why no man has captured you yet. What is wrong with English men?'

'Perhaps it is me,' she said, then could have kicked her-self. It was difficult to think straight with him being so close. 'I mean, being too picky.'

He laughed down at her, his teeth white in the dark. 'You should be picky,' he said. He tangled his hands in her hair and, with his thumbs under her cheek bones, raised her face to his. 'You are so beautiful. So perfect.'

No, she thought wildly. *Don't think that!* He mustn't think she was perfect. He'd only be disappointed.

He lowered his head and brought his mouth down on hers and then she couldn't think any more. This was what she'd been imagining almost from the moment she'd first set eyes on him and it was everything she'd dreamed it would be. As his kisses deepened she clung to him, almost dizzy with desire.

When he moved away she gave a little gasp of disappointment. But he lifted her in his arms and carried her over to a soft patch of grass where he laid her down.

'Are you sure?' he asked as she gazed up at him.

'Sure?' She almost laughed. She pulled him down to her. 'What took you so long?' she murmured against his lips.

Later, they lay wrapped in each other's arms, gazing up at the stars. She'd never felt so peaceful, so thoroughly made love to. He'd been demanding, gentle and teasing and had touched her in ways she couldn't remember being touched before, until she'd cried out with her need to have him inside her. She blushed as she remembered how she'd dug her fingertips into his back, how she'd called out to him as wave upon wave of pleasure had rocked her body.

But she didn't really care. This wanton, this woman he'd unleashed, was a revelation to her and she never wanted to go back to the one she'd been before. She smiled to herself. This was what sex should be like.

The moonlight shone on his naked body. It was every bit as she'd imagined—better than any of the Greek statues she'd seen. No wonder she hadn't been able to stop thinking about how he would feel under her hands. A smile curved her lips and she laughed with sheer joy.

He propped himself on his elbow and gazed down at her. Instinctively she reached for her blouse to cover her nakedness, but as she moved her hand he caught it in his fingers. 'Don't,' he murmured. 'I don't think I could ever get enough of just looking at you.'

The new wanton Katherine revelled in the desire she saw in his eyes.

She reached up to him and wrapped her arms around his neck.

As the horizon turned pink and apricot they lay in each other's arms, looking up at the star-sprinkled sky, their hands entwined. 'There's something I need to tell you,' he said softly.

Oh, God, here it was. *This was wonderful but...*

'Remember I told you that I was training to be a surgeon when Sophia died,' he continued.

'Yes.'

'And I said I was working all the time?'

She wasn't sure where this was going. 'I know how competitive the speciality can be.'

'When Sophia fell pregnant with Crystal I was so happy. And so was she. If at times I caught her looking wistful I just put it down to her being homesick for Greece. It suited me to believe that's all it was. Looking back, I think she knew it was the end of her dream to become a concert pianist.

'I was determined to make it in surgery, but you know how it is—the competition is fierce, especially for the top positions, and only the best job in the most prestigious hospital would do me. I had it all planned out. I would qualify for a consultant post then I would apply to the Mayo Clinic in America and do some further training there. I'd already sat my board exams when I was a resident in my final year at med school so getting a post wouldn't be an issue as long as I stayed focussed.

'Sophia backed me all the way. She said she could play

her music anywhere. I knew that wasn't necessarily true—not if she wanted to play professionally—but I chose not to listen to that particular voice. I was a selfish bastard back then—completely focussed on what I wanted to achieve. I told myself I was doing it for all of us, for me, for Sophia—and for the baby on the way.

'What I chose to forget was that she'd already put her career on hold for me. A musician's career is, if anything, more competitive than medicine—they have such a short time to "make it" and she'd already jeopardised her chances by coming with me to the UK. But, as I said, I planned to make it up to her. One day when I'd got to where I needed to go, I would slow down, let my career take a back seat and let her enjoy the limelight for a while.

'We both wanted a family and I told myself that by the time I had reached the top, the children would be of an age to allow her time for herself. There was always going to be more than one child. We both wanted at least three. Call me clever, huh? If I'd done the math I would have realised that if everything went to plan she would have been thirty three by the time the youngest was born. I thought it was simple. We'd have children. Sophia would stay at home until the youngest was six weeks or so and then we'd employ a nanny. And Sophia went along with it. Until Crystal was born. Then she could no more see herself putting any child of hers into a nursery than she could have left them home alone. She loved being a mother. If she found it boring she never said so and I never asked.

'She always made friends easily and the house was always filled—at least so I heard as I was rarely home long enough to see for myself. It was as if she'd gathered around her friends to be the family she'd left behind in Greece. I told myself she was happy. But when I thought about it later, I couldn't remember the last time she'd played the piano. At the time I told myself that that was good—that she wasn't really driven enough to make it as a concert pianist. Why is everything so much more obvious in hindsight?'

Katherine rolled over so she could see his face. 'We all see things differently later, don't we?' she murmured, although every word he'd said about Sophia cut her like a blade.

'I never stopped loving her. She was my best friend, my lover, the mother of my child, but I stopped seeing her—really seeing her.'

The sadness in his eyes twisted her heart.

'She deserved more than I gave her. Perhaps I didn't love her enough. If I had I wouldn't have put my needs so far above hers.'

'She was lucky to be loved the way you loved her. She would have known she was deeply loved,' Katherine whispered.

'I'm glad you told me about her.' And she was. She wanted to know everything about him. Even if hearing about how much he'd loved Sophia hurt.

'I had to. You have to know why I'm not sure I can ever promise more than what we have here tonight. I care too much about you not to tell you the truth about myself. And there's more…'

She stopped his words with her fingertips. The here and now was all they had. After what he'd told her, how could she ever tell him about Poppy? And not telling him meant they could never have more than what they had now. 'Let's not think about the past,' she said. 'Let's only think about now.' She moved her hand from his lips and taking his head between her palms lowered herself on top of him.

* * *

When they returned to the village she led him by the hand up the path and into her home. Her heart was beating so fast she couldn't speak.

He kicked the door closed behind him. '*Agapi- mou*,' he breathed into her neck. 'I want you. I need you.'

She stepped into his arms feeling as if, at last, she'd come home—even if only for a while.

They spent every day of the next week with each other, until Alexander's leave was over. Crystal came to the house often. If Katherine was working, the child would take the colouring book she'd brought with her and lay it on the table next to Katherine's papers, and quietly, her tongue caught in the corner of her mouth, use her crayons to colour in, stopping periodically to admire her work or to study Katherine from the corner of her eye, waiting patiently until Katherine stopped what she was doing to admire her efforts. Increasingly, Katherine would find herself, at Yia-Yia's invitation, at the family home, pitching in to make olive tapenade or some other Greek dish. Then, instead of sitting and looking out at the beach, they'd retire to the bench at the front of the house and sit in silence, enjoying the heat of the sun and letting the ebb and flow of village life happen around them. Katherine's rusty Greek was improving by leaps and bounds and she and Alexander's grandmother were able to communicate reasonably well.

She'd also become confident enough with her Greek to stop to chat with the other villagers when she was passing through the square. Soon small gifts of ripe tomatoes and zucchini, enormous squashes and bunches of fat grapes still on the vine appeared on her doorstep, and before long she had more plump olives than she could hope ever to eat and more bottles of home-made olive oil than she knew what to do with.

She often thought of her mother. It was as if she'd planned this, knowing that Greece would weave its magic around her and that Katherine would discover what she had missed out on in life. It was, Katherine realised, her mother's final gift to her and one she wanted to savour. As it had done during the epidemic, her thesis lay largely ignored—dotting the 'i's and crossing the 't's didn't seem as important as they once had—although Katherine knew she would never submit it until it was as perfect as she could make it. Greece hadn't turned her into a complete sloth.

But she *was* less than perfect here. She no longer blow-dried her hair every morning before twirling it into a tight bun. Instead she wore it lose around her shoulders or twisted carelessly into a ponytail, no longer caring if it frizzed a little around the edges. She felt freer without the tights, the buttoned-to-the-neck shirts, tailored trousers and sensible shoes she'd worn when she'd first arrived. Now it was bare-shouldered sundresses, skimpy shorts and strappy T-shirts. She'd even repainted her nails in the same blood red as Crystal had—leaving Crystal's handiwork would have been a step too far! With Alexander back at work, she saw little of him during the day, but most evenings they drank cold beer and nibbled olives and fresh figs, spoke about work and history while Crystal played in the square. He made her laugh with his amusing stories of the villagers and his patients and although her skin still fizzed every time he looked at her, she was able to relax in his company in a way that she hadn't done with anyone, apart from Sally, in years.

It was, Katherine thought, the happiest time of her life. For once, nothing was asked of her, nothing demanded, no one expected anything of her. Sometimes Crystal came with them and sometimes they went on their own. He took her to Cape Souinon and she could see straight away why he loved it. The ruins of the temple of Poseidon looked out towards the sea and she could easily imagine Lord Byron sitting with his back against one of the pillars, writing poetry.

Often they spent the day on the beach with Crystal, swimming, picnicking and sharing intimate smiles. In the evenings he would call at her house and together they would climb the path to the village square, releasing their hands by unspoken consent moments before they reached it. But it was the nights she longed for most. When his daughter was asleep he'd come to her house and they'd make love, either in her bed or down in the little bay. He'd wake up early and leave her to return to his home so that he'd always be there when Crystal woke up. And every day she fell just a little more in love with him.

She didn't know how she was ever going to say goodbye.

Alexander was whistling as he showered. In a short while he'd be seeing Katherine. It had been a long time, he reflected, since he'd felt this good. Not since Sophia had died.

And it was all down to Katherine. He grinned remembering the night before. How could he ever have thought she was reserved—when it came to making love she was anything but.

Unfortunately his lunchtime date with Katherine was going to be curtailed. He had a patient who needed a home visit. Perhaps Katherine would come with him? He didn't want to waste any of the little time they had left.

But why should she leave?

He stepped out of the shower.

She could come to live with him in Greece. He was certain she would find another job here easily. Or he could find one in England. He quickly dismissed the thought. He couldn't uproot Crystal again. At least not until she was older. Katherine would understand. She knew how important it was for Crystal to be brought up around family.

But would she stay? They would get married of course. The thought brought him up short. Marriage! He almost laughed out loud. He'd been so certain he'd never marry again, but that was before he'd met Katherine. Now he couldn't imagine the rest of his life without her.

Although she hadn't said, he was certain Katherine was in love with him. But enough to marry him? Give up her life in the UK?

There was only one way to find out. 'What do you think, Sophia?' he murmured. 'Do I deserve another chance at happiness?'

CHAPTER EIGHT

KATHERINE WAS PORING over her computer, trying and failing to concentrate on finishing her paper, when there was a knock on the door. No one in the village ever knocked and certainly not Crystal, and although she was expecting Alexander any minute, he always marched in, announcing himself by calling out her name. She quickly saved the file she was working on and went to answer.

When she saw who it was her heart almost stopped beating.

'Poppy?'

Her daughter pushed by her and dropped her rucksack on the floor. 'I'm surprised you know who I am.'

Admittedly, for a brief moment Katherine hadn't. Her daughter had changed so much since the last photo she had seen of her. Gone was her long, golden hair. Gone was the awkward yet beautiful, fresh-faced teenager. In her place was an angry-looking young woman with black spiky hair, kohl-ringed panda eyes and a lip-piercing.

'Of course I know who you are,' Katherine whispered. She'd dreamed of this moment for so long but in her imagination it had taken the form of getting-to-know-you phone calls followed by lunches and shopping trips. In her head, Poppy had been like her as a teenager; demure, well spoken and beautifully mannered. Nothing in her dreams had prepared her for this. But despite her dismay, a warm, happy glow was spreading from her stomach towards her heart.

Poppy flung herself down on the sofa. 'I thought you might be staying in a villa or something. But this place is pokey. I don't see a pool.'

'That's because there isn't one.' She was still stunned. 'But there's an ocean to swim in.'

'Oh, well. I suppose it will have to do. Anything's better than being at home with *them*.'

'Them?'

'Liz and Mike. The people who call themselves my parents.'

Katherine's head was whirling. 'How did you know I was here? Do Liz and Mike know you're with me?'

'I had your email address, remember? I emailed your work address and got an out-of-office reply, so I phoned them and told them I needed to know where you were. I told them it was urgent—a family emergency—and luckily I got through to a receptionist who didn't know you had no family.' The last was said with heavy and pointed emphasis on the 'no'. 'And as for Mum and Dad, no. They don't know I'm here. They don't care where I am!'

'Poppy! They must be out of their minds with worry! You must—'

'All they care about is their new baby. It's Charlie this and Charlie that. God, why did they adopt me if they were going to go and have a baby of their own?'

Mike and Liz had had a baby? Well, it wasn't unheard of for couples who believed themselves infertile to conceive spontaneously when they'd given up all hope of having a child, but Katherine wished Liz had written to tell her.

It had been a long time since she'd heard from Poppy's

adoptive mother. Not since a year ago when Poppy had turned sixteen and Liz had emailed Katherine, telling her that any further contact would be up to Poppy. In the meantime, if Katherine chose to continue writing, not emailing if she didn't mind as Liz couldn't monitor those, she would keep the letters but only pass them on to Poppy when and if she asked.

It hadn't been written to hurt her, although it had. In her heart, Katherine had wanted to argue but in her head she'd agreed. At sixteen Poppy was old enough to decide for herself whether she wanted to stay in touch. Katherine had always hoped that she would decide to—but not like this.

'I didn't know they had another child,' Katherine said. 'That must have been a surprise.'

'They didn't have *another* child. They had a child. I'm not their child. Not any longer. What is it with you lot that you can cast off your children when it suits you?'

'They put you out?' Katherine said, astonished and outraged. 'But that's—'

Poppy stared down at the floor. 'They didn't *exactly* put me out,' she mumbled. 'I mean, they never said in so many words that they wanted me to go—but it was obvious.'

'And they don't know where you are?' Katherine asked, beginning to recover. 'They'll be frantic You need to let your parents—'

'They're not my parents!'

'According to the law, they are. They've probably alerted the police. How did you leave without them knowing? *When* did you leave?'

'Yesterday morning. I said I was going to a sleepover at my friend Susan's'

Katherine was aghast. 'You *lied* to them?'

'Well, I could hardly tell them where I was going, could I?'

'If you're so convinced they don't care, why didn't you try it?' Katherine winced at the tone of her own voice. Now she sounded as snarky as her daughter.

Poppy glowered. 'They have to pretend, don't they, that they care? Even if it's all a big, fat act.'

'Of course they care and they need to know where you are. They need to know you're safe.'

'I don't want to talk to them.'

Katherine retrieved her mobile from her bag and held it out. 'Phone them. Now.'

'No.'

Katherine was tempted for a miniscule moment not to phone Liz and Mike. They might phone the police to return Poppy or at the very least insist Katherine put her on the next plane and she couldn't bear not to steal a day or two with her child. Her child! She gave herself a mental shake. Of course she couldn't possibly do that to Mike and Liz.

'You can't stay here unless you do. I'll have to notify the police.'

Poppy got up from the sofa and picked up her rucksack. 'In that case, I'm off. I should have known you wouldn't want me either. Jeez, I'm so stupid. You got rid of me once. Why on earth would you want anything to do with me now? I just thought you might have a little leftover maternal feeling—if not a sense that you owe me something at least.'

Katherine knew she was being manipulated, but even so, she couldn't let Poppy leave. Not now, not like this. If Poppy walked out her life, would she ever get another chance with her again? And under the sullen exterior Katherine glimpsed the lonely, confused child within. It took all her resolve not to march across the room and envelop her daughter in her arms. Somehow, instinctively, she knew that wasn't the way to handle the situation either. Best to remain calm and reasonable. After all, there must be *some* reason for Poppy to have sought her out—even if part of her motive was to hurt her adoptive parents as much as possible. She had to tread carefully.

'Poppy, please. I don't want you to go, that's not what I meant. I can't tell you how…' her heart swelled '…thrilled and delighted I am to see you.' She gestured towards the sofa. 'Please, sit back down. Let me phone your parents, talk to them. I'll ask if you can stay here for a couple of days. It'll give us a chance to talk…'

Katherine held her breath, her heart beating in her throat, while Poppy considered what she'd said. Now that Poppy was here—here! In front of her! she couldn't bear not to grab this chance to talk to her, maybe hold her… even once.

Just when she thought her daughter was going to bolt for the door, she dropped her bag again.

'Okay.'

Relief made her legs weak. 'Great.'

'But I'm not going back. Ever.'

'We'll talk about it later.' Katherine sat down then stood up again. 'Look, why don't you have a shower—freshen up while I phone Liz and Mike? Then I'll make us something to eat, okay?'

Poppy's contemplated her from under her fringe for a few moments before nodding sullenly.

'I could do with a shower,' she admitted. 'I feel as if I've been in a sauna with my clothes on.' Now that she mentioned it, they did have a faint whiff of body odour. 'Then after that I could do with crashing. Is there a spare bedroom?'

'Yes. Let me get you some towels for your shower and check that the bed's made up.'

'Towels would be good, thanks. I don't think I brought one.'

Katherine hid a smile. It seemed that Poppy had forgotten to forget her manners. And as if she'd realised the same thing, the scowl returned with a vengeance. 'No need to make the bed if its not already. I'm so bushed I could sleep in a pig's pen.'

As soon as she heard the shower running, Katherine dug her diary out of her handbag. She could still hardly believe that Poppy was here. And wanting to stay. It was what she'd always wished for, but in her imagination it had been organised in advance and arranged to perfection. Fear, excitement, nerves—a whole tumult of emotions coursed through her. But first things first: she had to let Poppy's parents know she was safe and well. Flicking through the pages until she found Mike and Liz's number, she sat down on the sofa and rested the phone on her lap. Twice she had to stop pressing the numbers her fingers were shaking so much.

'Poppy?' Liz sounded harassed and hopeful when she answered the phone. Katherine could hear an infant crying in the background. That had to be Charlie.

'No, it's Katherine.' It had been years since they'd spoken, all subsequent communication after the adoption having taken place by letter or email. 'But Poppy is here. Don't worry, she's fine.'

'Katherine? You say Poppy's with you? Thank God!' Liz started to cry. Katherine waited until she was able to speak. 'We've been beside ourselves. We didn't even know if she was alive. She just upped and disappeared.

We thought… Oh, God. She's with you? And definitely all right?'

'She's a little travel weary. Nothing a sleep won't put right.' It was clear that whatever Poppy believed, Liz did care about her.

'Where are you?' Liz continued. 'We'll come and get her.'

'I'm in Greece. Working.'

'Greece? Poppy's in Greece?'

'She found me through my work email.' Katherine lowered her voice and glanced behind her to make sure Poppy hadn't suddenly come into the room. However she could still hear the sound of the shower running.

'She did? Mind you, she's a bright girl—almost too bright for her own good. That's why I wanted her to go to university, but she's not been working… I don't know if she's going to pass her A-levels. She's been going out till all hours despite being grounded and refusing to study. She's changed!'

Katherine smiled wryly.

'I gather you've had a baby. She seems upset about that.'

'Charlie? Oh, I know I've been caught up in caring for him. He's such a demanding baby. Not like Poppy at the same age. That doesn't mean we don't care about her, Katherine. We love her. She's our daughter!'

Katherine winced inwardly. As if she needed to be reminded. Liz broke down again.

'Should we come? No, I can't. Not with the baby—I haven't got around to getting a passport for him…Mike's working… I…' Liz said between sobs.

'She can stay with me for as long as she likes.'

'Oh, that would be a relief. She'd be all right with you.'

They finished the phone call with Katherine promising

to keep Liz and Mike informed and also promising to try and convince Poppy to go home if she could. The problem was, Katherine didn't want her to go.

As she waited for Poppy to re-emerge, Katherine quickly laid the patio table and stood back to survey the results. She cocked a critical eye at the little vase of flowers she'd placed in the centre and hesitated. Too much? Definitely. Hastily she snapped it away but now the plain white tablecloth appeared too plain and unwelcoming so she placed the vase back. For God's sake, she was more nervous than on a first date—but this was way more important than that. Even with this little gesture she wanted Poppy to know how much she cared.

Hurrying back to the kitchen, she tossed the big bowl of salad and added a touch more seasoning. Was it too salty now? Did Poppy even like salt? Or figs, for that matter? Fish? Was she vegetarian, a vegan? She knew absolutely nothing about her, nothing. Not one single iota about her likes and dislikes. Well, perhaps a simple lunch was the place to find out.

The sound of the shower finally stopped. Nervously Katherine paced the small living room, preparing herself for Poppy's reappearance. *Keep conversation light and simple. Ask questions without probing. Get her trust.*

When the front door opened and Alexander walked in, Katherine could only stand and stare at him. With Poppy's sudden arrival, she'd completely forgotten they'd arranged to go out for lunch.

He strode into the room and gathered her into his arms, kissing her softly on the lips. 'I've missed you.' His eye caught the laid-out table. 'Oh, are we eating in, then?' He grinned. 'Smart thinking. I have to go and visit a patient later, but I have an hour or two before I need to leave—'

Katherine wriggled out his arms. 'Alexander, something's come up… Could we step outside a minute? There's something I have to tell you.'

He raised an eyebrow. 'Sounds ominous.' He studied her more closely. 'What is it? Something's really upsetting you. Have there been more meningitis cases reported?'

'No. It's not that.' She took him by the arm. 'We can't talk here.

'Hi. Are you her boyfriend?' Katherine whirled around to find Poppy, wearing only a skimpy towel, draped against the stairpost. When Katherine looked back at Alexander his eyebrows had shot even higher.

'I'm Alexander Dimitriou,' he replied, 'and you are?'

'Hasn't she told you? Well, that doesn't surprise me.' Poppy flounced into the room and sprawled on the sofa, her long thin, legs stretched in front of her. 'I'm Poppy.' She pointed at Katherine. 'And she's my mother. Or should I say the woman who gave birth to me. Not the same thing at all, is it?'

It was one of those moments when the room seemed to take a breath. Behind her scowl, Poppy seemed pretty pleased with herself. Unsurprisingly, Alexander appeared bewildered, and as for her, it felt as if her legs were going to give way.

'Would you excuse us for a moment?' she said to Poppy. 'Alexander, could we speak outside for a moment?'

Still looking stunned, he followed her downstairs and out to the patio. She closed the door behind them.

'You have a daughter?' he said.

'Yes.'

'You have a daughter,' he repeated, with a shake of his

head. 'You have a child and you didn't even mention her. Why the hell not?'

'I was going to tell you about her.'

'When?'

Good question. She had no answers right now. At least, none that would make sense to him.

'I didn't know she was coming.'

'Evidently,' he said dryly, folding his arms.

'I probably should have told you before now.'

He continued to hold her gaze. 'Probably. So where has she been all this time? Most women would mention they had a child and if I remember correctly you told me you were childless.'

'Oh, for heaven's sake,' she burst out, immediately on the defensive. 'It's not as if we— I mean…' What the hell *did* she mean? She couldn't think straight. 'It's not as if we made promises…' Damn, that wasn't right either.

His mouth settled into a hard line. 'Fool that I am, I thought we did have something. I thought it was the beginning.'

Had he? He'd never said. But she couldn't think about that now. Not when Poppy was upstairs, waiting for her. She glanced behind her, caught between the need to return to her child and the need to talk to Alexander. Right now her child had to take precedence. Explanations would have to wait.

'Can we talk about this later?' she pleaded. 'I could come down to the bay.'

He shook his head. 'I think you've just made it clear that you don't owe me an explanation and I doubt there is anything…'

Poppy chose that moment to appear from the house, wearing a bikini and a towel slung casually over her shoulder.

'I'm going for a swim,' she said. 'Where's the coolest place to go?'

'Coolest?' Katherine echoed.

'Where the boys hang out. You don't think I'm going to hang out with you all the time, do you?'

'The little bay just below the house is quite safe to swim in as long as you don't go too far out. Actually, perhaps it's better if you wait until I come with you before you go into the water. And if you're sunbathing, put factor thirty on. The sun here is stronger than you think.'

'I'm seventeen, not seven, you know. Besides, don't you think it's a bit late to do the maternal thing?'

Katherine winced. 'I've spoken to your mother. She knows you're with me. She's been worried about you.'

A faint gleam appeared in Poppy's eyes, to be replaced almost immediately by her habitual scowl. 'Serves them right.'

Katherine sneaked a look at Alexander. He looked confused. No wonder. 'Her mother?' She saw the dawning realisation in his eyes.

'Liz wants you to go home. They miss you,' she told Poppy.

'Well, I'm not going.' Poppy pouted. 'I always fancied a holiday in Greece.'

'We need to talk about that.'

'Whatever.' Poppy yawned, exposing her tongue and, to Katherine's horror, another piercing. She hid a shudder.

'I should go,' Alexander said stiffly.

Poppy sauntered past them and towards the bay.

Katherine turned back to Alexander. 'I'll see you later. Or tomorrow. I'll explain everything then—'

'As I said, you don't owe me an explanation. Hadn't you better go after your daughter?'

'I had to give her up,' she said quickly.

'Did you?' he said coldly. And with that, he turned on his heel.

Alexander left Katherine standing on her patio and strode towards his car. He was stunned. How come she'd never mentioned that she had a child? How old was Poppy anyway? At least seventeen. So Katherine must have been around the same age when she'd had her. Had she been too dead set on a career in medicine to contemplate keeping a baby? If so, he'd had a narrow escape. Thank God he'd found out before he'd proposed. He'd never understand how a woman could give up her child.

But what he found harder to forgive was why she hadn't told him about her. He'd been open and honest with Katherine—sharing stuff that he'd never shared with anyone before—and she'd flung his honesty in his face. He'd let himself believe that finally he'd met a woman who matched up to Sophia, but he'd been mistaken. He'd thought she was pretty damn near perfect. What a fool he'd been. What a bloody fool. He'd come damn close to asking this woman—or at least the woman he'd thought she was—to spend the rest of her life with him. How could have believed he'd find someone as true as Sophia?

He wrenched his car door open with such force it banged against its hinges. Damn.

If Katherine thought that the evening would be spent chatting with her daughter she soon found she was mistaken. Every time she went near Poppy she'd pick up her book and walk away, and, after only picking at her supper she'd excused herself and gone to bed, slamming the door behind her. Left alone, and feeling raw, Katherine had pulled out her photograph album and picked out the photo of Poppy that had been taken on the beach.

What would her life have been like if she hadn't relinquished the care of her daughter to someone else? She would have been the one holding her. She would have been the recipient of those ice-cream kisses. It was something she would never know, although she had questioned it then, when her tiny infant had been gently but firmly tugged from her arms, and she wondered more than ever now.

Early the next morning while Poppy was still asleep Katherine sent a text to Alexander asking him to meet her down on the beach around the corner from her house. She didn't want to go to his home and she didn't want him to come to hers. Not when they could be overheard at either. Whatever he said she owed him an explanation.

He replied almost immediately, saying that he'd be there in five minutes. She tied her hair into a ponytail and applied a touch of lipstick and let herself out of the house.

She was sitting on a rock when he appeared. Her heart jerked when she saw the grim expression on his face. What else had she expected? She *had* lied to him.

'I don't have long,' he said, stopping in front of her, his hands thrust into the pockets of his light cotton trousers.

She leaped to her feet, hating the way he towered over her, making her feel a little like a schoolgirl waiting to be told off by the schoolmaster. 'Thank you for coming,' she said stiffly.

'Look,' he said, 'I can see you have a lot going on at the moment. What we had was fun but as you pointed out, it was never going to be anything but short term, was it? You have your life…' he glanced towards her house '…back in Britain and I have mine here.'

He'd clearly made up his mind about them, then. She'd thought that after a night to think things over, he'd at the very least be prepared to listen to what she had to say.

'No,' she said softly. 'I can see that now. I came here to explain but if that's the way you feel…' She didn't wait for a response but, blinking back tears, turned back towards home—and Poppy.

Katherine paused outside her door and waited until she had her emotions under control before going inside. She gasped. It looked as if a tornado had hit it. There were empty cups and plates and a cereal carton scattered over the work surface. A damp towel was in a heap on the floor, along with several magazines. Her daughter's bedroom was in a worse state. Poppy's rucksack lay on her bed, clothes spilling from it, some on the floor. Instinctively Katherine began to pick up, folding the clothes as she went along.

She called out Poppy's name but there was no answer. She quickly searched the small villa and the garden, but there was no sign of her anywhere. Had she decided to go? But where? Back to Liz and Mike? Or somewhere else? It hadn't even crossed her mind that Poppy might up and leave. But if she had, wouldn't she have taken her rucksack? So where was she? Panic ripped through her. What if Poppy had ignored Katherine's warnings and had gone swimming and been dragged out to sea? She should never have left her alone. Underneath that sullen exterior was bound to be a desperately unhappy girl. Katherine had only just got her back and she'd failed her again.

She ran outside but there was no sign of her daughter. However, Alexander was still standing where she'd left him, apparently lost in thought.

She hurried over to him. 'I can't find her,' she said.

'Who? Poppy?'

'She's taken her swimming things but I looked—she's not in the bay.' She spread her arms wide. 'I can't see her anywhere.'

'I'll check the bay on the other side,' Alexander said. He squeezed her shoulder. 'Don't look so worried, she'll be fine.'

He couldn't know that for sure. She ran around to the bigger bay. On the small stretch of beach was another towel and a pair of sunglasses but no sign of Poppy.

She scanned the bay, searching for her, but apart from a couple of boats the sea was empty. A late-morning breeze had whipped it into frothy peaked waves. Had she gone for a swim and gone out too far?

'Where is she?' She grabbed Alexander's arm. 'We've got to find her.' She began tugging off her sandals.

'What the hell are you doing?'

'I'm going to swim out. I need to find her.'

Alexander gripped her by the shoulders. 'Calm down. Think about it. You'd see her if she's out there.' He cupped his hands and called out to one of the boats nearby. The man called back to him.

'He says he hasn't noticed a stranger, and he's been out here since dawn. He'll ask the other boats just to make sure. Come on, let's check the village. She's probably gone in search of a Coke. Someone will have seen her.

Filled with dread, Katherine followed him back up the steps. He stopped a woman and spoke to her in Greek. She shook her head. They asked several more people and they all denied seeing a young stranger. Katherine's panic was threatening to overwhelm her when the village store owner told them, his expression aghast, that, yes, he'd served a girl with short black hair and an earring in her lip. She was, he said, with Alexander's pretty daughter. The last was said with significantly more approval.

Inside Alexander's house, Grandmother was in her habitual place in the kitchen. In the small sitting room Crystal was lying on the sofa with her feet in Poppy's lap as Poppy painted her toenails. The little girl was giggling while Poppy seemed totally oblivious to the stir she'd caused. Katherine sagged with relief.

Then fury overtook her.

'Why the hell didn't you leave a note to say where you were?'

Poppy looked up in surprise. Immediately her face resumed its belligerent look. 'Why should I leave a note? You didn't and it's not as if you've ever known or cared what I do.'

'While you're staying with me, you're my responsibility. For God's sake, I thought you'd drowned. Your towel—all your things—were on the beach.'

Something shifted in Poppy's eyes. If Katherine hadn't known better she would have said it was regret.

'Well, as you can see, I haven't drowned. I went to the beach and came back to your house for a drink and Crystal turned up. She wanted some company.'

'Poppy's painting my toenails! See, Baba, she's made patterns on them.' When the child turned her face towards them, Katherine noticed that Poppy had also given her full make-up.

Alexander placed a restraining hand on Katherine's arm. 'Thanks for spending time with Crystal, Poppy.' He crossed the room and smiled down at his daughter. 'Have you seen my daughter, Crystal? She's a beautiful little girl with a clean, shining face who never needs make-up.'

Crystal glared at him. 'I am your daughter, silly. And I like my face the way Poppy has done it.'

Grandmother muttered something from behind Katherine. When she glanced at her she couldn't be sure whether it was amusement or disapproval on her face.

Alexander scooped Crystal into his arms. 'I think it's time for a wash.'

'But Poppy is going to do my fingernails next. Then we're going to get dressed up and go to the square.'

'Poppy, we need to go,' Katherine said firmly.

'Oh, all right.' She stood up. 'See you tomorrow, Crystal.'

'That woman is not good,' Alexander's grandmother told him when he returned from helping Crystal to dress. 'What kind of woman gives away her child? I am disappointed. I thought I had found the right woman for you.'

So Poppy hadn't wasted any time in telling Crystal and Grandmother her story. 'We shouldn't judge her, Yia-Yia. Not until we know her reasons.' But wasn't what she'd said exactly what he'd been thinking? Katherine clearly wasn't the woman he'd thought she was. No doubt she'd had her reasons for giving her daughter up for adoption—although he couldn't think what they could be. She'd lied about having a child—that's what he couldn't bring himself to forgive. He'd thought he knew her. Now he knew better.

But a few days later his heart kicked against his ribs when he saw her emerge from the village store.

She hurried along the street, a few steps in front of him, and he was appalled to find that the villagers no longer called out to her or smiled in her direction. Since Poppy had arrived the village had been alight with gossip about her and her mother. Word had it that Poppy had been abandoned as a baby—where, no one could say exactly, but it varied between a hospital doorstep and an alleyway, that she had been taken away from Katherine because she had been unfit to look after her, to all sorts of even crazier versions. One of the other rumours he'd heard had involved Poppy running away from adoptive parents who beat her to a mother who hadn't wanted her in the first place. It seemed now that they knew about Poppy and having made up their minds, they had decided to spurn Katherine. Alexander suspected that most of the gossip had originated from Poppy, who no doubt was making the most of the sympathy she was getting from the women in the village.

He'd seen mother and daughter yesterday, sitting on the downstairs patio. Both had been wearing shorts, revealing long brown legs, both barefoot. When they'd turned to look at him, two identical pairs of blue eyes had stared out from porcelain complexions. It was obvious they were closely related, although, given the gap in their ages, they might have been taken for sisters rather than mother and daughter—even with the radically different hairstyles and Poppy's piercing.

Feeling she was being unfairly accused was one thing, re-igniting their aborted love affair quite another. Nevertheless, it was about time the gossip stopped.

Furious with them, or himself—he couldn't be sure which—he called Katherine's name and ran the few steps to catch up with her. He took the shopping bag from her hand. 'Let me carry this for you.'

She looked up at him, defiance shining in her blue eyes. 'I can manage,' she said. 'You don't have to keep the fallen woman company.'

But behind the defiance he could see the hurt and

his chest tightened. No matter what she said, she'd been wounded badly by the villagers' attitude. She'd told him how much she'd loved feeling part of their small community.

'You'll be a seven-day wonder,' he said. 'Then they'll forget all about it.'

'I'm not so sure,' she said. 'But I won't be judged. Not by them—not by anyone.' She looked at him again. He knew she was including him in her statement and she was right. He had been as guilty as the rest of drawing conclusions without having the facts. 'Neither do I need you to stick up for me.'

'I know. You're perfectly able to do that yourself.' He was rewarded by the briefest of smiles.

'How is the prodigal daughter anyway?' he asked. 'I understand she spends a fair bit of time at my house.'

'She seems to get a kick out of being around your grandmother. She's shown her how to make soap from olive oil, how to dry herbs and how to cook. The things she was showing me before I fell out of favour. Don't get me wrong, I'm sure she's wonderfully patient with her and I'm happy Poppy has someone she feels good around.'

'She tells me Poppy is very good at entertaining Crystal. I suspect my grandmother sees a different side to Poppy than you do.'

She smiled sadly. 'I'm trying to get to know her. I'm trying not to nag, just to make her aware that I'm ready to talk whenever she's ready. I thought that she would have begun to unbend towards me a bit, but she seems as angry with me as she was the day she arrived.' Her shoulders sagged and he had to ball his fists to stop himself taking her in his arms.

'Give her time. She hasn't gone home so being here must mean something to her.'

'I don't think I'm anything more than a bolt-hole to her. And in many ways I'm glad just to be that. I took her to Mycenae the other day. I thought doing things together would help us to bond.' She laughed bitterly. 'I was wrong. It was nothing short of a disaster. She managed half an hour before she sulked off back to the car.'

Despite everything, he had to suppress a smile. 'You know the ruins of ancient cities aren't everyone's cup of tea. Especially when they're teens. From what little I know of Poppy she strikes me as more of a beach girl.'

'But I thought she'd be interested—I would have been at her age. I thought we'd have something to talk about at least. Something that was less emotional than our relationship and what's going on with her back home.'

She looked so disappointed he almost reached out for her. Instead, he dug his hands even deeper into his pockets. But was she really so naïve to think that dragging a seventeen-year-old around ruins was the way build a relationship?

'Have you asked her what *she* wants to do?'

'Of course! I'm not a complete idiot.'

'And her answer?'

'Let me use her exact words. "Duh. To chill."'

Alexander hid another smile. She'd mimicked the little he'd heard of Poppy's truculent voice exactly. 'Then just let her to do whatever she wants. If that means hanging around my grandmother's or sunbathing on the balcony or beach, just let her. She'll come to you when she's ready.'

'I've tried. But every time I go near her she gets up and walks away.' Her blue eyes were bewildered.

'Tell you what,' he found himself saying. 'There's some

caves with amazing stalactites and stalagmites not very far from here. And there's a good beach nearby—shallow, so it's great for swimming—so why don't the four of us go there tomorrow?'

'You must have other things you want to do.' But he could tell by the way her eyes lit up that she liked the idea. She looked like a drowning woman being tossed a float. He hadn't planned to suggest a trip together, but the words were out and he couldn't take them back. Not that he wanted to take them back. A day with Katherine was suddenly irresistible.

'Crystal would like nothing better than to spend the day with her new idol—especially if it involves a boat trip in caves followed by a picnic and a swim. No, I promise you that is my daughter's idea of a dream day and so it's mine too. Do you want me to ask Poppy?'

'I'll do it,' she said, taking her shopping from him. Suddenly she stood on tiptoe and kissed him on the cheek. 'Thank you,' she said.

To Katherine's surprise, when she told Poppy the next morning about Alexander's invitation, she seemed keen to go. She disappeared into the shower and returned an hour later dressed and carrying one of Katherine's bags. In the meantime, Katherine had prepared a picnic with some of the fresh bread she'd bought from the village store as soon as it had opened. She'd also made a fig and mozzarella salad, which she'd put in a plastic container. There were olives, cold meat, soft drinks, and crisps too. She hoped Poppy would find at least some of it to her taste. As she made her preparations her head buzzed. Did Alexander's invite mean he was ready to listen to her? Or was he simply sorry for her? Whatever the reason, she had to at least try and make him understand.

Crystal ran into the room ahead of her father. 'We are going to swim. We're going to see magic caves! And you are coming too.'

'Yeah,' Poppy said, sliding a look at Katherine. 'So she says.' Then her daughter's face broke into a wide smile and picked Crystal up. 'Let's get into the car.'

Alexander looked as gorgeous as ever in a pair of faded jeans and a white T-shirt and Katherine's heart gave an uncomfortable thump. She couldn't read the expression in his eyes when they rested on her. Perhaps at a different time they might have had something—perhaps if she'd been a different person... Timing had never been her strong suit.

'Ready?' he asked.

'As I'll ever be.'

Crystal did all the talking as they drove towards the caves. 'I can swim, you know,' she told Poppy proudly. 'Can you?'

'Of course,' Poppy replied. 'I swim for my school.'

Katherine was surprised. But delighted. They had this in common at least. 'I swam for my school too,' she remarked.

'Whatever.'

Katherine shared a look with Alexander. It would take time, it seemed, for Poppy to unbend towards her—if she ever did.

They parked at the top car park and, leaving their bags and the picnic, walked the rest of the way. The sky was a brilliant blue, feathered with the slightest clouds, and the sea was turquoise against the blindingly white shore.

They bought the tickets for the boat trip into the caves and the children were given life jackets to put on. Poppy looked as if she was about to refuse but clearly thought better of it. Katherine was relieved. No doubt if she had refused, Crystal would have too.

The girls clambered into the front of the boat, with Katherine and Alexander squashed together on one of the seats in the stern. She was painfully aware of the familiar scent of the soap he used and the pressure of his leg against hers. She closed her eyes, remembering the feel of his arms around her, the way her body fitted perfectly against his, the way he made her laugh. She shook the images away. They might never be lovers again, but did him being here now mean that at the very least he was still her friend?

As their guide used an oar to push the boat further into the depths of the caves she gasped. Thousands of spectacular stalactites hung from the roof of the cave, which was lit with small lights that danced off the crystal formations like thousands of sparks.

Crystal turned around, eyes wide, her small hands covering her mouth. 'It is a magic cave, Baba. It's like Christmas! Only better!'

Even Poppy seemed stunned by their beauty. She spent the trip with her arm around Crystal's shoulders, pointing out different formations. Katherine had read about them yesterday after Alexander had extended his invitation and was able to tell the girls how they'd been formed as well as a little history of the caves. Poppy asked some questions, appearing to have forgotten that she wasn't speaking to Katherine. Katherine glanced at Alexander and he grinned back. He'd been right. This was the kind of trip to impress a seventeen-year-old—inasmuch as *anything* could impress this particular seventeen-year-old.

Their trip into the caves finished, Alexander returned to the car for their costumes and their picnic, while Katherine and the girls found a spot on the grass, just above the pebbly beach, where they could lay their picnic blanket. As soon as Alexander came back Poppy and Crystal disappeared off to the changing rooms to put on their swimming costumes.

'Aren't you going to swim?' Alexander asked.

'In a bit. What about you?'

'What are the chances of Crystal letting me just lie here?' When he grinned she could almost make herself believe that they were still together.

The girls came out of the changing rooms and ran down into the sea, squealing as the water splashed over their knees.

'She's a good kid,' Alexander said.

'Yes. I believe she is.'

'What happened to her father?'

Katherine sighed. It was a question she'd been waiting for Poppy to ask. 'Ben? Last time I heard, he was married with three children and doing very well as a lawyer.'

'You must have been very young when you had her.'

'I was seventeen. Sixteen when I fell pregnant.'

'You don't have to tell me anything you don't want to. It's none of my business.'

'No,' she said. 'I'd like to. It's not something I've ever spoken to anyone about, but I think I owe it to you to tell you the truth.'

'I don't want you to tell me because you think you owe me, although I would like to understand. It's not so much that you have a child you gave up for adoption, it's the fact you didn't tell me. Hell, Katherine, I bared my soul to you.'

'I know…' She sighed. 'It's just—it's been a secret I've kept for so long, afraid of what people would think if they knew…'

'I can't imagine the Katherine I know caring about what people think.'

'We all care what people think if we're honest—at least, the opinions of those we love and respect.'

'If they love and respect us, then their feelings shouldn't change...' he said slowly. He was quiet for a long time. 'I promise I'll listen this time.'

'It's a long story.'

He nodded in the direction of the girls, who were splashing each other and laughing. 'Looks like they're not going to be out of the water any time soon.'

Seeing Poppy like this reminded Katherine how painfully young her daughter still was and how painfully young she herself had been when she'd fallen pregnant. A child really.

'Remember I told you that I won a scholarship to high school?'

He nodded.

'I was proud and excited to have won it but I was totally unprepared for the reality. Being there terrified me. Most of the rest of the pupils came from well-to-do families—the children of business people, doctors and lawyers. I was desperately shy as it was, and with my second-hand uniform I knew I stuck out. Unsurprisingly perhaps, they wanted nothing to do with me. I pretended I didn't care. At break times I'd take a book and read it. I knew I still had to get top marks if I wanted to be accepted at medical school.

'I was in my second year when I met Ben. I'd been roped in to swim for the school team in the swimming gala—it was the one sport I seemed naturally good at—and he was there. He was a couple of years older than me, as confident as I was shy, as good-looking as I was geeky—but for some reason he seemed to like me.

'We were friends at first. We spent our break times together, usually in the library or just walking around, talking about history and politics—even then he knew he wanted to be a lawyer—stuff that no one else was interested in discussing but that we both loved to debate.

'Being Ben's friend changed everything. I wasn't lonely any more. I now realised there were people just like me who didn't care about clothes and the latest hairstyle. Then when I was in fourth year and he was in sixth year—he already had a place to read law—everything changed and we became boyfriend and girlfriend. He'd come around to my house. By that time Mum and Dad had bought a small restaurant and were working all hours to get it established, but then Dad died suddenly. Mum, as you can imagine, was devastated and so was I. I clung to Ben and eventually the inevitable happened. We slept together.

'It didn't seem wrong—quite the opposite. It seemed a natural progression. We'd talked often about how, when he was a lawyer—famous and defending the poor and downtrodden, of course—and I was a doctor, the very best, of course...' she risked a smile in Alexander's direction, and was reassured to find he was looking at her with the same intent expression he always had when they talked '...saving lives and discovering new treatments and cures, we'd marry and have a family. But then I fell pregnant. Stupid, I know. We did use contraception but with the optimism and ignorance of youth we weren't as careful as we should have been.

'By that time, he was about to leave to start his law degree and I had just sat my A-levels. I expected, rightly as it turned out, to get all As and I was confident I would get a place in medical school.

'To say we were both shellshocked would be an understatement. We talked about getting married, but we couldn't see how. My parents' restaurant was struggling without Dad and barely making enough for Mum to live on, and she'd been recently diagnosed with multiple sclerosis. Ben's parents weren't much better off. There didn't seem any way to have the baby.'

'What about Ben? Didn't he have a say?'

'Terminating the pregnancy was Ben's preferred option.' She looked over to where Crystal and Poppy were splashing each other and her heart stuttered. Thank God she'd never seriously considered it. 'He said he couldn't see a way of supporting me or our baby—he still desperately wanted to be a lawyer—and one night he told me that if I continued with the pregnancy he couldn't be part of either of our lives.

'We broke up. With the pregnancy something had changed between us. It was as if all that had gone on before had just been us play-acting at being a couple. Maybe if we were older… Whatever, I couldn't blame him. I didn't want to marry him, I knew that then—just as I knew I wasn't ready to be a mother. But neither could I bear to terminate the pregnancy. Oh, I thought about it. I even went as far as making an appointment with the hospital, but when it came down to it I just couldn't go through with it. I knew then I had to tell my mother. It was the most difficult conversation I've ever had in my life. I could see her imagining her and Dad's dreams of a better life for me going down the plughole. She lost it and broke down.

'When she'd pulled herself together she said that she would look after the child. It would mean my delaying going to university for a year but we'd manage. Just as we always had. But she was ill—some days I had to help her get dressed—and even then I knew what a diagnosis of

MS meant. I knew she couldn't help take care of a child—
not when she would need more and more care herself. I
was in a bad way, Alexander. I felt so alone.' She took a
shuddering breath.

'I told her that I had decided to have the baby but that I
was going to give it up for adoption. I'd done my research,
you see. I knew that you could arrange an open adoption.
I would get to pick the parents—ones already pre-selected
by the adoption agency. My child would always know they
were adopted, and although I could never see him or her, I
could write care of the adoptive parents and in return they
would send me updates. If I couldn't keep the baby myself,
it seemed the only—the best—solution.

'My mother tried to argue me out of it—she couldn't
imagine how any child of hers could even consider giving
their child away, and I think she believed I would change
my mind.

'But she was wrong. I refused to imagine it as a baby.
Instead, I pored over the biographies of the would-be adoptive parents. The adoption agency did a thorough job.
There were photographs, bits of information about their
extended families, letters from them. It was heart-break-
ing, reading their stories. I could almost hear their desperation. They had to advertise themselves to me—they
had to make me want to pick them.

'When I read about these couples I knew I was doing
the right thing. At least I managed to convince myself
that I was. Far better for the child I was carrying to have
a home with a couple who would be able to give them the
love and attention I couldn't. In the end I picked out one
family. They weren't particularly well off—I wasn't so
naïve that I thought money was all that important—but

they were financially secure. Enough to give my child everything he or she could ever need.

'But more than that, it was them as people who made them shine. They seemed kind, loving and so desperate to have afamily to shower love on. They'd been trying for a baby for several years and were getting close to the age where they'd no longer be able to put themselves forward for adoption. This was, I knew, their final chance of having a child. They also said that they hoped, in time, to adopt an older child, a brother or sister for this one. I liked that. I didn't want my child to grow up, like I did, as an only child. I wanted him or her to have a sibling who would always be there for them. So I picked them. I could have picked any of a dozen couples but I picked them.

'I know you probably can't imagine how anyone could do what I did. But I thought, I really believed I was doing the best thing for her. I insisted on an open adoption—I wouldn't have chosen Mike and Liz if they hadn't agreed to that—because although I couldn't keep Poppy myself I wanted to know that wherever she was in the world she was all right.

'But Mum was right. I hadn't accounted for how I would feel as my pregnancy continued. I began to feel protective of this child growing inside me. I didn't know what to do. I had already committed to giving her up and I knew her prospective parents were longing to welcome her into her family. But even then I thought about changing my mind—even though I knew the grief it would cause them and even though I knew I was too young to bring up a child. I began to persuade myself that with Mum's help we would manage.'

She paused and looked out to sea. 'But then Mum's multiple sclerosis returned with a vengeance. She had to have a wheelchair and she couldn't do even the basics for herself. I wondered if the stress of my pregnancy had made her worse. I felt as if it was all my fault. I didn't know what to do. So in the end I kept to my original decision and gave her up.

'The day I gave birth to her was one of the worst in my life. The labour was easy compared to what came next. They allowed me a few hours alone with her to say my goodbyes. I hadn't realised how difficult it would be. Here was this tiny thing in my arms, looking up at me as if I was the only thing in her world. I felt such an overwhelming love for her it shook me to the core. But how could I go back on my decision then? I was only seventeen. I thought it was unfair to everyone if I did. So I let them take her from me.'

It was only when he leaned across and wiped the tears from her face with the pad of his thumb that she realised she was crying. He waited without saying anything until she'd regained control again.

'I wrote to Liz often and she wrote back, telling me about Poppy's progress and sending photos. I knew when her baby teeth fell out, I knew when she got chickenpox, I saw her in her school uniform on her first day at school. I had more regrets then—seeing the photos of her, watching her grow up, albeit from a distance, made her real in a way she hadn't been before. Of course, by then it was too late to get her back. Mike and Liz were her parents and there was no doubt they loved her and that she loved them.'

He said nothing, just waited until she was ready to continue.

'I sailed through my final year at school and all my exams at medical school. But I worked for it. I hardly went out, hardly joined any clubs or societies, just worked. It all had to be for something, you see? If I'd failed I don't think I could have lived with myself. Mum never spoke of it. It was as if we pretended it hadn't happened. But sometimes I'd see Mum looking at me with such sadness it ripped me in two. I caught her once. About six months after I'd had Poppy. She was in the small bedroom at the front, the one that we kept for visitors. She was kneeling on the floor with a pile of baby clothes in front of her. She was smoothing out each item with her palms, murmuring to herself, before she placed it in a little box. Tears were running down her face. I doubt she even knew she was crying. You see the adoption only became final after six months. I could have changed my mind up until then and, believe me, sometimes I thought I might. But when I thought of the couple who had Poppy, how happy they'd been, I knew I had done the right thing. But I know now that Mum always hoped I would change my mind.

'She didn't see me so I tiptoed away. What was the point in saying anything? Even if I'd wanted to it was too late to change my mind. I had to keep believing I'd done the right thing.

'We never spoke about it. Not once.'

She drew in a shuddering breath. 'By all accounts, she was a happy child. She grew up knowing that she was adopted—that was part of the deal—and I guess it was just something she accepted.

'So many times I wished I could have been there to hold her when she was sick, to hear her laughter, just see her.' She swallowed the lump that had come to her throat. 'But I knew I had given away all my rights. I was just pleased to be allowed into her life—if only in small slices.'

'And have you told her this?'

'I've tried. But every time I raise the topic, she gets up and walks away.'

'Yet she came to find you.'

'I'm not sure she came to find me for the right reasons. When Poppy turned sixteen, Liz said that she would no longer give her my letters unless she asked. She also said that she wouldn't pass on news of Poppy. She thought, at sixteen, Poppy had the right to decide what place, if any, I had in her life. I heard nothing after that. It seemed Poppy had made her decision and I couldn't blame her. I hoped when she was older that she might seek me out.' She laughed shortly. 'I just never imagined it would be now.'

'What made her come to find you?'

'I think it was the new baby. Liz and Mike didn't think they could have children—that's why they decided to adopt. I know they intended to adopt another child, but they never did. About eighteen months ago, Liz fell pregnant—as you know, it can happen long after a couple has given up hope. The child is eight months now. I suspect Poppy's nose has been put out of joint. A baby can be demanding and she's bound to feel a little pushed out. Liz also said she's been bunking off school and her grades have taken a turn for the worse. If she carries on like this then there will be no chance of her getting accepted at university.'

'And that's important to you and to Liz?'

'Yes. Of course. Wouldn't you want the same for Crystal?'

'I want Crystal to be happy. I found out the hard way that success at work isn't the same as having success in life. Nothing is more important than being with your family. Nothing is more important than their happiness. At least to me.'

She felt stung. Somehow she'd hoped that she could make him understand, but it appeared she'd been mistaken. She bent over and undid her sandals. 'I've told you everything. Now I'm going to join the children in the water.'

Alexander watched her tiptoe gingerly into the sea. Her legs had browned in the sun and appeared to go on for ever in the tiny shorts she was wearing. He cursed himself inwardly. She was right. Who was he to judge her? It wasn't as if he had nothing to regret. But he'd wanted her to be perfect—which was rich, given that he was anything but. He still loved her but he needed time to get used to this different version of the Katherine he'd thought he'd known.

'Baba!' Crystal called from the water. 'Come in!' He rolled up the bottoms of his jeans, pulled his T-shirt over his head and went to join them.

It was, Katherine had to admit, despite the tension between her and Poppy and her and Alexander, a happy day—one of the happiest of her life. Despite everything how couldn't it be when she was spending it with the people she loved most? They swam and ate, then swam some more. As the afternoon became cooler, Alexander bought some fish from a boat he swam out to and they built a small fire over which they roasted the fish.

By the time they drove home, Crystal and Poppy were flushed with tiredness and happiness. Poppy had even come to sit next to Katherine when Alexander had taken Crystal away to dry her off and help her change back into her clothes.

'It's cool here,' Poppy said. 'I think I'd like to stay until you go back. If that's all right with you?'

'Of course,' Katherine said, delighted. 'Until I go back

at the end of the month, at any rate. Will you let your mother know?'

'Sure,' Poppy said, and leaned back, hooking her arms behind her head. 'I kind of miss them. Even the crazy baby.'

'They miss you too.' She didn't want to say anything else, frightened of spoiling the fragile truce that had sprung up between them. There would be time to talk in the days to come. At the very least she owed it to Poppy to keep trying to explain why she'd given her up. Maybe Alexander was right. She shouldn't force it. Just tell Poppy she was happy to talk about it and leave it to her to bring it up when she was ready.

Back home, Alexander parked the car in the square and lifted Crystal into his arms. 'Perhaps we could do this again?' he said.

She looked at him. 'Maybe. I'm not sure.' She still felt hurt. They had been friends before they'd become lovers. Didn't that count for anything?

He nodded and, holding his daughter in his arms, turned towards his house. Back home, Poppy also excused herself, saying she had her sleep to catch up on. Katherine suspected that she wanted to phone Liz in privacy and she was glad.

She poured herself a glass of wine and took it out onto the balcony. She'd told Alexander everything. At least now there were no more secrets between them.

She didn't see much of Alexander over the next few days, although Crystal and Poppy continued to visit each other's houses.

Katherine went to call Poppy for supper one day to find

her up to her elbows in flour. 'I just want to finish these baklavas,' she said.

Alexander's grandmother looked at Katherine, shook her head and said something to Crystal in Greek. For one mortifying moment Katherine wondered if she was being told not to visit again, but to her surprise Crystal told her that her grandmother wanted her to come and sit with her outside on the bench by the front door.

Bemused, Katherine did as she asked.

They sat on the bench and Alexander's grandmother reached out and patted her hand. As people passed she kept her hand on Katherine's. Every time one of the villagers passed, her grip would tighten and she'd smile, while calling out a greeting. Many stopped and said a few words to Grandmother and greeted Katherine too, with a 'Hello' and 'How are you?'

So that was what the old lady was up to. Whatever she thought of Katherine's decision to give her child up for adoption, she was, in her own quiet way, telling the other villagers that she supported her. Tears burned behind Katherine's eyes. It was an unexpected, touching gesture from Grandmother and she wondered whether Alexander was behind it.

Speaking of which, he was coming across the square towards them. Katherine's heart leaped. Frightened he would see the desolation in her eyes, she lowered her lids until she was sure she could look at him calmly.

'Oh, hello.' He bent and kissed his grandmother on her cheek. He said something to her in Greek and she laughed. The old lady got to her feet and retreated back inside, leaving her space on the bench for Alexander.

'I think she had an ulterior motive for sitting with me here,' Katherine murmured. 'I suspect she's telling the

village to stop shunning me. Did you have anything to
do with it?'

'No one tells Grandmother what to do, least of all me,'
he said evasively. 'But I need to tell you, I've forgiven you
for giving up Poppy. I'm sure you did what you had to and
for the best possible motives.'

Katherine leaped to her feet. 'Forgiven me? Forgiven
me! How dare you? I wanted your understanding, not your
forgiveness. You're right about one thing. I should have
told you earlier. That was wrong of me. But if you think I
need forgiveness for giving birth to her then you are badly
mistaken. And as for giving her away, you make it sound
like tossing out so much rubbish. That's not the way I felt.
I gave her to two loving, stable parents and it ripped me
apart. You just need to spend time with her to know she's
a young woman any parent would be proud of.'

Tears burned behind her eyes. She didn't even care that
her outburst had garnered a bit of an audience. 'As far as
I'm concerned,' she hissed, 'if I never see you again it will
be too soon.' She whirled around to find Poppy standing
behind her. Her daughter grinned. 'Way to go, Katherine.
Way to go!'

Katherine and Poppy talked late into the night after Poppy
had witnessed her outburst. It hadn't been an easy conversation—there had been no instant falling into each other's
arms, but the tension and angst had begun to ease. There
would, Katherine knew, be many more such conversations
and bumpy roads but they had made a start. It would take
time for them to be totally at ease with one another, but
at least they were moving in that direction. And despite
the rift between her and Alexander, she was more content
than she had been in years.

* * *

'Crystal's great-grandmother isn't well,' Poppy told her a couple of days later. Katherine's heart tumbled inside her chest. She was deeply fond of the old lady but hadn't seen her since she'd made an absolute exhibition of herself by ranting at Alexander in public.

'Do you know what's wrong with her?'

'Crystal says she has a bad cold but she didn't get up this morning.'

If Grandmother had taken to her bed she had to be ill. 'Where is Crystal?'

'I left her at the house. I wanted her to come with me so I could tell you but she wouldn't leave Yia-Yia.'

Katherine snapped the lid of her laptop closed. 'Does Crystal's father know?'

'I don't think so.'

'Come on,' Katherine said, picking up the medical bag she'd brought with her. Luckily she had a whole case of antibiotics left over from the meningitis outbreak. Did Yia-Yia have a chest infection? If she did, it wasn't good. But she shouldn't get ahead of herself. It was possible Grandmother did have just a cold.

But as soon as she saw her she knew this was no ordinary cold. The old woman was flushed and clearly running a temperature.

'Poppy, could you take Crystal to our house, please? Stay there until I come for you. You can go down to the bay if you like but no further. Do you understand?'

Was it possible that the meningitis had come back in another form? No, that was unlikely if not impossible. However, until she knew for sure what it was, it was important to keep her away from the others.

For once Poppy didn't argue with her. She took Crystal

by the hand. 'Go fetch your costume. My mum will look after your great-grandmother.'

It was the first time Poppy had called her Mum and a lump came to Katherine's throat. She swallowed hard and made herself focus. She had a job to do.

After listening to Yia-Yia's chest and taking her temperature, which as she'd expected was way too high, Katherine phoned Alexander.

'I'll come straight away,' he said, when she told him.

'I'll give her oral antibiotics,' Katherine said, 'but she could do with them IV to be on the safe side. Do you want me to take her to hospital?'

'Wait until I get there,' he said. 'I'll be thirty minutes.'

While she waited for him to arrive, Katherine wetted a facecloth in cold water and wrung it out, before placing it on Grandmother's forehead. When the old lady tried to push her away she soothed her with a few words in Greek, grateful that it had improved to the point where she could reassure her.

'Alexander is on his way,' she said softly. 'He says you are to lie quietly and let me look after you until he gets here.'

'Crystal? Where is she?'

'Poppy has taken her to my house. Don't worry, she'll make sure she's all right.'

The elderly woman slumped back on her pillows, worryingly too tired to put up a fight.

Alexander must have driven as if the devil himself was behind him as he arrived in twenty minutes instead of the thirty he'd told her. He nodded to Katherine before crouching at his grandmother's side.

'Her pulse is around a hundred and shallow. She's

pyrexial. I've given her antibiotics by mouth. Crystal is with Poppy. I thought it best.'

When Alexander looked up she could see the anguish in his eyes. He took out his stethoscope and Katherine helped Grandmother into a sitting position while Alexander listened to her chest again.

'As I thought. A nasty chest infection. She's probably caught a dose of the flu that's been going around and a secondary infection has set in very fast.'

'Does she need to go to hospital?'

Grandmother plucked at Alexander's sleeve. 'She says she won't go,' he translated. 'She wants to stay in her own home.'

'In that case,' Katherine said, 'that's what's going to happen. We can easily put her on a drip and give her IV antibiotics that way. Poppy and I can help look after her. What do you think?'

'I think it's risky.'

'More risky than admitting her to hospital?'

His shoulders slumped. 'You're right.'

She wished she could put her arms around him and tell him everything would be okay, but nothing in his demeanour suggested he would welcome the overture.

'I'll stay here with your grandmother,' Katherine said, 'while you fetch whatever it is we'll need.'

Later when they had Grandmother on a drip and her breathing was better, Katherine slipped home to ask Poppy to take Crystal back to her father. A short while later she was standing on the balcony when she became aware that Poppy had come to stand beside her. 'Is she going to get better?' she whispered.

'I hope so.' She reached out for her daughter's hand and squeezed it. Poppy didn't pull away. Instead, she leaned into her. Katherine pulled her close. 'We're all going to do everything to make sure she will. But, sweetheart, I think you should go back to Liz and Mike. If flu is going around, I don't want you to get it.'

'But I could have it already and just not be showing the symptoms yet. If I go back I could pass it on to my baby brother.' It was the first time she'd referred to Charlie as her baby brother. 'So I'm staying,' Poppy continued in a tone that sounded much like her own when she wouldn't be argued with. 'I'll help you look after Grandmother and any of the villagers who need help. I can't nurse them but I can cook and run errands.'

Katherine's eyes blurred as she considered her amazing child. 'I'm so proud of you,' she said. 'Did I ever tell you that?'

Poppy grinned back at her. 'And I'm proud of you. Now, shouldn't we get busy?'

'I think it's time I went home,' Poppy said. She'd been a godsend this last two weeks, helping by playing with Crystal while Alexander and Katherine took turns caring for Grandmother. They barely saw each other, the one leaving as the other took over. She'd also helped care for some of the other elderly villagers who'd fallen ill with flu. But Grandmother was much better, as were the others affected. 'I think Mum can do with some help with Charlie.' She looked at Katherine, a small frown between her brows. 'You're okay…' she grinned self-consciously '…but she's still my mum.'

'Of course she is. She's the woman who's cared for you all your life, the woman who nursed you through all your childhood sicknesses. Who was always there for you. Of course she'll always be your mum. But I hope you'll always remember that I love you too. If it helps, think of me as an honorary aunt. Someone who will always be there for you.'

'You know, and I don't mean this to sound horrible, I'm glad you gave me up. I can't imagine anyone except Liz and Mike being my parents. I mean, they get on my nerves sometimes but, you know, they've always been there.'

Katherine winced at the implied rebuke in Poppy's words.

'Would you still have given me away if you had the chance to do it all over again?'

Katherine took her time thinking about her answer. She loved Poppy too much to be anything less than honest.

'I feel so lucky that you are part of my life now—to have been given this second chance to get to know you. And knowing you now, I can't imagine a scenario where I would ever give you up. But back then I didn't know you and I wasn't the person I am now. Remember I was about your age. Half grown up and half still a child. Everything seemed so black and white then.

'I do know that I thought of you almost every day and receiving the updates about you from Liz were the highlight of my year. Wait there. I'd like to show you something.'

She went inside and retrieved the album she always carried with her. She placed it on the patio table. 'Liz sent me a photo of you on every birthday and Christmas. This is you on your first birthday.' She passed a photograph to Poppy. She was standing in front of a birthday cake with a single candle. A hand belonging to someone just out of shot was supporting her and Poppy was grinning into the camera, two small teeth showing. Katherine handed her several more photos. 'Here you are on your first day at school, when you joined the Brownies, your first swimming lesson, your first trip to the beach. Liz sent me a letter with every photograph and sometimes a little souvenir from your life—like this picture you drew when you came back from a holiday in Spain. I wrote to you too.

'I'm not pretending any of that makes up for not bringing you up myself, but I knew you were happy and so I could live with my decision.'

'Why didn't you ever get married?

'The right person never came along. One of the things I promised myself when I gave you up was that I would concentrate on being the best doctor I could be.'

'And you did.' The admiration in her daughter's eyes made her want to cry.

'I'm human, Poppy. You of all people know that. Don't ever think anyone can be perfect.'

'You like Alexander, don't you?' Poppy said out of the blue. 'And I think he likes you too.'

It felt odd discussing her love life, or rather lack of it, with her seventeen-year-old daughter.

'He did once, I think.' She leaned across and wrapped her arms around her child. 'But I've got you now. And that's more than enough for me.'

Two days later, the tickets home were booked and Poppy had gone for a nap, exhausted after a day spent cooking and running errands. Her daughter was truly an amazing young woman.

Katherine had made supper but Poppy hadn't reappeared. She boiled the kettle and made her some of her favourite camomile tea. She loved how she now knew these small details about her child.

Taking the tea with her, she tiptoed into Poppy's bedroom. Her daughter was lying spreadeagled on the bed, the sheets tangled in her long limbs. Once more Katherine sent a silent prayer upwards for whatever had brought her daughter back to her.

But something about the way Poppy's face was screwed up—as if she were in pain—made her cross the room and place a hand on her child's forehead. At the feel of cold sweat alarm shot through her. Poppy had been complaining of a sore stomach the night before but this was something more.

Perhaps she had the same flu that had brought Grandmother and some of the other villagers low? Stamping down on the panic that threatened to overwhelm her, she gently shook her daughter by the shoulder. 'Poppy, wake up.'

Poppy opened her eyes, groaned and closed them again.

Her heart beating a tattoo against her ribs, Katherine knelt by the side of the bed and examined Poppy's limbs. To her horror she saw that her legs were covered with a faint but definite purpuric rash. It was one of the signs of meningitis. Worse, it was a sign that the disease had already taken hold.

Forcing herself to keep calm, she ran back to the sitting room and picked up her mobile. Her hands were shaking so badly she was almost not capable of punching in Alexander's number.

To her relief, he picked up straight away.

'Dr Dimitriou.' The sound of his voice almost made her sink to the floor with relief.

'Alexander. Where are you?'

'At home.' He must have picked up the fear in her voice. 'What is it? Are you all right?

'It's Poppy. I need you to come.'

'I'll be there in a few minutes.'

She went back to Poppy's room and tried to rouse her again but once more, her daughter's eyes only flickered. She needed to get antibiotics into her and soon. Perhaps she should have phoned for an ambulance instead of Alexander. But that would take longer. The ambulance would have to come here—at least an hour—and make its way back. And every moment could make a difference.

She sat on the bed and pulled her child into her arms. 'Hold on, darling, please, hold on.'

Alexander was there in less than five minutes, although it felt like hours. He took the scene in at a glance. Katherine looked over at him, anguish etched in every line of her face.

'She feels unwell and has a purpuric rash. I think she has meningitis. Help us, Alexander.'

Although he wanted nothing more than to take her into his arms, he automatically switched into professional mode. He felt Poppy's pulse. Rapid but still strong. She was clammy to the touch but the night was hot. He inspected her limbs and torso. There was a rash but it didn't quite look like the ones he'd seen on patients suffering from meningitis. However, given the recent outbreak, meningitis was still the most likely diagnosis.

'Let's get her to hospital,' he said, picking Katherine's child up. 'You sit in the back with her and phone ahead to let them know we're on our way.'

For once Katherine didn't complain about the way he

drove. She cradled her child in her arms, murmuring words of love and encouragement.

Later that night Katherine sat by the bed, holding her daughter's hand. Poppy had been started on IV antibiotics and it would be some time before they would know whether they'd caught it in time. Alexander had disappeared. He was going to phone Liz and Mike as soon as he'd spoken to the doctors again.

Was she going to lose her daughter again when she'd just found her? Why hadn't she forced her to leave even if she'd felt confident that there was zero chance of her daughter contracting the disease? Had she let her own desire to have Poppy with her get in the way of what was right for her child?

She murmured a prayer. 'God, if you're there, please don't take my child. I'll do anything—give up everything—if only you won't take her.'

A few moments later she heard a soft footfall behind her and looked up to find Alexander smiling down at her. Why was he smiling? Didn't he know she was in danger of losing her child?

'I have good news,' he whispered. 'Poppy doesn't have meningitis.'

'What do you mean? Of course she must have. The aches and pains, the rash...'

'It's the rash that got me thinking,' he said. 'It's very like a meningococcal one but I noticed it was only on her shins. I remember reading something about an illness that can mimic meningitis so I looked it up. Katherine, Poppy has Henoch-Schönlein purpura, not meningitis. When the kidneys get involved it can be nasty but Poppy's kidneys aren't affected.'

'She doesn't have meningitis?' Katherine could hardly believe it.

'No. She'll feel quite ill for a week or two, but I promise you she's going to be fine.'

Katherine's vision blurred as Alexander wrapped his arms around her. 'It's okay,' he murmured into her hair. 'You can let go now. I promise you, everything is going to be okay.'

'How is Poppy today?' Alexander asked Katherine a couple of days later when he visited them in hospital. She was a different woman from the one bent over Poppy's bedside when she'd thought her child was desperately ill. The worry and fear had left her eyes and the steely determination he knew so well was back.

'She's booked on this afternoon's flight to London. I'm going with her.'

'Of course.'

'Thank you for being here.' She held out her hand and he grasped her long, cool fingers. 'Thank you for recognising she didn't have meningitis.'

'Will you come back?'

She smiled wanly. 'I don't think so.'

'I love you, Katherine.' She needed to know that.

There was no response. She just looked at him with her cool blue eyes. 'Do you?'

'I was a fool, an idiot-think of any noun you like and it could apply to me, but I love you, more than I thought possible to love another woman. Just give me a chance and I'll prove it to you.'

She smiled wanly. 'I'm sorry, Alexander, but it's over.' She shook her head. 'I need to go if we're to catch our plane.'

He wanted to reach out to her but the coldness in her eyes held him back. Now was not the time to convince her to give them another chance.

He pressed her fingers. 'If ever you want to come back, if ever you need me, I'll be here.'

CHAPTER NINE

KATHERINE THRUST HER hands deep into her coat pockets and pulled her collar up. Almost overnight, the leaves had fallen from the trees, carpeting the ground.

In a week's time, Poppy would be coming to stay with her for the October school break. Liz and Mike were dropping her off before heading off to stay with Liz's family in the Cotswolds. After Poppy had a week with her, Katherine would drive her daughter up there and stay for the night, before returning to London.

It was amazing how quickly she'd become part of Poppy's family. As she and Poppy had discussed, she never tried to take Liz's place but instead acted the part of the trusted aunt or wise big sister. Poppy had applied to and was starting medical school the autumn after next should she get the grades she and her teachers expected.

Katherine's feet were beginning to freeze as the cold seeped through her boots, but she was reluctant to return home. The solitude that she'd cherished before she'd gone to Greece—before Poppy and Alexander—now felt disturbingly like loneliness.

The crunch of footsteps came from behind her and she whirled around.

At first she'd thought she dreamed him up.

He was every bit as beautiful as she remembered. His hair was slightly longer and he'd lost weight so that his cheeks were more prominent but laughter still lurked in his eyes.

He was wearing a thick trench coat over a thin jersey and jeans and heavy boots.

They looked at each other for a long moment. 'Katherine,' he murmured, and stepped towards her.

She'd been waiting for him to come to her since she'd left Greece. She'd told herself that he would but she hadn't been sure. Then, as the days had turned into weeks, she'd given up hoping.

What had brought him here now? Her heart hammered against her chest.

'How did you find me?' she whispered.

'You do know that Poppy and Crystal still write to each other? Crystal has been giving me regular updates every time your name is mentioned, which is pretty often, or so I gather.'

But it had taken him all this time to come and find her.

'Is Crystal with you?'

'Of course. I left her at the hotel with Poppy. It was Poppy who told me you'd be here and where to find you.'

'Poppy is in London?'

'She met us at the airport earlier.'

'It sounds as if she's decided to meddle. I think she's frightened I'll stay an old maid and she'll spend her adult years looking after me when I'm an old lady. That's why she asked you to come.'

It was a conversation they'd had as a joke—so why was she repeating it? Why was she babbling?

'Poppy didn't ask me to come, Katherine. I wrote to her and told her I was coming to see you and she asked me to keep it as a surprise.' He stepped towards her, his familiar soapy smell turning her bones to water. 'To be honest, I wasn't sure you'd want to see me.'

She stepped back and he halted where he was. 'How is Grandmother?' she asked.

'Looking forward to seeing you again. I think she's decided that you are already part of her family.'

Already part of the family?

He took hold of her collar and pulled her close. 'I've missed you,' he said into her hair. 'More than I thought possible.'

'You don't sound too pleased about it,' she mumbled.

'I am. I'm not. It depends.'

She placed her hands against his chest and although she wanted nothing more than to go on touching him for ever, to be held by him for ever, she pushed him away. 'Depends on what?'

'On whether you feel the same way.'

'I think you know how I feel.' She took a moment to steady her breathing. 'But I won't be with you and have you disapprove of me—or of what I did. I can't go through life thinking and feeling I have to pay over and over for what I did.' She tried to smile but it came out all wobbly. 'I've spent the last seventeen years of my life feeling as if I don't deserve to be happy. Being in Greece, being with Poppy changed all that for ever. I did what I felt I had to do at the time. That was the person I was back then and I can't change her. I'm not even sure I want to.'

'God, Katherine. Don't you understand what I'm saying? I love you. I love everything about you and that includes the person you were as well as the woman you are now. When I met you I didn't want to fall in love with you. I tried not to but I couldn't help it. So I told myself that

Sophia would want me to be happy, would want me to re-marry, especially someone who obviously cared for Crystal.' He looked at her with anguished eyes. 'I didn't tell you everything about Sophia. I have to tell you the rest so you can try to understand why I did what I did.'

He took her hand and led her across to a bench. 'I was six months away from being able to apply for the job in America. In the meantime I had been offered a consultant post at St George's, even though they knew I was going to America. In fact, they said it was one of the reasons they'd chosen me. While I was away they would employ a locum and my job would be kept open for me. It was a flatter-ing reminder of the esteem in which I was held, but at the time I saw it as nothing less than what I was due—what I had worked for over the years.

'But I didn't want to take my foot off the pedal, although I could have. I had the job I wanted—one that was mine for life. I had the post in America. I had done everything I'd set out to do. Now, if there ever was, it had to be Sophia's time. And I was prepared to shoulder more of the child care—or at least that's what I promised Sophia.

'She had an interview for one of the smaller orchestras. It wasn't the career as a concert pianist she'd hoped for but it would have been a start. I wasn't sure. I didn't know if she'd be expected to travel. And it would only have been for eighteen months. But she was so happy to be given the chance. Nervous too. She started playing the piano, prac-tising as if her life depended on it.

'Every hour that she wasn't looking after Crystal she was practising. Often I'd wake up in the night to hear the sounds of Mozart or Beethoven; I can barely listen to their music now. She was in a frenzy—so sure that this was her last chance. It was only then that I realised how much she'd sacrificed for me. And then she fell pregnant again. It wasn't planned, just one of those things, and that was that. Her chance was over.'

He paused for a long moment.

Katherine held her breath as she waited for him to continue.

'It was December and the winter had already been harsh. I left the house early—sometimes before six—but she always got up to see me off. That morning she'd been complaining of a headache. When I think back she'd been complaining of a headache the night before too. But I didn't take too much notice. I was already thinking of a complicated surgery I had that morning. She said she would take some painkillers and go back to bed for an hour or so. Crystal was staying with my mother for a few days. Sophia was thirty-two weeks by this time so I told her that I thought it was a good idea, kissed her and left.' He passed a hand across his face.

'If I'd stopped to look at her, really look at her, I would have seen the warning signs. I was a doctor, for God's sake. A couple of minutes—that's all it would have taken.'

A chill ran up Katherine's spine as she sensed what was coming.

'The roads were bad. The gritting lorries rarely came down the lane leading to our house so I'd taken the four-by-four. She sometimes drove me to the train station so she would have the use of the car, but because she had a headache she suggested I take it. I would leave it at the train station and catch the train from there. It would mean Sophia being without a car, but she said she wasn't intending to go anywhere anyway. She didn't need anything from the village and if she did, she would call me and I could pick it up on the way home.

'I was just relieved to get the use of the car. I needed to catch the six-thirty train if I was to make it to the hospital in time to see my patient before surgery was scheduled to start.'

Katherine's heart was beating a tattoo against her ribs. She sensed what was coming. 'You don't have to tell me any more,' she said softly.

'I do. I have gone over the day so many times in my head, trying to make it come out a different way, but of course that's impossible. We make these decisions in our lives, sometimes ones made in a split second, like the car driver who reverses without looking or overtakes when he shouldn't.'

'And sometimes we agonise over decisions for months but it doesn't mean that they turn out to be right,' she whispered. 'I, of all people, know that.'

'But you've come to terms with your demons. It's taken me this long to come to terms with mine. You need to know what happened so you can try and understand why I reacted to finding out about Poppy the way I did.'

'Tell me, then,' she said softly.

'Surgery that day went like a dream. I had two on my list—both major cases so I wasn't finished in Theatre until late. My secretary had left a note that Sophia had phoned and I tried to call her back, but there was no answer. I assumed she was in the bath—if I assumed anything. I went to see my post-operative patients and planned to try to get her again after that.

'Typically I got caught up and it wasn't until seven that I remembered I hadn't phoned her. I tried again and it went to voice mail. I still wasn't worried. She could be in the bath or in the garden and not heard the phone. She didn't keep her mobile on her unless she was away from home.

'But I was keen to get home—just to reassure myself. I had this uneasy sense of something not being quite right.

'The train seemed to take for ever. I kept trying to get her on the phone and when she still didn't answer I became more and more worried. I wondered if she'd fallen. There was no one nearby—no neighbours for me to call. Sophia would have known their names but I wouldn't even have recognised any of them.

'It did cross my mind to call the police, but I couldn't think of a good reason. My wife not answering her phone for an hour or two was hardly an emergency.

'I collected the car from the station, cursing the snow and praying that the road wouldn't be completely blocked, but nothing was going my way that night. I could only get as close as the lane leading down to the house before drifting snow made it impossible for me to go any further. There was nothing for it but to walk the rest of the way. All this time I was getting increasingly frantic. What if Sophia had gone outside and something had happened? What if she was caught in a snow drift?

'But I told myself that she was too sensible for that. Why would she need to go outside? By that time I was at the house. It was dark—it would normally be lit up like a Christmas tree. It could be a power cut—they weren't infrequent where we lived—but I couldn't fool myself any longer about something being seriously wrong.

'I let myself inside and called out for her. No answer. The lights were working so it wasn't a power cut.

'I found her in our bedroom. She had her mobile in her hand. She was unconscious. But she was alive. I could see that she'd been fitting and now I noticed that her ankles, hands and face were puffy.

'Eclampsia. And I'd been too damn into myself and

my career to even notice. But there was no time to berate myself then. If Sophia was to have a chance of surviving I had to get her to hospital and quickly.

'I called 999. They said they would send an ambulance straight away. I told them they wouldn't get any further than my car and that I would meet them there. They said it would take around twenty minutes to get to me, supposing the roads stayed clear. The baby had to be delivered. If I'd had a scalpel with me, so help me God, that's what I would have done.

'She came round briefly, enough to recognise that I was there, but she started fitting again. I waited until she stopped and then I wrapped her in a blanket and carried her to the car. Thankfully the ambulance arrived at almost the same time.

'They delivered our son. But it was too late. For either of them.'

Katherine wrapped her arms around him and held him. What could she say? All she could do for him was let him talk. No wonder he'd been so shocked when he'd found out about Poppy. Sophia had died bringing a child into the world, whereas, it must have seemed to him, she had casually given hers away.

'If it wasn't for Crystal I don't know how I would have got through the next months. In the end it was Helen stepping in that saved us both. As soon as she heard the news she jumped on the first plane. She was with us before night fell. I was like a madman. That I'd lost the woman who was my very heartbeat was bad enough, but the guilt that she might not have died had I been a different man was worse.

'I stopped going to work. I turned down the consultant job at St George's and the one in America—to be fair to them they told me to think it over, to take my time, but I knew I wouldn't take them up. You see, I no longer felt as if I deserved it. I guess, to be honest, I was sunk in self-pity. So far sunk in it I was wallowing.'

'How old was Crystal?'

'She was three. Old enough to miss her mother but not old enough to understand that she would never see her again and definitely not old enough to understand that this man—who she barely knew, remember—hadn't a clue how to look after her. Even if I had, I was so deep in my trough of self-pity I think I was in danger of enjoying it.

'And when Helen came to stay that gave me more opportunity to wallow. Now she was there to take care of Crystal, there was nothing to hold me back. I drank myself almost unconscious most nights. I rarely got out of bed until mid-morning and when I did I couldn't be bothered getting dressed or shaved. Sometimes I didn't even shower until mid-afternoon.

'God knows how long that would have gone on if Helen hadn't called in reinforcements. It was as if the whole of my extended Greek family had taken up residence. Helen, her mother, my mother and my grandmother too—if my grandfather and father had been alive they would have been there also. I'm pretty sure their disapproving ghosts were in the background, cheering them on and wagging their heads at me.

'Those formidable women kissed and hugged me and then marched me off to the shower. My mother threw every last drop of alcohol down the sink and then Helen and Yia-Yia cooked up a storm. They looked after Crystal, but most importantly they made me see it was my job to care for my child. They fed her and dressed her, but after that it was up to me to look after her.

'Do you know, she clung to them the first time I tried

to take my daughter to the park on my own? She gripped the sides of the door when I tried to lift her, so in the end my first trip outside with my daughter since the funeral was with my whole family in tow. It got better after that. I still mourned Sophia but my family made me see that she would have been furious if she'd seen the way I'd gone to pieces. And I knew they were right. I had stolen her dreams from her, and what kind of major creep would I be if I couldn't make a life—a good, loving, caring life— for our daughter?

'The rest, as they say, is history. I sold everything we owned in England and ploughed it into a small practice here in Greece. Then...' he smiled wanly '...I met you. I fought my attraction to you, but I couldn't help it. You were the only woman who had come close to measuring up to Sophia, the only woman I could imagine spending the rest of my life with. But I felt guilty. It seemed a betrayal of Sophia's memory.

'Then I found out about Poppy and it was as if I didn't know you at all. As if the perfect woman I had built up in my mind had disappeared in a breath of wind. I'd put you on a pedestal' you see. I guess we're not so dissimilar, huh? Both of us seemed to feel the need to atone.'

Katherine grimaced. 'I no longer feel I have to atone. As I said, I did what I did and I just have to look at the wonderful young and happy woman Poppy is today to know I made the right decision. I'm sorry I couldn't be perfect for you. But, you know, Alexander, I don't think I want to be perfect.'

'No,' he said softly. 'Of course you don't. You're human. Like us all.'

'So what changed your mind?'

'Nothing changed my mind. When you told me why

you gave Poppy up I realised why you'd felt you'd had no choice. And when I saw you with Poppy I could see how you felt about her. I was coming to beg your forgiveness when Grandmother became unwell. As soon as I was sure she was all right I was coming to ask you to stay—to marry me. That's when you phoned me about Poppy. I knew it wasn't the time to tell you how I felt. Every ounce of your attention was—quite rightly—focussed on your daughter. I knew there would be time later—when she was better.'

He rubbed the back of his neck. 'What I wasn't so sure about was whether you could forgive me. Then when you were about to leave and you looked right through me, I thought I had ruined any chance I had with you.' His Greek accent became more pronounced, as it always did when he was emotional.

She looked him in the eye. 'You said you forgave me! I wasn't looking for forgiveness. Not from you! How could I be with a man who thought I needed his forgiveness?'

'It was a stupid, thoughtless thing to say.'

'It was,' she agreed. 'I needed the man I loved to love me warts and all.'

His eyes burned. 'So you do love me?'

'I think I fell in love with you almost from the moment I set eyes on you. But I was frightened too. I wanted to tell you about Poppy but I just couldn't. At least, not then. I was planning to tell you, but then Poppy turned up. I never wanted you to find out that way.

'Then she became ill and I couldn't think of anything else. I thought I was going to lose her again. I made a pact with myself, with the gods, to anyone I thought might be listening. If they'd let Poppy live I would give you up. I know it's crazy but I was crazy back then.'

'But when she was better, why didn't you write to me?'

'It took a long time for her to recover completely. I couldn't leave her.' She smiled wryly. 'And I was keeping my pact. Then when she was completely better I wanted you to come to me. I needed to know that you wanted me. The woman I am, not the one in your imagination.'

'I would have come sooner, but I was arranging a job here. I've taken a year's sabbatical. I love you. I adore you. I don't want a life without you. I lost Sophia because I put my ambition before her needs. I won't do that to you. God, woman, put me out of my misery. I have to know if you love me—if you will marry me and live with me. If you say yes, I'll spend the rest of my life trying to make you happy.' A gust of wind blew the leaves around his feet. But she needed to be sure. She had to know she wouldn't be second best.

'What about Sophia?' she asked. 'I don't want to spend my life competing with the memory of a woman who was so perfect. Because we both know I'm not. None of us are.'

'You're perfect to me,' he said. When she made to protest he stopped her words with his fingertips. 'I don't want perfection, my love. It's too hard to live up to.' He grinned. 'But you'll do me. What about you? Can you put up with a man who doesn't always appreciate a good thing when he comes across it?'

She smiled back at him, her heart threatening to burst from her chest. 'You know what? I rather think I can.'

EPILOGUE

THE TINY WHITEWASHED church was perched on a small promontory overlooking the sea. Poppy had helped Katherine find the place where she would marry Alexander. And it was perfect.

It was a glorious spring day and even the small breeze that whipped Katherine's dress around her ankles was welcome.

Crystal could barely control her excitement. She'd been hopping from foot to foot all morning, keeping up a constant flow of chatter. Poppy wasn't much better. Although she'd tried to hide it, she was almost as excited and thrilled to have been asked to be Katherine's bridesmaid—to the extent that she'd removed her piercings in honour of the occasion, although Katherine had no doubt they'd be back in place tomorrow. Not that she cared. Poppy could have turned up in a paper bag for all she cared. All that mattered was that she was here today, celebrating what was the happiest day of her mother's life.

She glanced at the girls. Crystal with a basket of rose petals hooked over her elbow and Poppy holding the little girl's hand. Who would have thought a year ago that she would be standing here with her two children, because that's how she saw them. Crystal and Katherine had other mothers—women who would always be an important part of their lives—or, in Crystal's case, an important memory, but they had her too. And she would always be there for them—to hold them when their hearts got broken, to help them achieve their dreams, whatever those might be, to support them when life wasn't so kind and eventually to help them plan their weddings, if that's what they wished. Whatever lives they chose for themselves, she'd be there cheering them on, as she was certain her mother was cheering her on. Mum would be so proud.

Her gaze turned to the man beside her, more Greek god than gladiator in his cream suit and neatly pressed shirt. She'd earned her doctorate and had accepted a job in Athens for a couple of years. She was almost fluent in Greek now. After that? They didn't know, but they'd be deciding together.

She had the future—a wonderful future—to look forward to, and she'd be doing it with Alexander by her side.

* * * * *

HER LITTLE
SPANISH SECRET

BY
LAURA IDING

Laura Iding loved reading as a child, and when she ran out of books she readily made up her own, completing a little detective series when she was twelve. But, despite her aspirations for being an author, her parents insisted she look into a 'real' career. So the summer after she turned thirteen she volunteered as a Candy Striper, and fell in love with nursing. Now, after twenty years of experience in trauma/critical care, she's thrilled to combine her career and her hobby into one—writing Medical Romances for Mills & Boon. Laura lives in the northern part of the United States, and spends all her spare time with her two teenage kids (help!)—a daughter and a son—and her husband. Enjoy!

This book is dedicated to the
Milwaukee WisRWA group.
Thanks to all of you for
your ongoing support.

PROLOGUE

Four and a half years earlier...

KAT had never seen so much blood—it pooled on the floor and stained the walls of the O.R. suite. Dr. Miguel Vasquez, along with two other trauma surgeons, had worked as hard as they could to stop the bleeding but to no avail. Their young, pregnant patient and her unborn baby had died.

After the poor woman's body had been sent to the morgue, Kat was left alone to finish putting the supplies and equipment away while the housekeepers cleaned up the blood. Only once they were finished did she head over to the staff locker room. Thankfully, her shift was over, she was exhausted. Yet as tired as she was physically, she was emotionally keyed up, and couldn't get the horrific scene from the O.R. out of her mind. They hadn't had a case like that in a long time.

After she changed out of her scrubs into a pair of well-worn jeans and a short-sleeved sweater, she found Dr. Vasquez sitting in the staff lounge, holding his head in his hands. He looked so upset and dejected that she stopped—unable to simply walk away.

"Please don't torture yourself over this," she urged

softly, as she sank down beside him on the sofa close enough that their shoulders brushed. "Her death wasn't your fault."

Miguel slowly lifted and turned his head to look at her, his eyes full of agony. "I should have called the rest of the team in earlier."

"You called them as soon as you discovered her abdomen was full of blood and they came as soon as they could," she corrected. "No one knew she was pregnant, it was too early to tell."

"I should have examined her more closely down in the trauma bay," he muttered, more to himself than to her. "Then we would have known."

"Do you really think that would have made a difference?" she asked softly. "Even if the other two surgeons had been notified earlier, they wouldn't have been able to come right away. Dr. Baccus said they were resuscitating a patient in the I.C.U. All of us in the O.R. suite did the best we could."

He stared at her for a long moment, and then sighed. "I can't help thinking about what I should have done differently. I know we can't save every patient, but she was just so young. And pregnant. I can't help feeling I failed her."

She put her hand on his arm, trying to offer some reassurance. "If three of the best trauma surgeons in the whole hospital couldn't save her or her baby, then it wasn't meant to be."

A ghost of a smile played along the edges of his mouth, and she was glad she'd been able to make him feel a little better. Because what she'd said was true. Everyone talked about Miguel's skill in the O.R. He could have stayed here in the U.S. once his fellowship was finished, even though he'd made it clear that wasn't part of his plan.

She reluctantly slid her hand from his arm and rose to her feet. But she'd only taken two steps when he stopped her.

"Katerina?"

She hesitated and turned to look back at him, surprised and secretly pleased he'd remembered her first name. They'd operated on dozens of patients together, but while she'd always been keenly aware of Miguel, she had never been absolutely sure he'd noticed her the same way. "Yes?"

"Do you have plans for tonight? If not, would you join me? We could get a bite to eat or something."

She wasn't hungry, but could tell Miguel didn't want to be alone, and suddenly she didn't either. Word amongst the O.R. staff was that Miguel wasn't in the market for a relationship since his time in the U.S. was limited, but she ignored the tiny warning flickering in the back of her mind. "I don't have any plans for tonight, and I'd love to have dinner." *Or something.*

"Muy bien." He rose to his feet and held out his hand. She took it and suppressed a shiver when a tingle of awareness shot up her arm.

But she didn't pull away. Instead, she stayed close at his side while they left the hospital together.

CHAPTER ONE

"Down, Mama. *Down!*"

"Soon, Tommy. I promise." Katerina Richardson fought a wave of exhaustion and tightened her grip on her wriggly son. She couldn't imagine anything more torturous than being stuck in a plane for sixteen hours with an active soon-to-be four-year-old. She didn't even want to think of the longer flight time on the return trip.

Plenty of time to worry about that, later. For now they'd finally arrived in Seville, Spain. And she desperately needed to get to the hospital to see how her half sister was doing after being hit by a car. The information from Susan Horton, the coordinator for the study abroad program, had been sketchy at best.

"I can't believe the stupid airline lost my luggage," her best friend, Diana Baylor, moaned as they made their way out of the airport to the line of people waiting for taxis. "It's so hot here in April compared to Cambridge, Massachusetts. I'm already sweating—I can't imagine staying in these same clothes for very long."

Kat felt bad for her friend, who'd only come on this trip in the first place as a favor to her, but what could she do? Diana's lost luggage was the least of her concerns. "Don't worry, I'll share my stuff or we'll buy what you need."

"Down, Mama. Down!" Tommy's tone, accompanied by his wiggling, became more insistent.

"Okay, but you have to hold my hand," Kat warned her son, as she put him on his feet. She'd let him run around in the baggage claim area while they'd waited for their luggage, but even that hadn't put a dent in his energy level. She was grateful he'd slept on the plane, even though she hadn't. Kat grabbed hold of his hand before he could make a beeline for the road. "Stay next to me, Tommy."

He tugged on her hand, trying to go in the opposite direction from where they needed to wait for a taxi. Thank heavens the line was moving fast. Her son was as dark as she was blonde and if she had a nickel for every person who'd asked her if he was adopted, she'd be rich. Even here, she could feel curious eyes on them.

"No, Tommy. This way. Look, a car! We're going to go for a ride!"

His attention diverted, Tommy readily climbed into the cab after Diana. They all squished into the back seat for the short ride to their hotel. "Hesperia Hotel, please," she told the taxi driver.

"Hesperia? *No comprendo* Hesperia." Their cab driver shook his head as he pulled out into traffic, waving his hand rather impatiently. *"No comprendo."*

Kat refused to panic and quickly rummaged through her carry-on bag to pull out the hotel confirmation document. She handed it to him so he could read the name of the hotel for himself. He looked at the paper and made a sound of disgust. "Es-peer-ria," he said, emphasizing the Spanish pronunciation. "Esperia Hotel."

Properly chastised, she belatedly remembered from her two years of high-school Spanish that the H was silent. Being in Spain brought back bittersweet memories of Tommy's father, especially during their three-hour layover in Madrid. She'd briefly toyed with the thought of trying to find Miguel, but had then realized her idea was ludicrous. Madrid was a huge city and she had no idea where to even start, if he'd even be there, which she seriously doubted. He may have studied there but it was possible he'd moved on. "*Sí*. Hesperia Hotel, *gracias*."

The taxi driver mumbled something unintelligible and probably uncomplimentary in Spanish, under his breath. Kat ignored him.

"Are you going to the hospital today?" Diana asked with a wide yawn. "I'm voting for a nap first."

"I doubt Tommy will sleep any time soon," she reminded her friend. "And, yes, I'm going to head to the hospital as soon as we get the hotel room secured. I'm sorry, but you'll have to watch Tommy for a while."

"I know," Diana said quickly. "I don't mind." Kat knew Diana wouldn't renege on her duties, seeing as Kat had been the one to pay for her friend's airfare, along with footing the hotel bill. Kat hadn't minded as she'd needed someone to help watch over her son. "Wow, Kat, take a look at the architecture of that building over there. Isn't it amazing?"

"Yeah, amazing." Kat forced a smile, because Diana was right—the view was spectacular. Yet the thrill of being in Europe for the first time in her life couldn't make her forget the reason they were there. The knot in her stomach tightened as she wondered what she'd discover when she went to the hospital. Susan Horton, the director of the study abroad program at Seville

University, had called just thirty-six hours ago, to let her know that her younger half sister, Juliet, had a serious head injury and was too sick to be flown back to the U.S. for care.

Kat had immediately made arrangements to fly over to Seville in order to be there for her sister.

She and Juliet hadn't been particularly close. And not just because of the seven-year age gap. They had different fathers and for some reason Juliet had always seemed to resent Kat. Their respective fathers had both abandoned their mother, which should have given them something in common. After their mother had been diagnosed with pancreatic cancer, Kat had promised her mother she'd look after Juliet.

Juliet had gone a little wild after their mother's death, but had settled down somewhat after she'd finished her second year of college. At the ripe old age of twenty-one, Juliet had insisted on studying abroad for the spring semester of her junior year. Kat had been forced to pick up a lot of call weekends in order to pay for the program, but she'd managed. To be fair, Juliet had come up with a good portion of the money herself.

Kat felt guilty now about how she'd been secretly relieved to put her younger sister on a plane to Spain. But even if she'd tried to talk Juliet out of going, it wouldn't have worked. Juliet would only have resented her even more.

How had the accident happened? All she'd been told was that Juliet had run out into the street and had been hit by a car, but she didn't know anything further.

Getting to the hotel didn't take long, although there was another hassle as she figured out the dollar to Euro exchange in order to pay the cranky cab driver. As soon as Diana and Tommy were settled in the hotel room, Kat asked the front-desk clerk for directions to the hospital. She managed to figure out how to get there on the metro, which wasn't very different than using the subway back home.

Seville's teaching hospital was larger than she'd expected and that gave her hope that Juliet was getting good medical and nursing care. Kat found her sister in their I.C.U and walked in, only to stop abruptly when she saw Juliet was connected to a ventilator. Her stomach clenched even harder when she noted several dark bruises and small lacerations marring her sister's pale skin.

"Dear heaven," she breathed, trailing her gaze from her sister up to the heart monitor. She'd done a year-long stint in the I.C.U before going to the O.R. so she'd known what to expect, but had hoped that Juliet might have improved during the time it had taken her to make the travel arrangements and actually arrive in Seville.

A nurse, dressed head to toe in white, complete with nurse's cap on her dark hair, came into the room behind her. Kat blinked back tears and turned to the nurse. "How is she? Has her condition improved? What is the extent of her injury? Can I speak to the doctor?"

The nurse stared at her blankly for a moment and then began talking in rapid Spanish, none of which Kat could understand.

Kat wanted to cry. She desperately paged through the English/Spanish dictionary she held, trying to look up words in Spanish to explain what she wanted to know. *"¿Donde esta el doctor? ¿Habla Ingles?"* she finally asked. Where is the doctor? Speak English?

The nurse spun around and left the room.

Kat sank into a chair next to Juliet's bed, gently clasping her half sister's hand in hers. Maybe the age difference, and completely opposite personalities, had kept them from being close, but Juliet was still her sister. With their mother gone, they only had each other.

She had to believe Juliet would pull through this. Her sister was young and strong, surely she'd be fine.

Kat put her head down on the edge of Juliet's bed, closing her eyes just for a moment, trying to combat the deep fatigue of jet lag and her fear regarding the seriousness of her sister's injuries.

She didn't think she'd fallen asleep, but couldn't be sure how much time had passed when she heard a deep male voice, thankfully speaking in English. She lifted her head and prised her heavy eyelids open.

"I understand you have questions regarding the condition of Juliet Campbell?"

"Yes, thank you." She quickly rose to her feet and blinked the grit from her eyes as she turned to face the doctor.

His familiar facial features made the room gyrate wildly, and she had to grasp the edge of her sister's side rail for support. "Miguel?" she whispered in shock, wondering if she was dreaming. Had thoughts of Tommy's father conjured up a mirage? Or was it just the doctor's Hispanic features, dark hair falling rakishly over his forehead, deep brown eyes gazing into hers, that were so achingly familiar?

"Katerina." His eyes widened in surprise, and she couldn't help feeling relieved to know she wasn't the only one knocked off balance at this chance meeting. For several long seconds they simply stared at each other across the room. Slowly, he smiled, relieving part of the awkwardness. "What a pleasant surprise to see you again. How are you?"

She tightened her grip on the bed rail behind her because her knees threatened to give away. "I'm fine, thanks." She struggled to keep her tone friendly, even though for one beautiful night they'd been far more than just friends. Yet despite her fanciful thoughts during the Madrid layover, she hadn't really expected to see Miguel again.

He looked good. Better than good. Miguel was taller than most Latino men, with broad shoulders and a golden skin tone that showcased his bright smile. His dark eyes were mesmerizing. If not for his full name, Dr. Miguel Vasquez, embroidered on his white lab coat—she'd for sure think this was a dream.

She knew Juliet's condition needed to be her primary concern, but she had so many other questions she wanted to ask him. "I'm surprised to find you here in Seville. I thought you lived in Madrid?"

He didn't answer right away, and she thought she saw a flash of guilt shadow his dark eyes. She glanced away, embarrassed. She didn't want him feeling guilty for the night they'd shared together. Or for leaving so abruptly when notified of his father's illness. It wasn't as if they'd been dating or anything.

Neither was it his fault she'd let her feelings spin out of control that night.

When she'd discovered she was pregnant, she'd called his cell phone, the only number she'd had, but the number had already been out of service. She'd assumed he hadn't kept his old American phone once he'd returned to Spain. She'd looked for him on several social media sites, but hadn't found him. After about six months she'd stopped trying.

"I live here," he said simply. "My family's olive farm is just twenty minutes outside Seville."

"I see," she said, although she really didn't. Obviously, she hadn't known much about Miguel's family. She could hardly picture him growing up on an olive farm. She'd simply assumed because he was a Madrid exchange student that he'd lived there. She forced a smile, wishing they could recapture the easy camaraderie they'd once shared. "How's your father?"

"He passed away three and a half years ago." The shadows in Miguel's eyes betrayed his grief.

"I'm sorry," she murmured helplessly. She'd known that Miguel had needed to return to Spain when his father had been sick, but she was a little surprised that he'd stayed here, even after his father had passed away.

During the night they'd shared together he'd confided about how he dreamed of joining Doctors Without Borders. When she hadn't been able to get in touch with Miguel once she'd discovered she was pregnant, she'd imagined him working in some distant country.

Why hadn't he followed his dream? He'd told her about how he was only waiting to be finished with his family obligations. And his father had passed away three and a half years ago. He should have been long gone by now.

Not that Miguel's choices were any of her business.

Except, now that he was here, how was she going to tell him about their son?

Panic soared, squeezing the air from her lungs. She struggled to take a deep breath, trying to calm her jagged nerves. Right now she needed to focus on her sister. She pulled herself together with an effort. "Will you please tell me about Juliet's head injury? How bad is it? What exactly is her neuro status?"

"Your sister's condition is serious, but stable. She responds to pain now, which she wasn't doing at first. She does have a subarachnoid hemorrhage that we are monitoring very closely."

A subarachnoid hemorrhage wasn't good news, but she'd been prepared for that. "Is she following commands?" Kat asked.

"Not yet, but she's young, Katerina. She has a good chance of getting through this."

She gave a tight nod, wanting to believe him. "I know. I'm hopeful that she'll wake up soon."

"Katerina, I have to get to surgery as I have a patient waiting, but I would like to see you again. Would you please join me for dinner tonight? Say around eight-thirty or nine?"

She blinked in surprise and tried to think of a graceful way out of the invitation. She knew he was asking her out from some sense of obligation, because they'd spent one intense night together.

But she needed time to get the fog of fatigue out of her mind. Time to think about if and when to share the news about Tommy. Obviously Miguel deserved to know the truth, but what about Tommy? Did he deserve a father who didn't want him? A father who'd made it clear he wasn't looking for a family?

She didn't know what to do.

"I'm sorry, but I'm sure I'll be asleep by then," she murmured, averting her gaze to look at her sister. "I just flew in today and I'm a bit jet-lagged."

She steeled herself against the flash of disappointment in his eyes. Juliet's well-being came first. And Tommy's was a close second.

As far as she was concerned, Miguel Vasquez would just have to wait.

Miguel couldn't believe Katerina Richardson was actually here, in Seville.

He allowed his gaze to roam over her, branding her image on his mind. She wasn't beautiful in the classical sense, but he'd always found her attractive with her peaches and cream complexion and long golden blonde hair that she normally wore in a ponytail. Except for that one night, when he'd run his fingers through the silk tresses.

To this day he couldn't explain why he'd broken his cardinal rule by asking her out. Granted, he'd been devastated over losing their patient, but he'd been determined to avoid emotional entanglements, knowing he was leaving when the year was up. He knew better than to let down his guard, but he'd been very attracted to Katerina and had suspected the feeling was mutual. That night he'd given up his fight to stay away.

But then the news about his father's stroke had pulled him from Katerina's bed the next morning. He'd rushed home to Seville. His father's condition had been worse than he'd imagined, and his father had ultimately died twelve painful months later. His mother was already gone, and during his father's illness his younger brother, Luis, had started drinking. Miguel had been forced to put his own dreams on hold to take over the olive farm, which had been in the Vasquez family for generations, until he could get Luis sobered up.

His visceral reaction to seeing Katerina again

stunned him. He hadn't allowed himself to miss her. Besides, he only had three months left on his contract here at the hospital and he'd be finally free to join Doctors Without Borders.

And this time,nothing was going to stop him. Not his brother Luis. And certainly not Katerina.

He shook off his thoughts with an effort. Logically he knew he should accept her excuse, but he found himself pressing the issue. "Maybe a light meal after siesta, then? Certainly you have to eat some time."

There was a wariness reflected in her green eyes that hadn't been there in the past. He wondered what had changed in the four and a half years they'd been apart. He was relieved to note she wasn't wearing a wedding ring even though her personal life wasn't any of his business. He couldn't allow himself to succumb to Katerina's spell—he refused to make the same mistakes his father had.

"You've described my sister's head injury, but is there anything else? Other injuries I need to be aware of?" she asked, changing the subject.

He dragged his attention to his patient. "Juliet was hit on the right side. Her right leg is broken in two places and we had to operate to get the bones aligned properly. She has several rib fractures and some internal bleeding that appears to be resolving. Her head injury is the greatest of our concerns. Up until late yesterday she wasn't responding at all, even to pain. The fact that there is some response now gives us hope she may recover."

Katerina's pale skin blanched even more, and his gut clenched when he noted the tears shimmering in her bright green eyes. They reminded him, too much, about the night they'd shared. An intense, intimate, magical night that had ended abruptly with his brother's phone call about their father. She'd cried for him when he'd been unable to cry for himself.

"When can she be transported back to the United States?" she asked.

The instinctive protest at the thought of her leaving surprised him. What was wrong with him? He wrestled his emotions under control. "Not until I'm convinced her neurological status has truly stabilized," he reluctantly admitted.

Katerina nodded, as if she'd expected that response. "Are you my sister's doctor? Or just one of the doctors here who happen to speak English?" she asked. Her gaze avoided his, staying at the level of his chest.

"Yes, I'm your sister's doctor. As you know, I'm a surgeon who does both general and trauma surgery cases."

"Do any of the nurses speak English?"

Seville didn't have the same tourist draw as Madrid or Barcelona, which meant not as many of the locals spoke English. Miguel had originally learned English from his American mother, who'd taught him before she'd died. He'd learned even more English during his time at the University of Madrid. In fact, he'd earned the opportunity to live and study medicine in the U.S. at Harvard University.

There he'd ultimately become a doctor. And met Katerina. He dragged his thoughts out of the past. "No, the nurses don't speak much English, I'm afraid."

She closed her eyes and rubbed her temples, as if she had a pounding headache. Once again he found himself on the verge of offering comfort. But he didn't dare, no matter how much he wanted to.

"I would appreciate periodic updates on my sister's condition whenever you have time to spare from the rest of your patients," she said finally.

The way she turned her back on him, as if to dismiss him, made him scowl. He wanted to demand she look at him, talk to him, but of course there wasn't time. Glancing at his watch only confirmed he was already late for his scheduled surgery. "I'd be happy to give you an update later today, if you have time at, say, four o'clock?" He purposefully gave her the same time he normally ate a late lunch, right after siesta.

She spun around to face him. "But—" She stopped herself and then abruptly nodded. "Of course. Four o'clock would be fine."

He understood she'd only agreed to see him so that she could get updates on her sister, but that didn't stop him from being glad he'd gotten his way on this. "I look forward to seeing you later, then, Katerina," he said softly.

He could barely hide the thrill of anticipation racing through him, knowing he'd see her again soon, as he hurried down to the operating room.

CHAPTER TWO

"So what do you think? Do I really need to tell Miguel about Tommy?" Kat asked, after she'd caught up with Diana and Tommy at the park located right across the street from their hotel. The park was next to a school and seeing all the kids in their navy blue and white uniforms playing on the playground wasn't so different from the preschool Tommy attended back in the U.S.

"I don't think you should do anything yet," Diana advised. "I mean, what do we know about the custody laws in Spain? What if Miguel has the right to take Tommy away from you?"

The very thought made her feel sick to her stomach. "Tommy is a U.S. citizen," she pointed out, striving for logic. "That has to count for something."

"Maybe, maybe not. I don't think you should say anything until we know what we're dealing with. Miguel is a big important doctor at the largest hospital here. Maybe he has connections, friends in high places? I think you need to understand exactly what you're dealing with if you tell him."

Kat sighed, and rubbed her temples, trying to ease the ache. Lack of sleep, worry over Juliet and now seeing Miguel again had all combined into one giant, pounding headache. "And how are we going to find out the child custody laws here? Neither one of us can speak Spanish, so it's not like we can just look up the information on the internet."

"We could check with the American Embassy," Diana said stubbornly.

"I suppose. Except that seems like a lot of work when I'm not even sure Miguel will bother to fight me for Tommy. During our night together he told me his dream was to join Doctors Without Borders. He made it clear he wanted the freedom to travel, not settling down in one place."

"Except here he is in Seville four and a half years later," Diana pointed out reasonably. "Maybe he's changed his mind about his dream?"

"Maybe." She couldn't argue Diana's point. She still found it hard to wrap her mind around the fact that Miguel was here, in Seville. She'd stayed with her sister for another hour or so after he'd left, slightly reassured that Juliet's condition was indeed stable, before she'd come back to the hotel to unpack her things. Seeing Miguel had made her suddenly anxious to find her son.

Tommy was having a great time running around in the park, chasing butterflies. As she watched him, the physical similarities seemed even more acute. She realized the minute Miguel saw Tommy, he'd know the truth without even needing to be told.

Although Miguel wouldn't have to see him, a tiny voice in the back of her mind reminded her. Tommy could stay here with Diana and in a couple of days hopefully Juliet would be stable enough to be sent back to the U.S. Miguel didn't need to know anything about their son.

As soon as the thought formed, she felt a sense of shame. Keeping Tommy's presence a secret would be taking the coward's way out. Diana was worried about the Spanish custody laws, but Kat had other reasons for not wanting to tell Miguel about Tommy. Being intimate with Miguel had touched her in a way she hadn't expected. When she'd discovered she was pregnant, she'd been torn between feeling worried at how she'd manage all alone to secretly thrilled to have a part of Miguel growing inside her.

She knew he hadn't felt the same way about her. Men had sex with women all the time, and lust certainly wasn't love. She knew better than to get emotionally involved. In her experience men didn't remain faithful or stick around for the long haul. Especially when there was the responsibility of raising children. Her father and Juliet's father had proven that fact.

She gave Miguel credit for being upfront and honest about his inability to stay. He hadn't lied to her, hadn't told her what he'd thought she'd wanted to hear. It was her fault for not doing a better job of protecting her heart.

Telling Miguel about Tommy opened up the possibility that she'd have to see Miguel on a regular basis. If they were raising a child together, there would be no way to avoid him. She would have to hide her true feelings every time they were together.

Unless Miguel still didn't want the responsibility of a son? There was a part of her that really hoped so, because then he wouldn't insist on joint custody.

Now she was getting way ahead of herself. Maybe she could tell Miguel about Tommy and reassure him that she didn't need help, financially or otherwise, to raise her son. She and Tommy would be fine on their own. The way they had been for nearly four years.

"Don't agonize over this, Kat. You don't have to tell him this minute, we just got here. Give me a little time to do some research first, okay?"

"I guess," she agreed doubtfully. Diana was clearly concerned, but she was confident that Tommy had rights as an American citizen. "I won't do anything right away, although I really think I'm going to have to tell him eventually. I tried to call him when I discovered I was pregnant, even tried to find him on all the popular social media websites. Now that I know he's here, I need to be honest with him."

"Then why do you look like you're about to cry?" Diana asked.

"Because I'm scared," she murmured, trying to sniffle back her tears. "I couldn't bear it if Miguel tried to fight for custody."

"Okay, let's just say that the Spanish law is the same as the U.S. regarding joint custody. You mentioned he wasn't wearing a wedding ring, but we both know that doesn't always mean much. Miguel might be married or seriously involved in a relationship. Could be the last thing on earth that he wants is to fight for joint custody."

"You're right," she agreed, even though the thought of Miguel being married or involved with someone didn't make her feel any better. "Okay, I need to get a grip. Maybe I'll try talking to Miguel first, try to find out about his personal life before springing the news on him."

Diana nodded eagerly. "Good idea. Meanwhile, I'll see if I can call the U.S. embassy to get more information."

Kat nodded, even though deep down she knew she'd have to tell him. Because Miguel deserved to know. Besides at some point Tommy was going to ask about his father. She refused to lie to her son.

The spear in her heart twisted painfully and tears pricked her eyes. As difficult as it was to be a single mother, she couldn't bear the thought of sending Tommy off to be with his father in a far-away country. Although she knew she could come with Tommy, no matter how difficult it would be to see Miguel again.

If Miguel was truly planning to join Doctors Without Borders, maybe all of this worry would be for nothing. She and Tommy would go back home and continue living their lives.

Tommy tripped and fell, and she leaped off the park bench and rushed over, picking him up and lavishing him with kisses before he could wail too loudly. "There, now, you're okay, big guy."

"Hurts," he sniffed, rubbing his hands over his eyes and smearing dirt all over his face.

"I know, but Mommy will kiss it all better." Holding her son close, nuzzling his neck, she desperately hoped Miguel would be honorable enough to do what was best for Tommy.

Kat returned to the hotel room to change her clothes and freshen up a bit before going back to the hospital to see Juliet and Miguel. She'd left Diana and Tommy at the local drugstore, picking out a few necessities for Diana to hold her over until her luggage arrived. They'd also picked up two prepaid disposable phones, so they could keep in touch with each other. After fifteen minutes, and with the help of one shopkeeper who did speak a bit of English, they had the phones activated and working.

The metro was far more crowded towards the end of the workday, forcing her to stand, clinging to the overhead pole.

At her stop, she got off the cramped carriage and walked the short distance to the hospital. The temperature had to be pushing eighty and by the time she arrived, she was hot and sweaty again.

So much for her attempt to look nice for Miguel.

Ridiculous to care one way or the other how she looked. Men weren't exactly knocking down her door, especially once they realized she had a son. Not that she was interested in dating.

She hadn't been with anyone since spending the night with Miguel. At first because she'd been pregnant and then because being a single mother was all-consuming. But she didn't regret a single minute of having Tommy.

In the hospital, she went up to the I.C.U. and paused outside Juliet's doorway, relieved to discover Miguel wasn't there, waiting for her. Her sister had been turned so that she was lying on her right side facing the doorway, but otherwise her condition appeared unchanged.

She crossed over and took Juliet's hand in hers. "Hi, Jules, I'm back. Can you hear me? Squeeze my hand if you can hear me."

Juliet's hand didn't move within hers.

"Wiggle your toes. Can you wiggle your toes for me?"

Juliet's non-broken leg moved, but Kat couldn't figure out if the movement had been made on purpose or not. When she asked a second time, the leg didn't move, so she assumed the latter.

She pulled up a chair and sat down beside her sister, glancing curiously at the chart hanging off the end of the bed. She didn't bother trying to read it, as it would all be in Spanish, but she wished she could read the medical information for herself, to see how Juliet was progressing.

She kept up her one-sided conversation with her sister for the next fifteen minutes or so. Until she ran out of things to say.

"Katerina?"

The way Miguel said her name brought back a fresh wave of erotic memories of their night together and she tried hard to paste a *friendly* smile on her face, before rising to her feet and facing him. "Hello, Miguel. How did your surgery go this morning?"

"Very well, thanks. Would you mind going across the street to the restaurant to talk?" he asked. "I've missed lunch."

She instinctively wanted to say no, but that seemed foolish and petty so she nodded. She glanced back at her sister, leaning over the side rail to talk to her. "I love you, sis. See you soon," she said, before moving away to meet Miguel in the doorway.

As they walked down the stairs to the main level of the hospital, he handed her a stack of papers. "I spent some time translating bits of Juliet's chart for you, so that you can get a sense as to how she's doing."

Her jaw dropped in surprise and for a moment she couldn't speak, deeply touched by his kind consideration. "Thank you," she finally murmured, taking the paperwork he offered. Miguel had often been thoughtful of others and she was glad he hadn't changed during the time they's spent apart. She couldn't imagine where he'd found the time to translate her sister's chart for her between seeing patients and doing surgery, but she was extremely grateful for his efforts.

He put his hand on the small of her back, guiding her towards the restaurant across the street from the hospital. The warmth of his hand seemed to burn through her thin cotton blouse, branding her skin. She was keenly aware of him, his scent wreaking havoc with her concentration, as they made their way across the street. There was outdoor seating beneath cheerful red and white umbrellas and she gratefully sat in the shade, putting the table between them.

The waiter came over and the two men conversed in rapid-fire Spanish. She caught maybe one familiar word out of a dozen.

"What would you like to drink, Katerina?" Miguel asked. "Beer? Wine? Soft drink?"

"You ordered a soft drink, didn't you?" she asked.

He flashed a bright smile and nodded. "You remember some Spanish, no?" he asked with clear approval.

"Yes, *muy poco*, very little," she agreed. "I'll have the same, please."

Miguel ordered several *tapas*, the Spanish form of appetizers, along with their soft drinks. When the food arrived, she had no idea what she was eating, but whatever it was it tasted delicious.

"Do you want to review Juliet's chart now?" he asked. "I can wait and answer your questions."

"I'll read it later, just tell me what you know." She wanted to hear from him first. Besides, there was no way she'd be able to concentrate on her sister's chart with him sitting directly across from her.

He took his time, sipping his drink, before answering. "Juliet has begun moving around more, which is a good sign. She will likely start to intermittently follow commands soon. We have done a CT scan of her brain earlier this morning and the area of bleeding appears to be resolving slowly."

She nodded, eating another of the delicious *tapas* on the plate between them. There were olives too, and she wondered if they were from Miguel's family farm. "I'm glad. I guess all we can do right now is wait and see."

"True," he agreed. He helped himself to more food as well. "Katerina, how is your mother doing? Wasn't she scheduled to have surgery right before I left the States?"

She nodded, her appetite fading. "Yes. The result of her surgery showed stage-four pancreatic cancer. She died a couple months later." Despite the fear of being a single mother, at the time of her mother's passing, her pregnancy had been one of the few bright spots in her life. Things had been difficult until Juliet had gone off to college. Thankfully, her friend Diana had been there for her, even offering to be her labor coach.

"I'm sorry," he murmured, reaching across the table to capture her hand in his. "We both lost our parents about the same time, didn't we?"

"Yes. We did." His fingers were warm and strong around hers, but she gently tugged her hand away and reached for her glass. She tried to think of a way to ask him if he was married or seeing someone, without sounding too interested.

"I have thought of you often these past few years," Miguel murmured, not seeming to notice how she was struggling with her secret. He took her left hand and brushed his thumb across her bare ring finger. "You haven't married?"

She slowly shook her head. There was only one man who'd asked her out after Tommy had been born. He was another nurse in the operating room, one of the few male nurses who worked there. She'd been tempted to date him because he was a single parent, too, and would have been a great father figure for Tommy, but in the end she hadn't been able to bring herself to accept his offer.

She hadn't felt anything for Wayne other than friendship. And as much as she wanted a father for Tommy, she couldn't pretend to feel something she didn't.

Too bad she couldn't say the same about her feelings toward Miguel. Seeing him again made her realize that she still felt that same spark of attraction, the same awareness that had been there when they'd worked together in the U.S. Feelings that apparently hadn't faded over time.

"What about you, Miguel?" she asked, taking the opening he'd offered, as she gently pulled her hand away. "Have you found a woman to marry?"

"No, you know my dream is to join Doctors Without Borders. But I can't leave until I'm certain my brother has the Vasquez olive farm back on its feet. Luis has a few—ah—problems. Things were not going well here at home during the time I was in the U.S." A shadow of guilt flashed in his eyes, and she found herself wishing she could offer him comfort.

"Not your fault, Miguel," she reminded him, secretly glad to discover he hadn't fallen in love and married a beautiful Spanish woman. "How old is Luis?"

"Twenty-six now," he said. "But too young back then to take on the responsibility of running the farm. I think the stress of trying to hold everything together was too much for my father." He stared at his glass for a long moment. "Maybe if I had been here, things would have been different."

She shrugged, not nearly as reassured as she should be at knowing his dream of joining Doctors Without Borders hadn't changed. She should be thrilled with the news. Maybe this would be best for all of them. He'd go do his mission work, leaving her alone to raise Tommy. Miguel could come back in a few years, when Tommy was older, to get to know his son.

All she had to do was to tell him the truth.

Diana wanted her to wait, but she knew she had to tell him or the secret would continue to eat at her. She'd never been any good at lying and didn't want to start now. She swallowed hard and braced herself. "Miguel, there's something important I need to tell you," she began.

"Miguel!" A shout from across the street interrupted them. She frowned and turned in time to see a handsome young man, unsteady on his feet, waving wildly at Miguel.

"Luis." He muttered his brother's name like a curse half under his breath. "Excuse me for a moment," he said as he rose to his feet.

She didn't protest, but watched as Miguel crossed over towards his brother, his expression stern. The two of them were quickly engrossed in a heated conversation that didn't seem it would end any time soon.

Kat sat back, sipping her soft drink and thinking how wrong it was for her to be grateful for the reprieve.

"Luis, you shouldn't be drinking!" Miguel shouted in Spanish, barely holding his temper in check.

"Relax, it's Friday night. I've been slaving out at the farm all week—don't I get time to have fun too? Hey, who's the pretty Americana?" he asked with slurred speech, as he looked around Miguel towards where Katerina waited.

"She's a friend from the U.S.," he answered sharply. "But that's not the point. I thought we had an agreement? You promised to stay away from the taverns until Saturday night. It's barely five o'clock on Friday, and you're already drunk." Which meant his brother must have started drinking at least a couple of hours ago.

"I sent the last olive shipment out at noon. I think you should introduce me to your lady friend," Luis said with a sloppy smile, his gaze locked on Katerina. "She's pretty. I'd love to show her a good time."

The last thing he wanted to do was to introduce Katerina to his brother, especially when he was intoxicated. Luis had been doing fairly well recently, so finding him like this was more than a little annoying.

What was Luis thinking? If he lost the olive farm, what would he do for work? Or was this just another way to ruin Miguel's chance to follow his dream? He was tired of trying to save the olive farm for his brother while taking care of his patients. He was working nonstop from early morning to sundown every week. It was past time for Luis to grow up and take some responsibility.

"Go home, Luis," he advised. "Before you make a complete fool of yourself."

"Not until I meet your lady friend," Luis said stubbornly. "She reminds me a little of our mother, except that she has blonde hair instead of red. Are you going to change your mind about going to Africa? She may not wait for you."

Miguel ground his teeth together in frustration. "No, I'm not going to change my mind," he snapped. He didn't want to think about Katerina waiting for him. No matter how much he was still attracted to her, having a relationship with an American woman would be nothing but a disaster. His mother had hated every minute of living out on the farm, away from the city. And far away from her homeland. He was certain Katerina wouldn't be willing to leave her home either. "Katerina's sister is in the hospital, recovering from a serious head injury. She's not interested in having a good time. Leave her alone, understand?"

"Okay, fine, then." Luis shook off his hand and began walking toward the bar, his gait unsteady. "I'll just sit by myself."

"Oh, no, you won't." Miguel captured his brother's arm and caught sight of his old friend, Rafael, who happened to be a police officer. "Rafael," he called, flagging down his friend.

"Trouble, amigo?" Rafael asked, getting out of his police car.

"Would you mind taking my brother home?" He grabbed Luis's arm, steering him toward the police car, but his brother tried to resist. Luis almost fell, but Miguel managed to haul him upright. "I would take him myself, but I'm on call at the hospital."

"All right," Rafael said with a heavy sigh. "You'll owe me, my friend. Luckily for you, I'm finished with my shift."

"Thanks, Rafael. I will return the favor," he promised.

"I'll hold you to that," Rafael muttered with a wry grimace.

Miguel watched them drive away, before he raked a hand through his hair and turned back towards Katerina. As if the fates were against him, his pager went off, bringing a premature end to their time together.

"My apologies for the interruption," he murmured as he returned to the table. "I'm afraid I must cut our meal short. There is a young boy with symptoms of appendicitis. I need to return to the hospital to assess whether or not he needs surgery."

"I understand," Katerina said, as he paid the tab. She gathered up the papers he'd given to her. "Thanks again for translating Juliet's chart for me. I'm sure I'll see you tomorrow."

"Of course." When she stood, she was so close he could have easily leaned down to kiss her. He curled his fingers into fists and forced himself to take a step backwards in order to resist the sweet temptation. "I will make rounds between nine and ten in the morning, if you want an update on your sister's condition."

"Sounds good. Goodbye, Miguel." She waved and then headed for the metro station, located just a few blocks down the street.

Back at the hospital it was clear the thirteen-year-old had a classic case of appendicitis and Miguel quickly took the child to the operating room. Unfortunately, his appendix had burst, forcing Miguel to spend extra time washing out the abdominal cavity in order to minimize the chance that infection would set in. Afterwards, he made sure the boy had the correct antibiotics ordered and the first dose administered before he headed home to his three-bedroom apartment located within walking distance of the hospital.

It wasn't until he was eating cold leftover pizza for dinner that Miguel had a chance to think about Katerina, and wonder just what she'd thought was so important to tell him.

CHAPTER THREE

"Look, it's a shopping mall!" Diana exclaimed. Then she frowned. "I almost wish my luggage hadn't shown up this morning, or I'd have a good excuse to go buy new clothes."

Kat nodded ruefully. She was surprised to find Seville was a city of contrasts, from the modern shopping mall to the mosques and bronze statues straight out of the sixteenth century. "A little disappointing in a way, isn't it?" she murmured.

"Hey, not for me," Diana pointed out. "I mean, the history here is nice and everything, but I'm all in favor of modernization. Especially when it comes to shopping."

They'd walked to a small café for breakfast, and found the shopping mall on the way back to the hotel. "Maybe you can explore the mall with Tommy this morning while I'm at the hospital, visiting Juliet."

"Sounds good. Although don't forget we plan on taking the boat tour later this afternoon," Diana reminded her.

"I won't forget," Kat murmured. Sightseeing wasn't top of her list, but it was the least she could do for Diana as her friend spent a good portion of every day watching her son. Besides, sitting for hours at the hospital wasn't going to help Juliet recover any quicker.

"Here's the metro station," Kat said. "Call me if you need anything, okay? I'll see you later, Tommy." Kat swept him into her arms for a hug, which he tolerated for barely a minute before he wiggled out of her grasp.

"We'll be fine," Diana assured her, taking Tommy's hand in a firm grip.

"I know." She watched them walk away towards the mall, before taking the steps down to the metro station to wait for the next train. Despite the fact that she still needed to break the news about Tommy to Miguel, she found she was looking forward to seeing him again. Last night, before she'd fallen asleep, Miguel's words had echoed in her mind, giving her a secret thrill.

I've thought of you often over these past few years.

She doubted that he'd thought of her as often as she'd thought of him, though. Mostly because of Tommy since he was the mirror image of his father. Yet also because Miguel had taken a small piece of her heart when he'd left.

Not that she ever planned on telling him that.

She needed to let go of the past and move on with her life. Whatever her conflicting feelings for Miguel, she couldn't afford to fall for him. They wanted different things out of life. She wanted a home, family, stability. Miguel wanted adventure. He wanted Doctors Without Borders. He wanted to travel. The only time they were in sync was when they had worked as colleagues in the O.R..

And, of course, during the night they spent together. Walking into the hospital was familiar now, and she greeted the clerk behind the desk in Spanish. *"Buenos dias."*

"Buenos dias," the clerk replied with a wide grin. One thing about Spain, most people seemed to be in a good mood. Maybe because they had a more laid-back lifestyle here. She found it amazing that the shops actually closed down for three hours between noon and three for siesta. She couldn't imagine anyone in the U.S. doing something like that.

Yet if the people were happier, maybe it was worth it?

Kat took the stairs to the third-floor I.C.U., entered her sister's room and crossed over to the bedside, taking her sister's small hand in hers. "Hi, Jules, I'm back. How are you feeling, hmm?"

She knew her sister wasn't going to open her eyes and start talking, which would be impossible with a breathing tube in anyway, but Kat was convinced patients even in her sister's condition could hear what was going on around them, so she decided she'd keep up her one-sided conversation with her sister.

"Seville is a beautiful city, Jules, I can understand why you wanted to study here. I wish I knew exactly what happened to you. No one here seems to know anything more than the fact that you ran into the road and were struck by a car. Can you hear me, Jules? If you can hear me, squeeze my hand."

When Juliet's fingers squeezed hers, Kat's knees nearly buckled in relief. "That's great, Juliet. Now wiggle your toes for me. Can you wiggle your toes?"

This time Juliet's non-casted left leg moved again. It wasn't wiggling her toes, exactly, but Kat was still thrilled at the small movement. Her sister was truly doing better. Juliet would probably only follow commands intermittently, but each day she'd improve and do better.

Exactly the way Miguel had assured her she would.

"Good job, Jules. I'm so glad you can hear me. You're still in the hospital in Seville, but as soon as you're better, you're going to be sent to an American hospital back home. Can you understand what I'm saying? If you can understand me, squeeze my hand."

Juliet squeezed her hand again, and relieved tears blurred her vision. Her sister was going to make it. Juliet might have a long road to recovery ahead of her, but she was going to make it.

"Katerina?"

At the sound of Miguel's voice she whirled around and quickly crossed over to him. "She's following commands, Miguel!" she exclaimed. "She's starting to wake up!"

He caught her close in a warm hug. "I'm glad," he murmured, his mouth dangerously close to her ear.

She wanted to wrap her arms around his waist and lean on his strength, but she forced herself to step away, putting badly needed distance between them. What was wrong with her? It wasn't as if she'd come to Seville in order to rejuvenate her feelings for Miguel. Better for her if she kept him firmly in the friendship category. As if their one night together had been an aberration.

One that had produced a son.

There was no reason to feel as if being around Miguel was like coming home. Truthfully, she'd never been farther from home.

"I'm sorry," she said, wiping her tears on the back of her hand while searching for a tissue. "I didn't mean to get all emotional on you."

"Here." He grabbed the box of tissues from the bedside table and handed them to her. "Don't apologize, I know how worried you've been."

She blew her nose and pulled herself together, forcing a smile. "I hope this doesn't mean you're going to send Juliet home right away, are you?"

"Not yet. I would like your sister to be completely off the ventilator and more awake before she's transported back to the U.S."

"Sounds good." She was relieved to know they wouldn't have to leave Seville just yet. Especially as she hadn't told Miguel about Tommy. A wave of guilt hit hard. Should she tell him now? No, this wasn't exactly the time or the place for a heavy conversation. Besides, Miguel was working, making rounds. No doubt he had many patients to see.

She was about to ask him what time he got off work when he reached over to take her hand in his. "Katerina, will you have dinner with me tonight?"

She hesitated just a moment before nodding her assent. Wasn't this what she'd wanted all along? A good time and place to tell him about his son? A quiet dinner with just the two of them would be the perfect time to give him the news. "Yes, Miguel. Dinner would be wonderful."

"Excellent," he murmured. His gaze was warm and she had to remind herself this wasn't a date. Her son's future was what mattered here, not her roller-coaster feelings for his father.

"What time?" she asked.

"We'll go early as I know you're not used to our customs yet. Shall we say eight o'clock?"

A wry grin tugged at the corner of her mouth because eight o'clock wasn't at all early back home. "All right. Where should I meet you?"

"I will pick you up at your hotel. Which one are you staying at?"

"We— I'm at the Hesperia hotel," she said, using the correct Spanish pronunciation while hoping he didn't catch her slip.

"Excellent. There is a wonderful restaurant just a few blocks away." He glanced at his watch. "I'm sorry, but I need to finish making rounds. Did you have any questions about the chart copies I gave you?"

She'd read through his entire stack of notes early that morning, before Tommy had woken up. "I noticed her electrolytes keep going out of whack—do you think that's because of her head injury?"

"Yes, brain injuries cause sodium levels to drop, but try not to worry as we are replacing what she's lost."

She'd noticed the IV solution running through Juliet's IV was similar to what they'd use in the U.S. Except for the equipment being a little different, the basics of medical and nursing care were very much the same.

"Thanks again, Miguel, for everything," she said in a low voice, trying to put the depth of her feelings into words. "I'm so relieved to know my sister is in such good hands."

"You're very welcome, Katerina. I'll see you tonight, yes?"

"Yes," she confirmed. After he left, she walked back and sat down at her sister's bedside.

She was lucky that Miguel was here. Not just because he spoke English, which was a huge help, but because she knew he was an excellent surgeon.

Ironic how fate had brought her face to face with

Tommy's father after all these years. Her previously suppressed feelings for Miguel threatened to surface and she took a long, deep breath, ruthlessly shoving them back down.

She needed to protect her heart from Miguel's charm. And even more importantly, she needed to preserve the life she'd built with her son.

Miguel finished his rounds and then took a break to call his brother. Unfortunately, Luis didn't answer the phone so he left his brother a message, requesting a return phone call.

He rubbed the back of his neck, debating whether he should go out to see his brother after work or not. He should have time before dinner as he wasn't on call this evening. But at the same time, going all the way out to the farm and back would take at least two and a half hours, and he didn't want to be late for his dinner date with Katerina.

Miguel was pleased Katerina had agreed to see him again tonight. He felt the need to make it up to her for leaving so abruptly after finding out about his father's stroke. The night they'd spent together had been incredible. There had always been the hint of awareness between them while working together in the operating room. At times it had seemed as if Katerina could practically read his mind, instinctively knowing what he'd needed before he'd had to ask.

He'd been tempted to pursue a relationship, but had told himself it wouldn't be fair since he wasn't planning on staying. Maybe if things had been different…

No, he'd made his decision. He'd already given notice at the hospital that he was leaving at the end of the academic year, which was just three months away. He'd first heard about Doctors Without Borders in Madrid from one of his colleagues. He'd quickly decided that he wanted to join as well once he'd finished his training. He'd known early on he didn't want to stay on his family's olive farm. He'd wanted to travel. To learn about other cultures. He'd jumped at the opportunity to study in the U.S. and now couldn't wait to join Doctors Without Borders.

So why was he torturing himself by seeing Katerina again? If he had a functioning brain cell in his head, he'd stay far away from her until her sister was stable enough for transport back home.

Katerina wasn't the woman for him. He knew he shouldn't measure all women against his American mother, but after living in both cultures he understood a little better why his mother had reacted the way she had. The two lifestyles were very different. Maybe if the olive farm hadn't suffered two bad years in a row, there would have been money for vacations back in the U.S. Would that have been enough for his mother? Or would that have only emphasized her loss?

Truthfully, he couldn't understand why his mother just hadn't purchased a one-way ticket to New York and returned home if she'd been so desperately unhappy here. Instead, she'd stayed to become a bitter woman who'd made all their lives miserable. Until she'd unexpectedly died of an overdose, which had been determined to be accidental rather than a suicide attempt.

Miguel shook off his dark thoughts and concentrated on his patients. He loved everything about being a surgeon. There wasn't nearly as much trauma here in Seville as in Cambridge, Massachusetts, but he didn't mind. One thing he never got used to was losing patients.

Especially young patients. Like the twenty-five-year-old pregnant mother they'd lost during his last shift in the U.S.

After finishing his rounds on the adults in his case load, he made his way over to the children's wing, which happened to be in the oldest part of the hospital. He wanted to visit Pedro, his young appendectomy patient. The young boy would need to stay a few days for IV antibiotics before he could be discharged.

This was the other part he loved about being a doctor in Spain. There weren't large children's hospitals here, the way there were in the U.S. He was glad to have the opportunity to take care of both children and adults, rather than being forced to decide between them.

"*Hola,* Dr. Vasquez," Pedro greeted him when he entered the room.

"*Hola, Pedro. ¿Como estas?*"

"*¿*English, *por favor*? I'm fine."

Miguel grinned and switched to English for Pedro's sake. The youngster was part of a group of teenagers in Seville who were committed to learning English. Many of them didn't bother, but even when Pedro had been in pain in the emergency department yesterday, the boy had informed him he was going to America one day.

"May I examine your incision?" Miguel asked politely.

Pedro frowned, probably having trouble with the word "incision", but lifted his hospital gown anyway. "It's healing well, no?"

"Very much so," Miguel said, pleased to see there were no signs of infection. Although the bigger problem

Pedro faced was an infection in the bloodstream from the burst appendix. "Where is your mother? I think you'll need to stay for a couple more days yet."

Pedro smiled broadly as he drew his hospital gown back down. "She's caring for my younger brothers and sisters. She'll be here soon. And I'm glad to stay, Dr. Vasquez, because you will have more time for me to practice my English with you, yes?"

Miguel couldn't help but grin at the awkwardly worded sentence. "Yes, Pedro. We will practice while you are here, but even after you go home, we can practice when you return to clinic to see me, okay?"

"Okay. Thanks, Dr. Vasquez."

Miguel went on to see his second patient, a young girl who'd sustained a compound fracture of her left arm. They had orthopedic specialists, but since the fracture wasn't complicated he'd simply set it himself and casted it.

Marissa's room was empty so Miguel went to find the nurse, only to discover that the young girl was getting another X-ray of her arm.

He decided to return to the I.C.U., vowing to come back to check on Marissa later, but as he reached the third floor, the entire building shook and the lights flickered and went out. It took him a moment to realize what had happened, even though he'd been through this scenario once before.

Earthquake!

Kat was about to leave the I.C.U., intending to head back to the hotel, when she felt the building shake with enough force to make her fall against the wall.

The lights flickered and then went out. She froze, waiting for them to come back on.

Juliet's ventilator!

Instinctively, she ran back down the hall to her sister's room, able to see somewhat from the daylight shining through the windows. She saw Miguel going into another room but didn't veer from her path. After rushing over to Juliet's bedside, she reached for the ambu-bag hanging from the oxygen regulator. She turned the dial up, providing high-flow oxygen as she quickly disconnected the ventilator and began assisting her sister's breathing.

She forced herself to calm down so she wouldn't hyperventilate Juliet, hardly able to believe that the power was still out. Didn't they have back-up generators here? What had caused the shaking? Did they have earthquakes here? And where was everyone? She'd hadn't seen anyone other than the glimpse of Miguel going into another patient's room.

After what seemed like forever, the lights flickered back on, but only part way, as if conserving energy. At least Juliet's ventilator and heart monitor came back on.

She connected the ventilator back up to Juliet's breathing tube, but before she could go out and find the rest of the hospital staff, Miguel showed up in the doorway.

"What happened?" she asked.

"Earthquake. Nothing too serious, probably about a five or six on the Richter scale. We've had one similar to this before. But I need your help."

Earthquake? She was a little shocked, but strove to remain calm. "Me? What for?"

"I've just been told that a very old tree fell against

the corner of the building and we need to evacuate the patients. They are all pediatric patients in the children's wing located on the fourth floor. As it is a weekend, we do not have full staffing. We could use an extra pair of hands if you're willing to stay?"

"Of course," she said, knowing she couldn't simply walk away, even though she needed to know her son was safe. She was tempted to call Diana right away, except that she didn't want Miguel to ask questions. So she promised herself she'd wait until she could steal a few minutes alone to call her friend.

"Let's go," Miguel said, and she followed him out of the I.C.U. and down the hall, trying to make sense of what was happening. Clearly, the earthquake must have caused the tree to fall on the hospital building. What other damage had occurred? And what about the hotel? Was everything all right there?

As they walked down the hall, she peered through the windows to look out over the city. She was relieved when she didn't see any evidence of mass destruction. As she followed Miguel, she hoped and prayed Tommy and Diana were someplace safe from harm.

CHAPTER FOUR

KAT was horrified to see the amount of damage the building had sustained when they arrived in the children's ward. Many of the younger kids were crying, but one older boy had already stepped up to take charge. He'd obviously gathered all the children on several beds located as far away as possible from the crumbled corner of the building.

"Good job, Pedro," Miguel said as they rushed in. "Where's your nurse, Elouisa?"

"I'm not sure, but I think she went to get medication," Pedro answered. Kat was impressed that the boy spoke English and seemed to accept the responsibility of staying here with the children alone.

Miguel's mouth tightened, but he didn't say anything else. "Okay, then, we'll need to transport the sickest patients down to the I.C.U. first."

"DiCarlo is the worst, I think," Pedro said, pointing to a boy who was lying listlessly in bed. Kat estimated there were at least a dozen kids gathered on three beds surrounding the obviously very sick boy. "Elouisa said something about how he needed more antibiotics."

"She should have stayed here with all of you. He can get his antibiotics in the I.C.U.," Miguel said firmly.

"I'll take him down, but do you think it's safe to use the elevators?" she asked warily. She didn't mind transporting the sick child downstairs but the thought of being stuck in an elevator alone with him was scary.

Just then Elouisa returned, hurrying in with an IV bag in her hand. She came straight over to DiCarlo's IV pump to prepare the medication.

Miguel said something to her in Spanish, which she assumed was something related to the care of the children. She responded in Spanish as well, even while she hung the IV antibiotic. When they finished their conversation, Miguel turned to her.

"Okay, you and I together will take DiCarlo in his bed down to the I.C.U. Elouisa has promised to stay with the children." He turned to Pedro. "I am counting on you to stay here and to help Elouisa until I can return, okay? Once we have DiCarlo safe in the I.C.U., we can find other beds for the rest of you."

Pedro nodded. "I understand Dr. Vasquez. You should have trust that I will wait here for you."

"Good, Pedro. Thank you."

"Give me a quick rundown on DiCarlo's condition," she said to Miguel as Elouisa used an old-fashioned crank to lift the bed higher off the floor so it would be easier for them to push him. "I need to understand what to watch for."

Miguel set a small bin of emergency supplies on DiCarlo's bed, and again she was struck by the similarities between medical care here in Seville and in the U.S. When she worked in the I.C.U., they would always take a small pack of emergency supplies on what they called road trips, when patients needed to leave the I.C.U. to go down for certain X-rays or CT scans.

Miguel started pushing the boy's bed towards the elevator as he gave a brief report.

"What started as pneumonia has turned into full-blown sepsis. He's been fighting the infection as best he can, but he's had heart trouble since he was born so he's not as strong as most children his age."

She digested that bit of information as they left the children's ward through a long, empty hallway. As they waited for the elevator, which seemed to take a very long time, she looked down at DiCarlo's wan features, hoping and praying he'd survive the infection.

Miguel's impatience was obvious when he stabbed the elevator button a second time.

"Where is everyone?" she asked. Miguel's features tightened. "We were short-staffed to begin with, but some left, wanting to check on their loved ones. I honestly didn't think we would lose this many staff members."

She could understand why some staff had felt compelled to leave, and worry over the safety of her son gnawed at her. She pushed her fears aside. For one thing, Diana would have called her if something bad had happened. Their hotel was new and sturdy. Surely they'd be safe. The elevator arrived and she helped Miguel push DiCarlo's bed inside. The doors closed and she pushed the button for the second floor when suddenly the boy began coughing so hard his face turned bright red.

"Miguel, he's having trouble breathing," she said urgently, reaching for the dial on the oxygen tank and turning the knob to give him more oxygen. "Do we have a pediatric ambu bag?"

"Yes, along with intubation supplies." Miguel opened

the small bag of emergency supplies and pulled out the ambu bag. "We can intubate if we have to."

She hadn't assisted with an intubation since the time she'd worked in the I.C.U., but she nodded anyway. She gently placed the small face mask over DiCarlo's mouth and nose, and used the ambu bag to give him a couple of breaths.

DiCarlo squirmed beneath the ambu bag, fighting her at first, but then abruptly went limp, and she quickly reached over to feel for a pulse. "Miguel? His pulse is fading fast."

"I'll have to intubate him now, rather than waiting until we reach the I.C.U." He took the laryngoscope in his left hand and then gently slid the endotracheal tube into DiCarlo's throat. She took Miguel's stethoscope from around his neck and listened to the boy's lungs to verify the tube was in the correct place. Thankfully, it was. She quickly connected the ambu bag tubing to the end of the endotracheal tube so she could give DiCarlo several breaths.

Miguel secured the tube with tape and then gestured behind her. "Check his pulse and then push the button again. The doors have already closed."

She'd never heard the elevator ding. She made sure DiCarlo's pulse was stable before she turned around to hit the button for the third floor. This time it only took a couple of minutes for the doors to open.

She was very happy to see the critical care area. "Which bed?" she asked, as she walked backwards, pulling the bed as Miguel pushed, keeping one hand on the child's endotracheal tube.

"Twelve," he directed.

She knew the basic layout of the unit from visiting

her sister and quickly pulled the bed towards the vacant room number twelve. Nurses came over and assisted her with getting DiCarlo connected to the heart monitor overheard.

"Gracias," she murmured, smiling weakly. She glanced up and was reassured to note that DiCarlo's pulse had stabilized. Miguel spoke to them in Spanish, and they quickly brought over a ventilator. She stepped back, allowing the staff room to work.

Crisis averted, at least for the moment.

She hesitated, not sure if she should go back down to the children's wing alone or wait for Miguel. He was still examining DiCarlo, and the grave concern in his gaze as he listened to the boy's lungs wrenched her heart.

Would he look at Tommy like that?

Just then he glanced up and caught her staring at him. She swallowed the lump in her throat, holding his gaze for a long moment. Watching him, the way he was so gentle with DiCarlo, gave her hope and reassurance that he would never do anything to hurt their son. Including taking him away from her.

"He's fine for now," Miguel said, putting his stethoscope away. "Give me a few minutes here while I make sure his orders are up to date."

"Of course," she murmured, turning away, her hand on her phone. Outside DiCarlo's room, she made sure she was out of Miguel's hearing distance before she quickly pressed the number for Diana, holding her breath while she waited for an answer. Diana's voice brought instant relief. "Kat? Are you okay?"

"Yes. Are you and Tommy safe? Was there damage to the hotel?"

"We lost power for a while, and there seems to be a lot of confusion, but we're fine. No damage to the hotel that we know of."

Kat closed her eyes with relief. "I'm so glad. Listen, I have to stay here for a bit yet—will you be okay for a while?"

"Sure. We'll be fine."

"Thanks, I'll check in with you later." She closed her phone just as Miguel came around the corner of the nurses' station. She quickly tucked the phone back into her pocket.

"Ready to go?" Miguel asked.

"Of course." She felt bad for deceiving him, but obviously this wasn't the time or place for a conversation about his son. As they walked together toward the stairwell, their hands brushed lightly. A tingle of awareness shot up her arm.

"So, maybe I should apply to be a nurse here, huh?" she said jokingly, in a feeble attempt to break the closeness that seemed to grow deeper between them every moment they spent together.

"Are you planning to stay?" he asked, in shocked surprise. The brief flash of horror in his eyes pierced the tiny balloon of hope that had begun to grow in her heart.

"No! Of course not. That was a joke, Miguel." Ridiculous to be hurt that he didn't want her to stay. She preceded him down the stairwell, wondering if he'd change his opinion once she told him about Tommy.

She had to tell him about his son. The sooner, the better.

Miguel mentally smacked himself on the side of the head, understanding from the stiffness in her shoulders and the sharpness of her tone that he'd inadvertently hurt her.

He hadn't meant to make it sound like he didn't want her to stay. He'd just been taken aback by her statement, especially after they'd worked together to save DiCarlo. He couldn't help making comparisons with his mother. Maybe if his mother had been able to work in a career, other than helping his father run the olive farm, she would have been happier.

Could Katerina really be happy in Seville? And why did it matter as he himself wasn't planning to stay?

He hadn't slept well last night because all he'd been able to think about had been Katerina. And even now, in the aftermath of a small earthquake, he still wanted her.

But their situation was no different than it had been back when he'd met her in Cambridge. He'd already committed to Doctors Without Borders. He was finally going to live his dream. He couldn't start something with Katerina that he wasn't willing to finish.

A tiny voice in the back of his mind wondered if she'd be willing to go with him. But then he remembered Juliet. No, the Katerina he knew wouldn't pack up and leave her sister. Especially not when Juliet had a potentially long road of recovery ahead of her. Several months of rehab at least.

He pushed thoughts of Katerina possibly going with him to Africa aside to concentrate on the situation down in the children's ward.

Thankfully, Elouisa had kept her word, staying with the rest of the children. He was glad to see an additional staff nurse had come up to help.

"Which wing can we use as the children's ward?"

he asked, joining the group. "I'd like to keep them together if possible."

"We can use the east wing of the third floor," Elouisa
informed him. "I too would like to keep them together
if possible. How is DiCarlo?"

"Very ill. We had to intubate him in the elevator,"
Miguel said. "You were right to make sure he received
his antibiotic," he said by way of apology. He'd been
upset to find the children alone, but he understood she'd
prioritized the best she could.

"I was hoping to get him to the I.C.U.," Elouisa admitted. "But you were right, I shouldn't have left the
children alone."

"Difficult decision either way, so don't worry about
it." He noticed Pedro was listening to their conversation.
He was impressed with how the boy had taken charge
in Elouisa's absence. "Pedro, are you able to walk or
would you like us to get you a wheelchair?"

Pedro practically puffed out his chest. "I can walk.
I'm fine, Dr. Vasquez."

He could tell Pedro had some pain, but the boy wasn't
about to admit it. He vowed to make sure Pedro took
some pain medication as soon as they were all relocated
in their new rooms.

Elouisa gathered up several wheelchairs and between
the three of them they assisted getting all the children
ready for transport. Pedro helped, as if he were a hospital staff member rather than one of the patients needing to be relocated.

The elevator was too small for everyone to go at
once, so Elouisa and Pedro took three children first,
while the second nurse, Maria, took two patients with
her. Miguel and Katerina waited for the next elevator

with their three patients. They were lucky there hadn't been more patients in the children's wing.

"Pedro's English is amazing," Katerina said while they waited for the elevator. "I'm impressed at how he seems to understand everything we're saying."

"He takes learning English very seriously as he is determined to go to America one day," he admitted. "You'd never know he had a burst appendix last evening, would you?"

Katerina's eyes widened. "No, I certainly wouldn't. He's doing remarkably well."

"Yes, but as his appendix ruptured, I want him to get a good twenty-four to forty-eight hours of IV anti-biotics before he's discharged."

The elevator arrived and as they quickly maneuvered the three remaining patients into the elevator, Miguel found himself watching Katerina with awe. He'd always known she was an excellent O.R. nurse but seeing her interact with the young patients, managing to overcome the language barrier with smiles, simple words and hand gestures, he thought her skills would be better utilized in a position where she could care for awake and alert patients on the ward or in the I.C.U.

Or in the Doctors Without Borders program. They needed nurses to work with them, too.

Not that her career choices were any of his business.

It didn't take long to get the children settled on the east wing of the third floor. The entire layout of the area was very similar to the one where the building had collapsed. Even Pedro reluctantly took to his bed, and Miguel made sure he took a dose of pain medication that was long overdue.

Afterwards, he glanced at his watch, thinking he

should go up and check on DiCarlo. But he was hesitant to leave Elouisa here alone as Maria had been called away to help elsewhere. He walked up to the nurses' desk where Elouisa was busy organizing the charts. "Have you requested additional nursing support?" he asked.

"*Sí,* but so far Maria has not returned," she told him. "Thankfully, most of the children are very stable, especially now that DiCarlo is in the I.C.U."

"True, but I still think you should have someone with you. What if you have to leave the unit for some reason?"

Katerina stepped forward. "I can stay for a while," she volunteered. "I would just like a few minutes to check on my sister first."

He nodded, filled with gratitude. Even though Katerina wasn't licensed to practice nursing here in Seville, she could stay on the unit as a volunteer, offering a second pair of hands as needed. And her knowledge of nursing would be invaluable. He would feel much better knowing Elouisa wasn't here on the children's wing alone.

"Why don't you run over to see your sister, and I will wait here until you return?" he offered.

"Gracias," she murmured. "I promise to be quick."

He couldn't begrudge her the chance to make sure Juliet's condition hadn't changed since they'd been up there. "I will need to check on her too, but I will wait for you to return."

"¿Que?" Elouisa asked, indicating she hadn't understood his conversation, so he quickly translated for her. "Both of you go and check on her sister," Elouisa said firmly. "I will be fine alone here for five minutes

until Katerina returns. Pedro has been a huge help. He will get help in an emergency."

Miguel reluctantly agreed and led the way down to the I.C.U., using the stairwell as the elevator was so slow.

"You're going to have to make Pedro an honorary nurse, soon," Katerina teased as they walked towards Juliet's room. "Maybe after all this he'll decide to pursue a career in medicine?"

He chuckled. "There are not nearly as many male nurses here in Seville as there are back in America."

They entered Juliet's room and Katerina immediately crossed over to take her sister's hand. "I'm here, Jules," she said in a gentle tone. "Don't worry, you're still doing fine."

Juliet was moving restlessly on the bed, as if she was uncomfortable. Katerina tried to comfort her, talking to her in a soothing voice as Miguel took the clipboard off the foot of the bed and scanned the latest laboratory results and vital signs that had been recorded.

"Miguel?" He glanced up at Katerina's urgent tone. "Look! I think she's having a seizure!"

CHAPTER FIVE

"DISCONNECT the ventilator and use the ambu bag to assist her breathing," he directed quickly. He leaned over to hit the emergency call light and in less than thirty seconds two nurses came running in. He gave them orders in Spanish for a loading dose of IV dilantin followed by a continuous infusion. Also five milligrams of Versed to calm the effects of the seizure and for new IV fluids to correct Juliet's electrolyte imbalance.

His heart twisted when he saw the sheen of tears in Katerina's eyes. Thankfully, the seizure didn't last long, and within ten minutes he was able to put Juliet back on the ventilator. The medications he'd ordered worked beautifully, and Kat looked relieved when Juliet was resting quietly in her bed.

"She's going to be okay," he murmured to Katerina as they moved back, allowing the nurses to complete the dilantin infusion along with the new IV fluids he'd ordered. "This isn't a sign that her head injury is worse, but more likely as a result of her electrolyte imbalance."

Katerina rubbed her hands over her arms, as if she was cold, and he couldn't stop himself from putting a strong arm around her shoulders and drawing her close. "Are you going to do a CT scan of her head, just to be sure this isn't related to her intracranial hemorrhage?" she asked.

He hesitated because normally he wouldn't order such a test for that purpose. But he found himself wanting to reassure her in any way possible. "Let's wait to see how she does after the electrolytes are in, okay? If there is any change in her neuro status, I will order the scan immediately."

Katerina pulled away from him, turning to look at her sister, and he sensed she wasn't happy with his decision.

He wasn't used to explaining himself—especially not to a family member of a patient. "Listen to me, the earthquake has caused some chaos here in the hospital. I see now that your sister didn't get the new IV fluids I'd ordered during rounds. I truly believe, Katerina, her seizure is the result of an electrolyte imbalance."

She swiped a hand over her eyes, sniffed loudly and nodded. "All right, Miguel, we can wait to see how she does once the electrolytes are corrected."

He reached out to put a hand on her shoulder, wanting nothing more than to offer comfort, easing her fears. "I promise you, I'll take good care of your sister, Katerina."

For a moment he didn't think she'd respond, but then she suddenly turned and threw herself into his arms. Surprised and pleased, he hugged her close.

"I can't lose her, Miguel. I just can't," she said in a muffled voice. "I promised my mother I'd take care of her. She has to be okay, she just has to!"

Her despair tore at his heart. "I know, Katerina," he whispered, brushing his cheek against her silky hair, ignoring the shocked stares from the two nurses. "I know."

As soon as the IV medications were flowing according to his prescribed rate, the two nurses left them alone in the room. He continued to hold Katerina close, smoothing a hand down her back, giving her the emotional support she needed while trying to ignore the sexual awareness zinging through his bloodstream. He was stunned to realize how much he wanted her, even after all this time. And the feeling was impossibly stronger than it had been during the night they'd shared together four and a half years ago.

He hadn't left her by choice, returning home because of his father's stroke, but he hadn't sought her out afterwards, either. Had he made a mistake? Was he wrong not to have gone back to be with her again?

He pressed a kiss along her temple and the slight caress must have been too much for her because she pulled away abruptly, straightening her spine and swiping at the wetness on her face. "I'm sorry, Miguel. I don't know what's wrong with me. I'm usually not this much of a mess."

"Give yourself a break, Katerina. It's understandable that you're worried about your sister. And this has been incredibly stressful for all of us. Despite what you may think, we don't have earthquakes here often." He lifted a hand to wipe a strand of hair from her cheek. "You don't have to stay to help if you don't want to. Maybe you should go back to the hotel for some rest."

She bit her lower lip and he could sense her inner struggle, knowing she was tempted to take him up on his offer. But then she sighed and shook her head. "I can't leave Elouisa all alone with those sick children. I will stay, but only for an hour or so. Hopefully by then, some of the staff will have returned."

He nodded, admiring her strength and determination. "I would like to think so, too."

For a moment she simply stared at him, and then she totally shocked him by putting her hand on his chest and going up on tiptoe to kiss his cheek. It was everything he could do not to pull her into his arms for a real kiss. The feather-light touch was too brief and before he could blink, she drew away. "I'll see you later, Miguel," she whispered, before leaving to return to the children's ward.

His throat was so tight, he couldn't speak. He spent several long minutes wrestling his warring emotions under control. Part of him knew he was playing with fire, yet he couldn't stay away from Katerina. Couldn't keep himself at arm's distance. He longed to kiss her. To make love to her.

Taking a deep breath, he tried to relax his tense muscles. He hadn't forgotten their dinner plans for later this evening, but with the earthquake there was a possibility the restaurants would be closed.

But he refused to consider breaking their date. No, he could always cook for her at his place, if necessary.

The idea grew on him as he continued to make rounds on his patients. He would be happy to prepare Katerina a meal she would never forget. And maybe they could explore the attraction that simmered between them.

Kat tried to concentrate on distracting the children, but she couldn't stop worrying about her sister and her son.

Even though she'd spoken to Diana just a little over an hour ago, she wanted to talk to her again.

Tommy was pretty young to talk on the phone, but she needed to hear his voice, just for a moment.

She ducked into a bathroom, seeking a moment of privacy. She called Diana again, and her friend answered right away. "Hi, Kat."

"Diana, I'm sorry, but I'm still here at the hospital. Some of the staff left and I'm volunteering on the children's ward. How's Tommy?"

"He misses you, but we've been playing video games since the power has come back on. Truly, he's fine."

"Can I talk to him? Just for a minute?"

"Sure, just a sec. Tommy, say hi to your mama, okay? Say hi," she urged.

"Hi, Mama." Tears pricked her eyelids when she heard her son's voice.

"Hi, Tommy. I love you very much. Be good for Aunt Diana, okay?"

There was a moment of silence and then Diana came back on the line. "I know you can't see him, but he's nodding in agreement to whatever you said, Kat."

Knowing that made her smile. "I'm glad. I told him to be good for you. Diana, I'm sorry we can't go on the boat ride," she murmured. "Maybe things will be back to normal tomorrow."

"Sure. Just come back as soon as you can, okay?"

"I will. Take good care of Tommy for me." Kat had to force herself to hang up, or she'd be bawling again.

Okay, she needed to get a grip here. She was becoming an emotional basket case. She quickly used the facilities and then splashed cold water on her face, pulling herself together.

As she returned to the children's ward, she found herself looking for Miguel. Ridiculous, as he was obviously spending time with the sicker patients. She hoped DiCarlo was doing better as she made rounds on the sick children, pleased to note they were doing fairly well.

She saved Pedro for last, knowing he'd want time to talk. "How are you, Pedro?"

"Very good, miss," he said, although his smile was strained, betraying his pain.

"Please, call me Kat," she instructed, coming over to stand beside his bed. "When was the last time you took a dose of pain medication?"

He shrugged one thin shoulder and angled his chin. "I'm fine. I'm not sick like these other children."

"Pedro, you had surgery less than twenty-four hours ago," she reminded him gently. "Taking pain medicine is not a sign of weakness. You need to conserve your strength so your body can heal."

She watched as he seemed to consider her words. "Maybe it is time for a pill," he agreed reluctantly.

"I will ask Elouisa to come," she said, turning toward the door.

"Miss Kat?" His voice stopped her.

"Yes, Pedro, what is it?"

"Are you and Dr. Vasquez…" He paused and frowned, as if searching for the right word. "Boyfriend and girlfriend?" he asked finally.

She couldn't hide her shock. "No! Why would you ask something like that, Pedro?"

His dark eyes crinkled with humor. "Because to me it seems that you like each other very much," he said reasonably.

"Of course we like each other, we're friends, Pedro.

We're friends, nothing more," she said firmly, trying not to blush. The boy was too observant by far. She really needed to keep her emotions under strict control. "I will go and get your pain medicine, which you will take, okay?"

She didn't wait for his response, but went out to find Elouisa. So far, she and the nurse had managed to communicate with facial expressions and hand gestures, intermixed with brief phrases.

"Pedro—medication *para dolor*," she said, using the Spanish word for pain. She found it amazing how the occasional word from her two years of high-school Spanish flashed in her memory.

"*Sí,* okay." Elouisa seemed to know right away what she meant. As the nurse went to get the pain medication, she couldn't help glancing at her watch. She'd been here almost an hour, and as much as she wanted to stay and help, she also longed to return to the hotel to see her son.

Surprisingly, it was only two o'clock in the afternoon, although it seemed as if she'd been here at the hospital for ever. She vowed to stay just another thirty minutes and no longer. For one thing, she was very hungry. And for another, she wanted to hold her son close, kiss his cheek and reassure herself that he was truly okay.

Elouisa returned, holding out a small paper medication cup, very similar to the ones they used in the hospital back home. Kat and Elouisa went back to Pedro's room to give him his medicine.

They found him standing in the doorway, a frightened expression on his face. "Pedro? What's wrong?"

He brought his hand away from his abdomen, revealing a bright crimson stain spreading across his hospital gown. "I'm bleeding," he said, as if he could hardly believe it.

"Elouisa, call Dr. Vasquez, Hurry! *¡Rapidamente!*" The nurse rushed for the phone while she quickly crossed over to put her arm around Pedro's shoulders. "You've broken open your stitches," she told him calmly. "Come, now, you need to get back to bed."

Pedro murmured something in Spanish, and the fact that he was too stunned to practice his English worried her more than the blood staining his gown. She should have inspected his incision. "Stay still, Pedro, Dr. Vasquez will be here soon."

True to her word, Miguel strode in just moments later. "What happened?"

"I'm not sure," she was forced to admit. "I knew he was having pain, but I didn't realize he'd broken open his stitches."

"Everything he did today was too much for him." Miguel's compassionate gaze did not hold any blame.

"I should have examined his incision," she admitted softly. "I'm sorry, Miguel."

He shook his head as he turned toward Pedro. "Do not take this on yourself, Katerina. Will you please get me some gauze dressings? I need to see how bad the wound looks."

She knew he was trying to offer Pedro some privacy and quickly left the room, searching for the supply cart. She found the gauze without too much trouble and then returned to Pedro's room, hovering outside the doorway until she knew the boy was adequately covered.

"Do you have the gauze?" Miguel called, indicating it was safe to enter.

"Yes." The sheets were arranged so that his body was

covered except for his belly. The small gaping hole in Pedro's abdomen worried her, although she tried not to let it show. "Will he need to go back to surgery?" she asked as she opened the gauze packet for him, keeping the contents sterile.

He took the gauze with his gloved fingers and turned back to Pedro. "I'm afraid so. Pedro, I will need to fix this open incision right away, understand?" He spoke in Spanish too, likely repeating what he'd said.

"I understand," Pedro murmured.

"You'll need to talk to his mother. I'll ask Elouisa to get hold of her."

"Thanks."

She left the room, and made sure Elouisa understood she needed to call Pedro's *madre* before she returned. Miguel had just finished dressing the wound, stepping back and stripping off his soiled gloves. "I will call down to surgery to make sure they have a room available and staff to assist."

She chewed her lower lip nervously. "And what if they don't have staff to assist?" she asked.

Miguel hesitated. "I'm afraid I will have to ask for your assistance, Katerina. You are a skilled O.R. nurse and we have worked together many times."

She opened her mouth to protest but stopped herself, realizing Pedro was listening to the interaction between them. She didn't want to say anything to upset the boy. "I can certainly help as needed," she agreed.

Miguel hurried away, apparently to make the necessary phone calls. She forced a reassuring smile on her face as she crossed over to Pedro's bedside, taking his hand in hers. "You're going to be fine, Pedro. Dr.

Vasquez is a very talented surgeon. He will fix you up in no time."

"Will you assist him, Miss Kat?" Pedro asked, his eyes betraying a flicker of fear. "If there is no one else?"

"Of course I will do whatever is needed, Pedro. Don't you worry about a thing, okay? You're going to be fine."

"Gracias," he murmured, tightening his grip on her hand.

When Miguel returned, the tense expression on his face told her without words that her help would be needed. "There is a theater available, but the staff nurses who have stayed and the surgeon on call are busy with a trauma patient. Either Pedro waits until they are finished or you come down to assist me. It's your choice, Katerina. I know I have asked a lot from you today."

She didn't hesitate, knowing she could never let Pedro down. "I will be happy to help," she said firmly.

Miguel flashed a grateful smile. "Thank you, Katerina. This is a small surgery and shouldn't take too long."

She glanced down at Pedro's small brown hand clasped tightly in hers. She couldn't have left him any more than she could have left her own son. "I know. Remember, Pedro, Dr. Vasquez and I have worked together often in America. We made a good team."

"Yes, we did." Miguel's soft tone reminded her of the night he'd made love to her. She needed to protect her heart from his lethal charm.

"Dr. Vasquez?" Elouisa poked her head into the room and said something about Pedro's mother. Miguel excused himself and went out to take the call.

Within minutes he'd returned. "Your mother will try

to be here soon, but I'd rather not wait if that's okay. I need to repair the incision to protect against infection."

"I know. It's okay, she has my younger brothers and sisters to care for. I will be fine."

Kat's heart went out to Pedro, bravely facing surgery without his mother being here to hold his hand, to kiss him and to wish him well. She could tell Miguel felt the same way, from the way his gaze softened as he looked down at Pedro.

"You are very brave, Pedro," Miguel murmured. "I am extremely proud of you."

The simple words brightened Pedro's face and he beamed up at Miguel as if he were some sort of miracle worker. She couldn't help wondering about Pedro's father, why he wasn't here if his mother was home with the other children.

Miguel oozed confidence and kindness at the same time. Obviously, he cared very much for children. First DiCarlo and now Pedro. Both were patients under his care, but she knew that was only part of it.

Miguel would be the same way with his own child. With Tommy. The truth was staring her in the face.

As they wheeled Pedro's bed down to the elevator to go to the surgical suite, she knew that she couldn't put off telling Miguel about his son for much longer. She didn't know if he still planned on keeping their dinner date, so much had happened since then.

But even if their dinner plans had to be cancelled, she would have to tell him. Tonight.

No more excuses.

CHAPTER SIX

MIGUEL worked as quickly as he dared, first exploring the open wound in Pedro's abdomen and then irrigating with antibiotic solution. He believed the wound might have opened from a combination of an infection starting to take hold internally along with Pedro's physical exertions during the earthquake disaster.

He was lucky to have found an anesthesiology resident willing to stay after his shift. And Katerina was doing a phenomenal job of being his assistant. They settled into the old familiar routine as if the four and a half years hadn't gone by.

"Three-O silk," he said, but before he finished his statement Katerina was already handing him the pick-ups prepared with the suture. He grinned, even though she couldn't see behind the face mask, and gave his head a wry shake. "You always did have a way of reading my mind, Katerina."

She went still for a moment and he wondered if he'd somehow offended her. When she remained silent, he couldn't help trying to make amends.

"My apologies. I truly meant that as a compliment."

She lifted her head and looked at him, her beautiful green eyes probing as if she could indeed read his internal thoughts. "No apology necessary, Miguel," she finally said lightly. "I was thinking that I was glad that our roles weren't reversed and you were the one trying to read my mind."

"Really?" Closing the small incision didn't take long and he turned to face her as he set the pick-ups back down on the surgical tray. "Now you have piqued my interest. What is it you don't want me to read in your mind, I wonder?"

"Surely you don't expect me to answer that, do you?" Her green eyes crinkled at the corners, making him believe she was smiling. He relaxed, realizing he didn't like the thought of her being angry with him. "Pedro will be all right, won't he?"

"Yes, certainly. He must rest, though, and take care of himself. No more playing hero."

She nodded and there was a hint of relief in her gaze. "Good. That's very good."

She backed away from the surgical field and he had to bite back a protest, even though he knew her volunteer shift was over. Truly, she'd gone well above and beyond the call of duty. When she stripped off her face mask, he followed suit. "Katerina, I hope you will still allow me to take you to dinner this evening?"

She hesitated, and he sensed she wanted to refuse, but she surprised him by turning back to face him. "Of course, Miguel. But I need to return to my hotel for a bit. I'm still feeling the effects of jet-lag."

He couldn't blame her. The hour was still early, just three-thirty in the afternoon, and as much as he wanted to take her straight to his home, he couldn't begrudge her some down time. Especially not after everything she'd done for them today. "I will see you in a few hours, then?"

"Yes. I'll be ready." She glanced once more back at Pedro, where the anesthesiology resident was reversing the effects of his anesthesia, before she turned and disappeared through the doorway in the direction of the women's locker room.

He instantly felt isolated and alone after Katerina left, which was completely ridiculous. He stepped back, allowing the anesthesiologist to wheel Pedro's cart over to the recovery area.

As he washed up and changed his clothes, he spent time considering what meal he would prepare for her tonight. He wasn't a stranger to the kitchen. Living on his own, he'd been forced to learn how to cook, but he wanted to be sure the meal was to Katerina's liking.

For some odd reason he couldn't help feeling that tonight was incredibly important, a turning point in their renewed relationship.

And he was determined to make their evening together special.

"Mama!" Kat braced herself as her son launched himself at her, his chubby arms wrapping tightly around her neck.

"Oh, Tommy, I missed you so much!" She held him close, nuzzling his neck, filling her head with his scent, eternally grateful to have him in her life. The more difficult times of being a single mother were easily forgotten during joyous moments like this.

"We were just going to try and find something to eat," Diana said with a tired smile. "I'm glad you came home before we left."

"I'm so hungry I could eat a bear," Kat murmured, still holding Tommy close. For once her active son seemed content to stay in her arms. "I'm surprised you didn't order room service."

"Can't read the room-service menu, it's in Spanish," Diana muttered with a heavy sigh. "Besides, we've been cooped up in here long enough. Believe it or not, there is a small café that's open just a few blocks away. We should be able to get something to eat. I have to tell you, the earthquake was a bit scary. There's one person behind the desk downstairs who speaks English and told us to stay in our rooms for a while. But I've been looking outside and haven't seen much damage."

Kat hadn't seen much evidence of damage either, and wondered if the tree outside the hospital had been partially dead already to have fallen on the building. "I'm so glad you're both safe."

"We're fine. We took a walk and found a couple of broken windows and a couple of uprooted trees. Nothing too awful."

"All right, let's go eat." She knew she had to tell Diana her plans for later that evening. But first she desperately needed something to eat. The gnawing in her stomach was almost painful.

While they ate, she explained how she'd helped out at the hospital in the children's ward, including doing surgery on a thirteen-year-old boy. As much as she didn't like being away from Tommy, she couldn't deny the satisfaction she'd felt by helping out.

"Hmm." Diana sat back in her seat, eyeing Kat over the rim of her soft drink. "So basically you spent the entire day with Miguel, huh?"

Kat finished the *tapas* they'd ordered, not exactly

sure what she was eating but enjoying the spicy food just the same, before answering. "Yes. And you may as well know I'm having dinner with him later tonight."

Her friend's eyes widened in horror. "No! You're going to tell him?"

"Don't," Kat said in warning, glancing at Tommy slurping his soft drink loudly through a straw. "Not now."

"But…" Diana sighed heavily, understanding that Kat didn't want to have this conversation with Tommy sitting right there. "I haven't had time to call the embassy," she complained in a low voice. "You agreed to wait."

"Doesn't matter." Kat was pleased to note how Tommy enjoyed the Spanish food. Must be part of his natural heritage, a trait passed down to him from Miguel. "Trust me when I tell you I know what I'm doing."

But Diana was shaking her head. "You don't know Miguel well enough yet," she protested.

"We worked together all day, moving the sick pediatric patients out of the children's wing. I helped him intubate a small child in the elevator and operate on a young boy. I know enough, Diana. You have to trust me on this."

Diana didn't say anything more, although the disapproval in her expression was clear. Even though Kat knew she was doing the right thing, she understood why her friend was worried. Seeing Miguel at the hospital today, there was no denying the powerful standing he had within the community, not to mention being on friendly terms with a police officer. A minor detail she hadn't dared tell Diana about. She hadn't understood exactly what they'd been saying, but when the police officer had taken Miguel's brother away, she'd had the impression he'd acted out of friendship.

But deep down those reasons weren't enough to hold her tongue. She knew Miguel was incapable of hurting a child, especially his own son. And he'd been so incredibly nice and supportive of her. Right from the very beginning, when he'd translated Juliet's chart for her. Spending time together today had only made her admire him more. No matter what Diana said, she would not back down from her decision.

Telling Miguel was the right thing to do.

"I hope you're not making a big mistake," Diana said.

"I'm not. Are you finished eating? We could take a little walk, maybe check out the church over there." Kat was determined to change the subject. She had a good hour yet before she needed to return to the hotel room to shower and change.

Better she keep her mind occupied with sightseeing rather than dwelling on the sweet anticipation of seeing Miguel again.

Kat pulled on the only dressy outfit she'd packed, a long gauzy skirt with a white tank top that molded to her figure. She left her long blonde hair straight and loose, rather than pulled back in the usual ponytail, knowing Miguel preferred it that way.

"You're dressing up for him as if this is some sort of hot date," Diana observed mildly.

She couldn't deny it. "Wanting to look nice isn't a crime." She needed some semblance of being in control. And maybe a part of her wanted to remind Miguel of the night they'd shared. A night of passion. A night that had produced a son.

Tommy was already falling asleep, and Kat couldn't help feeling guilty that she was leaving, forcing Diana to stay in the hotel room again. "I promise we'll do more sightseeing tomorrow," she said by way of apology.

"It's okay." Diana shrugged, even though Kat could sense her friend's keen disappointment. "This is why you paid my way to come here, right? There's no way we could have predicted the added complication of Miguel."

Truer words were never spoken. She went over to give her best friend a quick hug. "Thanks for being here, Diana."

Diana hugged her back, her good humor seeming to return. "You're welcome. Now, you'd better go downstairs, Miguel might just decide to come up here."

"He can't. They would make him call up here first," she protested. Still, she quickly crossed over to her half-asleep son, brushed a kiss on his brow and murmured how much she loved him before taking the room key Diana held out for her and letting herself out of the hotel room.

The elevators seemed to take for ever, but since she didn't know where the stairwells were, she forced herself to be patient. When the doors opened to reveal Miguel standing there, she nearly screamed, her pulse leaping into triple digits.

"You scared me!" she accused, putting hand over her wildly beating heart. "What are you doing here?"

His teeth flashed in a bright smile, but he stood back, allowing her room to enter the elevator. "I'm sorry to have frightened you, but it's already five minutes past eight. I was worried you'd forgotten about our dinner date and had fallen asleep."

She struggled to breathe normally, but being in the small elevator so close to him was extremely nerve-racking. He was impeccably dressed in a crisp white shirt and black slacks, and his scent made her knees week. "How did you know what room I'm in? They're not supposed to tell you that. What if I didn't want to see you?" She was outraged that her privacy had been so easily violated.

"Hush, now, don't be so upset. The clerk at the front desk is one of my patients from the hospital. She knows I wouldn't hurt you."

As he spoke, the doubts Diana had voiced seeped into the back of her mind. Miguel knew everyone, had connections everywhere. He'd gotten her room number without any effort at all. What if he really did plan to take Tommy away from her?

She had to believe he wouldn't. But she wasn't willing to let him or the clerk off so lightly. "It's not right, Miguel. Just because she happens to know you, it doesn't mean she has the right to give you my room number. I intend to file a complaint."

He seemed taken aback by her biting anger. "I'm sorry, Katerina. The fault is mine. Please don't get her in trouble for my mistake."

She knew she was overreacting, but the near miss had rattled her. What if he'd gotten a glimpse of Tommy? She didn't want him finding out about his son by accident. Back in the hotel room she'd been confident they could work something out, but now she wasn't so sure.

It was tempting to beg off their plans, but keeping Tommy a secret was already eating at her. She couldn't hold off another twenty-four hours, so she did her best to relax and smile. "Okay, fine, Miguel. I won't file a complaint, although you know I have a right to be upset. You forget I'm a single woman in a strange country where few speak my native language. I have a right to be concerned about strange men being allowed up to my room."

He lightly skimmed a hand down her back in a caress so light she thought she might have imagined it. "You are right, Katerina," he murmured contritely, although with a hint of steel. "I would not be at all happy if any other man was allowed access to your room."

The macho tone put her teeth on edge, but when the elevator doors opened she quickly escaped, putting badly needed distance between them.

She needed to stay in control. This wasn't a date, and she realized she'd made a grave mistake by dressing up for him as if it were. She was on an important mission, one that would have a great impact on her son's life, his future. Her future.

This was not a date!

Miguel cursed himself for being so stupid. If he'd been patient, they wouldn't be starting the night off on the wrong foot with an argument.

Katerina was breathtakingly beautiful. He'd never seen her in a dress and it was taking all his will-power to keep his hands to himself. He'd wanted to sweep her into his arms, to kiss her the way he had over four years ago.

His car was waiting, and he gently cupped her elbow, steering her towards the vehicle. Of course she dug in her heels. "I thought the restaurant was close by?"

"Please, get in the car. The restaurant nearby is closed due to the earthquake." After a brief pause she did as he asked, sliding into the back seat. "I'm afraid I have another sin to confess," he murmured, once they were settled and the driver had pulled away from the curb.

Her brows pulled together in a frown. "Really? And what sin is that?"

He subtly wiped his damp palms on his pants, more nervous than he'd ever been in his life. He was used to women coming on to him, many made it no secret they wanted to be the one to help end his bachelor ways. But he suddenly cared what Katerina thought of him. It was telling that she hugged the door as if she might escape at any moment. He flashed his most charming smile. "I have made dinner for us tonight."

"You?" her eyebrows shot upwards in surprise. And then the full meaning sank in. "We're going to your home?"

She acted as if he intended to take advantage of her. Had he read her wrong? Was it possible that she didn't feel the same sexual awareness that he did? Or had his stupid stunt in going up to her room broken her trust? "If you'd rather not, we can wait until tomorrow to dine. Hopefully the restaurants will reopen by then. I'm more than willing to ask my driver to return to your hotel." He tried not to let his hurt feelings show.

There was a long pause before she let out a small sigh. "No need to go back, Miguel," she said softly. She lifted her gaze and he saw the faint glint of amusement there. "I must say, I'm stunned to learn you know how to cook."

He relaxed and lifted her hand to his mouth, pressing his mouth to her soft skin. "There are many things you don't know about me, Katerina."

She gasped and tugged on her hand, which he reluctantly released. "And maybe, Miguel, there are a few things you don't know about me."

He couldn't deny the burning need to get to know all her secrets. The driver pulled up to his home and she glanced out the window. "You live right by the hospital," she said, recognizing the landmarks.

"Yes, very convenient for those nights I'm on call," he agreed.

His home was on the top floor, and they rode the elevator up in silence. He unlocked the door and then stepped back, allowing Katerina to enter first.

"Wow, very nice," she murmured, and he was ridiculously pleased she liked his home. "Bigger than I expected for a man living alone."

She didn't sit, but wandered around looking at his things with interest. When she approached the hallway farthest from the kitchen, he said, "Feel free to explore. There are three bedrooms, although our rooms tend to be smaller than you're used to back in the U.S."

He turned to check on the food, which was being kept warm in the oven, and when he turned around he was startled to find her standing right behind him.

She was so beautiful, he ached. "Katerina, please don't be angry with me." He stepped closer, reaching up to thread his fingers through the silky golden strands of her hair. "I wanted tonight to be special."

A strange expression, something akin to guilt, flashed in her eyes, but then she smiled and he knew he was forgiven. "I'm not angry," she murmured.

"I don't think I've thanked you properly for your help

today," he murmured, moving closer still. She stared up at him, standing her ground, and he couldn't resist the soft invitation of her mouth for another minute. Without giving her a chance to say anything more, he gently cupped her face in his hands and kissed her.

CHAPTER SEVEN

KAT didn't know how she allowed it to happen but the instant Miguel kissed her, memories of the night they'd shared came rushing back to her, flooding her mind, making her melt against him. Instinctively, she opened her mouth, wordlessly inviting him to deepen the kiss.

One moment his mouth was gentle, the next it was demanding, needy, stirring up flames of desire she'd tried to forget, vowed to live without.

She'd missed this. Missed him. Missed the way he made her feel, alive, vibrant, attractive. She wrapped her arms tightly around his neck, hanging on for dear life as a storm of desire washed over her, nearly drowning her with its intensity.

"Katerina," he whispered, as he pressed soft, moist kisses down the side of her neck. "You are so beautiful to me. I've never forgotten you. Never."

For one long moment she almost gave in to his sinful temptation. His hand came up to gently cup her breast, his thumb stroking her nipple through the thin layer of cotton, and her body reacted, arching into his, desperately needing to feel his hands on her bare skin.

She wanted nothing more than to close her eyes and give in to the whisper of pure pleasure, but she wasn't that younger, carefree person any more. She was a single mother with responsibilities.

Appalled with herself, she quickly broke off the embrace, forcing herself to let Miguel go, stumbling in her haste to put the width of the kitchen table between them. She grasped the back of a chair so tightly her knuckles were white. "I'm sorry, but I can't do this. I didn't come here to—to pick up where we left off, Miguel."

She couldn't allow the flash of hurt in his eyes to get to her. Too bad if his macho pride had taken a low blow. He would survive. She had to think about Tommy now. She watched him struggle to pull himself under control and she was a little ashamed of herself for being glad he'd been as aroused as she had been. At least she knew for sure the attraction wasn't one-sided.

"Of course you didn't," he said slowly, as if articulating each word helped him to maintain control. "I promised you dinner and I always follow through on my promises."

Dinner? Food? He had to be joking. She couldn't have eaten a bite to save her life. She shook her head and took a long deep breath, before letting it out slowly. "Miguel, listen to me. I came here because I have something to tell you. Something very important." She forced herself to meet his gaze.

He seemed truly baffled and took a step towards her, and she instinctively took a quick step back. "What is it, Katerina? Are you all right? It's not…your health, is it?"

She couldn't help being touched that he cared enough to worry about her health. And if she was sick, would he stand by her? Or would he look for an excuse to leave? She didn't want to consider the answer to that question, so she ruthlessly shoved the thought aside.

Obviously, he wasn't going to be able to figure this out on his own. She'd have to come right out to say it. "I'm fine, Miguel. But there is something you should know." She took a deep breath and bravely faced him. "I have a son. *We* have a son. He will be four years old in a little less than three months."

He gaped at her in shock, and for several long seconds the silence was heavy between them. She wished she could read his mind to know what he was thinking. "A son?" he echoed, almost in disbelief.

"His name is Tomas. I named him after you." During the night they'd shared, Miguel had confided that Tomas was his middle name. And his father's name.

Miguel dragged a hand down his face, as if still hardly able to comprehend what she was saying. "I don't understand. How did this happen? We used protection."

She batted down the flicker of anger—hadn't she asked herself the same question while staring down at the positive pregnancy test? But having him think, even for a moment, that she might have done this on purpose made her grind her teeth in frustration. "Protection can fail, Miguel. I'm sorry to spring this on you so suddenly. You need to know I tried to find you after you left. I called your cellphone and searched for you on all the popular social media websites. When I couldn't find you, I assumed you were working somewhere remote with Doctors Without Borders, following your dream." She spread her hands wide. "I didn't know Seville was your home. Had no way of knowing you were here all this time."

Miguel looked in shock and he lowered himself slowly onto a kitchen chair. "A son. Tomas. I can barely comprehend what you are telling me."

Relieved to have the secret out in the open, she sank into a chair across from him and reached for her purse. "I have a picture. Would you like to see?" Without waiting for his reply, she slid Tommy's picture across the table. "He looks very much like you, Miguel."

He stared at the glossy photograph for several long moments before he dragged his gaze up to meet hers. "This is such a shock. I don't know what to say, other than that he's amazing. Thank you for bearing him."

There had really been no choice, not for her. The way Miguel stared at the picture, as if awestruck, made her a bit nervous. Was he already thinking of taking their son away from her? Beneath the table she linked her fingers together, tightly. "Miguel, I only told you about Tommy because you had a right to know. Please be assured, I'm more than capable of raising him. I don't expect anything from you."

For the first time since arriving in Spain she saw his gaze darken with anger directed at her. "I will not avoid my responsibility, Katerina," he murmured in a low tone. For just a brief moment she thought he looked upset, but then the fleeting expression was gone. In its place was grim resolution. "Of course I will provide for my son. And I would like to make arrangements to meet him. As soon as possible. I know Juliet will be here for a few more days, but I can make arrangements for the two of us to return immediately to the U.S."

She stared at him, realizing in some portion of her brain that Miguel didn't know Tommy was here in Seville with her. Was, in fact, sleeping soundly back in her hotel room. If she told Miguel he was there, she had no doubt he'd swoop in and wake him up, scaring the poor child to death. She strove to keep her tone level. "Miguel, be reasonable. He's a young boy, not yet four. He won't understand or recognize you. You will be a stranger to him. We need some time to think this through, to figure out what we're going to do. Besides, I don't want to leave Juliet yet."

Miguel slowly rose to his feet, staring down at her arrogantly. "If you think I will let you raise my son without me, you are sorely mistaken. I will be a part of his life, and nothing you do or say will change my mind."

The sick feeling in her stomach intensified as she stared up at him helplessly, knowing he meant every single word. And while she knew she'd have to share custody of Tommy with Miguel, she wasn't at all sure what that exactly meant regarding their future.

Would Miguel play at being a father at first but then lose interest in them? Would he decide to up and leave, just like her father had? The way Juliet's father had?

Seeing him with Pedro earlier, she'd thought Miguel would be a good father to her son. But now she couldn't prevent the doubts from seeping in. And she desperately needed time. Needed to understand exactly what the future truly held for them.

How much would she have to sacrifice for her son?

Miguel inwardly winced when Katerina eyes filled with wounded shock. He knew he'd crossed the line, had put her on the defensive by practically threatening her, but he couldn't seem to stop.

She'd borne his son. Had been raising him alone for years. Deep down he was outraged that he had been cheated of precious memories, yet logically he knew the situation wasn't her fault. He'd left to return home after his father's stroke, leaving Katerina to fend for herself.

He'd simply assumed she'd be fine. Bitter guilt for not talking to her again after he'd left coated his tongue. She'd had every right to believe he was working in some distant country—after all, he'd told her about his dream. And truthfully, if not for his brother's drinking problem, he would have already been in Africa, working with those in need. He wouldn't be here now, hearing the truth about having a son. And she'd searched for him, too.

For a moment his resolve wavered. For so long he'd dreamed of joining Doctors Without Borders. Now his dream would have to be put on hold once again. Indefinitely. Maybe for ever.

He squelched the feeling of despair and refused to allow himself to think about that now. Instead, he glanced once more at the glossy photograph of a young boy with light brown skin, dark hair, and big dark eyes. His bright smile was the only facial feature that resembled Katerina. He trailed his fingertips over the photo and had the strongest urge to hop onto the first plane to the U.S. to see Tomas in person.

"Miguel? I smell something burning," Katerina said in a tight voice.

He whirled around in surprise, having totally forgotten about the meal he'd prepared. He went over to pull the chicken dish from the oven, waving the smoke away. "I don't think it's too badly burned," he said, even though the chicken looked a bit on the overdone side.

"I'm not hungry," Katerina murmured. She pushed away from the table and rose to her feet. "I think it's best that I go back to the hotel now. We can discuss this more tomorrow."

He swung around to face her, unwilling to call an

abrupt end to their evening. "Don't leave," he said, his voice sharply commanding rather than pleading with her, the way he should. He forced himself to soften his tone. "If you could spare a few minutes, I would like to hear more about Tomas."

She stood indecisively, wringing her hands together, and he silently cursed himself for being so stupid. He'd frightened her, instead of reassuring her that he intended to be there for her and for Tomas. Maybe a part of him mourned the loss of his dream, but he refused, absolutely refused, to ignore his responsibilities.

He'd been selfish once, following his dream to study abroad, and his brother Luis had suffered for it. His father had suffered too. He would always regret not being there when his father had sustained his stroke. The fact that he'd saved countless patients' lives wasn't enough to make up for his failures regarding his family.

He couldn't bear to fail his son.

"There isn't much to tell," she protested. "He's hardly more than a baby."

Katerina avoided his direct gaze and he wished he could cross over and take her once again into his arms. Kissing her had felt like heaven and he'd nearly lost all control when she'd wantonly kissed him back.

"He's not stubborn, like his mother?" he asked, trying to lighten the mood by gently teasing her. "I find that difficult to believe."

She narrowed her gaze and flipped her long golden hair over her shoulder. "Believe me, Tommy gets his stubborn streak from his father."

He tried not to wince at the shortened version of his son's name. He didn't understand this American tendency to give nicknames rather than using given names. "I bet he's smart, then, too. Just like me."

Katerina rolled her eyes. "Of course he's smart. I read to him before he goes to bed at night and he has memorized every story. He attends preschool and already knows his letters and numbers."

Hearing about his son's life, bedtime stories and preschool caused helpless anger to wash over him. He'd missed so much. Too much.

She was right, his son didn't know him. He couldn't bear the thought of being a stranger to his own son. "I can't wait to see him, Katerina. I want to see him, to hold him in my arms. I feel like I've missed too much already."

Her expression went from tolerant amusement to frank alarm. "Miguel, you can't just barge into his life like a steamroller. You'll be a stranger to him. You have to give him time to get to know you. And what exactly are you suggesting? That we'll just move here to Seville to be near you? Neither one of us speaks the language here and, besides, Tommy is an American citizen. We have a life back home." As she spoke, Katerina edged closer to the door, her eyes wide with panic.

"I'm sorry, but this is too much stress for me to handle right now, Miguel. I came to Seville because of Juliet's injuries, remember? And after working all day, I can barely think straight. We'll talk tomorrow."

"Katerina…" he protested, but too late. She already had her hand on the front door. He knew he was pushing her too hard, too fast. "All right. We can talk more tomorrow. I'll be happy to take you back to the hotel."

"I'll ride the metro," she said, lifting her chin in the stubborn gesture he secretly found amusing. Except that her eagerness to get away from him wasn't at all comical.

"Katerina, please allow me to take you." When she still looked like a rabbit ready to bolt, he added, "If you insist on taking the metro, I will have no choice but to follow you. We will ride together."

Her mouth tightened, but after a moment she gave a small, jerky nod. "Fine. We'll take your car. But I'd like to go now, Miguel."

He couldn't think of a way to talk her out of it, so he simply nodded and reached for his cellphone. He called his driver, Fernando, and requested him to return right away. Fernando sounded surprised, but readily agreed. "My driver will be here in five minutes," he assured her.

Katerina didn't move away from the door, but simply looked at him from across the room, a long awkward silence stretching between them. He glanced over at the photograph of Tomas, still sitting on the kitchen table. "May I keep the picture of my son?" he asked in a low voice.

For a moment he thought Katerina was going to burst into tears, but she bit her lip and nodded. "Of course," she murmured in a husky voice. "I have others at home."

The way she said the word home, as if he wasn't included, made his temper flare, but he managed to hold his tongue. Thankfully, Fernando arrived quicker than expected.

Katerina didn't say more than a couple brief sentences on the way back to her hotel. He couldn't think of anything to say to put her mind at ease. Because even though he didn't want to upset her, there was no way on earth he was going to give his son up easily.

"Thank you for the ride," she said politely, when

Fernando pulled up in front of her hotel. "I'm sure I'll see you some time tomorrow."

He caught her hand before she escaped from the car. "Katerina, wait. How about if we agree to meet at eleven o'clock tomorrow morning? I will have finished making rounds by then. We'll meet in your sister's room and then we can go somewhere for a cup of coffee, okay?"

"Fine. I'll see you at eleven." She looked pointedly down at where his hand was locked around her wrist and he forced himself to let her go. "Goodnight," she said, and didn't wait for him to respond before slamming the door shut and practically sprinting into the lobby.

He watched her hurry away, trying not to panic at the realization that she could easily catch a flight home tonight, making it extremely difficult for him to find her. And his son.

"Ready, sir?" Fernando asked from the front seat.

He hesitated, fighting the urge to follow her upstairs to her hotel room before she could slip away, maybe for ever. He wanted to talk to her about how they would deal with this situation, to insist they finish their conversation right this minute.

He took several deep breaths, fighting to stay calm. Logically, he knew Katerina wasn't going to run away. She wouldn't leave Juliet, not when her sister had suffered seizures earlier that afternoon. Besides, no one had forced her to tell him about his son. Truthfully, Katerina could have kept Tomas a secret, simply returning home without telling him a thing. The fact that she had told him indicated she wanted their son to have a father. The thought calmed him.

"Yes, I'm ready, Fernando," he said, giving his driver the signal to leave. As they pulled away from the curb and headed home, Miguel sat back in his seat, his mind whirling.

He had until tomorrow morning at eleven to come up with a new plan. He needed some way to convince Katerina that Tommy would benefit from having them all be together as a family, rather than living apart. Surely she wanted such a thing as well, or she wouldn't have told him her secret.

Granted, the obstacle of living in different countries was no small thing. They both had family members to take into consideration as well. He had his brother Luis, who still needed support, and she had Juliet, who might need ongoing medical care.

The entire situation seemed impossible, but he was determined there would be a way to make things work out to everyone's satisfaction.

Grimly, he stared out through the night, knowing he would fight anyone and anything that stood in the way of establishing a relationship with his son.

CHAPTER EIGHT

KAT barely made it up to her hotel room where she collapsed in the chair beside the bed and buried her face in her hands, trying not to give in to mounting hysteria.

Miguel wanted to meet his son, and it sounded pretty certain that he would want custody. All this time she'd figured he wouldn't want the responsibility of having a family, yet he'd made it clear that he intended to follow her back to the U.S. in order to claim Tommy as his own.

"Kat?" Diana whispered from the bed. "Are you all right?"

She lifted her head and struggled to swallow her tears. Thankfully, Tommy was sleeping in the small roll-away bed as he would only be upset to see her crying. The room was dark, but they always left the bathroom light on in case Tommy needed to get up. "Fine," she whispered back, subtly swiping her hands over her wet cheeks. "We'll talk in the morning."

She wished Diana was asleep already too, because her emotions were too raw, too fragile to talk now.

Maybe Diana had been right to encourage her to wait before telling Miguel about Tommy. She wished she'd listened to her friend's advice. But it was too late now.

There was nothing to do except to move forward from here. Telling Miguel about his son was the right thing to do, but while she thought she'd prepared herself for the conversation, Miguel's reaction had overwhelmed her.

He'd assumed she'd left her son back home, and she hadn't possessed the courage to tell him otherwise. She could rationalize the reason was because Miguel would have come right up here to the room, demanding to see Tommy regardless of the fact that he was already asleep. Regardless of the fact that seeing a stranger might upset him.

But deep down she knew her reasons for keeping silent were far more selfish. She'd needed a little time to come to grips with how her life would change from this point on. Miguel's demand to return immediately to the U.S. had frightened her. The fantasy she'd harbored, where Miguel would allow her to continue to raise his son while he joined Doctors Without Borders, had exploded in her face.

She crept over to the side of the roll-away bed where Tommy was sleeping to gaze down at his sweet, innocent face. He was clutching his favorite stuffed animal, Terry the tiger, to his chest. She lightly brushed her fingers over his silky dark hair, being careful not to wake him up. She wanted to gather him close into her arms, as if to reassure herself that she wasn't going to lose him.

She pressed a soft kiss to the top of his head, before heading into the bathroom to wash her face and change into her nightgown. She crawled into her bed and stared blindly up at the ceiling, knowing she'd never relax enough to fall asleep.

Going back over the events of the evening, she couldn't help remembering, in vivid detail, the way

Miguel had kissed her. Before he'd known about Tommy. He'd clearly wanted her, his body's reaction had been no secret. Had he assumed that since they'd made love four and a half years ago she wouldn't think twice about doing so again?

It had been tempting, far more tempting that she wanted to admit, to give in to the passion that shimmered between them. Truthfully, Tommy was the main reason she'd pulled back. If not for her son, she knew that she and Miguel would have continued where they'd left off all those years ago.

Because she cared about Miguel. More than she should. And while they might be able to get along enough to share custody of their son, she wasn't sure how to get past her personal feelings for him.

"Mama, wake up!" Tommy said, climbing up on her bed. "I'm hungry."

Kat forced her gritty eyelids open, inwardly groaning. She'd been awake half the night, worrying herself sick about the future, and could easily have slept for several more hours. But as a parent she was used to putting her needs aside for her son. "I'm awake," she murmured, trying to focus on the clock across the room and wincing when she realized it was seven a.m.

"Do you want me to take Tommy down to the café for breakfast?" Diana asked as she came out of the bathroom. "You can probably catch another hour or so of sleep."

"No, that's fine. I want to come with you." Kat sat up, running her fingers through her hair. "I was thinking maybe we should go on the boat tour this morning, instead of waiting until later."

Diana's eyes lit up. "That would be great."

Kat didn't have the heart to tell her friend that by early afternoon she'd likely be arranging a meeting between Miguel and Tommy. Better to put that conversation off for a little while yet. "Give me fifteen minutes to get ready, okay?"

"Sure."

Kat freshened up in the bathroom, forgoing a shower to pull her hair back into its usual ponytail. During the long night, when she'd tossed and turned for hours, she'd decided Tommy needed his father, so she planned to present Miguel with her joint custody proposal. As much as it pained her, she thought that having Tommy spend summers here with Miguel, along with a few holidays, would probably be the least disruptive to their lives. And she could travel with Tommy to make sure things went well, at least for the first few years. She could only hope that Miguel would find parenting too much work. Although remembering the way he cared for the pediatric patients in the hospital, like Pedro and DiCarlo, she knew he wouldn't.

Tommy ran into the bathroom and grabbed her hand. "Mama, let's go."

"All right, all right. Slow down. Diana, do you have your room key?"

"Right here." Diana held it up.

"All right, here's mine. After we go on the boat ride, I'm going to head over to the hospital to see Juliet." And Miguel, although she didn't voice that last part.

"Do you want to stop on the way?" Diana offered.

She did, very much, but at the same time she was too afraid they'd run into Miguel. And since she'd promised Diana and Tommy a boat ride, she was determined to follow through on her promise. If she was back in the U.S., she could simply call the hospital to see how her sister was doing, but with the language barrier she had no choice but to actually go in to see Juliet for herself. And it didn't help that Miguel's eleven o'clock time frame hung over her head like a time bomb. "No, that's okay. Let's do the boat tour first."

As they left the hotel and walked down the street to their favorite breakfast café, she was determined to have this short time to play tourist with Diana and Tommy. A few hours alone, before their lives changed, for ever.

"Look at these bikes, Kat—isn't this the coolest idea?" Diana said as she gestured toward the bike rack located a few feet from the café. "I found out that this is a type of public transportation offered in Seville. For a small annual fee you can take one of these bikes, ride it to your destination, park it in another bike rack and then use it again to go home. No need to buy a bike of your own. These bike racks and bikes are located all over the city."

Kat smiled when she saw an elderly gentleman ride away on one of the red and white bikes, his front basket full of groceries. "Very cool idea."

"Have you notice the people walk or bike everywhere? No wonder they're healthier than Americans." Diana was starting to sound like a TV commercial sprouting the benefits of living in Seville.

"Remember, this is southern Spain where the weather is mild and we live in the northeast of the U.S. Biking in snow and ice isn't an easy task."

"Maybe," Diana murmured. "But I have to say, this trip has really opened my eyes to how other cultures thrive."

Kat couldn't disagree. They finished their breakfast and took the metro to the heart of the city, where the sidewalk vendors sold tickets for the boat tours. Tommy was happy to be on the move, running from one location to the other. She gave him room to run, knowing that his boundless energy had to be let loose some time.

They had to wait almost thirty minutes for the next tour, and Kat kept an eye on the time, knowing she needed to head back to the hospital in order to meet Miguel by eleven o'clock. As much as she wanted to enjoy the tour, her stomach was knotted with nerves.

The boat tour wasn't crowded this early in the morning and they had almost the entire upper deck of the boat to themselves. Tommy was thrilled when she lifted him up so that he could see over the railing.

The tour lasted almost an hour, and by the time they disembarked from the boat Kat knew they needed to head back toward the hotel. "No, we need to go this way, Tommy," she called, when he took off down the sidewalk.

Her son ignored her instruction and Diana glanced at her. "I'll get him," she offered.

"No, I'll go." Kat took off after Tommy, who was running and laughing as if they were playing a game of chase. She wanted to be mad at him, but just listening to him laugh made her smile. She gained on him and tried to get his attention. "Tommy, come on, now. We have to go for a ride on the metro."

A woman walking a dog was heading towards them and Tommy suddenly swerved right in front of them. The dog was on a leash but reacted instinctively by jumping up and nipping at him at the same time both Kat and the dog's owner shouted, "No!"

Tommy let out a wail as the dog's owner yanked the dog back and Kat rushed over, picking Tommy up and carrying him out of harm's way. "Shh, it's okay. You're okay, Tommy," she crooned as she tried to examine him for injuries.

Her heart sank when she found puncture marks in the fleshy part of Tommy's arm a few inches above the wrist. The wounds were bleeding, and she glanced up as Diana joined them, feeling like the worst mother on the planet. "The dog bit him."

Diana was a nurse too, and she looked at the wounds with a grimace. "We need to get that cleaned up right away."

"Yeah, but I think he'll need antibiotics too. Do they have clinics here? Or should we go straight to the hospital?" She hated knowing this was all her fault. She shouldn't have let Tommy run around. She should have anticipated something like this.

The dog owner was talking in rapid Spanish, clearly upset about what happened. Kat tried to smile, shaking her head. *"No comprendo Espanol,"* she said.

"They must have clinics," Diana was saying with a frown. But Kat had already made up her mind.

"We'll go to the hospital where Juliet is being cared for. I saw an emergency department there."

"Are you sure that's a good idea?" Diana asked. "We could run into Miguel."

"It's a risk, but Tommy needs good medical care. Miguel is a surgeon—chances are good that we'll be in and out of there without him knowing." And even if they weren't, she wasn't going to worry about Miguel's reaction at seeing them. Tommy's health was far more important.

Diana reluctantly agreed. Kat made sure they stopped in a restroom to wash the dog bite with soap and water, before taking the metro back to the hospital. As they walked into the small emergency room, Kat couldn't help glancing around for any sign of Miguel.

Tommy was, of course, her first concern. Miguel already knew about their son, but she didn't really want him to find out like this that Tommy was here in Seville. She would much rather tell him herself.

The woman at the desk in the emergency room didn't speak any English, and she showed her the dog bite on Tommy's arm, pulling out her Spanish dictionary to find the word for dog. *"Perro,"* she said, demonstrating the action of biting.

"Sí, un momento." The woman spoke to someone else in Spanish, and then took them back to a small exam room. Kat was glad to see the nurse bring in a wash basin.

She relaxed, feeling better now that they were actually getting medical care for Tommy. She glanced at her watch, realizing she was going to be late for her meeting with Miguel.

"I can stay with Tommy if you need me to," Diana offered, sensing her distress.

She slowly shook her head. "No, I can't just leave. Not until I know the wound is clean and that he'll get the antibiotics he needs."

If she had a way to call Miguel, she would. But as she didn't, she could only hope Miguel would have patience and wait for her.

Miguel arrived at the hospital early, unable to contain his excitement. He'd found a flight to Cambridge that was scheduled to leave early the next morning and he'd been tempted to go ahead and book it, except that he wasn't sure when Katerina's return flight was scheduled for. It wouldn't help him to get there before she arrived. Yet he was thrilled that he was closer than ever to meeting his son.

He went up to see how Juliet was doing, hoping that she would soon be stable enough to transfer home. He was pleased to discover that she was following instructions again and hadn't had any more seizures. Her electrolytes were back to normal, which was also a very good sign. He left orders to begin weaning her from the ventilator.

She wasn't quite ready for transfer back home but would be soon.

Since he was early, he decided to check on his other patients. First he checked on DiCarlo, who remained in the I.C.U. The boy was still critical, but his vitals were stable. From there, he headed over to the temporary children's ward to visit with Pedro.

"Hi, Dr. Vasquez," Pedro greeted him. The boy looked a little better, although still a little too pale and drawn. He didn't like seeing the dark circles beneath Pedro's eyes.

"Pedro, how are you feeling?" He crossed the room and checked the nursing notes on the clipboard. "Why aren't you taking pain medication?"

Pedro grimaced. "I don't like the way they make me feel."

"Maybe not, but I don't think you're getting enough rest. Sleep is very important. You will heal much faster if you take some pain medication at nighttime."

The boy flashed a wan smile. "You sound like Miss Kat. That same thing she explained to me yesterday."

Miguel nodded, sensing a bit of puppy love for Katerina in Pedro's gaze. "Katerina is a very smart lady. You would do well to follow her advice."

Pedro was quiet for a moment. "I thought she might come to visit me today."

He saw the stab of disappointment in the boy's eyes. "She is planning to come later, and I'm sure she will visit. I'll need to talk to your mother about keeping you here another day, Pedro."

"She won't care. She is too busy at home with my brothers and sisters."

Miguel wished there was something he could say to make the boy feel better. "That may be true, but you also help her, don't you? I'm sure she misses you."

"Of course." Pedro winced as he shifted in the bed. He put a tentative hand over his incision. "But I don't think carrying my brothers and sisters is a good idea right now."

"No, that would not be good," Miguel agreed. He lifted Pedro's hospital gown and gently peeled back the gauze dressing to examine his wound. The skin around the incision was a little red and he gently palpated the area to make sure there was no pus beneath the skin. There wasn't, but he decided to add yet another antibiotic just to be on the safe side. The risk of infection was high. "Looks good, but you have to take your pain medications. I need you to get up and walk the hallways. Staying in bed all day isn't healthy."

Pedro nodded. "Okay, I will do that."

Miguel called for the nurse and waited until Pedro had taken the ordered pain medication before he moved on to the next patient. He took his time making rounds, wanting to be sure to have everything finished before he spent time with Katerina.

He returned to Juliet's room at exactly eleven o'clock, frowning when he discovered Katerina hadn't arrived yet. He went back out to the nurses' station. "Has Juliet's sister been here to visit?" he asked in Spanish.

"No, Dr. Vasquez, she has not been here yet."

He gave a brief nod, hiding his impatience. He went back to DiCarlo's room, reviewing the chart to make sure his orders had been carried out, secretly watching for Katerina to arrive.

At eleven-thirty his temper began to simmer. Was it possible his worst fears had been realized? That she'd actually taken an earlier flight home in an attempt to hide Tomas from him? He didn't want to believe she would do such a thing, but as the minutes passed with agonizing slowness, he couldn't help believing the worst.

At noon he muttered an oath and left the hospital, calling his driver to take him to Katerina's hotel. He had to know she was still here in Seville. And if she was simply trying to avoid him, he would make certain she never did such a thing ever again.

His driver pulled up in front of the hotel and Fernando had barely put the car in park before Miguel shot out of the back seat, striding purposefully up to the front desk. "I need to speak with Katerina Richardson in room 212," he said.

"I will ring the room," the clerk said. After a few minutes he shrugged and hung up. "I'm afraid there is no answer."

"But she's still a guest here, right?" Miguel persisted. The time was almost twelve-thirty and most of the flights back to the U.S. left early in the morning, but there had been one early-afternoon flight.

"*Sí, señor,* she is still a guest. If you would like to wait, I suggest you have a seat in the lobby."

Miguel was too keyed up to sit in the lobby so he went back outside to let Fernando know he'd be staying for a while. He paced back and forth for several minutes, before taking a seat in the outside café adjacent to the hotel. He ordered a soft drink, although he was in the mood for something far stronger.

Within minutes a familiar voice reached his ears. "Walk, Tommy, don't run. Here, take my hand."

He went still, hardly able to believe his ears. Tommy? Slowly he turned in his seat in time to see Katerina walking up the sidewalk toward the hotel, holding the hand of a young boy.

The same boy in the photograph she'd given him.
Their son!

CHAPTER NINE

MIGUEL slowly rose to his feet, his anger towards Katerina fading as he drank in the sight of his son. Seeing Tomas in person was so much better than a photograph. The boy was so animated, Miguel could barely breathe.

Katerina abruptly stopped in her tracks, going pale when her gaze locked on his. But then she took a deep breath and said something in a low voice to her companion, a woman with dark hair who looked vaguely familiar, as she resumed walking.

He wanted to rush over and sweep his son into his arms, but remembering what Katerina had said yesterday about how he was a stranger to Tomas, it gave him the strength to stay right where he was. It wasn't until Katerina and Tomas came closer that he noticed the white gauze dressing on his son's left forearm.

"Hi, Miguel," she greeted him. "I'm sorry I missed you at the hospital. This is my son, Tommy, who had a small accident. And you remember my friend, Diana Baylor?"

He cleared his throat, striving to play along as if seeing his son in person hadn't completely knocked him off balance. "Of course I remember. Diana, it's good to see you again. And this is your son, Tommy?" He purpose-fully used Katerina's dreadful nickname and crouched down so he was at eye level with the child and wouldn't seem so intimidating. "Hi, Tommy, my name is Miguel Vasquez. I'm very happy to meet you."

Tomas stared at him with his large brown eyes and shrank back toward his mother, as if suddenly shy. Miguel didn't want to frighten the boy, but at the same time he couldn't help being frustrated that his son didn't know him.

He had to remind himself that the situation was his own fault. Not Katerina's. And certainly not the child's.

"It's okay, Tommy," Katerina said, brushing a hand over his dark hair. "Miguel is a good friend of mine. Show him where the dog bit you on the arm."

Tomas held out his arm, the one covered in gauze. "Bad doggy bit me," he said solemnly.

"Tommy, remember how you ran straight at the doggy? He only nipped at you because he was scared," Katerina said, filling in the gaps of what had happened for Miguel. "And the emergency-room nurse gave you a lollipop, didn't she?"

There was a hint of red staining the child's fingers and teeth as he nodded vigorously. "I'm a good boy."

"I'm sure you were a very good boy," Miguel said with a smile, relieved to know that his son had received appropriate medical care for the dog bite. Obviously, this was the reason Katerina hadn't met him in her sister's room. A very good excuse, except that it didn't at all explain why she'd let him believe Tomas was back in the U.S.

Although he'd assumed that, hadn't he? Katerina hadn't lied to him, but she had withheld the truth.

He would grant her a pass on this one, but now that she was here, with Tomas, he was determined to spend as much time with his son as possible.

And Katerina had better not try to stand in his way.

Kat had been shocked to find Miguel waiting for her outside their hotel, but by the time she noticed him it was too late as he'd already recognized Tommy. At least now there were no more secrets. She could see Miguel wasn't happy with her, but there wasn't much she could do. This had already been a rough day, and it was barely one o'clock in the afternoon.

"Katerina, do you think the three of us could take a walk?" Miguel asked, as he rose to his feet. "No offense, Diana, but I'd like some time alone with Katerina and Tomas."

Diana crossed her arms over her chest and shrugged, glancing over at her. "Kat? What would you like to do?"

Kat knew her friend would stand by her, if asked, but she'd known that Miguel would want to spend time with his son and there was no good reason to delay. "We'll be fine, Diana. You deserve some down time anyway. Should we meet back here at the hotel in an hour or so? Tommy will be more than ready for his nap by then."

"Sure thing." Diana's gaze was full of suspicion as she glanced over at Miguel. "Nice meeting you again, Dr. Vasquez," she said politely, before turning to walk away.

"I'm getting the sense she doesn't like me very much," Miguel murmured after Diana was out of earshot.

"Diana has always been there for me when I needed her. She was my labor coach and has helped me out more times than I could count, especially on days when I needed child care when Tommy was sick." Her temper flared. She was unwilling to allow him to put down her friend.

Miguel winced as her barb hit home. "In other words, she blames me for not being there with you."

Kat glanced down at Tommy and decided this wasn't the time or the place to argue about the past. "You wanted to take a walk, so let's walk. There's a park not far from here, down the block and across the street."

Miguel nodded and fell into step beside her, keeping Tommy between them. "Yes, I played at that park often as a young boy. See that school there?" He gestured toward the white building across the street. "That's where both my brother and I attended school."

She remembered seeing the young kids all wearing their navy blue and white plaid uniforms running outside at recess. Today was Sunday, so there weren't any children playing now, but she couldn't help wondering if Miguel was insinuating that he wanted Tommy to attend the same school he had. She struggled to remain calm. "Yes, I saw the students playing outside in their uniforms the other day. I was struck by how similar the school was to ours back home."

"Tommy, do you like school?" Miguel asked, turning his attention to their son.

"Yeah." Tommy seemed to be slowly warming up to Miguel. "School is fun."

"Do you play games at school?" Miguel persisted.

"Yep. I play with my friends."

Kat couldn't help smiling as Miguel tried to have a conversation with their son. Too bad that having a rational conversation with an almost four-year-old wasn't easy. Miguel was lucky to get anything more than one- or two-word answers to his questions.

When they reached the park Tommy tugged on her hand so she let him go, allowing him to run over to the water fountain. He looked over the cement edge, peering into the water.

"I can't believe you didn't tell me he was here," Miguel said in a low tone. "Do you realize I almost booked a flight to Cambridge this morning?"

"I'm sorry, Miguel. But Tommy was already asleep and I couldn't risk you marching into the room and waking him up. Besides, I honestly planned on bringing him with me to see you today. Unfortunately Tommy's dog bite prevented me from meeting you at the hospital, as we'd planned."

He sensed the truth in her words and forced himself to relax.

"But why would you book a flight without discussing your plans with me?" she continued. "You can't bulldoze your way into Tommy's life, Miguel. What we want doesn't matter here. The only thing that matters is what's best for Tommy." She turned to face him. "I told you about our son, first because you deserved to know, and second because Tommy deserves a father. I would like to think we could work something out together."

"Joint custody?" Miguel's nose wrinkled in distaste. "Impossible with both of us living in two different countries."

"Not impossible," she countered. "Tommy could visit you in the summer and maybe over the holiday."

"While he lives the rest of the time with you?" Miguel asked. "I hardly think that arrangement is fair."

"Fair? Do you think it was fair to leave me pregnant

and alone? I tried to find you, Miguel, but you certainly didn't try to find me. So don't stand there and try to tell me what is or isn't *fair*."

There was a charged silence between them as Kat tried to rein in her temper. She'd long ago accepted that the night she'd spent with Miguel meant nothing to him. Yet deep down she had to admit there was still a small kernel of resentment.

"You're right, Katerina. I must accept responsibility for my actions."

Miguel's acquiescence shocked her. So much that she didn't have any idea how to respond.

"I can only ask that you give me some time now to get to know my son. And, of course, we will need to agree to some financial arrangements."

"I don't want your money, Miguel," she protested. "We're not rich, but we're not poor either."

"I insist," he said. And she could tell by the edge to his tone that there was no point in arguing.

She let out her pent-up breath in a silent sigh. "Fine. We can discuss that more later." She should be thrilled that he hadn't put up much of a fight. But as Miguel left her side to cross over to where Tommy was digging in the dirt with a stick, she couldn't help feeling a sharp stab of disappointment that apparently they wouldn't be raising their son together.

As a family.

Miguel wanted to protest when Katerina insisted it was time to head back to the hotel, but even he could see that Tomas was getting cranky. He didn't doubt her wisdom regarding the fact that their son needed a nap.

He cared for pediatric patients in the hospital, but

obviously he didn't know the first thing about raising a child. How was he to know that almost four-year-olds still took naps?

"Up, Mama, up," Tomas whined.

"Is your arm hurting you?" she asked, swinging the boy into her arms and cuddling him close.

Miguel wanted, very badly, to be the one to carry his son, but suspected his offer of assistance wouldn't be welcomed by Tomas. He'd started to make friends with his son, but the boy still clung to his mother for comfort.

"Yeah," Tomas said, burying his face against her neck.

"I'll give you something to make your pain go away when we get back to the hotel room, all right?"

"They gave you pain medication?" he asked in surprise.

"No, but I have children's ibuprofen at the hotel, although I suspect he'll practically be asleep by then, anyway."

Katerina was correct. Tomas had closed his eyes and fully relaxed against his mother by the time they approached the hotel lobby.

"Wait for me here," Katerina told him, as she stabbed the button to summon the elevator. "I'll only be a few minutes."

He stepped back, resisting the urge to follow her up to their room. He was surprised she'd asked him to wait, figuring she'd want nothing more than to put distance between them. Although it was possible she simply wanted updated information on Juliet.

True to her word, Katerina returned a few minutes later. "Thanks for waiting, Miguel. I'm planning to head over to the hospital, and figured we could ride the metro together."

"I'm happy to ask Fernando to drive us there," he offered.

A grimace flashed over her features, but then she nodded. "I can't get used to the idea of having someone drive me around, but that's fine."

He called Fernando, and then gestured towards a small park bench sitting beneath the trees. "Have a seat. Fernando will be here in a few minutes."

"Why haven't you learned to drive?" she asked.

"I do know how to drive," he said testily, even though, truthfully, it had been a long time since he'd sat behind the wheel. "Fernando is a former patient of mine. He has a wife and three children. He lost his job after his accident and subsequent surgery, so I hired him."

She didn't say anything until Fernando drove up in Miguel's sleek black car. "That was very kind of you, Miguel."

He shrugged and strode forward, opening the back passenger door for her. Once she was seated inside, he closed the door, went around to the other side and slid in.

"Take us to the hospital, please, Fernando," he said in Spanish.

"Sí, señor," Fernando said, his gaze resting curiously on Katerina.

"Juliet is doing better today," he said, as Fernando pulled away from the curb. "Her electrolytes are all within normal range and she's following instructions again. I left orders this morning to begin weaning her off the ventilator."

Katerina smiled and relaxed against the seat. "I'm

so happy to hear that. I feel bad I haven't been in there to see her yet today. Sounds as if she'll be ready to return home soon."

Now that he knew Tomas was here in Seville, he wasn't so anxious to pronounce Juliet stable enough for transport back to the U.S., but obviously he couldn't keep Juliet, or Katerina for that matter, hostage here. Maybe he'd be booking that plane ticket to Cambridge after all. "Perhaps," he responded slowly. "But I would like to make sure she's off the ventilator first."

She raised a brow, as if she was able to read his mind. But instead of pushing the issue, she changed the subject. "Tell me, how are DiCarlo and Pedro doing?"

"DiCarlo is still in the I.C.U., but his condition is stable," he admitted. "Pedro is doing well, too. He asked about you this morning. I think he was hurt that you didn't come to visit him."

"I'll visit him this afternoon," she promised. "He's a good kid, Miguel. I know his mother has several other children at home, but it breaks my heart to see him lying in that hospital bed all alone."

"Mine, too, Katerina," he murmured. There was no denying the soft spot in his heart he had for the boy. "His father is off for weeks at a time as a truck driver, so she isn't ignoring him on purpose. Regardless, I know he'll be thrilled to see you."

The ride to the hospital didn't take long. He put on his lab coat and then gave Fernando some well-deserved time off, seeing as he was close enough to walk home from the hospital.

"I'd like to see Juliet first," Katerina said as they entered the elevator.

"Of course." Several of the staff greeted him as they

walked down the hallway of the I.C.U., and if they were surprised to see him once again with Katerina, they didn't say anything to his face. No doubt, there was plenty of gossip going on behind his back and he was glad no one else knew about Tomas.

"Hey, sis, I'm back," Katerina said, as she crossed over to Juliet's bedside. "I'm sorry I couldn't be here earlier, but Tommy was bitten by a dog and I had to bring him to the emergency room."

Miguel was pleasantly surprised when Juliet opened her eyes and turned her face to look at Katerina.

"Juliet! You're awake!" Katerina took her sister's hand and leaned over to press a kiss on her forehead. "I was so worried about you."

Juliet looked as if she wanted to talk, but the breathing tube prevented her from making a sound. Before Miguel could step forward, Katerina took control.

"Don't try to talk—you still have that breathing tube in. But don't worry, Dr. Vasquez is trying to get that removed very soon. Which means you have to cooperate with him. You have to show us that you can breathe okay on your own. Can you understand what I'm saying?"

Juliet nodded and pointed to the tube, demonstrating with hand gestures that she wanted it out.

He crossed over to pick up the clipboard hanging off the end of the bed. "Good afternoon, Juliet. I can see here that your weaning parameters look very good."

Katerina glanced at him, her eyes full of hope. "Does that mean we can get the tube out now?"

He hesitated. Juliet had suffered a seizure just twenty-four hours ago, but he'd been convinced all along that she'd be fine once he got her electrolytes under control. "Let me listen to her lungs first," he said, replacing the clipboard and pulling his stethoscope from the pocket of his lab coat. Katerina went down to crank the head of the bed up so that Juliet was sitting upright. He helped her lean forward so that he could listen to her lung sounds.

"Well?" Katerina demanded when he'd finished.

Even though he knew that this meant Juliet would be discharged back to the U.S. soon, he nodded. "Yes, her lungs sound clear. I will get the nurse to come in and assist."

Katerina looked relieved and stood back as he and Maria, Juliet's nurse, took out her endotracheal tube.

"Water," Juliet croaked.

Katerina quickly came over to hold the small plastic cup and straw up so that Juliet could take a sip.

"Hurts," Juliet whispered hoarsely, putting her hand up to her throat.

"I know. Try to rest," Katerina said, putting a hand on her arm. "Breathe slow and easy. You're going to be just fine, Jules."

"Where's Mom?" Juliet asked.

Katerina tossed him a worried look. "Mom's gone, Juliet. She passed away three years ago."

"Remember, she's still recovering from her head injury," he murmured.

"Don't talk, Jules. Just relax."

"I thought you were a dream," Juliet said, rubbing her obviously sore throat.

"I'm not a dream. I came as soon as I heard. I love you, Jules. Very much." Bright tears filled Katerina's eyes.

Miguel slipped out of the room, giving the two sisters

time to be alone. He was pleased with Juliet's progress, even though he knew she still needed time to recover fully. Yet his heart was heavy as he went back to the nurses' station to write new orders. Obviously, if Juliet continued doing this well, she'd be stable enough to move to a regular room in the morning.

That would give him no choice but to deem her stable enough for transportation back to the U.S. as soon as arrangements could be made.

As he wrote instructions for breathing treatments and another chest X-ray in the morning, he vowed to let his boss know he needed a leave of absence as soon as possible. He couldn't bear the thought of Katerina and Tomas leaving so soon. He'd barely spent an hour with his son. And even though he would consider Katerina's proposed custody arrangements, he wasn't going to give up that easily.

There was no way he was going to settle for some long-distance relationship with Tomas. He was going to need that plane ticket after all.

CHAPTER TEN

KAT spent several hours with her sister, enormously relieved that she seemed to be doing so much better. But
Juliet was also still very confused, not understanding
that she was in Spain or that their mother was gone.

When Kat finally left, she was surprised to find
Miguel sitting out at the nurses' station, clearly waiting
for her. He rose to his feet when he saw her approach.

"Do you have time to visit Pedro?" he asked, meeting her halfway.

She nodded, ashamed to realize she'd completely
forgotten about the young teen. "Of course. But you
didn't have to stay, Miguel."

"I wanted to," he said simply.

She was touched by his dedication, even though logically she knew that he was glued to her side because of
Tommy more than anything. Still, when he put his hand
in the small of her back, her traitorous body reacted by
shivering with awareness.

When the elevator doors closed, locking the two of
them inside, the tension skyrocketed, his familiar scent
filling her head. For a moment she couldn't think of
anything except the heated kiss they'd shared.

She sneaked a glance at him from beneath her lashes,

wondering if she was losing her mind. Why did she have this strange attraction to him? She'd avoided personal entanglements with men because she didn't want to be left alone, like her mother had been.

Yet here she was, wishing for another chance with Miguel.

The doors opened and she stepped forward quickly, anxious to put space between them.

Thankfully, Pedro was a good distraction, greeting her enthusiastically. "Miss Kat! I'm so glad you came to visit."

"Hi, Pedro," she said, going over to take his hand in hers. She gave him a mock frown. "I hear you're not taking your pain medication as Dr. Vasquez ordered."

"Yes, I am," he corrected. "I took some earlier today when you were here, Dr. Vasquez. Don't you remember?"

Miguel sighed. "Pedro, that was almost eight hours ago. Do you mean to tell me you haven't taken anything since?"

He ducked his head sheepishly. "I wanted to wait until it was nighttime. You said that sleep was important."

Kat put her hands on her hips. "Pedro, you promised me you would take the pain medication."

"I'm sorry. I will take more tonight. Why are you so late here at the hospital?"

"Well, it was quite a busy morning," she said, as Miguel went out into the hall, probably to flag down Pedro's nurse. "I have a four-year-old son named Tommy and he was bitten by a dog so I had to take him to the emergency department to get antibiotics."

"I didn't know you have a son," Pedro said in surprise, and she belatedly realized she hadn't mentioned Tommy earlier. For a moment Pedro seemed almost disappointed by the news, but then he recovered. "Having a dog bite is very scary. Is he okay?"

"He's fine." She refused to look at her watch, not wanting Pedro to think she was in a hurry. Even though she knew Tommy would be up from his nap and ready to eat dinner soon. "But tell me how you're doing, other than not taking your pain medication."

"I walked today, the way Dr. Vasquez told me to. I went up to visit DiCarlo." Pedro grimaced and shrugged. "But I'm bored here with nothing to do all day. One of the nurses did play a word game with me, but she would only use Spanish words. How am I to learn English without practice?"

She'd noticed the game next to his bed. "How about we play a game before I leave? But our rule will be that we only use English words. Okay?"

"Really? You would do that for me?" He looked so happy that she wished she'd thought of it earlier.

"Of course." She pulled out the game and then sat next to his bed. She couldn't just leave, no matter how much she wanted to see Tommy.

"May I join you?" Miguel asked.

"Yes, more players will be more fun," Pedro said excitedly.

As Miguel pulled up a second chair, she realized Miguel would make a wonderful father.

But even as she acknowledged that truth, she knew there was no way to know for sure if he would be just as good a husband.

At the end of the second game Kat threw up her hands in defeat. "I give up. It's embarrassing to lose to both of you when I'm the one who speaks English."

Miguel flashed a conspiratorial grin at Pedro. "What do you think, amigo? Maybe we should have let her win one."

Pedro nodded. "I think we should have. It's only polite to allow a woman to win."

She rolled her eyes and stood. "I don't need either of you to do me any favors. You each won fair and square. But I'm afraid I need to go. Pedro, I'll visit again tomorrow, okay?"

"Okay. Thank you for staying," Pedro said. "I had much fun."

Miguel also stood. "I'll take you back to the hotel. And, Pedro, take your pain medication, please."

"I will." Pedro looked sad to see them go, but she'd already stayed far longer than she'd planned. She gave him a quick embrace before heading down the hall, anxious to get back to the hotel.

She glanced at Miguel as they waited for the elevator. "I can ride the metro back, there's no reason for you to go out of your way."

He didn't answer until they were inside the elevator. "I would like to see Tommy again, if you wouldn't mind. I thought I would take you all out for dinner."

She wanted to refuse, because being around Miguel was wearying. She was constantly on edge, trying not to let her true feelings show. But glancing up at him and seeing the hope in his eyes, she found she couldn't say no. "Tommy can't wait that late to eat. We usually have dinner at six or six-thirty."

"That's fine with me." When the elevator doors opened on the lobby level, he once again put his hand in the small of her back, gently guiding her. "I will take every moment possible to see my son."

She nodded, realizing with a sense of dread that they would have to make more specific plans for the future, especially now that her sister was doing better. How much longer would Juliet be allowed to stay in Seville? Probably not long. She swallowed hard and tried not to panic.

She wasn't surprised to see that Fernando was waiting outside for them. Now that she knew the reason Miguel had hired him, she found she was happy to have him drive them around. "*Buenos noches,* Fernando," she greeted him.

He flashed a wide smile. *"Buenos noches, señorita."*

"And that's pretty much the extent of my Spanish," she muttered wryly, as she slid into the back seat.

"I'd be happy to teach you," Miguel murmured after he climbed in beside her. "Tomas should learn both languages too."

She bit back a harsh retort, turning to gaze out the window instead. Her anger wasn't entirely rational, yet the last thing she needed was Miguel telling her how to raise her son.

Their son.

Her lack of sleep the night before caught up with her and tears pricked her eyelids. Telling Miguel about Tommy had been the right thing to do so there was no reason to be upset.

"Katerina, what is it? What's wrong?" Miguel asked. He reached over to take her hand and she had to struggle not to yank it away. "Becoming bilingual is a good thing. If my mother hadn't taught me English, I would not have been given the opportunity to study abroad. We never would have met."

And if they hadn't met, Tommy wouldn't exist.

She momentarily closed her eyes, struggling for control. "Miguel, can't you understand how difficult this is for me? Tommy has been my responsibility for almost four years. I was pregnant and alone. I did the best I could. Now it seems like you're planning to barge in and do whatever you want. Without bothering to consult with me."

His hand tightened around her. "Katerina, I am more sorry than you'll ever know about how I left you alone. I will always regret not keeping in touch with you after leaving the U.S. And not just because of the time I missed getting to know my son. But because I realize now how much I missed you."

She sniffed and swiped her free hand over her eyes. "You don't need to flatter me, Miguel. If I hadn't shown up here to visit my sister, we wouldn't have met again. You never would have tried to find me."

There was another long pause. "Katerina, do you believe in fate? Believe that some things just happen for a reason?" His husky voice was low and compelling. "It's true that my dream was to join Doctors Without Borders, and if not for the difficulties with my brother, I probably would not have been here when your sister required emergency care. But I was here. And you arrived with our son. What else could this be if not fate?"

"Coincidence." Even as she said the word, she knew it wasn't entirely true. Was there really some cosmic force at play here? Drawing the two of them together after all this time? She generally believed that hard work and taking responsibility for your choices was the way to get ahead, but she couldn't totally renounce Miguel's beliefs.

"Fate, Katerina," Miguel whispered. "I believe we were meant to be together."

Together? As in as a family? She didn't know what to say to that, and luckily Fernando pulled up in front of her hotel. She gratefully tugged her hand from Miguel's grasp and reached for the doorhandle. "*Gracias,* Fernando," she said, before climbing hastily from the car.

But as quick as she was, Miguel was that much faster. He caught her before she could bolt and gently clasped her shoulders in his large hands. "Katerina, please talk to me. Tell me what has caused you to be so upset?"

She tipped her head back and forced herself to meet his gaze. "I'm more overwhelmed than upset, Miguel. And I'm not sure how you can stand there and claim we were meant to be together. We're not a couple. We're simply two adults who happen to share a child."

One of his hands slid up from her shoulder to cup her cheek. "You can't deny what is between us, *querida.*"

She was about to tell him not to call her darling, but he quickly covered her mouth with his, silencing her with a toe-curling kiss.

She told herself to pull away, even lifted her hands to his chest to push him, but instead her fingers curled in his shirt, yanking him closer as she opened for him, allowing him to deepen the kiss.

All the pent-up emotions she'd tried so hard to ignore came tumbling out in a flash of pure desire. She forgot they were standing on the sidewalk in front of the hotel. Forgot that Fernando was still there, watching them with a huge, satisfied grin.

Forgot that she wasn't going to open herself up to being hurt again.

Everything fell away except this brief moment. A stolen fragment of time when they were able to communicate perfectly without words.

"*Querida,* Katerina, I need you so much," he murmured between steaming-hot kisses. "I can't understand how I lived all this time without you."

She pulled back, gasping for breath, bracing her forehead on his chest, wishing she could believe him. Wishing he'd felt a tenth of what she'd felt for him back then.

"Kat?" the sound of Diana's shocked voice had her jumping away from Miguel.

"Good evening, Diana. Hello, Tommy." Miguel smoothly covered the awkward pause. "Katerina and I were just about to ask you both to join us for dinner."

Kat avoided Diana's accusing gaze as she went over and gathered her son close. "Hi, Tommy, I'm sorry to be gone so long. Are you hungry?"

Tommy nodded. "I'm starving."

"Well, then, let's get going," Miguel said. "I understand there is an American restaurant nearby that serves great food, including hamburgers."

As much as she enjoyed the tangy bite of Spanish food, the thought of a simple American meal was tempting. "We can go somewhere else," she offered.

"Actually, other than smaller places that serve only *tapas*, the main restaurants don't open this early," Miguel said with a note of apology.

"I'm all in favor of having good old-fashioned hamburgers," Diana said. "But let's hurry, okay? Tommy's bound to get cranky if he doesn't eat soon."

Kat couldn't help feeling guilty all over again. She

shouldn't have stayed at the hospital so long. And she really, really shouldn't have kissed Miguel again.

The American restaurant was within walking distance, so Miguel sent Fernando away for a couple of hours. Diana's sour mood evaporated as they enjoyed their meal. When they were finished, Miguel took Tommy over to play a video game, leaving the two women alone.

"Kat, do you think it's smart to get emotionally involved with Miguel?" Diana asked in a low voice.

"I'm already emotionally involved with him, Diana," she responded wearily. "He's Tommy's father, remember? It's not like I can avoid him."

"Avoiding him is very different from having sex with him."

"It was a kiss, Diana." Although she suspected that if they'd been somewhere private, without the added responsibility of caring for Tommy, nothing would have stopped them from making love. "Besides, we'll be going home pretty soon. Juliet woke up and is off the breathing machine. She's still confused, but she's doing a lot better. I'm certain she'll be stable enough to be transferred home very soon."

"Already?" Diana looked disappointed with the news. "But we've hardly had time to sightsee."

"I know. I'm sorry." She did feel bad that Diana had been stuck babysitting Tommy. "Maybe tomorrow I can take Tommy to the hospital to visit Juliet, giving you time to go see the cathedral. I hear it's spectacular."

"All right. But what about Miguel? What's he going to do?"

Good question. "I'm not sure, but I suspect he'll

come visit me and Tommy in Cambridge. After that, I just don't know."

Diana was silent for a moment. "Are you going to move to Seville?"

"No!" Kat stared at her friend in shock. "Of course not. What on earth gave you that idea?"

Before Diana could respond, Miguel and Tommy returned to the table. "We blowed things up," Tommy said excitedly. "Bang, bang, bang!"

Kat grimaced and glanced at Miguel, who didn't look the least bit repentant. "Tommy has very good hand-eye coordination," he said proudly. "We scored many points."

They left the restaurant a little while later so that Miguel could enjoy this time with his son. They went for a long walk, enjoying the warm night air.

When they returned to the hotel, Tommy was definitely looking tired. "I'll take him upstairs, he'll need a bath before bed," Diana said.

Kat enjoyed giving Tommy his bath, but before she could utter a protest, Miguel spoke up. "Thank you, Diana. I have a few things to discuss with Katerina."

"No problem," Diana said with false brightness. "Say goodnight to your mom, Tommy."

"G'night." Tommy held out his chubby arms for a hug and a kiss. And then he shocked her by reaching over to give Miguel a hug and a kiss too.

"Goodnight, Tomas," Miguel murmured, as he finally set Tommy down on the sidewalk.

They stood for several moments until Diana and Tommy had gone into the elevator of the hotel. Kat rubbed her hands over her arms, suddenly chilled in her short-sleeved blouse and Capri pants, uncertain what exactly Miguel wanted to talk about.

"Katerina, would you join me for a drink?" Miguel asked, as Fernando pulled up.

A drink? Or something more? The kiss they'd shared simmered between them and suddenly she knew he planned to pick up where they'd left off before Diana had interrupted them.

"Please?" He reached over to take her hand in his.

She hesitated, feeling much like she had four and a half years ago when Miguel had asked her out after losing their young patient. But she was older now, and wiser. She shouldn't be a victim to her hormones.

When he lifted her hand and pressed a kiss to the center of her palm, her good intentions flew away.

"Yes, Miguel," she murmured. "I'd love to."

CHAPTER ELEVEN

MIGUEL could barely hide the surge of satisfaction when Katerina agreed to have a drink with him. He took her hand and turned to head outside where Fernando was waiting inside the car parked out at the curb.

"Where are we going?" she asked, when they stepped outside into the warm night air.

"My place will provide us with the most privacy," he murmured, gently steering her towards the car. When she stiffened against him, disappointment stabbed deep. "Unless you'd rather go somewhere else?"

He practically held his breath as she hesitated. Finally she shook her head and prepared to climb into the back seat of the car. "No, that's okay. Your place is fine," she agreed.

His relief was nearly overwhelming, and as he rounded the car to climb in beside her, it took every ounce of willpower he possessed not to instruct Fernando to break the speed limit to get to his apartment as soon as possible. Once he was seated beside her, he reached over and took her hand. "I want you to know, Katerina, I think you have done an amazing job with raising our son."

She glanced at him in surprise. "For some reason, I keep expecting you to be angry with me."

No, he was only angry with himself. "After tonight it is easier for me to understand your desire to protect Tomas from being hurt." He'd been surprised at the strong surge of protectiveness he'd felt when he'd spent time with his son this evening. "But I hope you can also trust me enough to know I would never willingly do anything to upset him."

"I do trust you, Miguel." Her soft admission caused the tension to seep from his shoulders, allowing him to relax against the buttery-soft leather seats. "Somehow we'll find a way to work this out."

He wanted to do more than to just work things out, but he refrained from saying anything that might cause an argument, unwilling to risk ruining their fragile truce. He wanted this time they had together to be special. So he kept her hand in his, brushing his thumb across the silky smoothness of her skin.

Katerina was always beautiful to him, no matter what she wore. Even dressed casually, in a short-sleeved green blouse that matched her eyes and a pair of black knee-length leggings that displayed her shapely legs, she was breathtaking.

Fernando pulled up in front of his apartment and he reluctantly let her go in order to open the door to climb out. She didn't say anything as they made their way up to his apartment. Once inside, he crossed over to the small kitchen. "What would you like to drink?" he asked.

"Um, a glass of red wine would be nice," she said, clutching her hands together as if nervous.

"Excellent choice." He pulled out a bottle of his favorite Argentinean wine from the rack and quickly removed the cork before pouring them two glasses. She stood awkwardly in the center of the living room as he approached and handed her the glass.

"I feel like I should make a toast," he murmured as he handed her one glass and tipped his so that the rims touched. "To the most beautiful mother in the world."

She blushed and rolled her eyes, taking a step backwards. "Exaggerate much?" she asked, her tone carrying an edge.

He wasn't exaggerating at all, but he could see she was struggling to hold him at arm's length, as if uncomfortable with drawing attention to herself. Or believing in herself.

That thought brought him up short, and he paused, wondering if his leaving so abruptly after their magical night together had caused her to lose some of her self-confidence.

If so, he'd wronged her in more ways than one.

"Katerina, why do you doubt my feelings?" he asked softly. "Surely my attraction to you is no secret by now. Four and a half years ago I succumbed to the keen awareness between us. And obviously that same attraction hasn't faded over time."

"But you still left," she pointed out.

"Yes, but if my father hadn't suffered his stroke, I'm sure that we would have continued to see each other." He knew that he wouldn't have possessed the strength to stay away. Even for her sake.

She eyed him over the rim of her wineglass. "You don't know that, Miguel. Rumor amongst the O.R. staff was that you didn't want any emotional attachments because you weren't planning to stay in the U.S. I doubt that you would have changed your mind about that, even for me."

He shouldn't have been surprised to know his plans had been fodder for gossip, but he was. There had been many women who'd expressed interest in him, and he'd often used that line to avoid entanglements. "I can't deny that I wasn't planning to stay. I didn't keep my dream of joining Doctors Without Borders a secret. And even then I was hesitant to start a relationship with an American."

She looked shocked by his revelation. "Why?"

He wished he hadn't gone down this path. "My mother was American and she wasn't happy living here in Spain. But that part isn't important now. Suffice it to say that had I stayed three more months to finish my trauma surgery fellowship, I would have been there when you discovered you were pregnant. If not for my father's stroke, we could have handled things very differently." He wasn't sure exactly how, but at least he would have known about his son.

She stared at him for several long moments. "Maybe. But playing the what-if game isn't going to help. We can't go back and change the past."

"I don't want to change the past, Katerina," he countered. "I wouldn't give up Tomas for anything. Yet this evening isn't about our son. It is about you and me."

Her lips parted in shock, making a small O, and she carefully set down her wineglass as if afraid she might drop it. "I don't understand."

Obviously he wasn't being very articulate. "Perhaps you would allow me to show you what I mean instead."

When she didn't voice an objection, he stepped closer and drew her deliberately into his arms. He didn't pounce but stared deep into her eyes so that she could read his intent and see the desire he felt for her. When she still didn't utter a protest, he lowered his mouth to capture hers.

She held herself stiffly in his arms, and just when he thought she would push him away, she softened against him and opened her mouth, welcoming his kiss.

Desire thundered in his chest and he gathered her closer still, pulling her softness firmly against his hard muscles and tipping her head back so that he could explore her mouth more fully.

He forced himself to take his time, savoring the exotic taste, when all he really wanted to do was to rip their clothing out of the way so that he could explore every inch of her skin.

"Miguel," she gasped, when he finally freed her mouth in order to explore the sexy curve of her jaw, the hollow behind her ear.

"Say yes, Katerina," he murmured between kisses. He wanted to make love to her, right here, right now. "Say yes."

He continued his leisurely exploration, kissing his way down her neck, dipping further to the enticing valley between her breasts, as if waiting for her answer wasn't killing him.

"Yes, Miguel," she whispered in a ragged voice, arching her back to give him better access to her breasts. "Yes!"

He didn't trust his voice so he swept Katerina up into his arms and strode down the hall to his bedroom, hoping and praying that she wouldn't change her mind.

* * *

Kat didn't allow herself to second-guess her decision, every nerve-ending was on fire for Miguel. She hadn't felt this way since their one and only night together. No other man made her feel as beautiful and desirable as Miguel did.

When he swept her into his arms, she pressed her mouth against the hollow in his neck, nipping and licking, savoring his scent and enjoying the way his arms tightened around her in response.

In his bedroom he flipped on a single lamp and then paused near the bed. He gently slid her body down the front of his so that she could feel the full extent of his desire. She shivered, but not with cold, when he unbuttoned her blouse and shoved the cotton fabric aside, revealing her sheer green bra and then ultimately the matching sheer green panties.

She was grateful she'd worn decent underwear, even though it didn't stay on long. She should have felt self-conscious to be naked before him, but she wasn't. His gaze devoured her as he quickly stripped off his own clothes.

"Katerina, *mi amore*," he muttered as he gently placed her on his bed, before covering her body with his. "I don't deserve you."

She was pretty sure he had that backwards, but then she wasn't thinking at all because he'd lowered his mouth to the tip of her breast. She writhed impatiently beneath him but he took his time, giving equal attention to both breasts before trailing kisses down her abdomen to her belly button. And then lower still.

There was a brief moment when she worried about the faint stretch marks along her lower abdomen, but when he swept long kisses over every single one, the last vestiges of doubt vanished. She was practically sobbing with need when he finally spread her legs and probed deep, making sure she was ready.

"Now, Miguel," she rasped.

His dark eyes glittered with desire but he simply shook his head and dipped his head again, this time replacing his fingers with his tongue. Something he'd done that first time they'd made love.

Her orgasm hit fast and hard, deep shudders racking her body. He quickly rose up, rolled a condom on with one hand before he thrust deep, causing yet another orgasm to roll over her.

She was sure she couldn't take much more, but he whispered to her in Spanish, lifting her hips so they fit more snugly together, gently encouraging her to match his rhythm. Slow and deep at first, and then faster and faster, until they simultaneously soared up and over the peak of pleasure.

Kat couldn't move and not just because of Miguel's body sprawled across hers. Every muscle in her body had the consistency of jelly, making it impossible to move even if she wanted to.

Which she didn't.

After several long moments Miguel lifted himself up and rolled over, bringing her along with him, so that she was now lying fully against him. She rested her head against his chest, listening to the rapid beat of his heart.

The chirping sound of a cellphone broke the silence and she froze, trying to remember if that was how her small disposable cellphone sounded. Was Diana calling because Tommy needed her? Maybe the dog bite on his arm was getting infected?

When Miguel muttered something in Spanish beneath his breath, she realized the call wasn't for her. It was for him. There was a strong sense of déjà vu as she remembered the phone call he'd received the morning after the night they'd spent together. She forced herself to lift her head, to look at him. "Do you need to get that? Is that the hospital?"

"I'm not on call tonight," he said with a dark scowl. "Whoever it is can wait."

After several rings the phone went silent and she relaxed against him. When she shivered, he pulled up the sheet and blanket to cover her. She would have been happy to stay like this with him for the rest of the night, but she knew she should go back to the hotel in case Tommy needed her.

She couldn't help thinking about what he'd revealed earlier about his mother being American and not liking it here in Spain. She'd known his mother had spoken fluent English, which had been how he'd picked up the language so quickly.

But what did this all mean about the future?

A loud buzzer sounded, echoing loudly across the apartment, startling her. Miguel muttered something rude before pulling away from her.

He fumbled for his clothing, pulling on his pants before heading out to answer the door. She was grateful he closed the bedroom door, giving her privacy.

She didn't hesitate but quickly found her clothes and got dressed, hardly able to contain her curiosity about who'd come to Miguel's home at ten o'clock at night. She crossed the room, trying to listen, unsure if she should go out there or not. When she heard a female voice speaking in rapid Spanish she froze, the blood draining from her face.

Was it possible that Miguel was actually involved with a woman after all?

Miguel wasn't the least bit happy to see the woman his brother used to date standing on the other side of the door. He tried to rein in his temper. "What do you want, Corrina?"

"Luis is missing, Miguel. I need you to help me find him."

Corrina was a pretty girl with dark wavy hair, who for some unknown, self-destructive reason was still hung up on his brother, despite the fact that Luis had broken her heart more than once.

"Come in," he said rather ungraciously, stepping back to give her room to enter. "How do you know he's missing?"

"He spent last night at my place but this morning he was gone. I've looked everywhere for him, Miguel. He's not at home or working on the olive farm or at any of his usual hang-outs." Corrina's eyes filled with tears. "I'm afraid something has happened to him."

He suppressed a sigh. His brother wasn't exactly known for his tact and could very easily have been looking for an excuse to avoid Corrina. "Did you notify the police?"

"Yes, but they said there's nothing they can do." Corrina stared up at him defiantly. "I know everyone thinks he's avoiding me, but I don't think so. Something is wrong, Miguel. I feel it here," she said, dramatically putting her hand over her heart.

The concern in her eyes was real enough, but he

didn't share her fears. Besides, he didn't want to end things so abruptly with Katerina. Not again. Not when their time here in Seville was so limited.

But then his bedroom door opened and Katerina emerged, fully dressed, and with a sinking heart he knew their evening had already come to an end. "Excuse me, I was just leaving," she said, avoiding his gaze as she swung her purse over her shoulder and headed for the door.

"Katerina, wait. This is Corrina Flores, my brother's girlfriend. It seems she believes Luis is missing."

There was a flash of surprise on Katerina's face and she paused, glancing back with concern. He realized she'd assumed the worst, believing Corrina was one of his former lovers. He was frustrated by her lack of trust yet at the same time grimly pleased that she cared enough to be jealous.

"Missing since when?" Katerina asked.

"Just since this morning. I'm sure he's fine, there's no need to rush off." Selfishly, he wanted her to stay, needed her support as he looked for his brother.

She grimaced and toyed with the strap of her purse. "Actually, I really should go, Miguel. I want to be there in case Tommy wakes up. The dog bite may cause him some pain."

He understood, even though he didn't want to let her go. There was so much yet that they needed to discuss before he released Juliet to return home. He'd used the short time they'd had together to make love, rather than planning their future.

Something he couldn't quite bring himself to regret.

"All right, let me call Fernando, he'll drive you back to the hotel. Why don't we plan to get together first thing in the morning? I'll take you and Tommy out for breakfast and then we'll visit your sister."

"Ah, sure. But don't bother Fernando this late," she protested. "I'll take the metro."

"It's no bother. He's probably just finishing dinner and I'll need his assistance myself, anyway." He certainly wouldn't allow her to go back to the hotel alone. And as much as he wanted to spend more time with Katerina, he couldn't bring himself to ignore Corrina's concerns about Luis.

"I hope you find your brother," Katerina murmured.

"I'm sure we will. And it's about time he learns to take responsibility for his actions. Luis can't expect me to keep bailing him out." He didn't bother to hide his annoyance.

Corrina wisely kept silent as he called Fernando and then walked Katerina outside.

"Thank you, Katerina, for an evening I'll never forget," he whispered, hugging her close and giving her another heated kiss.

"Goodnight, Miguel," she murmured, breaking away from his embrace and climbing into the back seat of the car. He couldn't help feeling as if he'd said something wrong when she ignored him to chat with Fernando.

Grinding his teeth together, he had little choice but to shut the car door and step back, allowing Fernando to drive Katerina away. He stared after the red taillights, fighting the urge to demand Fernando return at once so he could figure out what had caused Katerina to be upset.

Annoyed with himself, and his brother, he reluctantly turned and went back upstairs to where Corrina waited. All he could think was that he'd better not find out that his brother was simply trying to avoid his old girlfriend or he wouldn't hesitate to box Luis's ears.

This was the second time his family problems had pulled him away from Katerina. And he was determined that it would also be the last.

CHAPTER TWELVE

THE following morning, Kat was surprised when Miguel didn't show up as promised. As Tommy was hungry, she and Diana took him out for breakfast. As they enjoyed fresh pastries, she couldn't help wondering if Miguel had found his brother or if he'd stayed up the entire night, searching for him.

"I'll take Tommy with me to see Juliet now that she's doing better," she offered. "That way you can go and see the cathedral before we have to leave."

"If you're sure you don't mind," Diana said, before shoving the last bit of pastry in her mouth.

"I don't mind at all." In truth she would have loved to see the cathedral too, but coming to Seville hadn't been a vacation for her. She'd only come because her sister had been injured.

And there was a strong possibility she'd be back in the not-too-distant future if Tommy was going to be spending time with his father. She glanced around, silently admitting that, as beautiful as Seville was, she couldn't really imagine living here.

Once again she found herself thinking about Miguel's mother. Clearly he'd avoided dating anyone back in the

U.S. because he didn't plan to relocate to the U.S. on a permanent basis.

And considering the problems he'd had with his brother, she couldn't imagine him changing his mind. Which left them where? Back to a joint custody but separate countries type of arrangement?

She would have been satisfied with that before, but not any more. Not since making love with Miguel. She wanted it all.

She wanted a true family.

"Mama, go. Now," Tommy said insistently.

"Okay, I'm ready." She paid the bill and then used a wet napkin to clean up Tommy's sticky fingers. "We're going to go visit Aunt Juliet. Won't that be fun?"

He nodded vigorously and dropped from the chair, making her grin at the amount of energy radiating off his tiny frame. Had Miguel been the same way as a child? She suspected he had been.

She started walking toward the nearest metro stop, holding Tommy's hand as they took the stairs down to the lower level. There was a strong possibility that if Miguel had gotten home late, he'd decided to simply meet her at the hospital.

Suspecting that her sister might have already been moved out of the I.C.U., she stopped at the front desk. "*¿Donde esta mi hermana*, Juliet Campbell?" Where is my sister?

There was a flood of Spanish that she didn't understand. When she looked blankly at the woman, she wrote down the room number and handed it to Kat.

"*Gracias,*" she murmured, looking down at Juliet's new room number, 202. "This way, Tommy," she said, steering him toward the elevator.

Juliet was sitting up at the side of the bed, finishing her breakfast, when they entered. Kat was very relieved to find her sister looking much better. She crossed the room to give Juliet a hug. "Hey, sis, how are you feeling today?"

"Kat! You brought Tommy, too?"

"Yes. Tommy, you remember Aunt Juliet, right? Can you say hi to her?"

"Hi," Tommy said, and then ducked his head, refusing to relinquish Kat's hand.

"Hi, Tommy. It's good to see you. Wanna see my cast?" Juliet said, moving the blankets off her right leg.

Ever curious, the cast was enough to draw Tommy forward. He knelt beside Juliet's right leg, lifting his fist to knock on the fiberglass cast.

"Don't worry, that's the one part of my body that doesn't hurt," Juliet muttered dryly.

"Are you in pain, Jules?" she asked, moving closer. "Dr. Vasquez told me that you had some cracked ribs, too."

"Everything hurts," her sister admitted. "And don't bother asking me what happened, I honestly can't remember."

"Don't worry, I'm sure your memory will return in time." Although there was certainly no guarantee. The numerous bruises and lacerations were already starting to fade, but Kat could well imagine that her sister's muscles were also still sore.

She wanted to ask her sister more questions, to make sure Juliet wasn't as confused as she had been yesterday, but they were interrupted by a knock at the door.

"Good morning, Juliet," a plump woman greeted her

sister. "And you must be Katerina Richardson. Nice to meet you in person."

Kat stared at the woman, certain she hadn't met her before. She would have remembered someone speaking English, for one thing. The familiarity of the stranger's greeting was unnerving.

"My name is Susan Horton and I'm the study abroad program coordinator. I'm the one who contacted you about Juliet's accident, remember?"

Of course she remembered now. So much had happened since the first day she'd arrived, she'd completely forgotten about the woman. "Yes."

"I'm glad you're both here," Susan said, "because we need to make immediate arrangements for Juliet's transfer back to the United States."

Kat tried to hide her shock. "So soon? Don't we need Dr. Vasquez to sign off on Juliet's case first?"

"There's another doctor covering for Dr. Vasquez today, and he's already given his approval. So, if you'd come with me, we'll begin making the necessary arrangements."

"Right now?" Kat cast a helpless glance toward her sister, before following Susan out of the room. She could only hope Miguel would show up soon or they might have to leave without saying goodbye.

Miguel shouldn't have been surprised to find Luis in jail. His friend, Rafael Hernandez, had finally called him to let him know Luis had been driving under the influence. He'd called Corrina to make sure she knew, but then he debated with himself over whether or not to post Luis's bond. It wasn't the money but the principle of bailing his brother out of trouble again.

In the end they wouldn't let him post bail until the morning. Which ruined his plans to meet Katerina and Tomas for breakfast.

"Thanks for picking me up," Luis said, wincing at the bright light.

"Luis, you're either going to kill yourself or someone else if you don't stop this," Miguel said with a heavy sigh. "You'd better figure out what you want to do with the rest of your life, and quick."

"Don't worry about me, just go on your stupid mission trip," his brother muttered, scrubbing his hand over his jaw.

"I'm not going to Africa, I'm going back to the U.S., at least temporarily." He glanced over to where Luis was slouched in the corner of the car. "I have a son, Luis. A son I didn't know about until just a few days ago. But he and his mother live in Cambridge, Massachusetts."

Luis lifted his head and peered at him with bloodshot eyes. "You're going to live there? With them?"

He hadn't realized until just now how much he wanted to be with Katerina and Tomas on a full-time basis, but he wasn't keen on living in the U.S. for ever. Yet he couldn't ask Katerina to move here, not when she had her sister to worry about. And even once Juliet was better, he didn't want to risk the same thing happening to Katerina that had happened to his mother. He couldn't wait to see Katerina and talk to her about his idea of moving to the U.S. temporarily.

"I'm not sure where I want to live, but I do want to be a part of my son's life," he said slowly. "But I can't leave you like this, Luis. You need help. Professional help."

His brother was silent for a long moment. "Will you let me sell the olive farm?" he asked.

Shocked by the question, Miguel nearly swerved into the other lane. "You want to sell the farm? Why? What will you do to support yourself?"

"I've always wanted to work in construction," Luis admitted. "I hate farming. I want to build things. Houses, buildings."

Build things? He turned to stare at his brother, stunned by his revelation. Granted, Luis had built a new warehouse on the farm last year, but all this time he'd had no clue that his brother hated farming.

"Are you sure about this, Luis?" he asked. "Once you sell the farm, there's no going back."

"I'm sure. Corrina's father wants me to help in his construction company. I've been trying to get up the nerve to ask you about selling the farm."

"Do you think working for her father is wise? You haven't treated Corrina very well these past few years."

"I know I've made a mess of my life," Luis said in a low voice. "But I really want to do this, Miguel. I know the farm has been in our family for generations, but I feel trapped there. It's too far from town, for one thing. I realized when I built the new warehouse that I gained more satisfaction from doing that than all the years I've spent picking olives. And I care about Corrina. I kept breaking things off because I couldn't imagine raising a family on the farm. I keep remembering how Mom died there."

He couldn't hide his surprise yet at the same time he understood how Luis felt. "Why didn't you say something sooner?" he asked.

"I was afraid you would be upset. You and Papa always talked about how the Vasquez farm had sustained families for generations. That it was a family tradition."

Miguel winced, knowing Luis was right. He hadn't stayed on the farm, choosing to go into medicine at the university as soon as he'd been able to. It shamed him to realize he hadn't ever asked Luis what he wanted to do. "I'm sorry, Luis. I never realized how badly you wanted to leave the farm, too."

"So you're not mad?" Luis asked, looking pathetically eager despite his rough night in a jail cell. "Because Señor Guadalupe once asked me about selling. I would like to call him to see if he's still interested. If he will buy the farm, I can start working for Corrina's father right away."

"I'm not mad, Luis," he said. "By all means, call Señor Guadalupe. If he's not interested, let me know. I'll see what I can do to help."

Fernando pulled into the driveway of the Vasquez olive farm, and for a moment Miguel simply sat there, staring out at the rows upon rows of olive trees.

It was a little sad to think of selling the farm to strangers, yet at the same time he was a doctor. A surgeon. Saving lives was important and satisfying. He'd never planned on working the farm himself, yet had he subconsciously forced Luis into the role because he hadn't wanted to let go of the past?

The idea was humbling.

"Thanks for the ride," Luis said as he climbed from the car.

"Let me know when you have a buyer lined up."

"I will." Luis looked positively happy and waved as Fernando backed out of the driveway. He then headed into the house.

"Are you really moving to the U.S.?" Fernando asked from the front seat.

He met the older man's gaze in the rear-view mirror. "Yes, for a while, Fernando."

Fernando nodded. "Señor Vasquez, I wonder if you would be so kind as to give me a reference before you go so that I can apply for a job."

Miguel mentally smacked himself in the forehead. Why hadn't he thought of this earlier? "Fernando, how do you feel about being an olive farmer?"

"I would be willing to learn."

He grinned and reached for his cellphone. Everything was going to work out just fine. Luis didn't need to bother Señor Guadalupe after all.

Fate had helped him out once again.

Kat could only sit in stunned silence as Susan Horton finalized her sister's travel arrangements. Everything was set. They would be leaving Seville by one-thirty that afternoon. It was the latest flight out, and they wouldn't arrive back in the U.S. until nearly ten o'clock at night, but when Kat had tried to protest, Susan had remained firm that Juliet would be on that flight, regardless of whether or not Kat wanted to go with her. Given that choice, she'd quickly arranged for additional seating for herself, Diana and Tommy.

She'd also called Diana right away, arranging to meet back at the hotel immediately. The airport was only thirty minutes away, but they would need to get there by eleven-thirty, two hours before departure time, and it was already almost ten now. They had just over an hour to get back to the hotel, pack and check out of the hotel.

She left the hospital, carrying Tommy to make better time. Luckily the metro ran often and it didn't take her long to get to the hotel. She didn't waste any time tossing stuff into their suitcases.

"I can't believe they're making us leave today," Diana said as she helped Kat pack Tommy's things. "Like letting your sister stay one more day would make such a big difference?"

"I know. Although I suspect if they had come to visit Juliet on Sunday, they would have made us leave on an earlier flight."

"I suppose. Okay, that's everything," Diana said. They'd worked like speed demons, and had managed to get everything together in twenty-minutes flat.

Kat made one more sweep of the room, making sure Tommy hadn't left anything behind. "All right, let's haul all this down to the lobby so we can check out."

"What about Miguel?" Diana asked, as they crowded into the elevator.

"As stupid as it sounds, I don't have his phone number." Miguel was on Kat's mind, especially after the night they'd shared, and because they still hadn't made plans for the future. Kat had hoped that Miguel would show up at the hospital before they left, but she hadn't seen him. And now they'd be leaving the hotel shortly. "I'm sure he'll figure out what happened once he discovers Juliet has been discharged." She wished she didn't have to leave without saying goodbye, though.

"Did you guys decide on some sort of joint custody arrangement?" Diana asked.

"I'm not sure if we really agreed on that or not," she said truthfully. She hadn't told Diana about the evening she'd spent making love with Miguel either. Had she done the right thing by saying yes to Miguel? If only she'd waited. Obviously, it would have been smarter of her to avoid getting emotionally involved. Again.

"Stay here with Tommy while I check out." Kat crossed over to the counter, asking for the bill and for a taxi to take them to the airport where they would meet up with Juliet.

They arrived at the small Seville airport with time to spare, so they stopped for something to eat. Kat could barely concentrate—she kept scanning the area, looking for any sign of Miguel.

Where was he? Surely once he'd gone to the hospital and realized Juliet had been discharged, he would know to come and find her at the airport. Something bad must have happened to Luis for him to not be here.

Unless he'd changed his mind about being a part of Tommy's life?

No, she couldn't believe that. Not after the way he'd made love to her. Not after everything they'd shared.

Although she couldn't help coming back to the fact that he'd never wanted to be with an American. Like her.

"Kat, look, there's your sister."

She looked over in time to see Susan Horton pushing Juliet in a wheelchair through the small terminal, followed by an airport employee wheeling Juliet's large suitcase. "Watch Tommy for a minute, okay?" Kat said, before hurrying over to her sister.

"Hey, Jules, how are you?" Kat tried not to be upset at the way they were being rushed out of there. "Are you in pain?"

"I have her pain medication right here," Susan said before Juliet could answer. The woman's brisk, impersonal attitude made Kat grind her teeth in frustration.

"Now, is there anything else you need? If not, I'll be leaving Juliet in your hands."

Kat wrestled her temper under control. "We'll be fine," she said, taking over the task of pushing Juliet's wheelchair.

"Are you ready to go through security?" Diana asked, holding onto Tommy's hand. They needed the assistance of two airport employees to manage their luggage.

She sighed, glancing back over the crowd of people one more time, wishing more than anything that Miguel would come. But there was still no sign of him. As much as she wanted to wait, getting Juliet and Tommy through the airport security line would be difficult and time-consuming. She didn't dare wait much longer.

"Sure thing. Let's go."

Going through security took far longer than she could have imagined, especially with Juliet needing so much assistance. She tried not to think about the fact that they would have to change planes four times, before arriving at home. Once they were finished with security, they put their carry-on luggage back together and made their way down to their assigned gate.

Diana flopped into one of the hard plastic chairs with a groan. "Somehow, going home isn't nearly as much fun," she muttered.

Kat pasted a smile on her face, unwilling to let on how much she was hurting inside, as she made sure Juliet was comfortable.

She'd really, really, expected Miguel to show up here at the airport. And now that he hadn't—she wasn't sure what to think.

Had he changed his mind about wanting to be a father to Tommy? Did he regret making love to her? She wished she knew more about Miguel's mother. He'd mentioned she'd died several years ago, when he'd still been in high school. Whatever had happened had made him determined not to become emotionally involved with an American.

With her.

Her heart squeezed with pain and tears pricked her eyes as she realized she'd foolishly fallen in love with Miguel.

CHAPTER THIRTEEN

MIGUEL strode into the hospital, knowing he was beyond late. He wasn't due to work today but he knew Katerina would come to visit her sister.

He walked into room 202 and stopped abruptly when he saw an elderly man lying in the bed. He frowned and glanced at the room number, making sure he had the correct one.

After murmuring a quick apology, he spun around and went back to the nurses' station. They must have moved Juliet to a different room for some unknown reason.

But, no, her name wasn't on the board at all. With a frown he picked up the phone, intending to call down to the front desk, when he saw his colleague, Felipe. "Felipe, where's my patient, Juliet Campbell?" he asked.

Felipe turned around. "Miguel, what are you doing here? I thought I was to cover your patients today?"

"You are, but I was actually looking for Juliet's sister, Katerina. What room did Juliet get moved to?"

Felipe looked puzzled. "I discharged her, Miguel. Señora Horton from the study abroad program wanted her to be sent back to the U.S., so I went ahead and gave the discharge order."

"What?" A knot of dread formed in his gut and he grew angry with himself for not anticipating that something like this might happen. He'd known the minute he'd given the orders to have Juliet transferred to a regular room that her time here was limited. "When? How long ago?"

Felipe shrugged. "I'm not sure, maybe two or three hours?"

Three hours? No! He struggled to remain calm as he glanced at the clock. It was almost eleven-thirty already. "Was that when you wrote the order? Or when she actually left?"

"I didn't pay attention," Felipe admitted. "Miguel, what's the problem? Clearly, she was stable enough to travel."

He forced a smile, knowing none of this was Felipe's fault. "I trust your judgment. Excuse me but I need to catch up with them." Before Felipe could say anything more, he left, lengthening his stride to hurry as he called Fernando, instructing his driver to meet him outside.

"We need to stop at home, so I can get my passport. From there we're heading straight to the airport," he said, the moment he slid into the back seat. A few days ago, when he'd reviewed flights out of Seville heading to the U.S., he'd noticed the last flight was at one o'clock in the afternoon.

He grabbed his passport, and not much else. He'd have to buy what he needed once he arrived in the U.S. Back in the car, he called the airline in an attempt to book a seat as Fernando navigated the city streets.

"I'm sorry, but we can't book any more seats at this time," the woman said. "We stop selling tickets two hours before the flight."

He resisted the urge to smack his fist on the counter. "I need to get on that flight. I'm sure you can make an exception."

There was a pause, and he held his breath. "I'll check with my supervisor," she finally said.

He tightened his grip on the phone, willing Fernando to hurry. But the traffic was heavy today, and they were moving at a snail's pace. The airport was normally a thirty-minute drive, and he could only hope and pray that the traffic would break soon. He had to get there in time. He had to!

"I'm sorry, Señor Vasquez. We are not able to sell you a ticket."

He closed his eyes and swallowed a curse. He forced himself to be polite. "Thank you for checking."

"Problems?" Fernando asked, catching his gaze in the rear-view mirror.

He shook his head. "Just get to the airport as soon as possible. I want to see Katerina before she leaves."

He'd have to buy a ticket in order to get past security, but at this point he was willing to do anything to see Katerina, talk to her one more time before she and Tommy boarded that plane. The panic that gripped him by the throat surprised him. He hadn't realized until she was gone just how much he cared about Katerina.

It wasn't just that he missed his son. Katerina would agree to share custody, he knew. But at this moment he didn't care about custody arrangements.

He cared about Katerina.

When the airline attendant asked for all passengers needing help to board, Katerina stood up. "I think that means us. Are you ready to go, Juliet?"

"Sure." Her sister already looked exhausted and they hadn't even started their long flight. Kat couldn't suppress a flash of anger toward Susan Horton for rushing Juliet out so fast. As Diana had said earlier, what was one more day?

Maybe she should have put up more of a fight, even though Susan Horton hadn't been interested in listening to reason. Besides, it was too late now. She bent over to release the locks on the wheelchair and then pushed her sister forward, leaving Diana and Tommy to follow.

Getting Juliet safely transferred into an aisle seat was no easy task. The only good thing was that they were given a spot in the front row of a section, leaving plenty of room for her leg that was still in a cast. Juliet groaned under her breath as she used the crutches, favoring her right side where she had her cracked ribs.

They were both sweating by the time they were finally settled. Diana and Tommy were immediately behind them, which was a mixed blessing.

"Tommy, stop kicking the seat," she said for the third time, trying not to snap at him. "It feels like you're kicking me in the back."

"Sorry, Mama."

"Do you want me to switch places with him?" Diana asked, leaning forward anxiously as if sensing her frayed nerves.

"No, he'll only end up kicking Juliet." She was tense and crabby but did her best not to let it show as her bad mood certainly wasn't Tommy's fault. Or Diana's. Or Juliet's.

She was upset because she'd really expected Miguel to come to the airport to find her. But for all she knew, he was still looking for his brother. She tried to tell herself that this way was for the better. Things had moved pretty fast between she and Miguel so a little time and distance would likely be good for both of them.

Yet regret at leaving Seville so abruptly filled her chest, squeezing her lungs. There hadn't been time to say goodbye to Pedro. As the plane slowly filled up with passengers, she wondered how Miguel would manage to find her in Cambridge.

If he decided to come at all.

Miguel purchased a ticket to Madrid and managed to get through security in time to find Katerina's plane had just started to board. He rushed over to the gate and swept his gaze over the group of passengers. After several long moments he was forced to admit they must have already boarded. Which made sense, as Juliet had a broken leg and had probably needed help to get into her seat.

He went up to the desk. "Excuse me, but I need to speak to passenger, Katerina Richardson. I think she may already be on the plane."

"I'm sorry, but there's nothing I can do. You're not allowed on the plane without a boarding pass," the attendant said with a false smile.

So close. He was so close! "Just five minutes. You could ask her to come back out here and I promise she'll be back on the plane in five minutes."

"I'm sorry, Señor, I can't help you." The woman's false smile faded and he could see a security guard making his way over. She glanced past him as if he weren't there. "May I help you?" she asked the next person in line.

Miguel quickly left the counter, preferring to avoid

the security guard. He still had a ticket to Madrid, and from there he was sure there would be a better selection of flights to the U.S. But considering his flight didn't leave for two more hours, he knew there was no chance in the world of arriving in time to see Katerina or Tomas.

He called his police friend, Rafael, asking for help in finding Katerina's address back in Cambridge. Rafael called him back within twenty minutes with the address. At least that was one problem solved.

With a heavy sigh he crossed over to his own gate and settled into one of the uncomfortable plastic chairs. He wished more than ever that he'd spent more time talking to Katerina last night, rather than making love. Not that he regretted that part. He just wished they would have talked first.

He could only hope she would be willing to listen, to give him another chance, once he arrived in the U.S.

Nineteen and a half hours later Kat, Tommy and Juliet finally arrived home. Diana had gone to her own apartment and Kat couldn't blame her friend for wanting to sleep in her own bed.

Kat was exhausted, but she was far more worried about her sister. Juliet's pain had gotten worse the more they'd moved, and changing planes and then taking a train back to Cambridge had obviously been too much for her.

She was tempted to take Juliet straight to the hospital, but since the time was close to midnight, she decided against it. Rest would be the best thing for her sister, so she helped Juliet get into bed before giving her more pain medication. She'd have to arrange for follow-up doctor's appointments in the morning.

Unfortunately, Tommy wasn't nearly as tired. Just like on the way over to Spain, he'd slept on the plane and she wanted to burst into tears when he started bouncing on his bed.

After several minutes of fighting she gave up. "Okay, fine, let's go downstairs and watch a movie."

She put in a DVD and stretched out on the couch, holding her son in front of her, determined to get in at least a short nap. With any luck, Tommy would be tired enough to sleep after the movie was over.

Between Tommy's messed-up sleep cycle and her sister's pain, Kat only managed to get about four hours of sleep. Not nearly enough, but she would just have to make do. After making breakfast and encouraging Juliet to eat, she spent a good hour on the phone, making arrangements for Juliet to be seen by a doctor who specialized in head injuries.

Her sister was still slightly confused, but she was certainly better than she'd been when the breathing tube had been removed. At least she wasn't asking about their mother any more.

There was a loud knock at her front door at ten-thirty in the morning, and Kat fully expected to see her friend Diana had returned.

When she saw Miguel standing there, she stared in shock, wondering if her eyes were playing tricks on her. She blinked, but he didn't vanish. As she stared at him, she realized he looked as disheveled as she felt, indicating he must have been traveling all night. On one level she was glad to see him, but at the same time his timing couldn't have been worse.

"Miguel? How did you find me?" She didn't mean to sound ungracious, but lack of sleep made it difficult to think clearly. She was shocked to see him, but she couldn't deny she felt a warm glow at the knowledge that he'd come all this way to find her.

"I just missed you at Seville airport. I'm sorry we didn't get a chance to talk before you had to leave." He stared at her for a long moment as if trying to gauge her reaction. "May I come in?"

She smiled, although her eyes were gritty with lack of sleep. "Sure, but unfortunately, we're just getting ready to leave. Juliet has a doctor's appointment with a neurologist at Cambridge University Hospital." She stepped back, allowing him to come into her home. She frowned when she realized he didn't have so much as a suitcase with him.

For a moment her tired brain cells couldn't make sense of it all. Was Miguel planning to stay here with her? No, it made more sense that he must have left his luggage back in his hotel room.

"I think that is a good idea," Miguel was saying. "The doctors there will make sure she's really okay. Is she still confused?"

"A little. Not as bad as before, though."

"She probably just needs a little time." Miguel fell silent and she wondered what he was thinking as he glanced around her small home. After her mother had died, she had taken over the house payments and promised Juliet her half when she graduated from college.

"Maybe we can get together later on?" she suggested, glancing at the clock. If they didn't leave soon, they'd be late.

"I could stay here with Tomas, if you think that would help," Miguel offered.

She opened her mouth to refuse, even though going to the doctor's appointment would be much easier without dragging Tommy along. Tommy had only met Miguel twice and she couldn't bear to leave him with someone he probably still considered a stranger. "I don't know if that's such a good idea," she said slowly.

Glancing over her shoulder, she noticed Tommy hovering in the kitchen doorway, staring at Miguel with wide eyes. He wasn't crying, but he wasn't rushing over to greet Miguel either.

"Please?" Miguel asked. "I think he'll be fine. He doesn't seem afraid of me."

"Tommy, do you remember Mr. Vasquez?" she asked.

Tommy nodded, sticking his thumb in his mouth, something he only did when he was really tired. And suddenly, knowing that Tommy would probably fall asleep sooner than later, she made up her mind to take Miguel up on his offer.

"All right, you can stay here with Tommy. I would suggest you put a movie on for him as he's probably going to fall asleep soon. His days and nights are a little mixed up from the flight home."

Miguel's smile warmed her down to her toes. "I think I can manage that."

She forced herself to look away, trying not to think about the fact that Miguel was here for his son first and foremost. Obviously, Miguel wanted more time to get to know his son. But she couldn't help feeling a pang of resentment that Miguel was acting as if the night they'd spent together hadn't happened. "All right, we'll be back in a couple of hours."

Miguel helped her get Juliet out to the car, before going back inside. Leaving him in her house felt weird, but she kept her attention focused on her sister.

She could only manage one crisis at a time.

Kat was thrilled when Dr. Sandlow announced that Juliet's head injury seemed to be resolving without a problem. After a long exam, blood work and a follow-up CT scan of her head, he'd decided Juliet was stable enough not to be admitted. "I'd like to see her back in a week," he said. "And she also needs to start attending physical therapy three days a week."

She tried not to wince, wondering how in the world she'd be able to return to work while taking Juliet to therapy three days a week. She still had at least another week of vacation time saved up, but after that was gone, she'd need to apply for a leave of absence.

Time to worry more about that later.

The appointment had lasted longer than she'd anticipated, which was fine, except that they'd missed lunch. She stopped on the way home and picked up a bucket of fried chicken, mashed potatoes and coleslaw in case Miguel and Tommy were hungry too.

She parked her car in the driveway, rather than pulling into the garage, so that it was easier to maneuver Juliet out of the front passenger seat. She was somewhat surprised that Miguel didn't come out to help as she hooked her arms under Juliet's armpits to help her stand.

"Are you okay?" Kat asked, as she grabbed the crutches from where she'd propped them against the door.

"Fine," Juliet murmured, although her upper lip was beaded with sweat.

"Just a few more feet and you can rest, okay?" Moving around was obviously good for Juliet, but it was almost time for more pain medication. The way Juliet winced and groaned with every single swing of the crutches made Kat feel bad.

They managed to get into the house without incident and she immediately steered her sister towards the guest bedroom. Once Juliet was settled, she went back out to the main living area to look for Miguel and Tommy.

She found them on the sofa in the living room, both of them asleep. Miguel held Tommy close against his chest.

She stared at the two of them, father and son, feeling abruptly alone. The two had bonded while she'd been gone and Tommy clearly needed his father the same way Miguel needed him. She should be thrilled that they were together at last.

But she couldn't shake the sense of desolation. All this time she'd told herself she wanted a family. But she'd had a family, with Tommy and Juliet.

Now she was forced to realize what she really wanted was for Miguel to love her as much as she loved him. But did Miguel have the capability of loving her the way she wanted him to? Would he stick by her and Tommy not just in the good times but through the bad times as well?

Or would he leave the minute things got rough, just like her father?

CHAPTER FOURTEEN

MIGUEL felt a soft weight being lifted off his chest, and his arms tightened, instinctively holding on. He forced his eyes open and found Katerina leaning over him, her exquisite green eyes snapping with fury.

Confused, he tried to comprehend what he'd done to upset her. For a moment he didn't even remember he was in the U.S., until he glanced down to see Tomas was fast asleep on his chest. Abruptly all the memories tumbled to the surface.

"Let him go, Miguel. I need to put him down in his bed," Katerina said curtly. Still foggy with exhaustion, he released his hold so that she could lift their son into her arms. He instantly missed the warmth radiating from Tomas' soft body.

She disappeared from the living room and he used the few moments alone to pull himself together. How long had he been asleep? He couldn't remember.

With a guilty glance at the clock, he knew he'd slept longer than he should have. A part of him was disgusted that he'd wasted a good hour sleeping when he could have been making up for lost time with his son.

Although they would have plenty of time to get to know each other. Wouldn't they? On the long flight to the U.S. he'd finally realized that where he and Katerina lived wasn't important. Being together was all that mattered.

He kept waiting for the reality of his decision to sink in, but he didn't have the itchy feeling of wanting to leave. Was it possible that joining Doctors Without Borders really wasn't his dream?

Had it just been a way to escape?

He frowned and stretched in an effort to shake off his deep thoughts. Lifting his head, the distinct scent of fried chicken made him realize how hungry he was. He followed his nose into the kitchen.

There were bags of food lying haphazardly on the table, as if they'd been set down in a hurry. Before he could reach for one, Katerina returned.

"Tommy will be down soon, he wouldn't go back to sleep." Her slightly accusing gaze made him wonder if she believed that was his fault. Maybe it was. "We'll have lunch and then you'll need to leave, Miguel. I can't deal with you right now. I have Tommy and Juliet to care for."

He wanted to argue, but the lines of fatigue on her face tugged at his heart. She looked so exhausted he wanted to sweep her up and take her to bed. But, of course, he couldn't.

Somehow he'd thought she'd be happy to see him. But so far she'd seemed more annoyed. Had he misunderstood her feelings towards him? His heart squeezed in his chest.

He told himself to have patience, even though it wasn't easy. Tomas came running into the room and he helped Katerina pull out the fried chicken, mashed potatoes and coleslaw. He noticed that she made sure

Tomas had some food on his plate and that she made a plate for her sister, before worrying about eating anything herself.

"I'll be right back," she murmured, taking the food down the hall towards a small bedroom. He felt guilty all over again, knowing that Katerina had managed to get Juliet inside without his assistance.

He watched Tomas eat, determined to wait for Katerina. She returned quickly enough, dropping into a chair across from him.

"How is she?" he asked.

"Sleeping. Dr. Sandlow said she's fine, though. She needs to start physical therapy three times a week. I'll help her with her lunch later." She took a healthy bite of her chicken, and then seemed to notice he hadn't eaten. "Don't you like fried chicken?" she asked.

"Of course. Who doesn't?" He flashed a reassuring smile before turning his attention to his own plate. He wanted to help her, but sensed he was treading on thin ice. For some reason, she'd been angry with him for falling asleep. Either because she thought he'd put Tomas in danger, or because he'd slept when she couldn't. Or maybe because he'd made himself at home. Regardless, he knew he could help ease her burden by staying, if she'd let him.

"Lean over your plate, Tommy," she said gently when pieces of fried chicken dropped from his mouth and hit the floor. "Don't make a mess."

"No mess," Tomas said with his mouth full.

"Is the shopping mall still located a few miles from the hospital?" he asked. "I need to purchase clothes and toiletries."

She frowned. "Did the airline lose your luggage?"

"No. I didn't bring anything except my passport. I was racing to catch up with you and Tomas. As you'd already boarded the plane, they wouldn't let me talk to you. I ended up going through London to get here."

She looked shocked to hear he'd followed her. After several long moments she finished her meal and sat back in her chair. "Yes," she murmured. "The shopping mall is still there."

"Katerina, we need to talk." He glanced at Tomas, who was starting to wiggle around in his booster chair. He was tempted to smile at how their son had smeared mashed potatoes and gravy all over himself.

"Not now. As I said, I have other things to worry about at the moment. Tommy needs a bath and then I need to care for my sister. I'm sorry, but I'm afraid you'll have to wait until I get things caught up around here." She stood and picked up Tommy. "Goodbye, Miguel."

She turned and left, no doubt intending to give Tomas a bath. He wanted nothing more than to help, but she'd made her wishes very clear.

With a sigh he pushed away from the table and began clearing the dirty dishes, storing the leftovers in the fridge. Maybe she wanted him gone, but he wasn't about to leave this mess for her. Not when she looked like she was dead on her feet.

He wanted to believe that Katerina was just tired and jet-lagged, that she didn't mean what she'd said.

But since he'd arrived, she hadn't given any indication of wanting to pick up their relationship where they'd left off. If not for his brother going missing, they would have had time to talk. To plan. Surely there was a way to make this work? Surely Katerina felt something for him?

So why was he feeling as if she wished he hadn't come to the U.S.?

As he washed and dried the dishes, he racked his brain for a way to bridge the gap that had somehow widened between them.

Because if she thought he was giving up that easily, she was dead wrong.

Kat ran warm water and bubble bath into the tub for Tommy, knowing she'd been unfair to Miguel. He'd come all this way, had actually followed her to the airport in Seville, flying all night, only to have her demand that he leave. She hadn't even asked about Luis.

She set Tommy into the tub, kneeling alongside to keep a close eye on him. Tommy played in the water, splashing bubbles everywhere. She was so exhausted, so emotionally drained that she didn't even notice bubbles had landed on her hair.

She'd been badly shaken by the sight of Miguel holding Tommy, both of them looking adorable as they'd slept. She was a terrible mother to be jealous, even for an instant, of her son's love for his father. And the sad truth was that Tommy didn't even know that Miguel was his father yet.

But he would, soon.

For a moment she rested her forehead on the smooth, cool porcelain of the tub. She should be glad Miguel wanted to be a part of Tommy's life. She should be glad that he'd come here to Cambridge, rather than asking her to consider moving to Seville.

Yet, she couldn't help wishing that they would have

time alone, to explore the passion that simmered between them. She knew Miguel wanted her, but she
didn't know if there was any way he'd ever come to
love her. She felt confused and exhausted.

She had her sister to care for, and Tommy too. And
soon she'd have to go back to work. There wouldn't be
time for her and Miguel to renew their relationship. But
there would be plenty of time for him to establish a relationship with his son.

She lifted her head, instantly ashamed of herself for
being selfish. Her son was what mattered, not her own
ridiculous feelings. Giving her head a shake to clear the
troublesome thoughts, she quickly washed Tommy's
hair and then pulled him out of the water, engulfing
his slippery body in a thick, fluffy towel.

After getting Tommy dressed in clean clothes, and
straightening out her own disheveled appearance, she
went back out to the kitchen, half-afraid Miguel would
still be there. He wasn't, but she was pleasantly surprised to find her kitchen was spotless, every bit of
mess cleaned up, including the floor around Tommy's
booster chair.

His kind thoughtfulness only made her feel more
miserable for her earlier abruptness. Was it too late to
catch up to him? She almost headed for the door when
she heard thumping noises coming from Juliet's room.
Juliet was up, trying to navigate with her crutches, leaving her no choice but to hurry down to help her sister.

Forcing her to push thoughts of Miguel firmly out
of her mind.

An entire twenty-four hours went by without any word
or visit from Miguel. Kat should have been relieved to

have one less thing to deal with, but instead she was on edge. Had something happened to him? Had he decided she was too much of a witch to deal with? Had he decided to return to Spain after all?

She still didn't know his phone number, or if his cellphone from Spain would even work here in the U.S. She felt much better after getting a good night's sleep and was pleased to note that Juliet was also doing better every day.

Getting her sister to therapy wasn't too bad, especially as Juliet insisted on doing things for herself. There was a truce between them, a closeness that hadn't been there before Juliet had left to study abroad. Kat hoped that this terrible accident would bring them closer together.

"Where's that Spanish doctor?" Juliet asked, when they'd returned from therapy.

Kat shrugged. "I'm not sure. Why?"

"Come on, sis, you're not fooling me. He's obviously Tommy's father. And you love him, don't you?"

She wanted to protest, but really what was the point? "My feelings don't matter as he doesn't feel the same way."

Juliet stared at her for a long moment. "You never asked me what happened. I mean, how I ended up getting hit by a car."

Kat pulled up a chair to sit beside her sister's bed. "Jules, you were in the I.C.U. on a ventilator when I came to visit. And by the time you'd recovered, you were confused and told me you couldn't remember. Has that changed? Do you remember what happened?"

Juliet took a deep breath and let it out slowly. "I fell in love with a guy named Enrique. He was much older and so mature. I never told him how I felt, but I thought we had this great connection. Until I found him with another woman."

Kat sucked in a harsh breath. After having both of their fathers leave their mother, she knew that would be the worst betrayal of all. "Oh, Jules…"

"I was so upset I started crying and ran into the road." Juliet shrugged. "Thankfully, I don't remember much after that."

"I'm so sorry." Kat reached out and took her sister's hand. "I'm sure that was really difficult for you to see him with someone else."

"Yes, it was. After the way my dad left, I spend half my time waiting for the guy I'm dating to show his true colors. But now I wonder if I just liked Enrique because he was safe. I think I've been avoiding relationships, Kat. Because of our fathers."

Kat tried to follow her sister's logic. "But you just said you fell for Enrique. Wasn't that a relationship?"

"Not really. He was older and friendly with me. But it wasn't like we even kissed or anything. There was another guy who liked me, who was closer to my age, but I avoided him. I told myself it was because I liked Enrique, but the truth of the matter was that I was avoiding being hurt." Juliet tightened her grip around Kat's fingers. "Don't do that, Kat. Don't avoid Miguel because you don't want to get hurt."

Juliet's words struck a chord deep inside. For someone so much younger, Juliet had great insight. "It's more complicated than that, Jules. He's Tommy's father. We have to get along, for his sake."

"Tell him how you feel," Juliet insisted. "Don't let your pride or fear get in the way."

Was her sister right? Had she avoided talking on a personal level with Miguel because she was afraid of being hurt? They'd never really talked about their joint custody arrangement because she'd avoided the topic. The realization made her wince.

Maybe her sister was right. "Get some rest Jules, okay?" she said, changing the subject. "We'll eat around six o'clock. I have a pot roast in the slow cooker for dinner."

"Okay," Juliet murmured, closing her eyes.

Kat left her sister's room to head for the kitchen. She was surprised to hear the sound of voices.

"Meegl," Tommy shouted and it took her a minute to figure out that it was a mangled version of Miguel.

"Tomas!" Miguel responded, and she entered the kitchen in time to see her son launch himself at his father. Miguel laughed and clasped Tommy close, looking dangerously attractive wearing casual clothes, jeans and a long-sleeved denim shirt. "I've missed you," he said, nuzzling Tommy's neck.

"Me too," her son said, hugging him.

For a moment, seeing the two of them together, father and son, made her want to cry. But then Miguel lifted his head and caught her gaze, with such intensity she could barely breathe. "Hi, Miguel," she said inanely.

"Katerina," he murmured, and for a moment she thought she saw frank desire in his gaze, before he bent over to set Tommy back on his feet. "Would you allow me to take you out for dinner this evening?"

"I'm sorry, I would but I don't have a babysitter," she said, tearing her gaze from his. She figured that he wanted to finalize their co-custody agreement and was determined not to continue avoiding the topic.

Thankfully, she felt better prepared now after a good night's sleep. She forced a smile. "I have a pot roast in the slow cooker if you want to stay."

"Diana said she'd come over to babysit. And she's more than capable of watching over Juliet as well." He took a step toward her, holding out his hand. "Please?"

He'd called Diana? She could hardly hide her surprise. And now that he'd taken that excuse away, she couldn't think of a reason to refuse. "All right," she agreed. "But I need some time to change."

"I'll wait," he said.

The next few hours flew by as she showered, changed and then greeted Diana, who seemed glad to be back on American soil. As Miguel held the door of his rental car open for her, she felt a bit like a girl going out on her first date.

"Are you sure you know how to drive?" she asked, as he slid behind the wheel. "Maybe you should have brought Fernando here with you."

His teeth flashed in a broad smile. "Fernando is taking over the Vasquez olive farm. Believe it or not, my brother Luis has decided he wants to build things, instead of being a farmer."

"So he's okay, then?" she asked. "You found him all right?"

"He's fine. He was afraid to tell me how much he hated the farm." For a moment a dark shadow crossed his face, but then it was gone. "I'm convinced he's going to be fine now that he's following his dream."

Dread knotted her stomach, and she had the most insane feeling he was about to tell her he was going to follow his own dream. His dream of joining Doctors Without Borders. "I'm glad," she said in a choked tone.

He slanted a glance in her direction as he pulled into the driveway of a well-known hotel located mere blocks from her house. "I hope you don't mind if we have a quiet dinner here?"

"Of course not."

He led the way inside to the fancy restaurant located just off the hotel lobby. There weren't too many people dining, but it didn't matter as they were led to a small quiet table in the back.

Miguel treated her courteously, holding her chair for her and then asking what she'd like to drink. They started with a light appetizer and a bottle of Shiraz.

"Katerina," he said, reaching over to take her hand. "I have something very important to ask you."

She felt surprisingly calm, despite knowing they were about to settle their future joint custody arrangement once and for all. Her sister's advice echoed in her mind.

"Yes, Miguel?" She took a sip of her wine and carefully set it down.

In a flash he was out of his seat and kneeling in front of her chair. She stared at him in shock when he flipped open a small black velvet ring box, revealing a large diamond ring. "Katerina, will you marry me?"

For a moment her heart soared and she wanted to shout yes at the top of her lungs.

Except he hadn't said anything about love.

"Miguel, we don't have to get married," she said, tearing her gaze away and wishing she'd ordered something stronger than wine. "We'll work something out so that we'll both be actively involved in Tommy's life. I'll even consider moving to Seville, after Juliet is better, if that's what you want. You don't have to do this."

He never moved, still kneeling before her, his gaze steadily holding hers. "Katerina, I love you. I was foolish to leave you four and a half years ago. I let my mother's bitterness affect my outlook on life. It's true that I want to be a part of my son's life, but that's not why I'm asking you to marry me. I'm asking because I can't imagine my life without you."

She felt her jaw drop open in shocked surprise. She wanted so badly to believe him. Trusting men wasn't easy for her, but wasn't this what she'd secretly wanted? She couldn't allow her mother's tragic life to affect her ability to find happiness.

"Miguel, are you sure? Because there's no rush. Besides, I thought you always wanted to work with Doctors Without Borders? I don't want you resent us at some future point because you didn't get to follow your dream."

"My dream isn't to join Doctors Without Borders any more," he said. "It pains me to say this, but I realize now I've been partly using that dream to avoid getting close to anyone. Until I met you. I've fallen in love with you, Katerina. And I don't care where we live, here or Seville, it doesn't matter. Nothing matters except you and our son. And any other children we decide to have."

He loved her? She wanted so badly to believe him. Her small sliver of doubt faded when she saw the pure emotion shining from his dark eyes. And somehow she managed to find the courage to open her heart to him. "Yes, Miguel," she murmured huskily. "I will marry you. Because I love you, too. And I can't imagine my life without you either." She felt wonderful saying the words, knowing deep in her heart that they were true.

"*Te amo,* Katerina," he murmured, taking out the

ring and slowly sliding the band over the fourth finger of her left hand. She barely had time to enjoy the sparkle when he stood and then drew her to her feet before pulling her gently into his arms. He kissed her, gently at first and then with such passion she almost forgot they weren't alone.

He gently pulled back, simply staring down at her for a long moment. "I love you, so much, Katerina," he whispered. "I promise to show you just how much I love you every day for the rest of our lives."

"I love you, too, Miguel." She lifted up on tiptoe to kiss him again, ignoring the waiters and waitresses clapping in the background. "And I want Tommy to have at least one brother and one sister."

He laughed. "Anything you say," he agreed huskily, before kissing her again.

As she clung to his shoulders, reveling in the kiss, she realized that with a little faith and love...dreams really could come true.

EPILOGUE

MIGUEL was pleased and humbled that Katerina had
wanted to be married in Seville. He stood at the front of
the church, amazed at how crowded it was. Apparently
everyone in Seville wanted to be there to share in their
wedding. Juliet was there too, standing as Katerina's
maid of honor. She was fully recovered now from her
accident and was determined to finish her semester
abroad. His brother Luis hadn't touched a drop of alcohol since selling the farm, and he stood straight and
tall next to Miguel as his best man.

There were many friends and family in the church,
some even having come all the way from the U.S. to be
there. And he couldn't help smiling when he saw Pedro
sitting near the front, wearing his Sunday best, craning
his neck to get a glimpse of the bride.

When the music began, the first one to walk down
the aisle was Tomas. Miguel grinned when his son
walked slowly as if afraid he might drop the small
satin pillow holding their wedding bands. When Tomas
reached the front of the church, Luis stepped forward
and took the rings. Miguel put a hand on his son's shoulder, keeping him at his side.

"Hi, Daddy," Tomas said in a loud whisper. "I didn't drop them."

"Good boy," he whispered back.

Juliet was next, walking with only the slightest bit of a limp, hardly noticeable to anyone except him.

And then Katerina stepped forward, so beautiful his chest ached. The entire church went silent with awe, but when she caught his gaze and smiled, the love shining from her eyes made him catch his breath. He forced himself to stay right where he was when he wanted very badly to rush forward to greet her.

They had two priests, one who spoke English for Katerina, even though she was already broadening her knowledge of the Spanish language.

"Mama's beautiful, isn't she?" Tomas said again, in a loud whisper.

"Very beautiful," Miguel agreed. "Be quiet now, Tomas, okay?"

"Okay," he agreed, nodding vigorously. When Katerina reached his side, he took her hand in his and together they turned to face the two priests.

As anxious he was to have Katerina become his wife, he planned to enjoy every moment of this day, the first day of their new life, together.

* * * * *

MILLS & BOON®
By Request

RELIVE THE ROMANCE WITH THE BEST OF THE BEST

1017/05

MILLS & BOON®

Why shop at millsandboon.co.uk?

Each year, thousands of romance readers
find their perfect read at millsandboon.co.uk.
That's because we're passionate about
bringing you the very best romantic fiction.
Here are some of the advantages of
shopping at www.millsandboon.co.uk:

* **Get new books first**—you'll be able to buy
  your favourite books one month before they
  hit the shops

* **Get exclusive discounts**—you'll also be
  able to buy our specially created monthly
  collections, with up to 50% off the RRP

* **Find your favourite authors**—latest news,
  interviews and new releases for all your
  favourite authors and series on our website,
  plus ideas for what to try next

* **Join in**—once you've bought your favourite
  books, don't forget to register with us to rate,
  review and join in the discussions

Visit **www.millsandboon.co.uk**
for all this and more today!